WRECKED HEARTS

RUBY RIDGE SERIES
BOOK 3

A.M. FERNANDEZ

ALSO BY A.M. FERNANDEZ

Ruby Ridge

Wild Hearts

Defensive Hearts

Wrecked Hearts

A Wild Hearts Novella

Forever Wild

WRECKED HEARTS

RUBY RANCH

BOOK 3

A.M. FERNANDEZ

YOU'VE BEEN WARNED, SUNSHINE

If you're not into spice, here are the chapters containing it so that you can enjoy their love story without all the filth.

Now, be a good girl, and open up for me.

- Chapter 22
- Chapter 25
- Chapter 28
- Chapter 33
- Chapter 48
- Epilogue

First Edition: 2026

Printed in the United States of America.

ISBN: 979-8-9940040-2-9

TRIGGER WARNINGS

While this book has a cute cover, comedic relief, swoon-worthy moments, and a slow burn that'll make you scream, there are some topics discussed in this book that should be brought to your attention.

Please take care while reading.

- On page Domestic violence & emotional abuse
- On page Physical assault & aftermath injuries
- On page Anxiety, nightmares, and lingering PTSD symptoms
- Rape (Not from the main MMC)
- Mentions of suicidal thoughts/self-destructive behavior
- Grief
- Strong language & explicit sexual content
- Cheating

If you or someone you know is experiencing domestic violence or thoughts of self-harm, please reach out for help:

- National Domestic Violence Hotline (U.S.): 1-800-

799-SAFE (7233) or thehotline.org—available 24/7 by call, chat, or text.

• Suicide & Crisis Lifeline (U.S.): Dial 988 for free, confidential support anytime.

You Matter.

WRECKED HEARTS
OFFICIAL PLAYLIST

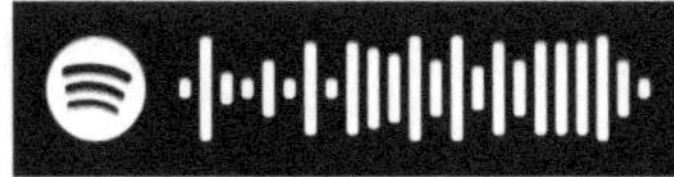

- Where's My Love - SYML
- Half A Man - Dean Lewis
- Fade Into You - Mazzy Star
- 505 - Arctic Monkeys
- back to friends - sombr
- Mine - Sleep Token
- crystallized (feat. Inéz) - John Summit, Inéz
- Drag Path - Twenty One Pilots
- iris - mgk, Julia Wolf
- Siren Sounds - Tate McRae
- GIVE ME YOUR LOVE - Chris Grey
- Empty - Letdown
- Talking To The Moon - Bruno Mars

To my past self, you were always enough to leave, and you did it.

In doing so, you found your soulmate.

To those who have been in Layla's shoes, I send you the biggest hug, my love.

And, to those who have always felt insecure with the way they look, you are beautiful, baby, and I hope you see that.

AUTHOR NOTE

Ruby Ridge began as a quiet thought late at night, the moment Carter and Catalina first came to mind. I didn't know then that one story would grow into an entire world; that a found family would take shape; that new voices would emerge; and that these characters would slowly become a home I would return to again and again.

Writing this series gave me space to sit with my own shadows, untangle pieces of my past, and let them exist without shame. Every character carries something of me—my darkness, my humor, my softness, my grief, and my healing.

They are imperfect, emotional, and stubborn, and they love fiercely, even when it scares them. They were never meant to be perfect. They were meant to be real.

Thank you for trusting me not only with my debut but also with these stories and the characters who live within them.

Thank you for allowing them to be messy, raw, and real. Thank you for staying when things hurt and for believing in the hope threaded through every chapter.

As we say goodbye to Ruby Ridge, we also say goodbye to some of our favorite couples; the ones who laughed too loud, loved too hard, and made this little town unforgettable. But don't be sad. Every ending is the beginning of something new, and a new series is already waiting on the horizon.

And who knows... You might see a few familiar faces along the way.

Ruby Ridge became a place of solitude, growth, and comfort, and I will always be grateful for the readers who walked these roads with me.

Xoxo,

A.M. Fernandez

PROLOGUE

Layla

Don't text him. Don't text him. Don't text him.

Layla, you silly girl, don't do it.

I stare at my phone sitting idly on my acrylic desk, begging to be touched. Spinning around in my chair, I think of all the reasons why I shouldn't text Reed.

1. I'm engaged.
2. He's older than me.
3. All of the above doesn't mean shit.

It's taunting me, that stupid little box is taunting me. I've never once thought about cheating on Brian, but lately, he's been an asshole.

I know, I know, why now? Well, he wasn't always like this. I've been with him since I was seventeen; he was my first everything. Fast forward ten years, my social media fame had grown; he changed.

He went from bringing me my favorite flowers, sunflowers, every day, along with a cute little note, to nothing at all. Now, he ignores me, cheats on me (which he thinks I don't know, but as women, we know), and sex? Only when he wants.

So the question I ask myself is, why do I stay? Well, Layla, if you must ask, we have over five million followers for our couple content, and I'm scared that if I leave him, no one will watch my content anymore.

You're so stupid, Layla. People are dying.

I let out a long, exasperated sigh, still staring at my phone. Whatever, I should plot out content to film. With that, I scoot my chair toward my desk, pushing my phone far away from me before I grab my yellow spiral notebook.

Scribbling out ideas, getting in the zone, the door to my office slams open, hitting the wall, causing me to bounce up in shock.

My heart falls straight into the pit of my stomach, sending a wave of dread through me.

Brian walks in with a look of disdain written all over his face. He doesn't even look at me when he drops the bouquet on my desk.

He's not ugly. Not at all. Six foot four, broad shoulders, and muscles that used to make me melt just by looking at him. His black hair is always perfectly styled, every strand in place, like he's auditioning for a magazine cover.

And those piercing blue eyes, yeah, once they made me weak. But now? Now they're cold. Empty. All that polished, perfect packaging doesn't matter when the personality inside ruins everything.

A bouquet lands on my desk with a dull smack. My eyes move from my pen to the sad little bouquet, of course, they're not sunflowers. It's never sunflowers anymore, just some sad-ass tulips with drooping stems and browning tips.

"There," he says, his blue eyes piercing into mine.

"Since you're always bitching about me not getting you flowers."

My pen freezes over the page of my notebook, where half-finished content ideas are scribbled in loops of purple ink. He notices what I'm doing, and he scoffs with a sly smile stretching across his lips.

"Get your little ideas ready so we can film and actually make some money," he adds, dusting his jacket off.

Then he's gone, turning on his heel and slamming the door hard enough to make the vase wobble on my desk.

I stare at the tulips. Pathetic, wilted, wrong. They resemble the apology he'll never give me—half-dead, careless, already discarded.

Fuck him and his shitty tulips.

I snatch my phone in fury, scrolling through my contacts, until I find *his*.

Type. Delete. Type. Delete.

Ughhhhhh, why is this so hard?

Grow a sack, Layla, do it.

My thumbs move swiftly across the glass screen, clicks sounding throughout my office.

LAYLA

When's a good time for me to film at Boots & Bourbon?

I slam my phone face down on my desk, the echo reverberating across the acrylic. Oh God, I did it.

I'm not cheating on my fiancé, I'm just helping a business owner get more views and customers for his bar.

No harm, no foul.

My hands sift through my hair as I tug at the strands, leaning against my desk on my elbows. My legs bounce up and down in a nervous rhythm, my stomach fluttering with nerves.

Buzz. Buzz. Buzz.

I crane my neck quickly, my eyes landing on my phone, snatching it up and reading the message that came through.

REED

Whenever you want. Doors are always open for you.

I press the phone to my chest, shutting my eyes for a second. Relief washes through me, chasing away the heavy silence Brian left behind.

Tulips might wilt on my desk, but at least there's one place where I don't.

Ruby Ridge.

Fuck, have you ever felt like you're being tugged and pulled by an invisible string?

Have you ever met someone and immediately felt that spark just by looking at them?

I shouldn't have felt that way.

Not when I'm engaged, even though he's an asshole. Not when every corner of my life was painted in curated perfection for people on the internet. But the moment I locked eyes with him behind the bar, broad shoulders bent over a bottle of whiskey, green eyes catching mine across the noise, everything I thought I wanted suddenly felt... wrong.

Now, sitting here with a vase of drooping, pathetic tulips on my desk, I can't stop thinking about the way Reed looked at me, like he truly saw me.

And all I can think about is every time Brian opens his mouth, I fall a little harder for someone who isn't him.

ONE
LAYLA

The hustle and bustle of Santa Monica hums outside my window, a blur of traffic and voices, but inside my apartment, it's suffocatingly quiet.

My phone is warm against my ear as Amelia's voice fills the silence, telling me about Maverick, her words spilling fast and sweet. I smile, even as my chest aches, staring out at the Santa Monica pier lights blinking against the dark water.

"He still hasn't sold it," she says, and I can hear the smile in her voice. "My apartment in LA. He said it's ours. For whenever we want to come back, or when we go to Moss Cove, we'll always have a place for us."

I sink onto the couch, pushing my knees under me. My throat constricts as I fight back the tears threatening to escape.

God, she says it so casually, but it knocks the air right out of me. Maverick refuses to let go, so that they'll always have a place to return to, to cherish the spot they have together.

Someone who fucking cares about her and the little

things, someone who cherishes the things she loves, despite the cost.

I want that. I want someone to care about me like that—to stay, to think about me before I even think about myself, to want to spoil me without anything in return.

My memory drifts back to the glass vase on my acrylic desk in my office. The tulips inside are wilted, their stems drooping, petals browned at the edges. They resemble an apology that was never truly sincere. I clench my jaw, heat bubbling beneath my ribs.

Anger tends to sneak in, right beneath the sadness. And that's what I've been feeling lately, sad. Despite having this "sunny demeanor," as Catalina says, no one truly knows how I really feel.

Amelia keeps talking, giggling between words as I hear Maverick kissing her, laughing between kisses. I swipe the tear threatening to escape beneath my lower lash line. I murmur something supportive back because she deserves to gush.

She deserves to have this.

When the call ends, the silence is worse than before.

I grab my phone, my thumb hovering over the screen, my pulse pounding in my throat. I type quickly before I can overthink it.

LAYLA

Hey Reed, would Friday work for me to come by? I mean, it's not like I can teleport there lol

I stare at my message, the cursor blinking as if daring me to take it back. My thumb hovers, hesitating, then I hit send.

My phone lands on the couch beside me, screen fading to black.

After sending the text, I stay busy doing the dishes that didn't really need scrubbing, refolding clothes that were already folded, and then folding them again. Anything to keep my hands moving so my mind won't spin.

Minutes drag on, and my phone remains silent. I try to tell myself not to care, that this is just business anyway—filming, content, the excuse I'm telling myself, but beneath that, my chest tightens with something that feels suspiciously like *hope*.

Buzz. Buzz. Buzz.

I snatch my phone before I can second-guess, sucking in a breath when I see his name glowing on my screen.

REED

Friday works.

That's it. Nothing more. But it's enough to make me smile.

A sliver of light in the darkness.

"Why the fuck are you smiling?"

My head snaps up. Brian's standing in the doorway, keys jangling in his hand, his brows furrowed.

"Nothing," I say quickly, tucking the phone against my chest before slipping it into my pocket.

He scoffs, his lips curling into that smirk I've come to hate. "Don't wait up. I'm hanging with Rebecca tonight, going to Downtown."

I swallow hard, rise to my feet, and walk past him before he can see how much it affects me.

In my room, I grab my phone and open the group chat with my girls. Fingers flying before I can lose my nerve.

LAYLA

Change of plans. Leaving for Tennessee next Monday turned into leaving early bc i hate it here

CATALINA

👀 bitch, spill

CATALINA

If Brian did something, tell me right now so I can fly to LA and set his shit on fire.

AMELIA

Same.

AMELIA

Except I can't fly since I'm 9 months pregnant. I'll mail him Rex's shit

CATALINA

Who even thinks like that 😨

CATALINA

Anyway, come here early. Carter can deal. I'll make him sleep in the barn if he complains.

LAYLA

You and I both know that man is glued to your hip

LAYLA

Brian didn't do anything

AMELIA

ur lying

CATALINA

don't lie bc i will find out

CATALINA

Okay, but are we talking Ruby Ridge early, like tomorrow?

LAYLA

Yes bitch, aren't you paying attention?

AMELIA

good i need girls time.

CATALINA

wow layla rude

LAYLA

catalina shut up

For the first time all day, my smile doesn't feel forced; my girls, my soul sisters.

But it kills me that I lie to them about how Brian really treats me. I just don't want to say anything, *I can't.*

I stand there, that small spark still in my chest, and begin opening drawers. My duffel bag falls onto the bed with a thud. I fold clothes, roll up jeans, and pack toiletries into side pockets.

Our bedroom door creaks open again. Brian's heavy footsteps reverberate off the wood, and the soft jangle of his keys comes into auditory reach. My stomach drops before I even hear his voice.

"Where the hell do you think you're going?"

He leans against the doorway with his arms crossed, his eyes narrowing at the half-packed bag on our bed. He scoffs. "You think you can just dip out? Who's gonna make *us* money?"

I straighten slowly, my hands stilling on the zipper. My heart pounds, but my voice comes out even. "I'm going to Tennessee. Trying out some new content."

He stares at me, long enough that the silence stretches, prickling across my skin. He scoffs again, rolling his eyes this time. "Whatever. It won't work because you need me."

Need him? But I suppose I'm the idiot for staying.

I refuse to flinch at his cruel words. Instead, I bend, grab my bag, and sling it onto my shoulder. My jaw aches from how hard I'm clenching it, but I don't look away.

He pushes off the doorframe, his lips curling into that sly smirk that makes my stomach twist. "Pay for your own shit," he tosses over his shoulder, already walking out. "Gonna go hang with my girl."

That fucker.

The sound of the door slamming rattles the walls, but I don't let myself crumble.

Not this time.

I suck in a breath through my nose, then let it out through my mouth, forcing my shoulders back, and focusing on the weight of my bag digging into my palm.

Tennessee is waiting.

TWO
REED

My phone buzzes, her last reply lighting the screen.

I should be used to it by now: the silence that follows messages I want to respond to, the way my chest stirs as if it remembers what hope feels like. But I'm not. The second her name lights up the bar top, it hits me in the gut.

Butterflies. Goddamn butterflies. I don't even recognize the sensation. It feels strange, wrong, somehow, like my body's betraying me for something it shouldn't want.

Tucking my phone into my pocket and letting the dull ache settle, I reluctantly grab the worn rag. The counter is spotless, with the wood gleaming beneath the soft light, but I scrub anyway.

It's routine. It's something to do with my hands while my head spins in circles.

The bar is alive tonight; perhaps a bit too lively. Laughter crashes like waves against the walls, boots thump on the floor, and glasses ring as they're set down a little too hard. Perfume blends with whiskey and wood smoke, creating a thick haze in the air.

In the corner, my brothers are wrapped up with their wives. Maverick's grin is wide enough to split his face in two, with his hand resting on Amelia's rounded stomach, admiring her and caressing her belly as she carries his son. She cradles his face in her hands, kissing his lips in gentle, continuous pecks.

Carter, Christ, the man is soft clay around Catalina. She talks loud enough to drown out the music, and he watches her like she's the only reason he bothers breathing.

They have the kind of love people write songs about. The kind I stopped allowing myself to believe in.

I force a smile, but it doesn't reach my eyes, not when I notice the looks sent my way across the bar. Women let their eyes drift over me, but not for long. Some pause a second too long on the jagged lines crawling down the peak of my cheekbone, down my neck, beneath the collar of my shirt. Their gazes harden. Lips curl—a whisper here, a quick nudge to a friend there.

They see me the same way everyone does.

Scarred. Disfigured. Less than.

A freak.

I've heard the word hissed before when they thought I couldn't. I've seen how they flinch when the light hits just right, when my face turns, and the skin pulls tight. I've felt the recoil when I brushed against someone in a crowded room, and they jerked back in disgust.

It never gets easier.

Pushing away those harmful memories, I move the rag in continuous circles against the wooden counter; the rag squeaks as my hand presses harder than needed. I let it. The sting in my palm is easier to hold than the hollow ache in my chest.

I want what my brothers have. Someone who doesn't

look at me and see the wreckage first. Someone who sees *me*.

But that's not my life. Not anymore.

So I wipe the bar again, cling to the silence between my ribs, and pretend I'm not still thinking about the way her name looked glowing against my screen.

I continue cleaning the glasses with more force than necessary, my palm pressing until the scar tissue tugs. Every stretch, every twist of my arm comes with that deep burn. The itch never fades, burrowed under my skin like a reminder I'll never escape.

Setting the glass I was cleaning too hard, I flex my hand against the ache, pushing my glasses back up the bridge of my nose.

I fucking hate them. They slip, they fog, and they remind me that even the parts of me untouched by fire are breaking down now.

"Would you look at that," Maverick's voice cuts through obnoxiously. His heavy arm slams across my shoulders, jolting the raw skin beneath my shirt. "Baby brother's all grown up. Got himself some glasses. Next thing you know, he'll be giving us lectures about bedtime."

I shoot him a glare over the rim. "Get your bitch ass arm off me."

He grins, leaning harder. "What's that, Professor Hayes? Can't hear you with all that wisdom weighing down your frames."

Carter comes over to us, carrying two empty pint glasses. He sets them down and looks at me with that steady, unimpressed expression. "He's right. You do look like a schoolteacher."

Maverick explodes with laughter. "See? Even Carter

agrees. Our baby brother is now Clark Kent, but with a mustache."

I grit my teeth, reaching for the tap. "Glad you two assholes find this entertaining."

"Entertaining?" Maverick grins so wide it's stupid. "Reed, this is the highlight of my week. Amelia nearly spit out her drink when she saw you. She said you looked like a tortured, broody bartender."

Heat creeps up the back of my neck. "She said that?"

Maverick leans closer, his voice dropping into a conspiratorial whisper. "Don't worry, you're not that broody."

Carter finally cracks, the corner of his mouth twitching. "Broody's an understatement."

I shove Maverick's beer toward him, sharper than I need to. "You two are insufferable."

Maverick lifts his glass. "And you love ussss."

I shake my head, turning back to the bottles. My skin burns, my chest aches, but for a second, the weight eases.

Even if I'm the youngest, even if I'll always feel like the one left behind, they're still my brothers.

And that's enough to keep me standing behind this bar a little longer.

The rag's still in my hand when I hear the scrape of chairs and the shuffle of familiar voices drawing closer.

"Reed," Amelia groans as she waddles up, joining the conversation. Her hand cradles her belly, as the other clutches a glass of water. "Do you have any idea how miserable it is to be nine months pregnant? My ankles look like tree trunks, my back feels like it's breaking in half, and if your brother doesn't stop hovering over me, I swear—"

Maverick ducks his head, smirking, his arm already sliding around her waist. "She loves it. Don't let her fool you. Can't get enough of me." He leans down, pressing a kiss to her temple. "My girl just doesn't know how to admit she's obsessed."

Amelia shoots him a look, but her fingers curl in his shirt anyway, anchoring herself there.

"God, you're insufferable," she mutters, but kisses him anyway.

"Insufferably handsome," he corrects, winking at me.

I roll my eyes and turn to grab a clean glass, anything to distract from the ache still simmering in my skin. Every movement tugs at the scar tissue, with the burn and itch constant and unforgiving. But I keep moving, because that's what I do.

"REEEED!"

Her shriek pierces the bar like a siren. Catalina charges ahead, Carter following behind with his usual scowl that softens the moment she grabs his arm.

"Reed! Reed, oh my GOD—Layla is here!" Catalina's chestnut eyes are wide as her manicured hand claps over her mouth. "She's finally here!"

My world stutters.

I freeze, the rag limp in my hand, chest tight as though all the air's been sucked from the room.

My pulse ticks erratically, my nerves spiking like electricity under my skin. For a second, I can't move. The laughter, the clink of glasses, and the noise of Boots & Bourbon all blur into each other.

She's here.

And suddenly, I'm not the steady, quiet bartender anymore. I'm just a man with scars crawling up his skin and butterflies tearing through his stomach, wondering what the hell she's going to think when she sees me again.

THREE
LAYLA

My driver slows to the curb in front of Boots & Bourbon, the bar I've visited a handful of times when I came to see Catalina many moons ago. I tighten my bag against my side, gripping the strap tightly, something to hold onto as my nerves surge through me.

"Thanks," I say, handing him a folded bill.

He nods, smiling, and I step out onto the cracked sidewalk.

The red neon sign above the door buzzes faintly in the early evening light.

Windows glow with a soft tinge of terra-cotta, promising warmth, noise, and maybe even a distraction. Catalina and Amelia had told me to get here immediately.

They all live there or something, I don't fucking know.

Taking a long, deep breath, I push through the heavy wooden door, and the atmosphere hits me immediately.

The intertwining smells of whiskey and polished oak smack me in the face first. Warm light spills from Edison bulbs strung across the ceiling, catching on the rows of multicolored bottles behind the bar, amber liquid glowing beneath the dim lights.

Boots scrape against wood as people laugh, talk too loudly, and clap each other on the back. The low hum of country music threads through it all, giving this place a warm, rustic feel.

My phone buzzes in my back pocket. I glance at the screen, and my stomach drops.

BRIAN

Don't forget why you're there. Content, Layla. YOU need to make us more money.

Bile rises fast, but I don't answer. I click my phone on do not disturb and shove it deep into my bag. Lifting my chin higher, I take another step inside, canvassing the bar, looking for my best friends.

My eyes scan the patrons, laughing and drinking their beer, their voices colliding, until they lock onto the bar, and there he is.

Reed's behind the bar, rag in hand, broad shoulders under a burnt-yellow flannel. The sleeves are pulled down, covering his arms, but from here I can see a glimpse of the scar tissue on the left side of his face, dipping down into the collar of his flannel.

My gaze lingers on the edge of ink there too—tattoo lines I can't quite make out, disappearing beneath the fabric.

He's wearing glasses now. They catch the light when he tilts his head, framing those sharp features that haven't dulled in the slightest. His dark brown hair is longer than I remember, brushed back but a little tousled, and the beard-mustache combo only makes his jaw look more chiseled, more striking.

God, I'd forgotten. I'd forgotten how handsome he was, devastatingly so. The attractiveness that makes your chest stutter and your throat go dry all at once.

My heart trips, stumbling over itself.

Reed continues wiping a glass until his eyes finally look up to lock onto mine.

Oh my God.

His eyes lock onto mine across the crowded room. The chatter of the bar drops out, silence rushing in like a wave, and it's just him, staring at me like nothing else around him matters.

It feels like an invisible string pulls straight from his chest to mine, tugging us together before I even take a step.

This metaphorical string between us tightens, pulling, but my feet carry me forward before I even think. My heart's still doing that wild stutter, but I paste on a grin, the kind Catalina always teases me for, because that's what I do. I smile, even when my insides are tangled in knots.

The crowd parts enough for me to spot them.

Catalina's already waving both her arms. "Laylaaaa!" she screeches, drawing half the bar's attention. Carter winces at the volume, but his mouth curves as he pulls her against him, pebbling kisses on her cheek.

I squeal right back, darting straight to Amelia first. She's perched at a table with Maverick practically glued to her side, his hand spread wide across her very pregnant belly.

"Oh. My. God," I gush, crouching slightly to press both palms to Amelia's stomach without asking, because boundaries don't exist in our friend group. "Look at this bump! You're glowing, babe."

Amelia arches a brow, grumpy as ever. "It's sweat. Don't let him fool you into thinking otherwise." She jerks her chin toward Maverick.

"Excuse you," Maverick cuts in, his blue eyes twinkling as he tightens his arm around her shoulders. "She glows because of me, don't you, baby?"

"You're lucky I love you," Amelia mutters, but she doesn't move his hand.

I laugh loudly, wrapping her in a careful hug, mindful of her belly. Once I let her go, I fling myself at Catalina, who shrieks and nearly topples backward before Carter steadies her with one big hand.

"You're here bitch!" she cries into my hair. "Oh my God, we have so much to do, so much to talk about—"

"Obviously," I tease, squeezing her tight before turning to hug Carter, who pats my back.

"Good to see you, Layla," he rumbles.

"And you," I chirp, then move on to Maverick, who engulfs me in a bear hug before I can dodge. "Maverick," I laugh against his chest, "don't crush me, please."

He sets me down with a grin, and just like that, the chaos settles into warmth. My girls are on either side of me, and the boys are steady anchors in the background. For a moment, it feels like I belong here, like I always have.

My gaze flicks back to the bar.

Reed's still behind the counter, rag limp in his hand, his steady eyes locked on me.

My throat goes dry, and I force my legs forward, each step heavier than the last, until I'm standing at the bar.

"Hi, Reed," I say softly, my smile wobbling just a little.

The string between us hums, pulling tight enough that I swear I can feel it thrumming under my skin.

For a heartbeat, he doesn't move, nor does he blink, as he stands there with that rag limp in his hand, his eyes locked on mine like he's searching for something I don't even know if I have to give.

Up close, he's even more intimidating. The glasses accentuate his green eyes, giving me a small glimpse of blue threaded within. His beard is neatly trimmed, but there's a ruggedness about him, something unrefined—like he doesn't bother to smooth out the rough edges.

Don't even get me started on his mustache, talk about hot.

The flannel he wears with the sleeves rolled down to his wrists conceals most of him, but I catch faint glimpses of scar tissue when he turns to grab something or when his collar gapes. A shadow of ink curves along it, a rose, disfigured from his scars.

My heart stutters so hard I swear it skips.

I grip the bar top, grounding myself in the cool wood beneath my palms because he's looking at me like I'm the only thing in the room. And I don't know what to do with that.

"Hey," he finally says, his voice low, rough around the edges.

One word, just one, yet it hits me like a stone dropped into water, rippling outward until I feel it everywhere.

I force a laugh, overly bright, because if I don't, I'll burst under the weight of his gaze. "What, no hug for me? Catalina nearly tackled me, and Maverick lifted me off the ground. You're slacking, Reed."

A flicker. The corner of his mouth twitches, as if he wants to smile but has forgotten how.

Catalina pipes up instantly, "Reed doesn't do physical touch, Layla, get with the program."

"Yes, he does," Amelia cuts in, rolling her eyes. "He hugged me at our baby shower, you guys saw."

"That was a side hug," Maverick calls, already laughing. "Doesn't count."

The group erupts with loud, overlapping voices, but Reed never looks away from me.

It feels like the noise around us turns into static. Like it's just me, leaning against the bar, and him, standing firm in the chaos as his eyes are locked onto mine.

My smile softens. "It's good to see you."

His jaw flexes as his eyes sweep over my face like he's memorizing it. When he finally answers, it's quiet, so quiet I almost miss it over the noise of Boots & Bourbon.

"You too, sunshine."

Sunshine? SUNSHINE?! HELLPPP.

My heart practically skips a beat. Butterflies hit me so hard I almost lose my breath.

I give him a curt smile, turning my attention back to the group.

Catalina's laughter rings above the music, her hands flying as she recounts some dramatic story, and Carter watches her like she hung up the moon and the stars, holding on to her tightly as he kisses her knuckles.

The sight of that makes me tear up, but I swallow it down.

I want that.

Amelia mutters under her breath about swollen ankles and heartburn, but the second Maverick presses a kiss to her temple, she softens, leaning into him despite her grumbling.

I jump right in, loud and laughing, rubbing Amelia's belly every chance I get until Maverick swats at me, groaning that she's his wife.

Weirdo.

Catalina and I scream-laugh at that, and Carter pinches the bridge of his nose, sighing, while tugging her into his lap.

The chaos swirls around us, and this is the only place I truly feel like I can be myself and have fun when I'm with my friends, my soul sisters, and I guess their wild husbands, too.

It's easy to get caught up in it, easy to forget the ache in my chest, the text burning a hole in my bag, the reason I left in the first place.

Every time I glance up, Reed's eyes are always on me, not once wavering.

Always steady. Always watching.

When our eyes lock, he looks away just as quickly, dropping his focus back to a glass, a rag, or the bottles lined neatly behind him.

Hours slip by, drinks and laughter flowing until the night stretches long. One by one, my friends peel away—Amelia crying about her feet hurting as Maverick carries her out, Catalina dragging Carter toward the door while mumbling about it's their facemask and bubble bath time.

Just like that, the noise is gone.

I'm perched at the bar, scrolling through my phone, checking my stats as Reed wipes down the same glass, all while doing everything in his power not to look at me.

He clears his throat, the sound making me sit up straighter. "Where are you staying?"

I bite my lower lip, glancing toward the door my friends disappeared through. "I... didn't want to intrude. They deserve their privacy with their obsessed husbands." My voice softens around the last words, a smile curling my lips. "I found a place outside of Ruby Ridge, called the Lone Star Motel."

"The Lone Star Motel?" His voice rumbles low, "Layla, that place is barely standin'. The roof leaks when it rains, and the locks don't always stick. You shouldn't be staying there."

The rag in his hands is abandoned, tossed onto the bar.

His eyes find mine, and my chest tightens under the weight of them.

"You don't need to tuck yourself away because you think you're intruding," he says, softer now, almost careful. "You're not. Not with them. Not with me."

His words land heavier than I'm ready for, heat rushing to my cheeks. My lips part, but nothing comes out, because all I can do is watch him shift his weight, clearing his throat like he's trying to swallow back something raw.

"Stay at my place," he says finally. The words are simple, but they feel like they crack something open in my chest. "It's safe. And I'd... I'd feel better knowin' you weren't out there alone."

For the first time all night, he doesn't look away.

FOUR
REED

Fuck.

I offered for her to stay with me like a complete idiot. But the thought of her being alone in a town she doesn't know that well makes my stomach twist.

The second the words left my mouth, my gut clenched. I don't do this. I don't invite anyone into my space, into the four walls that have been nothing but silence and shadow since the accident.

I've secluded myself in solitude, only communicating with my brothers. Who would want to talk to a freak like me? Who would want to start a family with someone who has baggage and scars like mine that run deep?

I don't let anyone in because people are quick to see my image, never giving me a chance to show them who I really am, who I want to be, to love someone unconditionally.

Unfortunately, people are quick to judge others based on appearance. One glance at me, and they see a man who doesn't meet their standards.

A monster. Ugly.

I circle back to the thought that my home isn't meant for

company—it's where I disappear, where the weight presses hardest.

But I can't take it back. Not when she's looking at me like that.

She looks like the sunrise I thought I'd never see again.

So fucking beautiful.

"Are you sure?" she asks, taking me out of my daze.

My throat feels tight, but I nod anyway. "Yeah," I manage, fiddling with the glass cups underneath the bar. "It's fine. Let me clean up here, and I'll take you over. You can get settled and..." I clear my throat, buying time, hiding my nerves. "...if you want, we can go over your content stuff."

Her whole face lights up with an essence of beauty that makes my heart constrict.

Her bright smile spreads quickly, effortlessly, and it's like someone dragged the sun into this dim bar. Her blue eyes light up, catching the glow of the Edison bulbs strung overhead. She leans forward just slightly, her blonde hair falling over her shoulder, and I swear the Earth stops spinning off its axis for *her*.

I've seen beautiful women before, sure, but not like *this*.

She radiates warmth in a way that feels foreign, dangerous. Sunshine bleeding into the cracks I've spent years patching shut.

I grip the rag tighter, my knuckles aching as the scar tissue pulls beneath my sleeve. The itch flares sharp and unrelenting, the pain crawling up my arm. My hand stills against the counter, but my eyes don't leave her.

I drink her in like a starving man.

The curve of her rosy cheeks where the light hits, the soft mauve gloss on her plump lips shining when she presses them together. Her lashes flutter as she glances down and then up again, catching me staring.

Her laugh bubbles out of her a second later, bright and carefree, as if she's not afraid to take up space. Hearing her laugh? Yeah, that's something I could listen to and never get tired of hearing.

Fuck, I'm in awe.

I'm not supposed to be. But I am.

Around us, the bar hums with leftover noise: distant laughter, the clink of a glass somewhere down the room. But it all blurs, fading into nothing.

All I see is her, standing there in front of me, smiling as if she doesn't notice the scars on half of my face, crawling down my neck, or the glasses perched on my nose, or the way my body feels too damn tight inside my own skin.

For a moment, I allow myself to think: maybe she doesn't notice the wreckage at first. Maybe she only sees me, and that thought terrifies me more than the fire ever did.

A few stragglers are finishing their drinks before leaving. I go through the motions of closing up; wiping down counters, stacking chairs, and ringing out the till.

My scars itch with every stretch and twist, a dull burn that sticks around no matter how many times I readjust my sleeves.

She sits perched on a stool, her duffel at her feet, as her legs swing back and forth. She's been talking nonstop since the others left, words spilling out faster than I can keep up, but I don't mind.

"Did you know flamingos aren't actually born pink?" she says suddenly, propping her chin on her hand. "It's from the shrimp they eat. Without it, they're like this sad, gray color."

I pause mid-wipe, arching a brow. "Flamingos."

"Yes, flamingos!" she grins, eyes sparkling. "I saw it in a documentary. Nature is weird. Imagine being stuck with just one color because of your diet. Like, what if I ate too many Cheetos and turned orange?"

I snort. "Maverick would."

She slaps the counter, giggling. "Oh my God, he totally would. Amelia would hate her lifeee."

Her giggle, fuck.

I shake my head, stacking clean glasses. "She already puts up with too much."

She leans forward, conspiratorial. "Between us, I know she secretly loves his chaos. Don't tell her I said that."

I glance at her, lips twitching. "Your secret's safe with me."

She beams, satisfied, then jumps into another tangent. "Oh! And Catalina texted me the other day about the Big Dipper, but she swears it looks like a frying pan. Can you believe that? She ruined it for me. Every time I look up now, all I see is a pan waiting for eggs."

"Fits her," I mutter.

She gasps, clapping a hand over her mouth. "Reed Hayes! Did you just make a joke? About your sister-in-law?"

"Don't tell her."

She laughs so loudly it bounces off the walls, and I can't stop the small smile tugging at my mouth.

Her words keep tumbling out, facts about Ruby Ridge she read online, stories about filming content in LA, complaints about airport security. She talks with her hands, blue eyes wide, like she's afraid silence will swallow her whole.

And I listen to every damn word.

Because I enjoy the sound of her voice filling the empty spaces, I like how her smile softens when she thinks I'm not looking. I even like how her engagement ring flashes in the low light, even though it feels like a punch to the ribs.

Lucky bastard. Whoever he is.

Finally, I finish counting the register and pull my keys from my back pocket, as her legs are still swinging idly, her mouth still moving a mile a minute.

I clear my throat. "Ready, Layla?"

She lights up, clapping her hands together. "Yessss!"

And just like that, she turns closing time, usually my loneliest hour, into something I don't want to end.

I shake my head, lips twitching, and head for the door. The familiar feel of the keys jingles in my hand as I flick off the last of the lights, plunging Boots & Bourbon into darkness. The neon sign outside bleeds a burnt red through the windows, casting a faint glow over the bar.

She hops off the stool, her duffel bouncing against her hip, and skips after me. Her sneakers squeak against the floor, her energy practically vibrating.

Out on the sidewalk, the night air is crisp, carrying the scent of pine and damp earth. The town feels quieter now, with Ruby Ridge settling into its bones, but with her beside me, the silence doesn't feel as heavy.

"Well," I mumble, fishing behind the door frame where I keep the spare, "I usually never have anyone with me." I turn and hold out the matte black helmet. "Wear this."

Her nose wrinkles as she stares down at it. "What?"

I jerk my chin toward the curb. "This."

She follows my gaze and gasps.

My BMW S1000RR gleams under the streetlamp, with black matte shimmering beneath the light, and a leather seat worn from years of rides that always ended with me alone.

Her hand flies to her chest, eyes wide. "Reed Hayes. You ride a motorcycle?"

"Yeah," I say simply, pressing the helmet into her hands.

"Oh my God." She laughs, the sound bright and bubbling. "That's-that's hot. I did not expect that."

Warmth spreads up the nape of my neck. I look away, hoping she doesn't catch me blushing, and slide on my gloves. "Put it on."

She fumbles, her cheeks flush as she gets it settled. Then she tilts her head at me, a smile tugging at her lips. "What about you? Aren't you supposed to wear one, too?"

I stand near my bike, my boots solid against the pavement, and meet her gaze head-on. "As long as you're safe, that's all that matters."

Her grin falters, softening into something different, something that makes my chest crack. She blinks, and I really look at her, noticing the way the inner corner of her eyes swells with the faint hint of tears, but she quickly brushes that off.

Silence stretches between us, and for once, I don't mind it as long as it's with her.

I take her in, analyzing her as she fixes the helmet on her head.

The helmet looks too big on her as she fumbles with it. She laughs softly, trying again, hair spilling around her shoulders. Sunshine incarnate, sitting on a cracked Ruby Ridge sidewalk, making even the asphalt seem worth smiling about.

"Got it," she announces, tugging the helmet on fully, and all I can see are her crystal blue eyes.

I don't trust my voice, so I nod, swinging my leg over the bike, and settle onto the worn leather seat. My bike roars to life as I turn the key, vibration crawling up my arms.

Layla steps closer, tentative for the first time tonight.

I glance over at her, steadying myself as I reach out my

hand. She hesitates before grabbing mine. Once our hands touch, it feels like her hands were always meant to be intertwined with mine.

She swings her leg across, climbing onto the back of me. The duffel rests awkwardly between us until she adjusts, pressing closer.

Letting go of my hand, she readjusts until both her arms wrap around my waist.

The air leaves my lungs all at once. My scars flare under my flannel, but the warmth of her touch cuts through it. Her chest presses against my back, her legs bracketing mine, and I swear I can feel her heartbeat pounding through both of us.

She leans in close, her helmet brushing against the back of my shoulder. "Okay, Reeed," she yells, mumbling over the rumble, "don't kill me, alright?"

The laugh that escapes me is quiet, buried in the roar of the engine. "You'll be fine."

She gasps dramatically. "Fine? That's not very reassuring!"

I can't help it, I smirk as I twist the throttle, the bike growling low. "Hold on tight."

The tires grip the pavement as we move forward, the night air rushing cold against my face. Her grip tightens instantly, her arms wrap around me as her body presses close to mine.

Cool wind whips, tugging at her laughter when it escapes, muffled through the helmet but loud enough to wrap around me. She points at the stars with her hand before clutching me tighter again, squealing when I take a curve.

Every bump in the road pulls at my scars, pain erupting

in jagged lines. But I barely notice, not when she's holding onto me like I'm the only steady thing in the world.

Her head rests briefly against my back, and it unravels me. The weight I've carried for years feels just a little lighter, like she siphons some of it away without even realizing.

I shouldn't let myself think it, but I do.

She's sunshine in my darkness.

And for the first time in a long time, the ride doesn't feel lonely.

FIVE
LAYLA

Reed coasts into a gravel driveway tucked deep into the hills. I hold on tighter than I mean to, not ready for the ride to end, not prepared to lose the steady warmth of him against me.

He cuts the engine, and the sudden silence is almost deafening. Crickets take over as the wind rustles through tall grass, the faint creak of trees shifting against the night.

I slide off the bike, legs shaking, my pulse still pounding in my throat. He hops off after me, and with just a tilt of his head, he grabs my duffel from my grasp and guides me forward.

We walk in sync as I take in my surroundings.

His house rises in front of me, half-hidden in shadow, but even in the dark, I see it's nothing like the sterile glass condos of LA. It's rustic, built from weathered timber and stone, the kind of place that looks like it's been here forever, rooted into the hillside itself.

Huge windows span across the front, tall panes catching slivers of moonlight and reflecting it like water. Even from the porch, I can see straight inside. Warm lamps softly illuminate his living room, the edges of the leather furniture softened by the spill of light.

The porch stretches wide, framed by dark beams and hanging Edison bulbs that sway in the night breeze. They cast everything in a soft, golden hue, transforming the space into something comforting and inviting.

I grip the sleeve of my sweater, my chest aching because this house is so Reed—rugged, scarred, and yet beautiful.

All I can think about is the ride here. My arms around him. His voice, low and steady, telling me to hold on. The way he called me sunshine. I can still feel the vibration of the engine in my bones, the press of his body against mine. I'm spiraling, tumbling fast into places I have no business going.

I tug my phone from my bag, fingers moving before I can think.

LAYLA

Staying with the girls.

The lie tastes bitter, but I send it anyway.

His reply comes instantly.

BRIAN

I don't fucking care.

Ew, fuck him.

Just get your shit together, Layla, then we can leave him.

Even though I'm mentally checked out, my throat still tightens, and tears prick hot at the corners of my eyes. He's an asshole, sure, but when you give every piece of yourself to someone you thought was your soulmate, it hurts.

And the thought of leaving isn't as easy as you think it is.

I shove my phone back into my bag as I lift my chin,

putting on a fake smile, and follow Reed up the steps to his door.

As the twinkle bulbs flicker above us, casting him in amber, I think if I'm not careful, this house, this man, might undo me completely.

He steps in front of me quickly, grabs his keys, and unlocks the front door, ushering me inside.

The door swings open with a low creak, and I step inside before I can second-guess myself.

His house smells faintly like oakmoss and sandalwood, that rugged mix of wood and warmth that makes you want to breathe deeper.

The first thing I notice is the light. Those massive windows I saw outside also stretch across the walls here, flooding the living room with natural light. Even at night, with only a few lamps turned on, the space feels expansive, as if the darkness itself can't quite intrude.

His living room centers around a large dark brown leather couch, positioned opposite a brick fireplace with a wooden beam atop it.

A pile of split logs sits in a metal bin nearby, a small detail that feels intimate and personal. The wooden mantle above is empty, except for a couple of framed photos that are too far away for me to see clearly.

Wide-plank oak flooring runs through his home, covered in a simple rug that softens the center, with muted yellow hues woven into geometric patterns. Shelves run along one wall, sparsely filled with old books and a few records.

I stand just inside the door, my heart racing as I take it all in because it feels like him, and I don't know what to do with that.

He places his keys in a small dish on an end table near

the door, but he doesn't look at me right away, and maybe I'm grateful because I'm not sure I could handle the weight of his gaze while I stand here, drowning in the feeling that I don't belong.

Brian's words—*I don't fucking care*—still sink their poisonous claws into my mind. I want to crumble. To let the tears out. But instead, I straighten my spine, paste the smile back onto my face as if it'll keep me from falling apart.

"This place is..." My voice cracks, and I clear my throat, forcing it steady. "It's beautiful, Reed."

He finally looks at me, his green eyes soft in the dim light. And for the briefest second, the heaviness inside me lifts, like maybe I'm not carrying it alone.

Reed moves further into the house, and I follow behind him, my sneakers whispering over the wood floors. He flicks on a lamp in the hallway, casting saffron rays that spill over the simple lines of his space—clean, uncluttered, yet heavy with the feeling of someone who lives alone.

He pauses at the end of the hall, his hand resting against the doorframe of a bedroom. "So..." His voice is low and rough, like gravel being turned over. "I only have one bed."

My heart flips.

He rubs the back of his neck, his eyes fixed on the floor as though the grain of the wood is suddenly fascinating. "You can take it. I'll crash on the couch."

I shift on my heels, my pulse pounding in my ears. The thought of him giving up his bed for me, the idea of him lying awake on a couch while I stretch out in his space, it tightens something in my chest.

"Reed, I don't want to—"

"It's fine," he cuts in, still not looking at me. His voice is steady, but his jaw flexes. "I've slept on worse."

The silence stretches awkwardly, and suddenly every inch between us feels significant.

I finally risk a glance at him, the flannel stretches across his broad shoulders, the reflection of his glasses catching the lamplight—the scar tissue stark against his cheekbone. My fingers itch with the urge to touch, to reach out, to close the gap, but I curl my fingers inward, my nails biting against my palm.

"It's late," I blurt out nervously. My smile wobbles, and I force it wider. "We can talk about the content ideas tomorrow."

He finally looks up, those fiery eyes pinning me in place, softer now but still sharp enough to make my stomach flip.

"Looking forward to it," he says quietly.

The awkwardness transforms into something else, something dangerous, a hum under my skin like static ready to spark.

He steps aside, his broad shoulders filling the doorway, before gesturing me in. I swallow hard, taking my duffel from his hand, and slip past him into his room.

I look over my shoulder, whispering, "Goodnight, Reed."

"Goodnight, Layla," he says, a small twinkle in his eyes.

He closes the door softly for me, the sound of his footsteps retreating into the living room.

I let out the breath I was holding, my gaze sweeping over his room.

It feels... intimate.

His space is simple but deeply personal, the kind of room that carries a man's weight in its silence. A king-sized bed sits against the far wall, sheets dark and crisp, tucked with military precision. A heavy, worn quilt lies folded at the edge of the bed.

There's a nightstand with only the essentials: an alarm clock, a small stack of books, and a half-empty glass of water. One wall is bare except for a large window that lets in the night, moonlight spilling in silver streaks across the floorboards.

Faint traces of bourbon and vanilla waft up, smelling like him.

My stomach twists into knots. It feels too much, stepping into a place that holds his sleep, his quiet, his solitude. I shouldn't be here, but I have this strange sensation of not wanting to be anywhere else.

I slip into the small adjoining bathroom and turn on the light. The mirror shows my flushed cheeks and wild hair from the helmet. I splash cool water on my face, scrubbing until I feel more stable. My makeup smudges into faint shadows, but I don't mind.

Tugging on the oversized T-shirt I shoved into my bag at the last second, the one with a cartoon raccoon sprawled across the front, bold letters reading *Too Cool For U*; it hangs loose over my thighs, the soft cotton tickling my skin.

Ridiculous and entirely me.

I catch sight of myself in the mirror again, groaning, and mumble to myself, "I'm a sexy bitch, I know."

Shutting off the bathroom lights, I pad back over into his bedroom and sink into Reed's bed. His mattress is plush, smelling faintly like *him*—before I can let myself delve into the way he smells, instinctively clenching my thighs, my phone lights up, buzzing against the worn, wooden nightstand.

I turn over, grabbing my phone as the screen lights up, flooding my phone with text messages from my unhinged group chat with my girls.

CATALINA

Okay, but where are you STAYING tonight? You didn't say anything to us, bitch.

I chew my lip, grin, and type.

LAYLA

ummm.. Reed's place.

My phone instantly pings.

CATALINA

EXCUSE THE FUCK OUT OF ME.

AMELIA

WHAT THE FUCK.

CATALINA

WHY DIDN'T YOU SAY ANYTHING AT THE BAR?!

AMELIA

We were literally RIGHT THERE.

I snort, my thumbs flying across the screen.

LAYLA

Because you were too busy in your love fest with your husbands. Didn't want to intrude.

CATALINA

BITCH. You sound so dumb

AMELIA

Pregnant. Carrying my six-foot-eight husband's baby. My ankles look like balloons. My pelvis feels like it's been split in two.

AMELIA

AND YOU think you're intruding??

CATALINA

Carter has been ravaging me bc we've been trying to get pregnant, but my vagina needs a break. Layla pls help

AMELIA

Honestly, come sleep in our bed and take Maverick's side. He's sweaty and annoying.

CATALINA

SAME. Carter's a fucking furnace

LAYLA

Wow, thanks for the offers. But no thanks. I'll stick with Reed's bed. He gave me the whole thing and is on the couch.

CATALINA

OH MY GOD???

AMELIA

That's so sweet

CATALINA

Couch = love declaration, you fuck.

LAYLA

stfu. He's just being nice.

AMELIA

Men aren't "nice." Trust me. If another woman breathes around Maverick, he gags.

CATALINA

Same. Carter once glared at a grocery store clerk because she said I had nice hair.

LAYLA

...you guys are insane.

CATALINA

And you're blind.

I roll my eyes and toss my phone onto the nightstand. Their chaos lingers, but the truth presses harder the longer I lie there.

I'm in Reed's bed, and I don't want to leave.

SIX
REED

The leather couch groans when I push myself upright, the cushions sagging like they're as worn-out as I am. My back protests immediately, scar tissue stretched tight across my shoulder blades, the ache deep in my muscles lingering from a night of shifting and never finding rest.

My house is silent, heavy in the early hours before dawn. Fog covers the early morning light, blanketing the trees in sheer mist.

I rake my fingers down my mustache, the coarse stubble catching against my fingertips, and push to stand. My body aches in protest, scars itching like they always do when I move first thing in the morning.

Mustering under my breath, I glance toward the kitchen; coffee can wait.

I need to use the bathroom more, but the only one is in my bedroom.

Where *she* is.

My chest caves in, nerves coiling tightly as I walk down the hallway, my bare feet making the wood groan with each step. The door is slightly open, silver-gray light from the first signs of morning seeping through those wide windows, casting a soft, muted glow around the edges of the room.

I quickly look around the room until my eyes lock onto Layla's relaxed body, tousled between the sheets.

She's tangled between the quilt and a thin gray sheet. Diagonal across the mattress, her leg is hooked in the quilt, the other hanging off the side. Her arm rests on her stomach, her hand hanging limply, fingers curled between the sheets.

Her mouth is slightly open, lips parted in a relaxed, unselfconscious way. A faint little snore escapes, barely audible, and the sound stirs something loose in my chest.

Her hair, wild from sleep, a golden, messy halo, spills across my pillow, catching faint streaks of dawn that make the strands glow.

She looks so at ease pressed into my pillow, like she's always belonged here.

I grip the doorframe harder than I should, my scars itching, pulling, burning like they want to remind me of what I am.

But for a moment, I let myself forget.

I let myself admire her.

Her chest rises and falls steadily, her lips twitching with some dream I'll never understand. She's wild, even while asleep; sprawled out, ungraceful, ridiculous.

And somehow the most beautiful thing I've ever seen.

My throat tightens. A faint, reluctant smile tugs across my lips, a genuine one.

I shouldn't linger, I shouldn't let my mind wander down the dangerous path it wants to.

I imagine this as something ordinary; I fantasize about waking up with her here, in my space. In my life.

She's engaged, Reed. You're being considerate and letting her stay here so she doesn't feel alone.

Fuck.

Shoving my internal thoughts aside, I push myself forward, careful as I slip past my bed, each step calculated so the floor doesn't creak.

The bathroom door clicks shut behind me, but the image stays burned in my mind: Layla sprawled in my sheets, soft and unguarded, like she belongs nowhere else.

And God help me, I want to see it again tomorrow.

Flushing the toilet, hoping it doesn't wake her, I quickly wash my hands, turn off the light, and head back out to make my escape back to the living room. The bathroom door clicks softly behind me as I step back into the bedroom.

I expect her to still be out cold, sprawled, and snoring like she was when I walked in.

But she isn't.

Shit.

She shifts, groaning as she rolls onto her side, her hair sticking up in every direction. Her eyes blink open, hazy but alert in that way only morning people can manage. A yawn cracks across her face before she props herself up on one elbow.

"Busted," she rasps, voice still thick with sleep. "Were you just watching me drool on your pillow?"

Heat crawls up the nape of my neck. Clearing my throat, I avert my eyes. "Needed the bathroom."

She grins slowly and mischievously. "It's okay, Reed. You just wanted to watch me sleep, admit it."

"Bullshit," I mutter, rubbing a hand over my jaw.

Her laugh is quiet yet bright, filling the room in a way that makes my chest ache. She sits all the way up, her ridiculous shirt slipping off one shoulder, her hair wild around her face. "For the record, I do not drool. I am a very dignified sleeper."

"Right," I deadpan, arching a brow. "Looked real dignified, half hanging off the bed."

Her mouth drops open in mock offense. "You could've fixed me, you know. Tucked me in or something. Isn't that southern hospitality?"

"Didn't want to lose a hand," I shoot back, finally letting the corner of my mouth twitch.

Her laugh erupts as she flops back onto the mattress, covering her face with both hands. "God, I can't believe I'm getting roasted by you at six in the morning."

I lean against the doorframe with my arms folded, just watching. Her sunshine burns away the quiet and heaviness until I almost forget it's there.

"Coffee?" I ask finally.

She peeks at me between her fingers, smiling. "Only if you promise not to make fun of my pajamas."

"No promises," I mutter, but the smile lingers as I turn toward the kitchen.

For the first time in a long damn while, the morning doesn't feel so heavy.

The coffee pot gurgles to life, filling the kitchen with the smell of dark roast. I lean against the counter with my arms crossed, watching the steady drip, waiting for the mug I know I'll need to get through the day.

She drops into one of the chairs at the breakfast nook, with her legs tucked under her, and starts talking before I can even ask how she takes her coffee.

"Your house is crazy, Reed. These windows? They're huge! Do you even have curtains? Because if not, you're basically giving the squirrels a free show. Not that I'm judging. I think they'd enjoy it."

Only she would be concerned about squirrels.

I shake my head, turning back to pour the coffee. "Don't need curtains."

"Bold of you to assume your neighbors aren't peeking through binoculars," she teases, chin in her hand. "If I lived across from this place, I'd totally creep."

I snort, sliding a steaming mug across the counter toward her. She brightens immediately, wrapping both hands around the ceramic mug.

"Oh my God," she sighs after the first sip. "You might have just saved my life. No offense to LA coffee shops, but this actually tastes like coffee, not burnt like oat milk that costs thirty dollars."

I settle across from her with my own mug, watching as she rambles, her words spilling faster than the pot ever could.

"And this kitchen," she continues, waving one hand dramatically, "is sooooo amazing. The wood? The stone? The whole rugged man lives here, but somehow knows what color palette is the vibe? Did you design this yourself?"

I shrug, sipping my coffee. "Catalina and Amelia helped, mostly."

She rolls her eyes, setting her mug down with a clink. "Well, they did an amazing job."

Her grin is too bright, too effortless. And even though I only give her a slight shake of my head, I feel a warm spark ignite in my chest.

She doesn't notice, as she keeps rambling about different topics all at once.

She talks about wanting to change her content, but her nervousness makes me wonder why—mentions how Amelia once threatened to toss a crystal at Maverick if he didn't stop stealing her snacks. Describes how Catalina swears by lavender-scented candles, even though Layla thinks all flower-scented products smell the same.

Choosing not to say much, I sip my coffee and listen to her intently, yet I hang onto every word.

I barely finish half my mug, and she's already up again, padding barefoot across the wood floors until she's in front of my fridge. She swings open the stainless steel doors and bends at the waist, peering inside.

"Okay, first of all," she calls out, voice muffled by the shelves, "you have the most bachelor fridge I've ever seen. Eggs, beer, leftover takeout, and... oh my God, Reed, you actually have a jar of pickles. Amelia would cry tears of joy."

I arch a brow, leaning back in my chair. "You always go through people's fridges?"

She pops up with the jar of pickles in hand, grinning. "Only when I'm hungry. Which is always." She twists the lid, takes one out, and crunches happily before continuing like she never left off. "You're missing out, by the way. Pickles at breakfast? Elite move. Don't knock it till you try it."

I shake my head, amused despite myself.

"Why the interest in my bar?" I ask finally.

She pauses for a moment, jar still in her hand, then turns to look at me. The humor fades, and her expression becomes steadier, more vulnerable.

"Because it feels real," she says simply. "So much of what I film in LA is staged, curated, filtered. But Boots & Bourbon? It's... different. It's lived-in. People actually feel there. You've built something that has soul, Reed. And I want to show that. To film it, to capture the way it feels when you walk through those doors."

Her words hit harder than I expected, pressing against the part of me that always wonders if people only see my scars, never the effort I put into everything else.

I clear my throat, leaning back. "That's a lot of pressure."

She laughs, light and easy again, as she sets the pickles on the counter. "It's just honest. That's all people want, something that doesn't feel fake."

Before I can respond, she's already jumping into her next idea. "Okay, content ideas, hear me out. We could do a behind-the-scenes of you setting up for the night. Like, people love that kind of process stuff. Or a spotlight on local musicians you bring in. Maybe even a series about the regulars, you've got characters in there, I know you do."

Her eyes flick to me, bright and mischievous. "Though we might need to work on your on-camera face. Right now you're giving me 'I hate my life.'"

I let out a huff of a laugh, shaking my head. "Appreciate the honesty."

She beams with triumph and pulls out a notebook from her bag that she left on the counter last night. She's already scribbling, rambling about angles and lighting; about capturing the glow of the bottles against the shelves, and about filming small snippets of conversation between patrons.

I don't stop her.

Because as she talks, I realize something; she sees the bar the way I once did, not as a reminder of what I lost, but as a place worth building.

And damn it, that makes me want to see it through her eyes, too.

She's pacing now, with the pickle jar forgotten on the

counter, her notebook open in one hand while the other waves wildly as she talks.

"Okay, imagine this," she says, spinning on her heel, hair flying around her face. "A mini-series: Night at Boots & Bourbon. Like, quick clips; the neon glow outside, people laughing, glasses clinking. And then you're behind the bar, all broody bartender, but secretly soft. The internet would eat you up, Reed. I promise."

Her pen scratches across the page, creating messy loops and arrows connecting half-formed ideas. "We could do themed nights, too. Oh! Maybe a girls' night highlight where we show which cocktails pair with which songs. People love that interactive stuff. And—wait, wait—do you still have that dartboard? Because, Reed, I swear to God, we could make a whole thing out of 'drunk dart confessions.' Viral. Instantly viral."

She's smiling brightly, words pouring out faster than I can follow, stumbling over themselves as she rushes to say them. Her sunshine lights up every corner of the room, banishing shadows that have stayed too long.

I sit at the table, coffee cooling in my hands, just absorbing all her radiance and beauty.

The way her nose scrunches when she's excited; the furrow of her brows when she scribbles something down; the little bounce in her step as she moves from the fridge, to the counter, to the table, and back again, like her body can't contain the energy.

She doesn't even notice me staring, and I shouldn't be.

I know that, but I can't help it.

A faint but genuine smile touches my lips, feeling strange—foreign, almost—after years of forcing them for strangers at the bar. This one comes easily, sparked just by watching her be exactly who she is.

Her light. My shadows.

She talks and talks, and I let her because every word reminds me that maybe, just maybe, I don't have to sit in the dark forever.

SEVEN
LAYLA

I tug at the hem of my yellow tube top, the fabric fitting snug against my skin, while my baggy, ripped jeans hang loose on my hips. Sandals softly slap against the wood floors as I walk. My gold hoops catch the light, and layered necklaces gently twinkle against my chest. My hair falls in loose waves down my back, with the ends tickling past my shoulder blades.

Reed's already waiting by the door, dressed like only he can pull off—dark jeans, scuffed boots, and a flannel in muted navy that strains across his broad shoulders. The sleeves are rolled up to his forearms, revealing scarred skin and tattoos that wind up from beneath the fabric.

My gaze travels across his jawline, up to his trim beard and devastating mustache, until it reaches his dark, tousled hair. When he looks up at me with those steady green eyes, something sharp stirs in my chest.

It's then that I notice the dog tags hanging from a chain at his neck, half-hidden beneath the flannel.

"Reed," I murmur, stepping closer, my gaze snagging on the metal catching the light. "Are those yours?"

He stiffens instantly as his eyes dart to mine. For a split second, I see a glimpse of hurt, raw, and anxiousness flicker across his face before he pushes it away.

My stomach twists as I open my mouth, then close it again.

Words choke in my throat. I shouldn't have freaking asked.

God, Layla, why can't you shut up sometimes?

He doesn't answer or explain. He looks at me for a heartbeat longer before pressing the helmet into my hands, and this time a leather jacket.

"Let's get to work, Layla."

I swallow hard, forcing a smile even as my chest burns. "Right. Let's go."

Throwing on the jacket and sliding the helmet on, I push the panic down where it can't show.

He moves past me, the weight of him so solid, so steady, as he straddles the motorcycle. The bike roars to life, the sound filling the quiet afternoon.

I climb on behind him, my arms wrapping instinctively around his waist. The world narrows to the thrum of the engine beneath us, the press of him against me, and the endless hum of tension I can't seem to shake.

He pulls out of the driveway, gravel spitting under the tires, and we head toward Boots & Bourbon.

All I can think, heart pounding against his back, is that I'm playing with something dangerous here.

The bike roars down the open road, the afternoon wind rushing against my skin, tangling through my hair where it escapes the helmet. I clutch him tighter as he leans into a curve, my fingers spread against the hard plane of his abs beneath the flannel.

God, he's ripped just from the way my fingers flex against his body.

Every movement is steady and controlled, his body warm and unwavering beneath my hands. The engine's vibration hums through both of us, and I can't tell if the tremor in my chest is from the ride or from him.

I shouldn't feel this way.

He's six years older than me. He's the quiet bartender with scars he doesn't talk about, with a gaze that burns through me as if it sees everything I try to hide.

And I'm engaged.

The thought slices through me. Brian's ring still rests heavily on my finger, even though his words from last night sting.

"I don't fucking care."

I grip him tighter as the bike accelerates, my pulse pounding. My thoughts keep circling back to the fact that I'm in another state with another man, while my fiancé is back home.

Burying my thoughts deep, locking them away where they can't burn me alive, I tell myself it's just the adrenaline, just the rush of the ride, just the contrast between his silence and my chaos that makes me feel this way.

But when he shifts slightly under my arms as his muscles flex, the heat rising through me reveals every lie I try to tell.

And the scariest part is, I don't want to let go.

His motorcycle shifts to a softer growl as he downshifts, leading us down Ruby Ridge's quiet main street—morning sun bathes the rooftops, reflecting off the glass shopfronts, and the air carries the scent of cut grass, asphalt, and freshly baked bread from a bakery two doors down.

Finally, he pulls up to Boots & Bourbon, and my

stomach does a little flip. I've been here before, but only at night, when the neon sign buzzes against the dark, when laughter spills into the street, when the place feels like a heartbeat for the whole town.

In daylight, it's a different creature entirely.

The neon letters, faded by the sun, hang lazily above the door, their edges chipped from the weather and the passage of time. The wooden siding is rough and sun-bleached, each plank bearing a history you can't wipe away. The wide front windows catch the morning light, glowing amber against the dark interior.

I tug off the helmet, my hair falling in messy waves, catching sunlight's gold. My sandals, surprisingly, stayed on the whole ride.

Why in the fuck did I wear sandals?

Swinging my legs off the bike, my sandals crunch on gravel as I steady myself, legs shaky from the ride, or maybe because of him.

I can't tell anymore.

The fall breeze is chilly, carrying the faintest hints of pine from the hills. Aromas of old wood, stale whiskey, and cigarette smoke intertwine and permeate the moment we step near Boots & Bourbon; they seep into the building's bones, becoming part of it.

My throat tightens. This is exactly why I came. Places like this, gritty, alive, imperfect, are the ones that stick and mean something.

I turn, about to speak, and catch Reed watching me.

He hasn't moved from his motorcycle, his hand resting on the handlebar while the other tugs off his gloves. His eyes follow me, unblinking, as if he's memorizing my every reaction.

The weight of his gaze pins me in place.

I force a smile, tucking a strand of hair behind my ear. "It's even better in the daylight."

His jaw tightens, the faintest movement as if there's something he wants to say but doesn't trust himself to. Finally, he nods once, his voice low and rough. "Yeah. It is."

The quiet stretches between us, feeling heavy but not uncomfortable, thick with something I can't quite name. My chest tightens with it—his silence, my noise, the way I keep trying to close the distance between us.

He slips the keys from his pocket, the jingle sharp in the stillness. He pushes the heavy door open, the wood groaning in protest.

The air inside is cool, shadowy, thick with layered scents of whiskey, wood polish, and faint cigarette smoke sinking into the beams. Sunlight streams through the wide front windows, catching dust that floats lazily, casting golden streaks across the tables and bar top.

I step inside and stop, my sandals squeaking softly on the wood floor.

It feels so different without the crowd. Without Catalina shrieking greetings, without Maverick's booming laugh, without Carter scowling at anyone who looks at her. The silence is heavy but not empty. It's... sacred. Boots & Bourbon in daylight feels like stepping into the bones of a story.

My chest swells, and before I can stop myself, words tumble out.

"Oh my God, Reed. This, this is everything. Look at the light on the bottles. That bar back? Gorgeous."

I spin slowly in a circle, taking it all in: the scuffed pool table, the old jukebox tucked in the corner, the mismatched stools that somehow complement each other. "This is exactly what I was talking about. This place breathes. I swear I could create ten different content series just standing right here."

Behind me, he says nothing.

I glance back, and he's leaning against the bar with his arms crossed, just watching. His eyes track me like he's trying to figure me out.

Moving to the bar, I press both palms flat against the wood. "Here? Mixology clips. We could do quick cocktails with stories behind them; local names, ranch references. People eat that up."

I look up, grinning at him, my heart pounding in my chest. "Reed, you have no idea how much gold you're sitting on here."

His mouth curves; small, fleeting, but genuine. For a moment, I forget how to breathe.

EIGHT
REED

My fingers are cool beneath the oak bar top as I work, polishing glasses, resetting stools, falling into a rhythm I've known for years. My scars itch with every stretch, but I keep my sleeves pulled down, hiding the worst of them.

Routine makes the silence and pain bearable.

Except today, it isn't silent; Layla is everywhere.

Her sandals softly slap against the wood floors as she paces the bar with her camera in hand, and her blonde hair shimmers in the evening rays coming through the windows.

She's talking a mile a minute, narrating to the camera, laughing at herself, spinning in small circles to capture every angle.

Hopping onto the edge of the mechanical bull, she caresses the back of it. "This is sooo iconic. I know you bitches wanna sit on a bull and ride." She slides off, brushing dust from her jeans.

She moves as if she belongs here, like she's known this bar just as long as I have, and my heart squeezes at the sight of her.

This is my space. The only place I've managed to keep steady after everything. And here she is, invading it, filling it, lighting it up like she was made for it. Sunshine bleeding into darkness, I never thought I'd shake.

I catch myself smiling. Ducking my head to pretend to fix some glasses, I hope she doesn't see and wipe the same glass again, even though it's spotless.

Eventually, she returns to the bar, her cheeks flushed, blue eyes shining. "Okay. I think I have a substantial amount to edit, for now. This is... this is perfect, Reed." She tucks her phone away, smiling brightly. "I'll have to get some more footage when I'm back. I'm heading back home tomorrow, but I'll text you."

"Tomorrow?" The word slips out harsher than I intend it to. "So soon?"

She nods, her lips curving in a gentle apology. "Yeah, I have some brand meetings that can't be rescheduled. But I'll be back, I promise."

I grunt, setting the glass down more forcefully than needed. Her smile softens as her gaze lingers, and her blue eyes follow me as if she's memorizing me.

And fuck me, I want her to.

The bell above the door rings out, breaking the quiet moment between us. Two women walk in, sunglasses pushed up high on their heads, their voices loud and clear for the calm afternoon. They go directly to the bar, searching the shelves for their desired drink.

As their eyes are scouring the shelves of liquor, two sets of eyes land on me, and once they get a peek at the scar tissue that I can't hide.

It's the look I recognize all too well; the twitch of lips, the subtle curl of disgust. Their eyes flick over the scars on my cheek and neck, the ones the flannel can't conceal.

One of them whispers something behind her hand, and the other smirks.

The familiar burn spreads through my chest and down my arms. I keep my head lowered, my jaw clenched, and my fingers gripping the counter tightly.

Before I can open my mouth, Layla's voice slices through the air.

"Why the fuck are you staring?"

Both women freeze, blinking at her.

Layla steps closer, chin held high, sunshine replaced by fire. "Seriously. Order your drinks or get the hell out. This isn't a zoo."

My eyes meet Layla's, seeing her fire and her determination to protect someone she barely knows. My heart races, that butterfly sensation fluttering low in my stomach once more.

She turns back to me then, her blue eyes blazing and protective like I've never seen before. And for the first time in longer than I can remember, the shame doesn't feel so suffocating.

Because someone finally stood between me and the world, and it was her.

The women mutter something under their breath, then quickly order, their eyes darting anywhere but at me. I pour without speaking, jaw clenched, sliding the drinks across the counter. They throw cash on the counter and slink off to a corner table, their laughter now hushed.

Layla doesn't look at them again.

She's looking at me.

Her eyes are softer than I've ever seen them, no longer the fire from a moment ago, nor the playful demeanor she usually carries. Just warmth, fierce, and quiet all at once. Like she sees every scar, every fracture, and doesn't flinch.

I swallow hard, my throat thick. "You didn't have to..."

"Yes, I did," she interrupts softly, her voice a gentle contrast to the sharpness she'd just delivered. Her hand brushes the bar top between us, close enough that our fingers almost brush. "Don't argue with me, Reed. Let me care a little."

Her words sink in deeper than they should, burrowing into places I've kept locked away for years. My chest hurts with it, but it's not the usual pain; it's something dangerous.

Something that feels a hell of a lot like *hope*.

She reaches into her bag, pulls out a slip of paper, and scribbles quickly. When she slides it across the counter, her gold jewelry shimmering beneath the natural light.

"My address," she says with a half-smile. "Just... to have. In case. Or if you need it. Or, I don't know, if you wanna write me letters." She laughs softly, shaking her head at herself.

I stare at the paper, the neat loops of her handwriting blur for a second before my vision clears.

Her address?

A piece of her world is placed willingly into my scarred hands. When my eyes meet hers again, she's still watching me, eyes wide.

And I don't know what terrifies me more, how badly I want to keep it, or how impossible it feels to deserve it.

I let the silence hang heavy between us. The crumpled paper sits on the counter as my hand hovers above it, my rough fingers twitching, before I finally give in and slide it toward me.

When I glance up again, she's grinning at me.

"There," she says brightly, brushing her hands together as if she's accomplished something big. "Now, if you ever get tired of brooding in here, you can send me letters. Or, you know, a pizza. I accept both."

The corner of my mouth twitches, almost a smile. "Pizza, huh?"

"Obviously." She leans in closer, resting her chin on her hand, yellow-gold bracelets softly clinking. "Pepperoni with extra cheese, and cheese crust, duh."

I shake my head, but the warmth in my chest won't fade. "You talk too much."

She gasps, pressing a hand to her chest. "Excuse me, but that's my brand. Sunshine and sass. You don't like it?"

I meant to tell her I don't mind. I like it more than I should. But the words are stuck in my throat. Instead, I settle for something safer.

"It suits you."

She beams at me anyway, all teeth and fire, like I just gave her a crown.

For the first time in a long, damn time, I don't feel like my scars are the only thing people notice.

NINE
LAYLA

Brand meetings are over, and I'm piled with content that I need to film, edit, and post before a deadline. All of it requires my fiancé to be featured because, according to them, our couple content is booming, and these brands only agreed to these deals as long as Brian is involved.

The Santa Monica breeze hits me, the smell of exhaust and food trucks blends on the sidewalk, while the chatter of people on their phones merges into a restless hum. My heels click against the concrete as I walk to the parking garage, my shoulders tense, replaying the meeting over and over.

Pulling my keys out of my bag, I click the key fob, a beep reverberating throughout the garage, and open my car door.

The leather seats are hot, sticking to the back of my thighs as I toss my tote into the passenger seat and start the engine. The air conditioner blasts me in the face, but it doesn't do much to cool the heat prickling beneath my skin.

My engine roars as I peel out of the parking garage,

anger bubbling in my chest, causing me to grip the steering wheel tighter as I merge onto the street.

Traffic is a tangled mass of brake lights, crawling along Ocean Avenue. I rest my elbow on the window ledge, watching palm trees sway against the hazy blue sky.

A couple on scooters zooms past, laughing, their hair whipping in the wind, and the sound slices through me.

I want to laugh like that. I want to feel like that. Instead, I'm here, stuck in a box of metal and noise, wishing I were strong enough to leave, but I'm not.

I'm scared to leave, worried that my content will be nothing without him. I'm afraid of being all alone while my best friends have their happily-ever-afters.

That's all I really want, someone to call home. Someone to love me, for *me*, not just my content and a quick cash grab.

Pulling into the underground garage of my Santa Monica apartment, my jaw aches from clenching it. I slam the car door shut harder than necessary; the sound echoes off the concrete walls, and I take the elevator up.

The ride is silent except for the buzzing fluorescent light above me.

I pause in front of my apartment door, hesitating to go inside. Taking a deep breath through my nose, I exhale, finally unlocking my front door.

The familiar scent of peony and cherry blossom candles, along with the lingering aroma of takeout, greets me. It should feel comforting.

It doesn't.

Brian is exactly where I knew he'd be: sprawled across the couch, phone in hand, thumb scrolling as if it's the only muscle in his body that works. He doesn't even bother looking up when I come home anymore.

"We need to film a video," I say, dropping my tote on the entryway table. My voice is steady and practiced, just like my smile. "For the skincare collab."

He groans dramatically, dragging his eyes up at me for the first time since I walked in. "Fine."

I pace over to the hallway closet, dragging my tripod out from it, the legs squeaking as they extend. The ring light flicks on, buzzing faintly, and the apartment transforms under its glow.

He remains slouched on the couch, still scrolling through his stupid phone. His jaw tics when I adjust the angle.

"Hurry up," he mutters, not even looking at me.

I make my way over to the couch after the tripod is set up, sitting closely next to him.

The moment I press record, he becomes a different person.

His phone vanishes, his posture straightens, and suddenly there's a dazzling smile on his face; one he reserves only for strangers online. He slides an arm around my waist, pulling me into his side as if he can't get enough of me, his lips brushing my temple.

"Look at my girl," he says, grinning into the camera, voice full of fake warmth. "Her skin's glowing, right? This stuff is magic."

I laugh on cue, the sound rehearsed and hollow, leaning my head against his shoulder as I broadcast the skincare I'm using.

My stomach twists. Ten minutes ago, I was just background noise to him. Now, in front of the camera, I'm his everything.

He kisses my cheek once, then again, lingering longer,

tilting my face so the camera catches it. It looks sweet. It feels wrong.

His mouth is warm, but it's empty. His thumb strokes my jaw for show, not for me.

I faintly feel a flutter through my chest, a glimpse of how he used to be with me, but that quickly fades.

We go through the routine: the product demo, the exaggerated reactions, the flirty banter that makes my chest ache with how fake it is. I can feel the stiffness in his body, the way every gesture is calculated, every laugh a little too sharp.

I plaster on a wider smile, even as my insides feel smaller, because this is what sells.

Couple content. Happy, glowing, showing the world that we are the perfect couple.

But not for long, I hope my experiment works so I can finally leave him and do what *I* want to do.

Twenty minutes pass in a blur, a blur of muted noises, our voices colliding that I don't hear anymore.

It's all I can handle before I stop recording. My face aches from forcing the smile, as my stomach clenches, leaving my palms sweaty. I quickly stand, reaching for the camera, to get away from him, but he's already standing, muttering under his breath.

"I'm done with this shit," he snaps, shoving my shoulder as he pushes past me. "Have fun fucking editing, and zelle me the money when it's in."

The breath bursts out of me in a sharp scoff. "Whatever."

He laughs without even turning around, the sound hollow as the bedroom door slams shut behind him.

Silence swallows the apartment.

The ring light hums faintly, casting a false glow over everything, and the camera's red standby light blinks like a cruel reminder of the lie we just filmed.

I sink back onto the couch, pressing the heels of my palms to my eyes, trying to breathe past the tightness in my chest.

Unbidden, Reed's face flashes in my mind. He looked at me across the bar, never once looking away. How his voice dropped when he said I wasn't intruding, as if it weren't up for debate. It was just a moment, almost a breath.

But it felt like something real. Something I have been craving for years.

My phone is warm in my hand before I even realize I've picked it up. My fingers hover, hesitating, until I finally type.

LAYLA

Heyyyyy

Would you maybe want to keep me company while I edit sometime? I don't mind flying out there; I could use the distraction.

I stare at my message as my thumb trembles above the screen. I shouldn't send it. It's stupid and fucking reckless.

The whoosh of the sent message makes my heart skip a beat.

Three dots appear. Disappear. Reappear.

Ping.

REED

Yeah, say when. I'll be here to pick you up.

No questions or hesitation.

For the first time today, my smile comes unforced, curling slowly across my lips. The sensation of butterflies fluttering through me again makes me feel giddy with nerves.

I quickly switch apps as my thumb moves on instinct before I can talk myself out of it, feeling the weight of guilt press down on me.

No, Layla, it's nothing.

Expedia loads slowly, and my heart beats faster with every second the screen takes to load. Finally, rows of flights appear, and I tap the one leaving in two days, round-trip from LAX to Nashville.

My thumb hovers over the screen as I switch between tabs, checking the date, opening my calendar, and doing the mental math of how quickly I could disappear back to a place that makes me feel normal, happy.

A small, hopeful smile slips onto my face before I can stop it.

"What are you smiling for?"

Oh my God, I didn't even hear him walk out of our bedroom.

His words come from behind me, quiet but strong enough to make me jump.

Turning quickly, I drop my phone on the floor.

He's leaning over the couch with his arms crossed, watching me with a glare, like he was trying to see what I'm doing on my phone.

"I— I'm not," I say too quickly, turning fully towards him, crossing my hands and praying to whatever God he doesn't pick my phone up off the floor.

He walks around the couch slowly, studying my face. When he stops in front of my phone, he picks it up and gently sets it down on the glass coffee table in front of me.

Once he sets the phone down, he reaches out and presses his hand against my shoulder, pushing me enough to fall back into the cushions.

"You know," he murmurs, leaning in until our noses are touching. "I should be the only one who makes you smile like that."

He says it like it's a joke, like it's sweet.

Like I should feel some kind of way that my man is jealous. But I'm not. All I feel toward him is emptiness, nothing, an ache where my love for him used to be.

He leans back enough to look at me before claiming my mouth with a searing kiss, his tongue pressing past my lips as nausea swirls through me.

I push him off of me, and he glares at me. Without a word, he walks back into our bedroom and slams the door shut. A faint sound of his game turning on a second later.

The knot in my chest tightens, and the excitement I felt just a moment ago fades away.

Walking toward the kitchen, I grab a dish towel and turn back to the sink, the thought of Nashville slowly fading as I continue moving through the kitchen.

Crouching down as I scour the cabinets, I grab the kettle, fill it with water, and place it on the stove.

The kettle shrieks, a sharp whistle that cuts through the silence, and I pour boiling water over a tea bag, watching amber seep into the steaming cup.

On the balcony, I hold the mug against my chest and breathe in the ocean air.

Below me, Santa Monica hums with the noise of traffic, chatter, and screams spilling out along the pier. It's everything I used to love, everything I thought I'd built for myself. But right now, the city feels like a backdrop, and I'm the only one who doesn't belong in the scene.

When the tea cools, I make my way back to the kitchen and rinse the mug, load a few stray dishes into the dishwasher, and wipe the counters.

Back on the couch, I open my laptop again. The files automatically load, the rainbow wheel of doom spinning until Brian's face fills the screen. His grin's wide, charming, and directly aimed at the camera.

I press play, watching him slide his arm around me and tilt my chin so the camera captures his kiss. It looks perfect. God, it'll sell.

But my stomach knots. Because I see the emptiness in his eyes that no one else will notice. The calculation behind every gesture. The way his thumb stroked my jaw was as if I were a product, not a person.

I cut the clip, trim the edges, and brighten the frame until we glow. The edits pile up, my fingers moving on autopilot while my heart aches with every keystroke.

Quickly, I glance at my phone.

Reed's reply is still there, eleven simple words.

Yeah. Just say when. I'll be here to pick you up.

It shouldn't mean so much, but it does.

I run my thumb over the screen, reopening our thread and rereading the message until I memorize it. I almost typed something else—*Are you sure? I don't want to bother you.*

But I delete it before it's even sent, my breath getting stuck in my throat.

I let the words play back in my mind: his steady, gruff voice and his quiet confidence.

For the first time today, my lips curve into something unpracticed.

The video stays paused on the laptop screen, frozen mid-laugh. But I'm no longer paying attention to it.

Instead, I'm staring at Reed's name glowing on my phone, wondering how someone who began as a friend suddenly feels like the quiet place my heart has been searching for all along.

TEN
REED

I drag my broom across the living room floor, its bristles catching on a loose thread in the rug. I shake it free with a grunt and keep going, making steady strokes back and forth until the wood grain reappears.

Dust gathers in the pan with each sweep, tiny flecks catching the lamplight. I empty it into the trash, then lean the broom against the wall in its spot, lined up next to the mop.

Routine. Always routine.

The house is too quiet otherwise.

I wipe down the kitchen counters next, the rag damp with cleaner, the sharp scent of ocean breeze filling the air.

Scrubbing until the surface shines, I then fold the cloth over itself, smoothing the edges before setting it back under the sink.

My boots creak against the hardwood as I walk down the hall. The lights are off in the bedroom, shadows stretching across the floor. My shoulders ache, but I keep going.

As I enter the bathroom, steam from my shower still lingers on the mirror, leaving faint streaks that fog the glass.

I grab the towel hanging by the sink and slowly drag it across the surface, clearing a patch.

My reflection looks back at me; my beard has grown in, lines etched deeper into my face than I remember, and my eyes look way too tired.

My gaze drops to the chain at my neck.

The dog tags rest against my chest, cool metal brushing against my shirt as I shift. I lift them, feeling the familiar weight in my palm, my thumb tracing the grooves of the letters etched into the steel.

Beau.

My throat tightens as I lean closer to the mirror, tags dangling between my fingers, the bathroom light glinting off their edges.

The memory slips in before I can stop it; Beau's laugh, his big, stupid grin as we cleaned the fire apparatus, always messing around.

His voice was always cocky as hell, promising he'd beat me one day for my time at tying knots.

One stupid accident during a fire containment drill, and I remember it all.

Smoke filled the air, and alarms blared overhead. Flames raced faster than our feet could carry us.

We both collapsed from lack of air, our SCBAs beeping, alerting anyone else in there that our oxygen was low.

I tried to drag him out, but he pushed me away, and his words will forever haunt me.

"Go, brother, it's okay, go."

His shout was cut off too soon. I was lucky to get out of there when I could, but the survivor's guilt I carry consumes me every fucking second of the day.

The fire should have taken me instead, but now I'm left with this grief and disfigurement that's too heavy to bear most days.

My grip on the porcelain sink tightens as I feel the cold surface beneath my hands.

Squeezing my eyes shut, I try to push the images away, but the memories claw at the inside of my mind until a single tear escapes, sliding down my cheek.

I bow my head as my shoulders tense, and my dog tags clink softly against my chest with a hollow sound that echoes in the bathroom.

My phone rattles against the counter, sharp in the quiet. I flinch, dragging my rough hand over my face, before reaching for it.

The screen lights up the bathroom in a pale blue glow, cutting through the fog on the mirror.

My throat tightens just looking at her name.

For a second, I stand there with my phone in my hand as my heart races faster than it should.

I unlock my phone, and her words fill the screen, small, simple, and sweet, asking if I'd keep her company while she edits.

I can't help it.

My lips pull into a grin before I've even finished reading.

It feels awkward at first, unfamiliar, like a muscle I don't use, but it settles in deep, tugging at something I thought was long gone.

Hell, I'm a grown man, scarred, worn down, and here I am, smiling at a phone like some idiot.

I rest my elbows against the sink, my dog tags clinking as they fall against my chest. My thumb hovers, hesitant, before I finally type back.

REED

When you comin'?

The bubbles pop up almost immediately.

LAYLA

mmmmmm why, miss me?

My pulse races, eyes locked on the screen as her reply shows up.

Something stirs deep in my chest. I swallow hard, adjusting my phone in my hand.

Fuck, what do I say to that?

REED

Just wondering, sunshine.

God, Reed, don't you know how to converse with a woman?

Stupid. Stupid. Stupid.

Not even a second passes before her name lights up again. This time, the words scroll across the screen like her voice in my head; bright, a little messy, and totally her.

LAYLA

Don't worry, Reed, i'll be there soon to brighten your day 😉

A genuine, deep laugh escapes me, echoing off the tile walls. It loosens something inside me, something tightly wound for years.

I bow my head, smile at the screen, and gently brush my thumb over her name before locking it.

Slipping my phone into my pocket, I lift my hand, brushing my stubble as I catch my reflection in the mirror again; same face, same scars, same tired eyes.

But with her words tucked warm in my pocket, the man staring back at me doesn't seem quite so *broken.*

I push away from the sink with a slow exhale, the dog tags tapping against my chest as if reminding me where I've been, and the possibility that, maybe, I'm no longer stuck there.

Turning off the bathroom light, I make my way to the front door, grabbing my keys from the empty bowl on the entry table. The night air greets me, carrying the faint scent of rain on asphalt. My truck door groans as I open it.

The drive into town is quiet as my truck's engine hums, its headlights slicing through the dark stretch of highway.

My mind should be on the list waiting for me: stock rotation, invoices, and the keg delivery I need to check this evening, but it drifts.

Always back to *her*.

I pull into the back lot of Boots & Bourbon, where the neon sign flickers to life, buzzing softly in the night.

Jade opens the bar for me, then closes it so I can reopen it and manage the night shift.

Pushing inside, I flip on the overhead lights one by one. The smell of oak, whiskey, and lemon polish hangs in the air, settling into my bones.

Falling into routine, I wipe down counters, stock clean glasses, and straighten stools that were left crooked. The jukebox hums to life in the corner, soft country twang filling the empty room. My body works, but my mind is elsewhere.

The lock starts shimmying on the front door, taking me out of my routine, and I know it's either Carter or my other dumbass brother coming to bother me.

"REEDDDD!" Maverick's voice rattles the bottles on the shelves. "Your favorite brother has arrived, and I come bearing a dire mission from my pregnant wife."

I don't even look up from the rag in my hand. "You're not my favorite anything."

He slams onto a stool, grinning like a lunatic. "Amelia is craving olives. Not just any olives. Your olives. The sacred, holy grail olives you hoard back here like they're liquid gold." He leans forward, whispering loudly, "If I don't bring them home, she'll bury me alive. You wanna be responsible for my untimely death?"

I grunt, reaching under the bar. "You're dramatic."

"Dramatic? DRAMATIC?" He slaps the counter with both hands. "Bro, if you'd seen the way she looked at me when I came back without peanut butter cups last week, you'd know this is survival. She's five-foot-two of pure rage."

I set the jar on the counter. "Here. Take it and get out."

He hugs it to his chest. "You're saving lives tonight, Reed. Specifically mine. I'll name my next kid after you."

I roll my eyes. "Maverick, please, shut up."

Before he can wind up again, my phone buzzes in my pocket. I pull it out, thumb swiping across the screen, and her name lights me up from the inside.

Her message sprawls across the screen.

LAYLA

you left me on read do u hate me

i'm totally joking, don't take me seriously

gif of screaming lizard

A laugh escapes me, making my shoulders shake. I pinch the bridge of my nose, grinning like an idiot.

Maverick leans over the bar, squinting. "Who the hell's got you laughing like that? What's this? Who is she? Tell me, or I'll pry it out of you."

"Mind your business."

"Oh, it's a *she*." His grin widens. "You've been holding out on me, bro. Turns out it's some mystery woman making you soft." He gasps, clutching his chest. "Don't tell me it's Catalina. Carter would kill us both, and I'm too pretty to die."

"Jesus Christ." I shake my head, pocketing my phone before he can grab it. "It's not Catalina."

The low laugh escapes before I can suppress it, and Maverick's eyes snap open.

"Holy shit. You laughed." He slaps the counter so hard the olive jar jumps. "Reed Hayes, ladies and gentlemen, has officially laughed again."

I shake my head and carefully set down a row of glasses. "You're exhausting."

"Exhausting? Nah, bro. I'm invigorating." He throws his arms wide. "I bring life to this dusty old saloon. Without me, you'd just brood into your whiskey until you fossilized."

"You're anno—"

His phone buzzes on the bar, screen lighting up. He grabs it, still smiling, but the color drains from his face in the blink of an eye. His jaw drops.

"What?" I ask, brows knitting.

"Catalina says—" His voice cracks. He swallows hard. "Amelia's water broke."

My rag stills in my hand, the jukebox humming low in the corner.

Maverick leaps to his feet so quickly that the stool crashes to the floor. "Oh my god. Oh my fucking god. This is it. This is happening."

He's pacing, his hair wild as he runs both hands through it, knocking his hat off onto the floor. "I can't—I'm not—I don't know what I'm supposed to do. Reed!"

I set the rag down, voice steady. "Start by getting to the hospital."

He freezes, then points at me. "Yes! Hospital! Fuck—yes. But—" He's spinning again, practically vibrating out of his skin. "I can't go alone. Reed, you gotta come with me."

"Maverick—"

"I'm serious!" His voice rises higher, sounding desperate. "I'm gonna pass out, forget the diaper bag, or drive to the wrong hospital, and Amelia's gonna divorce me before we even sign the birth certificate. You're the calm one. The rational one. You keep me from losing it."

I sigh, wiping my hands on a towel, but the truth is, I'm already moving for my keys. "You're a grown man, Hayes."

"Yeah, well, this grown man's about to be somebody's dad, and I'm two seconds away from shitting myself. Get in my car, shitbrick." He's already rushing for the door, olive jar still in his hand.

We spill out into the night. Maverick's already halfway to his truck, clutching that damn olive jar.

He fumbles with his phone as he yanks open the driver's side door, climbing in. "Cat!" he hollers the second the call connects. "Tell Amelia I'm coming! Reed's with me, we're on the road!"

I slide into the passenger seat, buckle my seatbelt, and get comfortable as he starts the engine with a shaky hand. His voice fills the cab, full of nerves and desperation.

On the other end, I can hear Amelia screaming. Not terrified, but furious. Her voice crackles through the speaker.

"MAVERICK HAYES, I'M IN LABOR, AND YOU'RE STILL AT THE BAR?!"

He winces. "Baby, wait, don't yell, it's bad for your blood pressure—"

"BAD FOR M—?! I WILL KILL YOU WHEN THIS CHILD IS OUT OF ME!"

Maverick's face twists, but he quickly tries to charm his way out. "Baby, you wanted olives. Please don't be mad at me, dollface, I'm bringing you olives! Reed saw, tell her, Reed!"

I grunt. "Drive."

"See?" Maverick points wildly at me, even though Amelia can't see a damn thing. "He agrees. Olives were essential. I'm a provider."

Her scream practically rattles the speakers. "I DON'T GIVE A SHIT ABOUT OLIVES! BABY, I NEED YOU HERE!"

"Baby! I'm coming!" He fumbles his phone into the cupholder, muttering, "Jesus Christ, she's hot when she's yelling at me." He laughs to himself. "Fuck, I'm gonna have to put another baby in her."

"Maverick, shut the fuck up and drive."

His Bronco rumbles down the highway, Maverick's knee bouncing against the steering wheel, his breathing ragged.

He mutters half-formed sentences—car seat, diapers, what if the baby hates him—but I'm only partly listening.

Because my phone buzzes in my pocket, again.

LAYLA

I'm excited to see u when i come out again

Fuck.

A grin slowly forms at my mouth, reigniting something I believed was gone. Maverick's losing his damn mind beside me, but my thoughts are fixated solely on her.

Always her.

ELEVEN
REED

Maverick's driving like an absolute asshole.

My hand grips the overhead handle as his Bronco fishtails around a corner, the olive jar rattling in the cupholder.

"Slow the hell down," I growl, bracing my boot against the floorboard.

"I can't slow down! My wife is in labor, you fuck! Do you want me to miss the birth of my first child?!" He's white-knuckling the steering wheel, blonde hair falling into his eyes, chest heaving. "Oh my god, what if I do miss it? What if the baby comes in the hallway? What if—"

"Mav," I cut in, firm. "She's fine. Carter and Catalina are with her. Just drive."

That seems to get through, if only just barely. He eases off the gas – though "eases" for Maverick still means ten over the limit.

His Bronco rattles with his muttering, half-prayers, half-panicked jokes about diapers and baby monitors, until the glow of hospital lights washes over the windshield.

He jerks his SUV into the drop-off lane, slamming it

into park before I've even unclipped my belt. "Come on, come on, come on," he chants, vaulting out of the driver's side.

I follow, calmer, steadier, my boots heavy on the pavement as we push through the sliding doors.

Maverick rushes straight to the nurses' station, voice loud and commanding. "WHERE'S MY WIFE? Amelia Hayes, she's in labor, I'm her husband, you gotta take me up right now!"

The nurse barely flinches. She blinks up at him, deadpan. "Sir, if you could just—"

"No, you don't understand, I have to be there. She'll murder me if I'm not. Do you want my wife to murder me?"

"Sir—"

"She's five-foot-two, but she's terrifying! She already screamed at me about olives—"

"Sir." The nurse's voice sharpens, clipped with authority. "Take a breath."

Maverick wheezes, slamming his palm on the counter.

I step up beside him, resting a heavy hand on his shoulder. "He's the husband," I say quietly. "He just needs someone to walk him through."

That finally softens the nurse's face. She makes a quick call, murmurs something into the phone, and within minutes, a staff member appears to lead him back.

Maverick's gone in a flash, throwing me one last wild-eyed look before disappearing down the hall.

And then it's quiet again.

I head toward the waiting area, my boots echoing on the tile. The harsh fluorescent lights make everything seem too bright and too loud in its silence.

Carter and Catalina are already in the lobby; she's perched on the edge of a plastic chair, fingers knotted together, while he stands behind her with one hand resting firmly on her shoulder.

Carter glances up as I approach, his blue eyes steady even in the wash of fluorescent light. "He make it in?"

I nod, lowering into the chair beside Catalina. "They took him back."

She exhales, a shaky little laugh slipping out. "Good. Amelia's gonna kill him, but... good."

I lean back in the chair as the hum of the vending machines fills the space, and for the first time since the night began, I let myself breathe.

The plastic chair groans beneath my weight as I settle back, the sterile hum of fluorescent lights filling the quiet. Carter leans against the wall, arms crossed, his hand still resting on Catalina's shoulder.

She's perched on the edge of her seat, knees bouncing, biting the inside of her cheek.

My phone buzzes in my pocket. I glance down, and her name lights the screen.

LAYLA

So... is it too early to request snacks? Like, do you even have In-N-Out, or am I doomed?

A low chuckle escapes me, quiet enough that Catalina shoots me a curious look. I clear my throat, typing back.

REED

Yes to In-N-Out, but the lines are hours long

Three dots dance.

LAYLA

Ughhh. This is a crisis. Do you deliver snacks to baggage claim? Asking for myself

My lips twitch.

REED

I'll deliver you. Snacks optional.

She fires back almost instantly.

LAYLA

Smooth, Hayes. Careful, I might start believing you're sweet.

I shift in my seat, the corner of my mouth lifting. My thumb hesitates over the keys before I type.

REED

Maybe I am. Just don't tell anyone.

Her reply makes me huff, laugh out loud.

LAYLA

Too late. I'm tweeting "Reed Hayes is secretly soft."

Carter cuts me a side-eye at the sound. "What's so funny?"

"Nothing," I say quickly, tucking the phone low, warmth buzzing in my chest.

Another buzz.

LAYLA

Seriously, though, thanks for texting me back. I needed it tonight. 😌

My throat tightens. I stare at the words for a long

moment before answering.

REED

Me too.

Before I can pocket the phone, a nurse pushes through the double doors. "Family for Amelia Hayes?"

Catalina jumps to her feet, Carter straightening up beside her. I also stand, my phone still warm in my hand, her name glowing on the screen.

The nurse only says Amelia's stable, and they'll update again soon. Catalina wipes at her eyes, Carter leans closer to her, giving her a soft peck, and I sink back into the chair, my phone still heavy in my hand.

It buzzes again.

LAYLA

Do Tennessee boys actually ride horses everywhere, or is that just in movies? 🤠

I huff a quiet laugh, thumbs moving slowly.

REED

We have trucks. Horses are optional.

Her reply comes fast.

LAYLA

Damn. I was picturing you on horseback, cowboy hat, riding in to rescue me at baggage claim.

My lips twitch.

REED

Don't tempt me. I've got the hat.

Three dots appear, then vanish, then appear again.

LAYLA

Pics or it didn't happen.

I shake my head, chuckling under my breath.

REED

You'll see soon enough.

She responds with a string of emojis—cowboy hats, hearts, a little horse—and then sends another message.

LAYLA

You know, for someone who claims he's not sweet, you're really good at making me smile.

My thumbs hesitate, then I type.

REED

Guess that makes two of us.

I pocket my phone, feeling the warmth settle deep, when the waiting room doors slam open.

Ten hours pass by in a motionless blur; we have been sitting here waiting for the birth of a new family member.

I twiddle my thumbs, staring at Carter and Catalina. Carter is massaging her shoulders, whispering things into her ear, and Catalina smiles. They've been together for four years, and I've never seen my brother smile like that with anyone.

My spiral quickens, but it quickly dies when the waiting room doors crash open.

Maverick storms in like a freight train. His face is streaked with tears, his shirt half untucked, and his hair sticking out every which way. He's still clutching that damn jar of olives.

"I'M A DAD!" His voice cracks, echoing through the sterile room. "Holy shit, I'm a dad!"

Catalina jumps to her feet, covering her mouth with both hands as tears start to flow. Carter wraps a firm arm around her waist, holding her steady as she trembles with emotion.

Maverick's pacing, laughing, and crying at the same time. "They're both fine. Amelia's... Jesus Christ, she's unbelievable. She swore at me the whole time, threatened to break my hand, and then she held him—" his voice fractures, his chest heaving, "—and I swear I've never seen anything more fucking perfect."

He drags a hand down his wet face, grinning through the mess. "His name's Leo Maddox Hayes."

Catalina breaks into new sobs as Carter kisses the top of her head. My chest tightens, pride swelling in a way I don't bother trying to hide.

Maverick laughs again, shaking his head as if he can't believe it. "He's so damn small. Got Amelia's nose, my ridiculous lungs. And he already looks at me like I don't know what I'm doing. He's right."

I shake my head with a smile, despite myself. That's Maverick—loud, chaotic, and full of heart.

My phone buzzes in my pocket.

LAYLA

Did Amelia really have the baby?? Catalina is blowing me up, but you know how she exaggerates.

A warmth spreads through me, cutting through the antiseptic hum of the hospital. My thumbs move slowly.

REED

Yeah. Baby boy. Leo Maddox Hayes. Both doing perfect.

Her reply comes fast.

LAYLA

Leo!! Oh my god, I'm crying in my apartment like an idiot. Tell Amelia I love her. And that baby better know I'm already his favorite aunt.

A quiet laugh escapes me. I tuck my phone back into my pocket, feeling lighter than I have in years, and look at my brother—loud, messy, crying with joy.

Work, sleep, repeat.

That's been my routine. But tonight? It's different. Tonight, it's about family. And thinking of Layla, miles away, crying happy tears into her phone, makes me think, I want more.

TWELVE
LAYLA

The soft hum of my laptop is the only sound in the apartment. I've been glued to my screen for hours, trimming clips from Ruby Ridge, Reed's bar glowing under string lights, the laughter spilling from Boots & Bourbon, the sound of my own voice talking about its decor, the mechanical bull, and other parts of his bar that I found fascinating.

Reed's voice echoes faintly in one of the clips, "You got the shot you need, sunshine?"

My fingers hover over the keyboard, replaying it once, twice, until the door clicks open behind me.

"Hey, baby."

Brian's voice sends a chill through me. I snap the laptop shut, my heart slamming against my ribs.

He's standing there with a smile that doesn't reach his eyes. A bouquet of white tulips dangles from his fingers. "What's this?" he asks lightly, gesturing to the laptop.

Tulips, I fucking hate tulips.

"Work," I say too fast. "Brand footage. Nothing interesting."

He hums, chewing on his lower lip as he steps closer.

His cologne hits before he does; sharp, expensive, suffocating. "You've been so busy lately," he murmurs, fingers grazing my shoulder. "How about we fix that? Let me take you out tonight."

I blink. "Out?"

What's gotten into him?

Brian hasn't wanted to "take me out" in months. The sudden sweetness feels off. "Uh, yeah. Sure," I say, because it's easier than arguing. Because I know he wants something, and pretending keeps the peace.

He grins, satisfied. "Perfect. Be ready by seven, okay?"

When he disappears down the hall, I exhale shakily, turning back to the laptop. My reflection stares back from the dark screen, perfectly painted, perfectly staged, perfectly *trapped.*

I drag myself to my bedroom to get ready, slipping into a white, flowy dress that looks right but feels unsettling. The whole time, my chest aches with the ghost of Tennessee air; of warm nights, laughter, and a certain bar owner's quiet eyes.

My phone buzzes on the counter, taking me out of my trance.

His name alone punches the breath out of me.

REED

Been thinkin' about you.

I grip the counter, heart pounding, caught between the reflection in the mirror and the one that still smells like oakmoss and sandalwood.

For a minute, I stare at Reed's text.

His words feel like warmth on my skin, like someone remembering me just because they wanted to, not because they needed something. My fingers hover above the keyboard.

I type it, erase it. Type again. Add a smiley. Erase that too.

Instead, I settle on:

LAYLA

Hey. Missed hearing from you.

Hitting send before I can overthink it. The little "delivered" bubble pops up, and I shove my phone away, the nerves settling low in my stomach.

I know this is wrong in many ways, but it feels like my relationship has been slowly suffocating me for almost eight years. I'm afraid to leave or speak up because a small part of me still believes he will change. I still hope he'll open his eyes and see that he has a good woman in front of him, but I'm tired of begging for scraps of attention. I don't need much, but I shouldn't have to beg for the bare minimum.

Brian has slowly been changing into a man who's comfortable with what he has; he's beginning to lose his temper, blaming it all on me, and I don't think I can hold on much longer.

Turning my focus back to the mirror as I curl my hair, I let out a long exhale. My hands are trembling when I put on mascara. I tell myself to breathe.

Maybe Brian really does want to make things right tonight.

Maybe he's trying.

Finally, I step out of the bedroom, my head spinning with my thoughts, making me feel a sense of queasiness.

Brian's already waiting. Freshly showered, clean-shaven, wearing the cologne I used to love.

"You look beautiful," he says easily, his smile too perfect, practiced.

"Thanks," I manage, smoothing the hem of my dress with shaky hands.

We walk through the parking garage, our footsteps echoing off the concrete. I watch our linked hands sway between us; his grip possessive, mine limp.

In the car, city lights blur across the windshield. For the first ten minutes, everything feels... almost normal. He discusses his friends, new contracts, and a brand's interest in having him promote a luxury watch line.

I nod when I should. Smile when it's safe.

"I saw that Lauren got engaged," I say lightly, scrolling through my phone. "She looks so happy."

Brian laughs once, a short, cutting sound. "Happy? Please. She probably trapped the guy."

I blink, thrown. "What? No, she's been with him for years."

He cuts his eyes toward me. "You'd know, huh?"

My stomach drops. "Brian, come on, it's not that deep."

His jaw flexes. "You always say stupid things like that and then act shocked when I call you on it."

Why is he mad about this?

"Brian, I was just saying—"

"Just saying," he mocks, slamming his hand against the steering wheel so hard the horn bursts for a second. "You never shut up, Layla."

"Please don't—"

"God, you're doing it again," he snaps. "Don't play the victim."

"I'm not—"

"Yeah, you are. Every time you cry, it's the same act." His hand crashes down on the dashboard; the glove box rattling. "Crybaby," he spits. "You think that works on me?"

My eyes sting. "I'm not trying to—"

"Save it. You know what? Maybe I should leave. Maybe I should walk away and find someone who actually loves me."

"What?"

He throws a humorless laugh into the dark. "Yeah. I could do it. Wouldn't be hard. You think you're the only one who wants me? Please."

I grip the edge of my seat, voice trembling. "Can you stop saying things like that?"

"Then stop giving me reasons to."

"Brian—"

"Don't," he snarls and slams his palm into the steering wheel again.

Tears slip down my cheeks before I can stop them. I turn toward the window, the cool glass biting against my skin.

"Layla." His voice sharpens.

I don't look, I can't because I'm so confused as to what is fucking happening.

"Layla, look at me."

Silence.

He reaches across the console, grabbing my chin, forcing me to face him. His grip is hard, the angle of his fingers pressing into the jawbone.

"Listen to me," he says, pushing his fingers deeper into my jaw. "Why do I have to yell, why do I have to threaten to leave, before you'll fucking listen?"

My breath catches, and a quiet sound escapes before I can swallow it. He holds my face there a moment longer, until my eyes start to water more, then jerks his hand away.

The rest of the drive is silent. Only the hum of the tires, the pulse in my ears, and the quiet question looping through my mind.

How did this become normal?

Thirty minutes of suffocating silence crawl by before we reach the restaurant.

We pull into the restaurant's valet line, and the argument disappears from Brian's face like it never happened. He quickly shifts back into charm mode, handing over the keys, complimenting the hostess, and smiling so broadly that strangers might think we're perfect.

Inside, the dim lighting is soft, casting a warm amber glow over the patrons. Everyone around us laughs, forks clinking against plates. I try to match the energy, pretending the bruised silence in my chest doesn't exist.

He orders for both of us without asking, his hand brushing mine across the table.

"Layla's been dying for a night out," he tells the waiter, tone easy, practiced. "Haven't you, baby?"

I nod, forcing a fake smile. "Yeah. It's nice to get out."

The waiter leaves, and I can feel Brian's gaze lingering, waiting for me to make things normal again. So I do what I've learned: I laugh softly at something that isn't funny while nervously picking at the linen napkin in my lap.

It's a performance, and I know my lines by heart. Strangers probably stare at us and wonder what a cute couple we make, but if they really knew what was going on.

He's laughing again, sharing a story about an ad campaign, gesturing with his glass as if he didn't just threaten to leave me thirty minutes ago.

I excuse myself quietly. "I'm just gonna use the restroom."

He barely looks up. "Don't take forever, okay?"

Making my way over to the restroom, I open the wooden door softly, letting out the breath I've been holding in. I lock myself inside a stall anyway and press my back to the door, swallowing down the tears.

My phone vibrates in my palm as Reed responds to the text I had just sent.

REED

When you comin' back out this way, sunshine? Bar's too damn quiet without you.

Shit. I never booked the flight.

I sit down on the closed toilet lid, open my travel app, and before I can talk myself out of it, make up some excuse as to why I shouldn't go; I book the damn flight.

Two days. Round-trip to Ruby Ridge.

It's impulsive, stupid, and in this moment, I don't fucking care.

I type back quickly.

LAYLA

Two days.

Don't make any plans without me. 😌

Three small dots appear instantly, then disappear just as quickly.

Buzz. Buzz. Buzz.

REED

Wouldn't dream of it.

I chew the inside of my cheek, pushing my phone back into my bag. Opening the stall, I walk over to the mirror to fix myself up before heading back out there.

Pushing open the restroom door, everything feels overwhelmingly loud again. The dim lighting, the gentle clinking of cutlery, the low hum of conversation; it's all too much.

Brian's laughter is the first thing I hear.

He's leaned back in his chair, talking animatedly with the waiter. He gestures with his glass, that confident tilt of his chin. The same man who'd slammed his hand against the dashboard not an hour ago now smiles as though he's never raised his voice in his life.

I slip quietly into my seat. His eyes flick toward me, the corners of his mouth lifting. "You okay?"

"Yeah," I lie.

He nods, reaching for the bottle on the table, topping off my wine before pouring more for himself. The waiter drops off our entrées, and Brian thanks him with that polished charm that used to make me melt.

We eat. Or rather, he eats. I move food around my plate, pretending.

He finally asks for the check, and I exhale quietly, my shoulders dropping half an inch. He slides his card to the waiter and leans back, drumming his fingers on the tablecloth. "You tired?"

"A little," I answer.

"Good dinner, though, right?"

I nod because disagreeing would make him mad.

He stands and helps me with his coat, the gesture so gentle that it almost feels cruel. The scent of his cologne clings to the fabric as he drapes it over my shoulders. His palm stays on my back a second too long. "C'mon, let's go."

We step out of the restaurant, and the night air is damp and heavy with city noise. Streetlights smear a hazy yellow across the pavement, and the valet's whistle echoes somewhere behind us. Brian's hand finds the small of my back as we walk, his fingers pressing just hard enough to guide.

He thanks the valet with that same polished grin, slips into the driver's seat without opening my door for me, and checks his reflection in the rear-view mirror before we pull away.

For a few minutes, there's silence—just the sound of tires sliding over slick asphalt and the low hum of the radio. I stare out the window, watching storefronts blur by like a reel I can't pause.

"So, I never asked how Tennessee was."

Oh, now he asks.

I glance over, caught off guard. "It was fine, nice seeing my friends, and filming new content for our page."

He snorts, one hand tightening on the wheel. "It better be good."

My pulse flickers. "It wil—"

"It better be, Layla," he interrupts, sarcasm curling around every word. "It'll do even better if I was in them."

I blink, unsure if he's serious. "It's something new I'm trying; you don't have to always be in my videos."

He laughs sharply. "*Our* content will always be better because of me. What, are you fucking someone out there?"

"It's not like that, Brian."

He slams his hand against the steering wheel; the sound cracks through the car. "Then how is it, Layla? Because it looks like you're trying to build a brand on me not existing."

My throat tightens. "It isn't personal—"

"It's personal when you don't include your fiancé!" he snaps. "People don't give a shit about you frolicking around hick town." He laughs under his breath, bitter. "But sure, keep pretending it'll do you some good."

I stare down at my lap, my nails digging into my palm.

He exhales hard, shaking his head. "You know what? Maybe I should stay out of it. You're nothing without me anyway."

I swallow. "I didn't mean to upset you."

"Yeah, well," he mutters, voice low, "you're good at it."

The rest of the drive unfolds quietly. The city disappears into quieter streets, then into the empty echo of the parking garage. When the sensor light flickers on, it casts a harsh white glow on his face, the same face that women melt over.

He parks, kills the engine, and leans back with a sigh that sounds almost tired. "Another trip coming up, I assume."

"Yeah." I force my voice steady. "Actually… I fly out in two days."

He scoffs, eyes still on the dash. "Of course you do."

"It's work."

"Right." His lips twist into a smirk that doesn't touch his eyes. "Whatever you say, Layla."

I unbuckle slowly, the click echoing like punctuation. My purse strap slips off my shoulder as I open the door. Cool night air pours in, fresh and unfamiliar.

Closing the door with a dull thud, I stand there for a moment, breathing in the quiet, the space, and the fragile sense that the world outside this garage still belongs to me.

Two days.

Just forty-eight hours until I can breathe again.

THIRTEEN
REED

Two days.

That's how long until she's back.

Even just thinking her name feels wrong. Like saying it out loud might summon something I can't control.

She's engaged.

I shouldn't be counting down the hours. I shouldn't be thinking about her smile, her laugh, or the way her eyes looked when she left Ruby Ridge.

But I am.

Because selfishness has a voice, and it's been whispering louder every damn night.

Fuck it.

I run a hand down my face, feeling the rough ridges of scar tissue; uneven, raised, still warm sometimes when the fire burns too hot.

My home's quiet, except for the crackle of the fireplace.

The firelight flickers on the photograph on the mantel—Mama and me, the summer I left for Los Angeles. Her arm is around my waist, her head tilted against my chest, both of us grinning.

She'd been so damn proud.

"Be brave, baby," she'd said, pressing her palm to my cheek. "But be careful. You don't gotta save the whole world to make me proud."

I never got to tell her she was right.

She died two weeks after I left for the academy. Maverick was the one who called, his voice breaking on the words. Carter told me not to come home.

"It's what she'd want, Reed. You stay. Finish what you started."

So I did.

Because they were right, because that's what she'd wanted, and maybe if I'd come home, none of it would've happened.

Maybe Beau would still be alive.

The tears come without asking.

They fall heavily against my palms as I sit in front of the fire, my shoulders hunched, the heat blurring my vision until the flames merge.

I try to swallow it down, but it's no use; the ache in my chest opens wide, spilling everything I've been holding.

I close my eyes, and when I open them, the room around me isn't my home anymore.

I'm taken back to the second-worst day of my life.

We were on day thirty-eight of training. It was a containment drill, and it wasn't supposed to go wrong.

The instructors had constructed a mock structure to simulate a live-fire environment. The rules were simple: containment, rescue, suppression.

I could recite them in my sleep.

Beau and I had run this drill five times before. He was in front, his voice even through the comms. "We're good, Hayes. Just another walk in the park."

But that hiss, that fucking hiss, changed everything.

It came from the far corner of the room, a sound that didn't belong.

I turned toward it, saw the gauge shaking, the line trembling where it fed into the gas system.

The pressure reading plummeted, and before I could give a warning—*BOOM*.

A flash of light and a roar like the sky tearing apart. Heat slammed into me so hard my helmet cracked the floor when I hit. I couldn't hear anything but ringing, the kind that drills straight into your bones.

Beau's voice came through the static. "We gotta move, brother! Now!"

Flames consumed the room in seconds, climbing the walls and curling over the ceiling.

The temperature soared—over eight hundred degrees. We found each other through the thick smoke, dropping to our bellies, crawling blindly through smoke so thick it turned day into night.

My tank alarm screamed, alerting me that my oxygen was low. So did his.

We had minutes, maybe less.

I looked back, saw his regulator sparking, the airflow dropping to nothing. "You're out!" I shouted, pulling at my own line. "Take mine!"

Beau shook his head, his voice breaking. "No. You got air. You can make it."

"Like hell I will!"

I ripped the mask off my own face, tearing at the straps, trying to shove it toward him. The heat punched into my skin, searing, eating through my turnout coat before I could blink.

The pain was instant, but I didn't fucking care.

"Put it on!" I yelled. "Don't argue, just take it!"

He shoved it back, eyes wild, the firelight flickering across his soot-streaked face. "Go, brother."

"Beau—"

"Go!" he barked, his voice raw. "You hear me? Go!"

The ceiling gave way.

The sound of collapsing beams crashing overhead drowned out everything else.

I lunged at him anyway, bare arms scraping against melting metal, the skin on my side blistering before I even felt it. I grabbed his turnout sleeve.

For one brief second, I had him.

Something heavy fell between us, the heat so intense it peeled the air right out of my lungs. The blast sent me backward. My vision tunneled, the edges going dark, the smell of burning gear and flesh fusing into one.

I tried to crawl, but my arms wouldn't move. The pain was overwhelming. The oxygen line hissed, empty.

The last thing I saw before everything went black was Beau's helmet, glowing orange, disappearing into the flames.

Squeezing my eyes shut, letting the tears fall, the memory runs through me, relentlessly.

I remember waking up to the hospital lights being too bright. My body didn't feel like mine. My left side was wrapped in gauze from the peak of my cheek to my waist, my arm bandaged to the elbow, the skin raw and new beneath. My throat was wrecked from the smoke.

They said I was lucky. That word still makes me sick.

My left arm always felt half-numb, the nerves too damaged to heal properly. I couldn't even shave without my hand trembling.

Beau didn't make it.

The academy called it a tragic malfunction.

I called it what it was, my fault.

When I was discharged, there was no turning back. My firefighting career ended before it truly began. My mama was gone. My best friend was buried.

And I was left with a face I didn't recognize.

I came home to Tennessee with nothing but guilt that still hasn't burned out.

My brothers helped me buy my liquor license, and I learned to bartend, turning an old feed store into my bar.

Boots & Bourbon smells like smoke and oak, and sometimes, when the lights dim and the crowd thins out, I still smell the fire, still hear Beau yelling my name.

The memory drags itself out of me, leaving only smoke behind.

I drop to my knees before I realize it, my hand gripping the edge of the coffee table as if it's the only thing keeping me upright.

My chest tightens, and raw breath scrapes through my throat. The air feels too thin and too hot. Still, I gasp for it.

"Fuck," I gasp.

The room spins. The smell of smoke isn't coming from the fireplace anymore; it's inside my lungs, my skin, that ghostly heat wrapping around me as if it's happening again.

I press a trembling hand to my chest, trying to breathe, but the air refuses to come.

"Not again," I whisper. "Please, not again."

My vision blurs as I fumble for my phone on the table, knocking over the half-empty whiskey glass, amber spilling across the wood.

My thumb swipes until I hit Carter's number.

Carter picks up on the first ring. "Reed?"

My voice cracks. "I can't—" A sob punches out of me. "I can't go to that dark place again. I need you, man. Please."

"Stay where you are," he says, already moving. I hear Maverick's voice in the background—*what's wrong?*—then tires on gravel, doors slamming.

It takes less than five minutes before I hear my brother's truck rumble onto my driveway.

I'm still on the floor, my palms pressed to my ribs, as my breath comes in shallow pulls.

Carter's the first through, his boots heavy against the boards. He drops to a knee beside me, his big hand gripping my shoulder.

"Hey, hey, look at me," he says quietly, moving his hand from my shoulder, holding my face.

Maverick crouches on the opposite side, his eyes wide and his voice softer than I've ever heard. "Breathe, Reed. Slow it down. In through your nose."

I take a shaky breath in, then another.

Carter's hand remains still as he stays there, grounding me with the kind of patience that only someone who's been through their own hell possesses.

The fire crackles softly, casting long shadows across the room, and the scent of spilled whiskey blends with the smoke.

Maverick leans back on his heels, exhaling. "You saw it again, didn't you?"

I nod, releasing myself from Carter's hold, wiping my face with the back of my wrist. "Every fucking second."

Carter's voice is low, careful. "You're not there anymore, Reed. You hear me? You made it out."

"I left him," I rasp. "I took off my gear, he told me to go, and I did."

Maverick shakes his head. "You didn't leave him; you tried to save him. That's what you do."

I look between them, Carter's jaw clenched, Maverick's

eyes bright with worry, and something in my chest finally breaks.

The tears come again, quickly.

Carter pulls me into a brotherly hug, holding me tight, and Maverick joins in.

For a long time, no one talks. The only sound is the soft crackle of the fire and the wind against the windows.

When the shaking finally stops, I pull back, clearing my throat. "Thanks for coming."

Carter squeezes the back of my neck. "You call us every time before it gets that bad. You don't do this alone again, you hear me?"

Maverick gives me that crooked grin that's half-joke, half-love. "We'd kick your ass if you didn't."

A broken laugh slips out of me.

I glance between them, my brothers, and give them a small smile.

Two days.

Layla will be here in two days.

Sunshine in the shape of a woman.

FOURTEEN
LAYLA

My suitcase sits open on the bed, half full of folded clothes and half full of nerves. The air feels heavy, like it always does when Brian's in one of his moods.

He's pacing back and forth across our apartment. "So you're leaving," he finally says, "Another trip."

I keep my eyes on the pile of jeans in front of me. "It's work, Brian."

"Work." He laughs softly. "Work this, work that. Must be nice to do whatever the fuck you want."

My eyes still don't meet his as I fiddle with my packed clothes, anything to keep my hands busy. "You knew about this weeks ago. It's for my—"

"Don't," he snaps. "Don't start with your 'my page' crap. Just answer me one thing."

He moves before I can prepare, crossing the room in three long strides.

My back hits the dresser, the edge digging into my lower spine. His hand quickly rises, his palm flat against my collarbone as his finger presses into my skin, right where the bone meets flesh.

It hurts; I feel pain blooming underneath, and all he's doing is pressing harder.

"Have fun on your little work trip," he says, the words dripping with venom. "You better not be cheating on me, Layla."

Pain radiates with his touch. I flinch, my hands trembling by my sides. His eyes are dark and unrecognizable.

He does it constantly; flirting, DMing models, coming home with lipstick stains on his collar, like I wouldn't notice.

But somehow, I'm the one being accused.

I mean, Layla, you are emotionally cheating. Fuck.

"Brian, you're scaring me," I whisper.

He tilts his head, eyes flickering like he's debating whether to keep pushing, but he scoffs instead. "Oh, please. Don't make me the bad guy. You love playing the victim."

He steps back, his tone already shifting back to casual, careless charm. "Have fun on your little work trip," he says. "Bring me something nice."

He stares at me for a beat that feels like forever, then scoffs again.

"And Layla?" he says, stepping back. "Maybe you should be scared."

His words hang in the air as he turns, grabs his keys, and slams the door so hard the picture frames rattle.

I let out a shaky breath, my hands gripping the edge of the dresser.

The spot where he pressed his finger throbs, already tender. I pull down the collar of my shirt, and I see the faint red marks where his finger was pressed, already knowing a bruise is going to form on my delicate skin.

Tears spill before I can stop them. I press my palms to my face, sobbing until I can't breathe anymore.

When the shaking finally subsides, I go back to packing. One shirt. Then another. My movements are slow, trying to keep myself moving so I can hold myself together.

My phone buzzes on the bed. I sniffle and reach to grab it, the bright light making me wince.

REED

You leavin' soon, sunshine?

Truck's ready. So am I.

I stare at his messages, the ache in my chest loosening just a little. My fingers tremble as I type back.

LAYLA

Yeah! I'll be there tonight. 😊

Three dots appear.

Ping.

REED

Can't wait to see you.

A tear hits the screen, splashing across his name. I wipe it away with my thumb and swallow the lump in my throat.

I zip my suitcase shut and stare at the very faint bruise already forming under my skin.

God, Layla, grow a pair and leave.

The thought hits hard.

It's not the first time I've said it to myself, and it won't be the last.

But then the other voice answers, the one that constantly makes excuses for him, the one that is scared to leave despite everything.

He didn't mean it. He's just stressed. You know how he gets.

I tell myself today is the day I'll leave, but when that day comes, it's either a good or bad day with Brian. On good days, I see a glimpse of the man I met in high school: sweet, charming, loving. On his bad days, I see someone I don't recognize—a monster—and he's progressively getting worse.

He verbally and emotionally abuses me, but tonight he physically hurt me, and I'm scared it's going to get worse if he gets mad again.

I can do it. I can do it. I. Can. Do. It.

But it's different when you're inside of it, when the person holding the match keeps whispering that the fire's your fault.

I'll find the courage, but right now, I'm running.

I'm tucked into a corner by Gate 14, my oversized hoodie pulled over my hair, pretending I'm just another traveler instead of a liar.

My suitcase sits between my boots, cherry-vanilla perfume leaking faintly from the zipper. I've already checked in, no turning back now.

My phone pings with messages from my group chat with the girls.

CATALINA

bitch, i miss you. when can you come and visit?

LAYLA

soon! i've just been busy with collabs and brian

AMELIA

ugh you suck, you need to meet leo

CATALINA

you hate us, its fine, miss you sm

LAYLA

miss you guys more, i love you

I press send and keep my gaze fixed on the screen. My throat tightens, and guilt creeps in. They'd kill me if they found out I went out there and didn't see them, but I'm running away to see *him.*

Aimlessly scrolling through my camera roll, I pretend to be busy, but every reflection, the window glass, the phone screen, reveals the same woman I'm trying not to recognize —the one with tired eyes and a bruise just below her collarbone, hidden beneath a layer of cotton.

The intercom crackles overhead, taking me out of my internal spiral.

Flight 612 to Nashville is now boarding Group 1-3.

That's me.

My phone vibrates in my hand, making my breath get caught in my throat when I see who's calling me.

I freeze, then swipe to answer before I can overthink it.

"Hey?" I say, too softly.

"Hey."

The deep cadence of his voice hits me hard, making it hard to breathe.

It's comforting, deep, and laced with a Southern accent, a kind of voice that stays with you long after the call is over. Behind him, I hear crickets and the soft hum of the night.

"You boardin' yet?"

"Just about to," I murmur. "They're calling my row."

"What time do you get in?"

I glance at my ticket. "Eleven p.m., your time."

There's a pause.

"I'll be there."

My chest tightens. "Reed, you don't have to, it's late, and I can just—"

He cuts me off, "Layla."

The way he says my name, it's a tether pulling me back down to something solid.

"I said I'll be there."

I swallow, my voice barely a whisper. "Okay."

"Text me when you land."

"I will."

"Good. See you soon, sunshine."

When the line clicks, the airport sounds flood back in—boarding calls, chatter, the hollow scrape of rolling suitcases—but now they sound muted.

I stare at my reflection in the terminal window as the lights outside blur into gold streaks against the darkness.

For the first time in years, my pulse feels like mine again.

I tuck my phone into my pocket, grab my carry-on, and step into the boarding line.

Four and a half hours in the air.

And a man waiting on the other end who calls me *sunshine* like it's a promise.

FIFTEEN
REED

The arrivals board keeps flickering between flight numbers and delays, but I really don't notice it anymore.

My hands are shoved in my jacket pockets, the hum of rolling luggage and chatter blend into static.

I've been standing at baggage claim C for nearly an hour, pretending to scroll through my phone when all I'm really doing is replaying her text in my head.

"Yeah! I'll be there tonight."

I told myself I was being a decent man by picking her up, so she wouldn't have to ride alone so late.

But decent men don't count the literal minutes or hours until sunshine walks back into their lives.

I've been standing here long enough for my coffee to go cold, as my boots are planted on the polished floor, tapping away in a nervous rhythm.

Tap. Tap. Tap.

My phone buzzes in my pocket as I grab it quickly, reading the message flashing across the screen.

LAYLA

Finally off the plane, headed to baggage claim 😮‍💨

I exhale as my thumb hovers over the screen.

REED

I'm by baggage claim C.

Before I can lock the screen, I spot her.

She's weaving through the crowd as she grips her purse, and her other hand is clutching her phone.

The hood of her bright yellow hoodie is half up, her hair spilling around her face. She's analyzing the crowd, her eyes scanning everywhere until they land on me.

And she smiles.

Her damn smile. She's so goddamn radiant, and she doesn't even realize how much of an effect she has on me.

When she reaches me, her words spill out, a cue that she's nervous.

"Hi—oh my god, hey—sorry, I'm talking too fast. I didn't sleep on the flight, and they ran out of pretzels—criminal, right? And some guy sneezed on my laptop, so now I think I have the plague—"

"Layla."

Her mouth snaps shut. "Yeah?"

"You're here," I say quietly, a ghost of a smile dances across my lips.

She laughs nervously. "Yeah. I'm here."

The noise around us briefly softens.

I notice the faint circles under her eyes and the exhaustion in her sagging shoulders, but she keeps trying to hide it, filling the silence with a bright smile.

She quickly adjusts her hoodie, pulling the fabric down, and in that movement, her features become more defined.

A blooming bruise, right below her collarbone.

My pulse quickens, the roar of my heartbeat drowning everything out. My jaw locks before my brain even catches up.

She doesn't notice me staring as she continues talking. "I don't think I've ever seen this airport so busy this late. You didn't have to wait, you know. You really didn't."

"Yeah," I say quietly. "I did."

Her voice falters. "You—you did?"

"Layla." I soften it this time, letting her name hang in the space between us. "You hungry?"

Her head pops up, surprised by the shift. "Starving."

"Good," I murmur, grabbing her suitcase before she can, as it comes around on the belt. "Figured as much."

"Oh my god, thank you, I swear it weighs less than it looks—actually, no, that's a lie, it probably weighs a ton—"

"Not heavy," I say, because she looks like she needs me to say it.

I set it upright beside me, my hand brushing hers for half a second.

"Truck's outside," I tell her.

"I can't believe you drove all the way here, that's like an hour. You didn't have to do that. I could've—"

"Layla."

"Right. You said you'd be here." She smiles again, softer this time. "You really meant it."

"Always do."

A faint blush colors her cheeks in this pretty hue of scarlet as she looks at me, really looks, and, for the first time since she stepped off that plane, she stops talking.

The silence remains, full yet comfortable, before I nod toward the doors. "C'mon. Let's get some food in you."

She falls into step beside me, her sleeve brushing my arm as we head for the exit.

Her perfume curls through the air—cherry and vanilla notes—and it makes the whole damn airport feel smaller.

Outside, the air is cooler with the distant promise of rain. The parking lot lights cast a soft yellow glow over the pavement, catching in her hair as she tugs her hood tighter.

"You cold?" I ask.

She shakes her head. "No, just... tired."

"Yeah," I mumble, unlocking the truck. "You and me both."

I steal a quick look at that bruise barely visible under her hoodie. A quiet, yet intense anger builds inside me, tightly coiled in my chest.

Whoever put that mark on her is never touching her again.

We don't talk as we walk. Her sneakers scuff against the concrete, and my boots clack.

The air carries that faint autumn bite that sneaks under your collar, sharp enough to make her tuck her chin into her hoodie.

Her suitcase rattles behind her, the wheels clicking unevenly over the cracks. I reach for the handle before I even realize it. She lets go without a word.

We keep moving as rain trickles in from the structure's open edges.

It dots her hair, darkening the strands where it lands. She tugs the hood tighter around her face, shivering once and remaining quiet.

I shift her suitcase to my left hand as I shrug off my jacket, draping it over her so she's warm.

An old reflex my mama drilled into me before I was tall enough to reach the door handle on her old truck.

"You take care of people, Reed. That's what we do."

I open the passenger door first. The rain has picked up now, a slow, rhythmic patter against the structure's roof.

"Careful," I murmur, as I brace my hand above the doorframe, so she doesn't bump her head.

She climbs in slowly, her movements small and cautious.

The overhead lights hit her face just enough for me to see the faint curiosity in her eyes.

She settles into the passenger seat, and I close the door softly, avoiding a slam.

I circle back to the driver's side, and she's looking out the window, not at the rain, but at me.

Her eyes are glossy in the dim light, not crying, but on the brink of it, that worn-out look people get after they've held too much for too long.

I load her bags into the back, along with her purse. She watches me through the rearview mirror the entire time. I can feel her eyes burning straight through me.

When I finally sit behind the wheel, the air inside the truck feels warmer. She's now turned toward me, her hoodie slipping off one shoulder. The bruise reflects the faint dashboard light. I look away before the anger comes back.

"Seatbelt," I say quietly.

She blinks, like she's waking from a thought, and reaches for it. The soft click echoes in the silence.

I start the engine. The hum fills the space between us, but she's still staring.

I finally glance her way. "What?"

Her lips twitch, a faint smile. "Nothing... you do all

that; carry the bags, give me your jacket, open doors, like it's automatic."

"Was raised that way."

"By your mom?"

I nod once, eyes on the rearview. "Yeah."

She looks down at her lap, her fingers tracing the seam of her jeans. "She did a good job."

Something twists in my chest. "Yeah," I mumble. "She did."

Outside, the rain begins to fall harder. The wipers move slowly as I pull out of the structure, headlights cutting through the darkness.

She leans her head against the window, watching the city lights blur past as her reflection meets mine.

The silence isn't awkward anymore like before, and honestly, I'm getting used to her company.

As we leave Nashville behind, I still feel her eyes on me, not with fear this time, but something gentler, something that feels a lot like trust.

The rain has faded into mist by the time we're halfway to Ruby Ridge. The truck hums steadily, its headlights cutting through the dark stretch of Tennessee highway.

She sits cross-legged in the passenger seat now, her hair loose around her shoulders. She's been talking for the last fifteen minutes.

And honestly, I'm not even pretending to dislike it.

She squeals, clapping her hands. "Let's play a questions game."

I sigh, nodding my head in approval.

"Okay, how old are you?"

I huff out a laugh. "Thirty-three, you?"

She giggles. "Twenty-seven, can't you see how radiant I am?"

I smirk. If only she knew her radiance is the only thing I look forward to.

She taps her chin dramatically. "Okay, favorite color."

I glance at her, a hint of a smile tugging at my mouth. "Green."

She hums, analyzing my answer. "Forest green or, like... muted cactus green?"

I let out a soft laugh under my breath. "Didn't realize there were different kinds."

"There are always different kinds," she says, pointing a finger at me. "Mine's yellow. Like the sun. Or sunflowers. Or traffic lights when you're already halfway through the intersection."

"Dangerous," I murmur.

"Fun," she counters, grinning.

Her laugh spills into the cab again, and I find myself wanting her to keep going; to fill the quiet, to keep laughing so I can hear that sweet noise again.

"Favorite flower," she says next, tucking her legs under her.

"Roses," I answer without thinking.

She blinks, surprised. "That's... unexpectedly sweet."

"My mama's favorite," I say with a shrug, as my hands tighten on the wheel. "It just stuck with me."

"Still sweet," she says, tucking her hair behind her ear, quickly saying her answer. "Mine's sunflowers. They always face the light, even when it rains."

"That fits you."

Her cheeks flush, and she looks away, tracing her finger along the fogged window. "So honest of you, Reed."

I grunt in response, not knowing what to say to her. She makes me nervous, and communicating hasn't always been my strong suit, but being near her makes me want to try.

Her blue eyes glance at me again, softer this time.

She's the only woman who can look at me with that curiosity in her eyes, and somehow it creates a look that makes my pulse race.

The moon slips out from behind a cloud, light pouring through the windshield just enough to highlight her face.

Her eyes aren't just blue, they're tinged with flecks of amber and honey, colors I've never seen on anyone else.

For a second, I forget about the road, about the rain, about everything but her.

Pay attention to the road, Reed, fuck.

She quickly looks away, and I drag my gaze back to the highway, clenching my jaw tightly, pretending I didn't just lose my breath over the simple fact of her eye color.

She clears her throat. "Okay, favorite movie."

"*Terrifier.*"

She gasps, her hand flying to cover her mouth. "Reed, that movie is terrifying, ha, get it?"

I snicker in response.

She grins, blurting out her answer. "Mine's *She's All That.*"

"Never heard of it."

Her jaw drops. "You're kidding. It's iconic. A high school makeover movie? Freddie Prinze Jr.? Paul Walker?"

"Doesn't sound like somethin' I'd watch."

"Well, I'm going ot make you watch it with me then."

I choke on a laugh, shaking my head. "Okay, sunshine, whatever you want."

"Whatever I want, huh?" she says, shifting closer, her tone teasing but her eyes saying something else entirely.

My hands tighten on the wheel. "You're trouble."

She leans forward, whispering conspiratorially, "The fun kind."

And without a thought, she absentmindedly reaches over the center console, her hand landing on my arm.

It's just a light touch, barely anything at all. Her fingers curl loosely around my bicep, and I feel every sensation of her touch, goosebumps erupting on my skin instantly.

My breath catches, as my eyes flicker down for a split second.

Her thumb brushes along the fabric of my flannel as she continues talking, something about art, paint colors, and canvases, completely unaware of what she's doing to me, not even realizing she's stroking my arm.

"I paint when I can," she says softly. "Not for anyone else. Just for me. It's quiet when I do."

I glance at her, my throat tight. "You good at it?"

She shrugs, still tracing little circles on my arm. "It makes me feel like I am."

Her touch lingers another beat before she finally pulls away, and the air that rushes in where her hand was feels too cold, too empty.

I clear my throat, trying to sound steady. "You miss it?"

"Every day," she whispers, her eyes turning back to the rolling pastures. "I get so busy with content creation and editing that I never have time to sit down, relax, and paint."

I grunt in response, not knowing what to tell her in this moment.

Her lips curve. "Maybe we can paint while I'm out here."

My eyes are focused on the road, but I can't help but smile. "I can make that happen."

She smiles in response, letting out a long sigh.

The cab settles back into silence, but it feels different now.

Her fingers brush the edge of her hoodie again, fidgeting as my knuckles tighten on the steering wheel.

I catch one more glance, her half-smile, her eyes heavy from traveling, and everything in me fights the urge not to reach for her.

The highway curves ahead as the world around us fades into the kind of night that only happens when two people are pretending not to fall for each other.

SIXTEEN
REED

"C'mon," I murmur, pushing my door open. "Let's eat before it gets cold."

She nods, climbing out, her hair shimmering beneath the porch light, and for a second, I watch the way she hugs her hoodie tighter, and the way the night wind tugs at her hair.

Damn, if it doesn't hit me right in the chest, that quiet, dangerous thought I've been trying to avoid since she stumbled into my life.

My house is dim when we walk in, the air cool and faintly tinged with whiskey and orange bitters. I set the takeout bag down on the coffee table and nod toward the couch.

"Hope you like semi-cold fries."

She flops down with a dramatic sigh, kicking her shoes off. "At this point, I'd eat airport carpet, so cold fries sound gourmet."

A laugh escapes me before I can stop it. She grins when she hears it, like she's proud of herself for pulling it out of me.

We settle in, wrappers crinkling, the room quiet except for the hum of the paused TV. *Terrifier* 3 is still frozen on the screen, *Art the clown's* grin stretched too wide.

"Of course you were watching this," she says, chewing on a fry. "Go ahead, I don't mind."

I glance at her, skeptical. "You sure?"

"Very sure."

"You asked for it." I grab the remote and hit play.

The movie continues to play, kicking back onto the shower scene, which I already know is going to be brutally gory. She squints at the screen, curious but a hint of horror flashing across her delicate features.

"Reed," she whines, "why does he look like that? It's gross."

"He's a horror icon."

"He's a nightmare," she whispers, clutching a fry. "The way he's smiling is freaking me out, like, why are his teeth black, please."

I smirk, leaning back. "You talk a lot when you're scared."

"I'm not scared," she shoots back immediately. "I'm just... narrating my trauma in real time."

The brutal, gory scene finally flashes across the screen, and I glance over at her, whose eyes are wide in shock.

She screams, actually screams, and bolts off the couch so fast she knocks her drink over. "NOPE. I'M OUT. ENJOY YOUR CLOWN!"

I choke on a laugh, setting my cup down before I spill it. "You alright?"

Her voice bounces from the kitchen. "Reed, what in the fuck is THAT?!"

Standing up from the leather couch, I make my way over to the kitchen, where I find her crouched behind the counter, her hair falling into her face, still clutching that sad fry, which is now limp in her fingers.

I crouch down across from her, resting my elbows on my knees, still fighting back a grin.

"You hiding, sunshine?"

"Yes," she whispers dramatically. "And I'm not coming out until that disgusting clown dies."

"Unfortunately, he doesn't die."

"Oh, well, that's fantastic!" she says mockingly with her hands thrown in the air, still clutching the fry between her fingers.

That draws another laugh out of me, the only person who can make me laugh so easily.

She peeks up through her lashes, cheeks flushed a pretty rosy pink, blue eyes bright, and for a moment, time stops.

Reaching out, I instinctively brush a loose strand of hair behind her ear. Her breath stutters slightly, her gaze snapping up to mine.

"There," I mumble. "Much better."

Her lips curve into a coy smile, a soft laugh slipping through. "Such a gentleman, Reed."

"Maybe."

But my voice comes out softer than it should. Her eyes linger on me, and suddenly it's too quiet, just the background noise from the TV spilling into the kitchen, her perfume mingling with the smell of fries.

She whispers, "You're still smiling."

I shrug, retreating my touch from her, and my thumb brushes against my knee. "Guess you're contagious."

Her laugh this time is smaller, almost shy, but it fills every inch of the room.

She blinks, a little stunned, then laughs nervously this time, but it fills the whole space anyway.

"Fine," she sighs. "But now, I'm forcing you to watch *She's All That.*"

"Deal."

She's still laughing softly as I stand and offer her a hand. Her fingers slip into mine, still trembling slightly from the scare. I help her up, and she stands there for a heartbeat too long, gazing up at me with that gentle, bright grin that always seems to disarm me effortlessly.

"Come on," I say quietly, nodding toward the living room. "We'll watch your movie, no more clowns."

"Thank God," she sighs, grabbing her limp fry from the floor. "My heart rate can't take cinematic trauma tonight."

We walk back to the couch, hand in hand. Once we're both seated, we let each other go, and the feel of her hand not intertwined with mine feels *wrong*.

I scroll through the streaming options until I land on the movie she wanted. She curls into the corner of the couch with her legs tucked under her, as she grabs one of my throw blankets and wraps it around herself.

The light from the screen flickers across her face, catching the beauty marks speckled on her cheek and neck. For a few minutes, she's quiet, and I think maybe she's winding down, but then she perks up again, turning to me.

"So, I've been editing all day," she says suddenly, like the thought just burst out. "Well, not today-today, 'cause plane Wi-Fi is garbage, but yesterday. The footage that I have is coming together nicely. We can film some more tomorrow."

I glance over at her as my arm rests on the back of the couch. "You got it, sunshine."

She grins, biting her lower lip, which drives me mad, as she turns her attention back to the movie.

The movie keeps playing, but neither of us is really watching.

She starts talking again—about camera angles, color grading, the way she wants to film in natural light next time—and I listen.

Her soft voice fills the room, cutting through the quiet that used to feel so heavy here.

She yawns and tucks herself deeper into the blanket, her words beginning to slow, her sentences stretched, and I know she's seconds from falling asleep mid-thought.

And somehow, with her in my house, half-asleep on my couch, I realize the quiet doesn't feel empty anymore.

It takes about five minutes for her to fall asleep, the movie still flickering on the TV, low enough that the sound barely reaches over the hum of the heater.

The blanket slips slightly off her shoulder, and her hair spills over the cushion in tangled, blonde waves.

I continue studying her, and her hair isn't just blonde; I'm able to see it now, beneath my glasses.

The color deepens toward the ends, fading from pale honey into warmer tones, with threads of auburn woven through. It's not perfect; a few pieces curl in different directions, and one strand rests against her cheek, caught on the corner of her mouth.

Her ivory skin looks soft, warm, and flushed even while she sleeps. Her cheeks have a natural, lingering pink.

A faint dusting of freckles appears near her nose, freckles I hadn't noticed before.

Her nose is small and gently upturned, the kind that wrinkles when she laughs or gets stubborn, which seems to be most of the time.

There are faint smile lines at the corners of her mouth, just barely visible, subtle reminders of every laugh she's ever forced into the world, even when it hurt.

Her dark, long lashes fan out across her cheeks, curling upward, and each time she exhales, they flutter just the tiniest bit.

And her lips, fuck, her lips.

I don't know how long I've been staring before I realize I am.

They're slightly parted, with a soft pink color that looks alive even in the pale light. Her lips are full, nearly shaped like a heart when parted.

She's beautiful.

My gaze drifts down to her hand resting on the blanket, her fingers loosely curled near her chest. That's when I notice that fucking ring.

Her engagement ring sparkles faintly in the TV light, glimmering.

It doesn't belong on her, not when she's here in my home, her chest rising and falling in that gentle rhythm that makes the whole damn world feel quieter.

The sight of that ring hits me harder than I expected.

It's an anchor, pulling me back to reality. A reminder that this isn't mine to want.

That *she* isn't mine to want.

But God, I want her anyway.

I want to hear her laughter echo through these walls every day.

I want to understand the thoughts behind those bright, reckless eyes. I want to learn the cadence of her voice when she's not performing for anyone. I want to hold onto this—this fragile, impossible peace between us—because it's the first time my house hasn't felt like a tomb.

And yet, I can't have it.

I can't have *her*.

She's here, asleep on my couch, wrapped in my blanket, and I'm sitting two feet away, quietly falling apart because she's the first person in years to make me feel alive again.

My gaze again follows her face, committing every detail to memory. I notice the curve of her jaw, the soft hollow under her cheekbone, the delicate shadow cast by her lashes, and the gentle rise at the corner of her lips.

I run my fingers through my mustache, attempting to look away, but it's futile.

Every fiber of my being is drawn to her.

I lean back against the couch, restraining my hands, fighting the urge to reach out and brush her hair aside. The restraint weighs more than anything I have ever lifted.

She quietly sighs in her sleep, her lips slightly parting, and her brows twitching as if reacting to something only she perceives.

I shouldn't be looking at her like this. I shouldn't be thinking about what it would feel like to touch her, to see those eyes open and find me there, to *kiss* her.

Something about her feels like sunlight breaking through every wall I've built to keep the world out.

I've been telling myself it's wrong, that it's nothing. That she's just a friend. A guest. A woman with a ring on her finger and a life that doesn't intersect with mine beyond this fleeting, stolen moment.

But the truth?

I already know this isn't temporary for me; it hasn't been since I first laid my eyes on her.

I sit there long after the credits roll, after the movie fades out and the screen goes black, after the only light left in the room is the light that spills through the porch window.

I sit there watching her breathe, memorizing every tiny detail because I know I shouldn't. Because it feels like the only thing I'll have.

Finally, I lean my head back against the couch as the ache in my chest becomes unbearable.

I close my eyes and let the sound of her breathing fill the room.

For the first time in a long time, I'm not sure if the silence is comforting or if it's killing me slowly.

SEVENTEEN
REED

I park two blocks away on purpose.

If I pull right up to Main Street, Layla won't look. She'll miss how Ruby Ridge opens slowly; the way the buildings lean toward each other, the way the air smells faintly of pine and coffee, the way everything feels... unrushed.

She hops out of the truck before I can even shut off the engine, already lifting her camera.

"Okay," she says, walking backward down the sidewalk while filming. "I need everyone to appreciate this cutie small town. LOOK at all the cute shops with western decor!"

I shut the door and catch up to her, my hands sliding into my pockets.

She's wearing a sundress today, the kind that moves with her, catching the breeze and brushing her legs.

My gaze travels along her delicate back, the curve of her natural hips, her sundress clinging to the right places.

Fuck, I shouldn't be looking.

I force my eyes back to the street, even though I desperately want to admire her.

"It's just buildings," I say.

She stops so abruptly that I nearly walk into her.

"Reed Hayes," she says solemnly, camera still rolling, "do *not* disrespect a good Main Street."

I snort. "I grew up here. It's allowed."

She grins and pivots, filming the bakery window, the handwritten menu, and the flower shop next door, with buckets of blooms spilling onto the sidewalk. She crouches low, captures a shot of petals scattered on the concrete, then pops back up.

"Do they always do that?" she asks.

"Do what?"

"Put flowers everywhere. Like they're trying to seduce people into staying."

I shrug. "Guess it works."

She glances at me, eyebrow raised. "Oh? You seduced?"

My pulse quickens as heat creeps up my neck. "That's not what I meant."

She laughs and turns back to her camera.

I watch her instead of the town now. I can't help it.

The way she talks with her hands, the way she rocks on her heels when she's thinking, the way she squints slightly at the screen as she's filming.

We pass the old movie theater, its faded marquee letters crooked and sun-worn. She slows, filming it from across the street.

"This is cute," she says. "Do they still show movies here?"

"Friday nights," I say. "Usually something outdated."

Her eyes light up. "I kinda love that, you should take me."

Oh.

"Yeah, sure, I can do that."

"Great! It's a date," she says, winking at me.

God damn it.

She walks backward again, narrating softly, nearly tripping over a crack in the sidewalk.

I reach out this time, my fingers brushing her arm just long enough to steady her.

She looks at me, surprised, then smiles. "Thank you for this."

"Anytime," I say, and mean more than just the moment.

We stop in front of a small boutique window; dresses, folded and stacked precisely on hangers.

She presses close to the glass, filming the street's reflection behind her.

"This might be my favorite so far," she murmurs.

"You say that every block."

"Because every block keeps trying harder," she says, glancing at me. "Unlike you."

I huff a laugh. "What's that supposed to mean?"

"You act like none of this is special," she says, sweeping the camera around. "But you know exactly where the good light is, which shop has the best coffee, and which street is quieter."

I don't answer as I watch her lower the camera and look at the town with bare eyes, like she's seeing something that belongs to her now, too.

She resumes filming, brushing past me, deliberately shoulder-bumping mine this time.

"You're smiling," she says casually.

"I am not."

She tilts the camera toward me.

I dodge it, laughing despite myself. "Don't."

"Smile for my fans," she teases.

"They don't need to see me."

She lowers the camera and looks at me, really looks. "I do."

My chest tightens, and I look away first.

I'm not used to anyone being interested in me. I've locked people out. Who wants to look at a freak like me?

At the end of the street, she turns slowly, capturing one last sweeping shot.

The sun catches her hair, her dress, and the tiny dust motes floating in the air.

I stand there quietly, analyzing every detail of her, memorizing the freckles that dance across her nose, the way her eyes crinkle when she smiles, and how they reflect the natural light, honey and amber swirling in the vast blue.

She's everything I could have ever dreamed of, but she isn't mine to want.

"Thanks for bringing me," she says, slipping the camera down into her purse.

I nod, my hands buried in my pockets, grounding myself. "Yeah."

The truth settles in anyway, watching her discover Ruby Ridge feels a lot like watching her find a place in my life.

She keeps drifting farther from me, rummaging in her bag before pulling her camera out again, capturing chipped fences and tall grass brushing the pavement's edge.

"This feels like a secret," she says, half to herself.

"It kind of is," I tell her. "Not many people walk this way."

She hums, pleased, as she scans the horizon.

Suddenly, she stops so abruptly that I almost bump into her again.

"Oh."

I follow her gaze, and it lands just beyond the road, past a low wooden fence.

There's a patch of land that never developed. I've driven by it a hundred times without a second thought.

Right now, sunflowers bloom. Just a scattered burst of them, their faces tipped toward the sun.

She makes a soft, breathless sound.

"Reed," she whispers.

Before I can answer, she grabs my hand.

Not my sleeve, not my wrist. My hand. My fucking hand.

Reed, relax, she's just a friend, this means nothing.

Her fingers curl around mine, and then she pulls me, actually pulls me, off the road and toward the fence.

"Wait, Layla—" I start, but she's already laughing and tugging me forward.

"Come on!" she says, breathless. "Please, please, please."

We run awkwardly at first, then we find our footing, my boots thudding on the dirt, her laugh ringing out.

I vault the fence half a second after she does, landing hard and still holding her hand like it's the most natural thing in the world.

She doesn't let go as she drags me into the middle of the sunflowers, spinning once, then twice, her hair catching the light, laughter spilling from her as if she can't contain it.

"Oh my god," she says, breathless. "This is—this is perfect!"

I'm not looking at the goddamn flowers. I'm looking at her.

Her cheeks are flushed, her eyes shine, and her fingers tighten around mine as she continues to twirl us around.

My chest feels too tight for my own good, as my pulse pounds in my ears.

She lifts her camera again with her free hand, filming the sunflowers swaying, the blue sky overhead, our shadows tangled on the ground.

"Okay," she says, giggling. "Tell me this town isn't magical."

I swallow the lump in my throat, choosing not to answer as she keeps spinning us in a circle.

She stops twirling us, turning to me then, still smiling, still holding my hand.

For a second, neither of us moves as the wind rustles through the flowers, brushing against us.

She looks down at our hands like she's just noticing them intertwined with one another.

"Oh, sorry," she says, but she doesn't pull away right away.

"That's okay," I say quickly.

Her smile shifts, smaller now as she finally lets go, and I wish she fucking didn't as she steps back just a little, but the space where she was feels cold immediately.

She lifts the camera again, filming the sunflowers from a different angle, humming softly as she smiles to herself.

I stand there with my hands loose at my sides, heart still racing, wondering how something so simple, running through a patch of sunflowers with her laugh echoing around us, can feel like it's changing something I can't undo.

And somehow... I don't want to. I don't want whatever this is between us to change. I want *more.*

She lowers the camera, taking two steps toward me. "Wait."

Before I can ask what she means, she reaches for my hands again, this time both of them.

Her fingers slide into mine as if they already know where to go.

"Layla—" I start.

"Trust me," she says, her eyes bright, already tugging.

She spins us again, and again, laughing as I stumble over my own feet.

Sunflowers blur around us, yellow and green streaking past my vision.

I'm painfully aware of how close she is, how her hands feel wrapped around mine, and how easy it would be to pull her in rather than let her lead.

"I don't dance," I protest weakly.

"You're doing great," she says. "Very... earnest."

I snort. "That's not a compliment."

"It absolutely is!"

She twirls this time, her dress flaring, her hair lifting in the breeze as she turns back to me, laughing too hard to keep her balance, and she trips.

I reach for her at the same moment she reaches for me, but momentum wins.

We go down together, hitting the ground amid laughter and soft dirt.

She lands on top of me, and the laughter fades, replaced by something quieter.

I can feel her curves through her dress as her hands are braced on either side of my shoulders, her breath warm against my face.

The sunflowers sway above us, shadows shifting, the world narrowed to this small space between us.

She blinks, her eyes flicking over my face as if she's suddenly aware of every inch of space, or lack thereof.

"Oh," she breathes.

My heart is pounding so hard I'm sure she can feel it. I don't move. I don't trust myself to do so.

"Sorry," she says softly, but she doesn't get up yet.

"It's...okay," I manage.

Her gaze settles on my glasses, slightly crooked from the fall. She lifts one hand slowly, as if giving me time to stop her.

I don't.

She nudges them back into place carefully, her touch feather-light on my cheek.

The contact sends heat straight through me.

"There," she says quietly. "Better."

I can feel my face burning. I know it's obvious. I know I'm blushing. There's no hiding it.

Fuck. Fuck. Fuck.

Something tender flickers across her expression, like she's seeing me clearly for the first time.

For a moment, neither of us moves.

"Sorry," she says quickly, her words tumbling out as she shifts her weight, suddenly very aware of herself. "I—I shouldn't be on you."

Her words hit me harder than the fall did.

"It's—no," I say at the same time she starts pushing herself up. "You're fine. I mean— it's fine. I didn't—"

We both stop, flustered, talking over each other.

She laughs nervously, brushing dirt off her dress. "I'm really clumsy. I swear I'm not usually this—"

"Layla," I say softly, and she looks at me.

Her expression changes, still bright, still warm, but there's something else there now.

A flicker of guilt.

"I'm sorry," she repeats, quieter this time.

Something twists in my chest.

"You don't have to be," I say, meaning it. "I should've... I don't know. I should've caught you better."

I push myself up first, then reach for her without thinking. My hands settle at her waist as my fingers curve instinctively around the soft warmth there.

Her skin is warm beneath my palms, the thin fabric doing nothing to help.

I'm suddenly hyper-aware of everything—how close she is, how easily my thumbs could move, how her hands hover for half a second before settling on my forearms.

I help her up slowly, taking a breath at a time before I lose it.

"There," I murmur once she's steady.

Neither of us lets go right away.

The sunflowers sway around us, brushing our legs. Everything is hushed except for the sound of my heartbeat pounding in my ears.

Her fingers curl slightly into my sleeves as my hands stay at her waist, my thumbs flexing once before I force them still.

I don't trust myself.

She swallows. "You okay?"

I nod, probably too fast. "Yeah. Just—uh. You're good?"

She smiles sheepishly. "Yeah. Thanks for... catching me."

"I didn't really," I admit.

"You did enough," she says.

It feels like she might say something else, something important. Her gaze flicks to my lips, then back to my eyes.

I let go first, and losing contact with her makes my heart ache.

She steps back, smoothing her dress, lifting her camera again to give her something to do with her hands.

"Well," she says lightly, clearing her throat. "Sunflowers conquered. Reed Hayes successfully twirled."

I laugh, rubbing the back of my neck. "I'm never living that down, am I?"

"Absolutely not," she says, grinning. "It's going in the vault."

She turns away to film again, but she glances back over her shoulder, her eyes soft, and she smiles at me.

Her smile could gut me completely.

I stand there for a moment longer, my hands still tingling, my heart still pounding, knowing one thing for sure, that the touch meant something.

And whatever this is between us, it's only just starting to burn.

EIGHTEEN
LAYLA

Yesterday with Reed was fun. Our friendship is turning into something interesting, and I'm lying to myself if I don't want more with him.

Layla, this is so wrong, but I can't seem to find a fuck to give.

It's late afternoon at Boots & Bourbon, the evening auburn rays of light slipping through the windows. The bar smells faintly like smoke and whiskey, that sweet-spice blend that clings to the air long after the doors open.

Reed's behind the counter with his sleeves rolled to his elbows. The more time we spend together, the more he's becoming comfortable showing me parts of himself he doesn't show others.

He moves with a quiet, careful rhythm that makes it feel like he's part of the place.

There's a half-empty bottle of bourbon by his elbow, a dishrag in his hand, and a pair of black-frame glasses resting low on his nose as he checks the register.

I'm perched on the far end of the bar with my laptop

open, earbuds in my ear, pretending to focus on my edits but mostly... watching him.

Okay, definitely watching him.

He's not doing anything special, but he looks unfairly good while doing it.

There's something about the way he moves, like he's unaware of the way people's eyes follow him.

Evening light reflects in his hair, turning the dark brown into shimmers of caramel hues woven in.

Every time he wipes the counter, the muscles in his forearm flex, ink shifting beneath his skin.

Focus, Layla. Edit the damn video.

I try, I really do. I replay the clips I filmed last week—snippets of laughter, clinking glasses, neon signs buzzing in the background—trying to find the right transition point.

Snipping the audio, I adjust the color balance and zoom in on a shot of the mechanical bull in motion.

But then I remember I have footage of him.

"Hey," I call, waving him over. "Come look at this."

He looks up with a raised brow. "What is it?"

"Footage from the bar," I say, turning the laptop toward him. "I have some good stuff, come looky."

He wipes his hands on a rag and steps closer as he leans over the counter. The light from the screen hits his face, and I watch the faint shadow of stubble along his jaw, his perfectly trim mustache, and the little crease between his brows as he squints.

Almost absently, he reaches up and readjusts his glasses, pushing them higher on his nose.

And all my self-worth is in the toilet, because holy shit.

It's such a small thing, pretty stupid—just a guy fixing his glasses—but something about it makes my body feel warm, a rush of heat making its way to my core, my pulse quickening from a straightforward action.

I instinctively clench my thighs together.

Jesus, Layla, relax.

His flannel sleeves are rolled up even higher now, and my eyes trace over every small detail.

The veins on his hands, the intricate muscles that naturally flex as he grips the bar counter, and don't even get me started on his forearm muscles.

My brain checks out, gone, vanished, evaporated.

He leans in closer to the screen, brows furrowed. "This from last week?

"Mm-hmm," I manage, but my voice comes out a little strangled.

He studies the footage, the corners of his mouth tugging faintly upward. "Looks good. You caught the light real nice here."

I nod, but I'm no longer looking at the screen.

Instead, I'm watching him; the way his glasses slide down again, the way he chews the inside of his cheek when he's thinking, the faint scar along his jawline, and the tiny flecks of blue that center his pupil.

He feels me staring. I can tell the moment he does.

His shoulders tense up, the relaxed focus on his face fading as his eyes dart anywhere else but me. His hand drops from the counter, and he takes a subtle half-step back, like he suddenly wants to fade into the background again.

The subtle movement knocks something loose in my chest; frustration, empathy, guilt, I can't tell which.

"You don't have to hide from me," I blurt out before my brain catches up.

He tilts his head slightly, eyes narrowing with confusion. "What?"

I swallow, instantly regretting my word vomit. "I just mean—" I wave vaguely toward him, my face burning. "You always do that thing. The, uh—backing away thing. You don't have to."

He blinks, silence stretching between us. His hand trails along the edge of the bar, thumb brushing the grain of the wood. "It's not—" he begins, then stops. The words get lost somewhere in his throat.

For a second, I think he might actually begin to open up to me.

He finally speaks, running his fingers through his hair. "It's not you I'm hiding from."

I suck in a breath at his honesty.

His eyes stay on the wood beneath his hands. "It's a reflex. You get used to taking up less space. It's easier that way."

Something heavy lodges in my throat. "Easier doesn't mean better."

He lets out a slow breath as his shoulders sag. "Maybe not. But it keeps things from hurting as much."

I lean closer without thinking. The distance between us feels wrong now. "Does it?"

"Not really."

His words are barely a whisper, but they undo me. Because for the first time, he's not trying to be unreadable. He's just... tired. Tired of hiding himself because of the way others look at him.

I want to reach for him, but I don't, opting to simply rest my hand flat on the bar between us, close enough that if he wanted to, he could bridge the gap.

"I notice when you pull away," I say quietly. "And I notice when you don't."

His gaze flicks to my hand, then to my face. There's a storm behind his eyes—fear, longing, maybe relief.

He looks at me as if he wants to say something, like he's struggling with whether he should.

"My bar is the only thing that's ever felt safe. I built it from nothing to have somewhere to be when everything else stopped feeling like home."

He stops there, the silence stretching, and I realize that might be the most he's told anyone in years.

My chest aches. "That's not nothing," I whisper.

His lips part, then press together again. "You make it sound simple."

"It doesn't have to be," I say. "Life isn't simple, it's messy."

For a long moment, neither of us moves as the clock ticks somewhere behind us.

He's still tracing the grain of the wood, but his hand drifts closer to mine, hesitating.

Our fingers finally touch; time seems to stand still, the noise of the world fades away, and it feels as if the universe itself is holding its breath, waiting for us to remember we have always been connected.

In that small, fragile moment, I sense him starting to let me in.

It's closing time, and I'm done editing for now. My phone buzzes in my pocket. I quickly pull it out, flinching at the bright screen.

BRIAN

a selfie of him with his friend, Rebecca.

Unreal. I throw my phone in my purse harder than necessary, scoffing at his stupid message.

He plays these mind games with me. Next, it'll be a message saying how much he misses or loves me. Then, like a switch, he'll be cruel, threatening, and hurting me with his words.

My focus snaps back to Reed.

He moves behind the bar with the same steady, methodical rhythm. The clink of glass against glass, the soft scrape of bottles sliding back into place. The neon sign out front casts a red glow through the windows, bathing everything in a gentle, muted maroon.

His shadow stretches long across the wooden floor, with broad shoulders outlined in warm illumination.

I'm still sitting at the bar with my chin propped in my hand, trying not to stew on Brian's text while watching him instead.

He doesn't talk much, but there's something about watching him move that feels like its own kind of conversation. The looseness in his shoulders, the way his brow furrows when he's counting bottles, the quiet focus that makes everything else fade away.

"Need help?" I finally ask because sitting still feels impossible.

He glances up, his eyes catching mine through the low light. "I've got it," he says, but his voice is softer than usual, not a real no.

I slide off the barstool anyway. "You always say that like it's a full sentence."

"It is."

I grin, walking around to the other side of the counter. "Too late, I'm helping."

He watches me for a moment, like he's trying to decide if it's worth arguing. Then he shakes his head, a faint smile curling around his lips. "Fine. Grab those receipts, and take 'em to the office in the back."

"On it."

I grab the stack of receipts he has piled on the counter neatly, the sound of paper crunching beneath my fingertips. Pushing past the bar, I make my way to the dimly lit hallway, entering Reed's office.

His office smells like him: oakmoss, whiskey, and faint traces of his cologne. The dark oak desk is neat except for a half-empty coffee cup and a few scattered papers. I set the receipts down on the corner of his desk, my fingers brushing against the worn leather blotter.

The low whir of the bar is distant from here, muffled behind the closed door.

I linger for a moment longer than I should. Maybe it's curiosity, or perhaps I like being surrounded by him; the quiet, and the warmth that seems to hang in the air even when he's not in the room.

Turning on my heel, I push open the wooden door and step back into the hallway, staring at my fingernails when I make it less than halfway before practically colliding into a wall of muscle.

Reed's hands grip my waist, steadying me.

I squeeze my eyes shut at the sudden contact.

Shit. Shit. Shit.

Finally, I open them, letting my gaze travel along his abs, broad chest, and massive shoulders until they meet his green eyes behind his glasses.

God, he's so tall it's unfair, really.

He's already staring down at me as his jaw tightens, his eyes flicking from my lips to my throat, and for a moment, I think he's going to close the distance. He doesn't, but God, I wish he would.

He releases my waist, resting his hand on the wall beside him, and gazes down at me. The hallway light washes over his face, and for a moment, neither of us moves.

"Sorry," I breathe, my voice wobbly. "Didn't mean to—"

"—run into me?" His mouth quirks, faintly.

He hesitates before he steps closer, as I try to move past him, but the space is too tight. The walls feel like they're shrinking to just him and me, the faint smell of whiskey, the warmth radiating from his skin, and only the sound of our breathing.

"Guess we've got a hallway problem," I mumble, smiling a little because I don't know what else to do with all this tension.

"Guess so," he says softly, taking off his glasses and tucking them in his back pocket.

We both stand there, close enough that the fabric of his shirt brushes my arm when he shifts his weight.

Without his glasses, he looks different. The scars along his cheek catch the light, each one a story he hasn't told me yet. His beard and mustache are trimmed close, framing his mouth, and I can't help but wonder what it would feel like if he kissed me.

The silence stretches, and I can hear the faint hum of the fridge behind the bar and the whisper of the neon sign outside. Every other sound feels miles away.

His gaze drifts, not in a creepy, deliberate way, but in a way that feels unavoidable. He starts from my eyes to my mouth, then back again, the muscle in his jaw tenses once before he looks away.

I should move.

He should move.

Neither of us does.

"You shouldn't stare at your nails as you walk," he says finally, his voice quiet but rough.

"You shouldn't run into people," I shoot back, because humor is easier than admitting my pulse is losing its rhythm.

His mouth curves just slightly. "You always have an answer for everything, don't you?"

"Occupational hazard," I whisper, my eyes flicking down to where his hand rests on the doorframe beside my shoulder. His fingers twitch slightly, and it feels like the entire room reacts with him.

He exhales slowly. "Layla..." he begins, but then stops, shaking his head as if trying to clear it.

"What?" I ask, too soft, too curious, too everything.

Kiss me.

He meets my eyes again, and for a moment, it feels like gravity shifts—like every rule, every line, every quiet promise he's made to himself is pulling tight.

But then he blinks, steps aside, and the spell shatters.

"Thank you for helping," he says, voice calm again, even though his hand is still braced against the wall as if he needs it to stay upright.

I swallow hard and nod, forcing a small smile. "You're welcome."

He huffs out a quiet laugh, looking down, and for a moment, I see it, the faint blush rising on his cheeks.

Maybe he doesn't say a word, but the silence between us speaks everything neither of us has the courage to say.

NINETEEN
REED

Sleep won't come.

I've been lying on the couch for what feels like hours, staring at the ceiling fan turning slow, steady circles in the dark.

Every creak of the house, every tick of the clock seems louder at night. I shift, rolling onto my side, then my back, tossing the blanket off again.

I keep replaying the moment at my bar; my hands on her waist, the warmth of her skin seeping through the thin fabric of her shirt, the soft hitch in her breath when I didn't let go right away.

She looked up at me with those bright blue, unguarded eyes, and for a second, it felt like the world had gone still, holding its breath for me to make a move I never made.

Fuck.

I exhale, dragging a hand down my face. My chest feels too tight, my thoughts too loud.

Faintly, from somewhere out back, music softly plays, but the beat is anything but quiet.

A gentle hum that gradually grows, enveloping the night air.

I sit up, every nerve in my body suddenly awake. The sound is coming from my backyard. I push off the couch and move toward the sliding glass door.

And there she is, barefoot in the grass.

She's wearing a matching pajama set, pale yellow with tiny brown teddy bears scattered across the soft fabric. The cami top is thin, loose in the breeze, the neckline dipping just enough to hint at the curves she usually hides.

I catch a glimpse of the bruise right beneath her collarbone again, and my breath turns ragged.

Heat crawls up my spine, and I force my hands to stay relaxed at my sides, but my knuckles are red from the sheer force of my clenched fists.

Her phone sits on the patio table, its speaker pulsing blue, softly playing *crystallized (feat. Inéz) by John Summit.*

The music wraps around her body like it's part of her as she moves with it, slow and wild all at once, her arms stretched over her head as her hips sway to the rhythm.

She starts to sing, and I just let myself listen to the sound of her voice through the glass.

And I could stand here, listening to her sweet voice sing, and be a happy man.

The next verse swells, and she sings louder, her voice slightly cracking, spinning beneath the open sky.

She stomps her bare feet into the wet grass, her head thrown back as she's yelling along to the chorus now, and I notice a slight sheen in her eyes, like she's been crying.

I stand there, half-hidden behind the glass, my heartbeat syncing to the song. The night hums, and all I can do is watch her glow under it.

The first drop of rain falls, the first speck dampening the strands of grass, swaying with the breeze.

She doesn't stop, of course she doesn't.

The drizzle deepens, speckling her skin, darkening her hair, making her pajamas cling to her.

Fireflies scatter, regrouping around her as she twirls, water spraying from her fingertips.

She screams the last line of the chorus, spinning once more before collapsing into laughter, breathless and gleaming under the moonlight.

Fuck, she's beautiful.

Not the kind of beauty you photograph.

The kind of beauty that hits you in the chest and makes you forget what air is.

She tilts her face toward the sky, her eyes closed, as rain runs down her cheeks, smiling. The light from the window flickers against her skin, mixing with the glow of fireflies and the silver shimmer of the storm.

I let myself stare, and it feels like balance is tilting, restraint slipping away.

She doesn't even realize she's doing it as she dances in the rain, looking like a promise I have no right to desire.

I've spent years thinking the world lost its color. That everything good belonged to someone else. That some people were just meant to live in the quiet while everyone else got the light.

But standing here, watching her sing and dance in the rain, surrounded by fireflies and moonlight, I'm not so sure anymore.

The song finally fades into the night, as the rain softens to a whisper.

She spins once more, this time more slowly, with her

eyes still closed, her lips parting in a gentle hum that echoes long after the last note fades.

I stand there, watching her like a creep, who's hopelessly in love with a woman who's promised to someone else.

She can't and won't fall in love with a freak like me.

She slows to a stop, still breathing hard, rain dripping down her nose. For a second, I think she hasn't noticed me, until her head tilts and her eyes lift toward the sliding door.

Fuck, she noticed me.

I think she's going to make a face at me and walk away, but then she smiles.

The same radiant, sunshine smile that could probably burn through fog.

She gestures for me to come outside, just a slight tilt of her hand, her fingers curling toward herself.

My palm is already sweaty against the cool metal handle of the sliding glass door, and I have to wipe it once against my flannel pajamas before I move.

I tell myself to calm down, she's just a *friend*, but my pulse is pounding so hard I can feel it in my ears.

The track squeaks softly as I unlock it and slide the door open, a rush of night air flooding into the room, threaded with the scent of rain and honeysuckle.

Outside, fireflies flicker brighter with the disturbance, scattered sparks drifting slowly.

"Dance with me, Reed."

My stomach drops, and the sensation of butterflies comes fluttering back. "What?"

Her laughter ripples through the rain, unbothered. "Come on!" she yells. "Dance with me!"

I blink, glancing down at myself. "I'm not dancing in the rain."

"Course you are," she says simply, like it's already decided. She takes a step closer, her wet cami clinging to her chest, her nipples hardening with each gust of wind.

Fuck.

"When I'm stressed, this helps. Moving, yelling, feeling the music. It's stupid, but..." she shrugs, gaze softening, "I relate to this song so badly it hurts."

Those two words hit me harder than I expected.

It hurts?

This woman, this vibrant, ridiculous, unfiltered burst of color, hurts?

The thought lodges somewhere deep. Because for all her laughter and brightness, there's something in the way she says it that cracks something open in me.

I step out onto the deck, rain soaking through my white Henley instantly. She's watching me, waiting, with her hand outstretched between us.

"Come on," she whispers. "What's the worst that could happen?"

A hundred things flash through my mind: embarrassment, slipping, falling, looking like an idiot, but none of it seems to matter when she's looking at me like that.

I hesitate for half a second, then I take her hand, interlocking our fingers.

She tugs me forward into the yard, laughing when I almost trip on the slick grass.

The music is still playing, softer now, fading into another remix.

She starts moving again, her hips swaying side to side as her hair flies as she spins. "You're too stiff!" she laughs, circling me. "Come on, Reed, let loose! Pretend no one's watching!"

I shake my head, rain dripping from my jaw. "You're watching me."

"So!" she says, spinning again. "Now move those hips!"

A real laugh escapes me, and it surprises me with how loud it is; it's been so long.

"You're out of your mind."

"Thank you!" she shouts back, over the music and rain. "Now dance!"

At first, it's awkward. I shift my weight, half-heartedly moving to the beat as she grins at me. But then she bumps her shoulder into mine, laughing when I stumble. She loops our hands together again, starts twirling under my arm, and I can't resist as I begin to move along with her.

The rain soaks through everything—my shirt, her pjs, the ground beneath our feet, but it doesn't matter.

She's still laughing with her head tipped back, and for the first time in years, I feel something like joy.

It's ridiculous, messy, and it feels *good*.

We dance until the music fades, and the only sounds left are our breathing and the soft hiss of rain.

"See?" she says quietly. "Told you it helps."

I look at her, really look at her, and my throat tightens. The rain clings to her lashes, catching in the corners of her mouth where her smile still lingers.

"Yeah," I say softly, voice barely audible over the rain. "Yeah, it does."

She brushes a wet strand of hair out of her face, catching me staring again. "What?" she asks, voice breathless.

I shake my head, the corner of my mouth twitching. "Nothing."

"Come on, Reed," she teases, stepping closer, rain

glinting on her lashes. "You've been staring all night. What is it?"

I swallow, hesitating before I lean down, reaching out and brushing her hair away from her face. My fingertips graze her hair lightly, barely touching her skin.

She inhales sharply, and my heart pounds against my chest. Her breath warms my knuckles as I let my hand rest near her jaw, not quite touching but close enough to feel her heat.

"I just... never seen anyone as beautiful as you."

Her lips part slightly as her eyes glisten, not from the rain, but from something else.

"Hey," I say, stepping closer. "I didn't mean to upset you."

She lets out a small laugh that breaks halfway through, her voice catching. "You didn't upset me," she says softly. "It's just... I haven't heard that in a long time."

I stare at her, trying to piece together how someone like her, who shines so bright it hurts to look at her sometimes, could ever go this long without hearing it.

I want to ask, and I want to fucking know.

But I don't have the right to pry.

So I stay quiet.

She inhales, wiping at her cheeks even though the rain does it for her, and smiles again, a little smaller this time. "I'm tired," she says, brushing it off with that same sunshine tone. "Think I'm gonna head to bed."

I nod, swallowing hard. "Yeah. Yeah, you should get some sleep."

She lingers there for a moment, as if she wants to say more, like there's something on her tongue neither of us is brave enough to speak.

The night air shifts, cooler now, and she wraps an arm around her chest, shivering.

Her toes curl into the damp grass before she steps. The blades bend and cling to her skin, dew glistening on her ankles.

She ambles, not because she's hesitant but because something in both of us wants to stretch out these last few seconds.

Fireflies make way for her, scattering in gentle bursts as she walks toward the house.

Her thin pajama shorts brush her thighs with each step, the teddy bear pattern looking both silly and heartbreakingly cute under the moonlight.

The porch lights cast a soft, amber glow on the wooden steps. They're slick with rain, and she carefully tests her footing, pressing her toes down gently.

She climbs one step, then another. She's almost at the door when she pauses.

Like she felt the exact moment my breath caught.

She turns her head just enough to reveal her profile in the dim glow from the porch light, highlighting the delicate line of her jaw, the curve of her cheek, and the faint shimmer in her eyes from the firelight behind them.

Then she fully looks back at me.

Rain falls in silver ribbons between us, with thin drops catching the light as they slide from sky to earth, and we just stare at each other.

She looks at me as if she wants to say something, but the hesitation in her movements tells me otherwise.

"Goodnight, Reed."

"Goodnight, Layla."

The door clicks softly behind her, and the yard feels different without her in it.

I stand outside for a while in the rain, watching the glow from the kitchen window fade as the lights inside turn off.

Layla, the woman who laughs loudly, talks too much, and brings color into every room she walks into.

And yet, I can't shake the memory of her voice cracking when she said she hadn't heard those words in a long time.

I run my hand through my wet hair, my chest heavy with an unnamed feeling.

Because now I can't stop wondering, the woman who radiates sunshine... is she hurting, just like me?

TWENTY
LAYLA

The morning sun's radiance spills across his kitchen with a natural brightness, sunrays warming the edges of the farmhouse table.

An open window carries the scent of damp earth and a faint trace of smoke from a neighbor's early burn pile.

A gentle draft drifts through the room, brushing the loose sleeves of my gray pajama set.

The cotton fabric feels soft against my skin, comfortably oversized, and for once, I don't feel the need to adjust myself to fit someone else's idea of me.

My laptop sits open in front of me, the cursor blinking patiently in the middle of a paused frame from footage I've shot this trip.

I'm supposed to be editing, but it's difficult to concentrate when the smell of strong coffee and freshly washed pine floors stands in quiet competition with my focus.

Grabbing the iced coffee Reed made for me earlier, I take a sip, savoring the brown sugar and vanilla.

It's the perfect mix of sweet, without overpowering the

coffee flavor. The cool liquid slides down my throat, easing the tension that built up overnight.

The pitter-patter of rain cooling my skin. Reed's uneven breath. His rough hand brushing my hair aside, and I can still feel the warmth of his fingertips. The way he looked at me was like I was the most beautiful woman in the world, and I wish he'd keep looking at me.

However, this guilt is consuming me.

Pulling my sleeves further over my hands, I immerse myself in the soft cotton.

I shouldn't be enjoying this so much. I shouldn't be enjoying his company as much as I am, and I especially shouldn't be lusting after a man who sees me as a person, not as dollar signs.

Buzz. Buzz. Buzz.

I don't even need to look; my stomach already knows who it is.

BRIAN

I hate how we left things.

I miss you.

The man who shoved his finger into my collarbone now says he misses me. My stomach twists. I flip the phone screen down and push it away slightly.

Brian's emotions fluctuate daily. One minute, it's apologies; the next, it's threats. My favorite is when he's sweet to me because he wants something.

The emotional pendulum never calms down.

I swallow hard, the coffee suddenly sour in my throat.

God, why does guilt always taste like I owe him something?

Before the familiar dread can grow inside me, a cabinet clicks shut in front of me, pulling me out of my spiral.

He moves around the kitchen, planting himself in front of his porcelain farmhouse sink as he rinses the skillet from breakfast, and places it on the drying rack without making unnecessary noise.

The atmosphere feels peaceful in a way that's unfamiliar to me. Muscles that are usually conditioned to flinch at every sudden sound find nothing to respond to here.

"You've been staring at that same frame for ten minutes," he says, his tone gentle, not teasing.

I close my laptop halfway and keep my fingertips resting on its edge. "I'm distracted."

He nods once, as if he understands more than I admit. He picks up two travel mugs from the counter and fills them with the freshly brewed pot. He places one in front of me, no words, just a steady offering.

I don't think I need any more caffeine, but who am I to say no?

"I think you need a break," he says. He slides the mug a little closer with a quiet gesture that feels more intimate than it should. "And I know exactly where we should go."

I lift my eyes to him. "Where's that?"

He leans against the counter, crossing his arms loosely over his chest. His posture remains relaxed, but there's a hint of attentiveness behind it.

"We've got several stops," he explains. "A whole morning of not thinking about anything except what's right in front of you."

I look down at my hands, where they wrap around the warm mug, the steam blurring the edges of my vision for a moment. My chest tightens, not quite painfully, more as a reminder of how long it's been since anyone asked what *I* might need.

I close my laptop fully and slide it away from me.

My phone buzzes again, but this time, I don't look.

Pushing myself to stand, the chair legs softly brush the floor, and he watches my movement without moving into my space or away from it.

"If you want," he adds after a brief pause, "I can give you five minutes to change." His attention flickers once to my pajama sleeves before returning to my eyes.

He doesn't comment on them—no smirk, no expectation—just an offer of privacy and comfort. The simplicity of that respect nearly unravels me.

"Five minutes is perfect," I manage.

As I walk toward the hallway, my bare feet press into the hardwood floor, and the house breathes around me; soft, sturdy, lived-in. Near the wall that opens up to the hallway, I stop and glance over my shoulder.

He's already turned away to rinse the coffee spoon, giving me space without making me feel abandoned. He pretends to focus on his task, but I can still sense the tenderness behind the pretense.

I observe my surroundings, the quiet patience of his presence, the sunlight filtering through the large windows, the day gently unfolding before us, and something in my heart flutters.

Hope is a fragile yet frightening thing, especially when it shows up where fear once lived.

I take another breath, steadying myself, and push open the bedroom door to get ready.

For once, I'm not performing for random people online, showcasing my curated, fake relationship and life.

I'm allowed to simply exist.

And that is a change I'm not sure how to handle.

The drive into Opal Springs is nothing like the quiet, sprawling landscape we left behind.

As the buildings come into view, the open fields give way to stadium lights and large vinyl banners advertising the upcoming rodeo finals.

Music drifts from open restaurant patios, mingling with the layered noise of laughter, distant cheers, and conversations overlapping as tourists spill down the sidewalks, iced lemonades in hand and shopping bags swinging at their sides.

A large marquee outside an arena flashes red letters in scrolling text.

Opal Springs Ice Dome; Renegades' Home Game Thursday

Street vendors line one side of the main street, selling handmade leather goods, sequined rodeo belts, and small jars of local honey.

He navigates through the slow traffic with practiced patience, his hand steady on the wheel while the other taps lightly against his knee in tune with a country song spilling from a truck beside us.

He pulls into a parking space along a row of lively storefronts. The shops are painted in cheerful colors—deep plum, sun-washed teal, old-fashioned brick facades with fresh signage.

A crowd gathers outside a souvenir store selling Opal Springs Rodeo merchandise, their voices rising with excited debate over which T-shirt design is best.

We step out of his truck, our footsteps in sync as we fall into stride side by side.

Reed guides me to a shop with a door painted in fresh sage-green. A hand-painted sign hangs above it.

The Wildflower Palatte.

I squeal with excitement, pulling out my camera to film. "Really?!"

A faint smile curves around the corner of his mouth. "Really, really."

He opens the door for me, guiding me inside, the ghost of his hand on my lower back.

The shop smells faintly of linseed oil and fresh paper—a calming scent after the electric buzz outside. Shelves run along the walls, filled with tubes of paint that catch the light like tiny gems. Smooth canisters of brushes stand in perfect rows, with bristles fanned out like flower petals.

Reed stands a few steps behind me, watching my reaction instead of the shelves. His hands slip casually into his pockets, shoulders relaxed, voice quiet, in contrast to the liveliness outside.

"Pick whatever you want," he says.

I stare at him, genuinely thrown. "Whatever I want? Reed, this stuff isn't cheap."

He shrugs calmly, his gaze steady. He doesn't attempt to lighten the moment with humor or soothe me with excuses. He stands by what he says.

"Anything," he repeats.

I turn toward the nearest aisle, filming the different shades of colors they have to offer. Acrylics in deep, earthy tones line the top shelf. Smaller tubes, vivid and punchy, colors that seem to pulse with life, filling the second row.

Running my fingertips along a shade of honey-yellow,

my breath hitches as I remember the last time I honestly sat down and painted, doing something for myself. Wanting things for myself has become complicated.

I select a set of acrylics that remind me of Reed's backyard—wild pine green, smoky horizon gray, and a muted rose like the reflection of sunset on a wild horse's coat.

Reed doesn't look at the different hues of paint; he's looking at me.

"I'll get these," I say softly, pocketing my camera to stay in the present.

I hesitate, shifting the box in my hands before finding the courage to look at him again.

"But only if you paint with me."

His eyes warm just a little, a subtle shift that might go unnoticed by anyone else.

He nods in agreement.

That simple agreement settles somewhere deep in my chest, as though a knot loosens without me noticing.

He takes the paint set from me with a slight nod and heads toward the front counter, his stride steady, the box held carefully in his hand.

I follow slowly as my fingers brush along the edge of a display of stretched canvases.

The clerk at the register greets us with a bright, friendly smile.

Reed places everything I picked up on the counter, including two canvases, the acrylic set I chose, and a pair of brushes with smooth, tapered handles designed for precision.

I reach for my wallet, and his hand gently rests on mine. He shakes his head once, firm but not unkind.

"I've got it."

"Reed, I can at least split—"

"No." His voice is low, not sharp, but it carries finality. He tilts his head down slightly, meeting my eyes with a look that asks for my trust, not my argument. "Let me do this."

The clerk busies herself adjusting something in the computer system, giving us a moment of privacy.

I swallow and lower my hand, feeling a strange mix of gratitude and discomfort wash over me.

Brian buys things to hold over me later, while Reed offers freely and asks for nothing in return. The difference sits uncomfortably in my chest.

The clerk finishes bagging the canvases and carefully slides them into a paper sack with their company logo stamped in green ink.

Reed thanks her, and we both wave goodbye.

We exit through the glass doors, stepping back into the lively energy of Opal Springs.

He walks slightly ahead, bags shifting at his side as he leads us to his truck, parked beneath a tree whose leaves have begun to turn a rust-red gold.

He doesn't rush me when I pause to look around, pulling out my camera again to film more of the scenery.

Once satisfied, we make it to his truck, and he opens the door for me, taking my purse and gesturing for me to get inside.

I finally settle into the passenger seat, and he waits until I'm comfortably in before closing my door completely.

He rounds the hood and slides in beside me, comfortably putting my purse and the paint supplies in the back seat.

The flannel across his shoulders shifts with his movement. He's rolled up his sleeves, revealing more of the scarred skin on his forearms.

My gaze lingers a bit longer than it should.

He presses the button, and his truck rumbles to life beneath us. As we pull away from the curb, the town's bright noise begins to fade again.

We turn onto a road lined with tall pines and glimpses of water through the trees. A lake unfolds into full view, reflecting the sky in broad strokes of blue and silver.

A few people sit along the shoreline with fishing poles stuck upright in the sand. Farther out, two kayakers glide in slow synchronization across the water.

He parks on a gravel patch near a cluster of wild grass.

The engine clicks softly as it cools in the open air. He then turns to me, and there is something incredibly steady in the way he looks at me.

"This is Sapphire Lake," he says. "We can set up just down by the pier."

He retrieves the supplies from the back while I grab the folded blanket he packed earlier. The grass brushes against my ankles with each step, as we walk closer to the water.

The breeze carries the clean scent of the lake and a faint, earthy undertone from the woods behind us.

He kneels to spread the blanket, smoothing his palms along the edges to keep it steady. He places the canvases gently and arranges the brushes within easy reach.

Lowering myself, I sit cross-legged as he sits beside me, our knees nearly touching. His flannel shifts, revealing more of the burn scars running up his arm.

I feel the question forming before I have time to soften it. My voice emerges barely above the natural hush of the lake.

"Reed... may I ask what happened?"

He pauses, his brush hanging midway over his palette, shoulders rising with a deep inhale before settling again.

Shit, I shouldn't have asked.

It isn't because I don't want to know, but because the second the question left my mouth, something in his demeanor changed.

His shoulders stiffen as his gaze drifts past me, out over Sapphire Lake, avoiding eye contact for a brief moment.

For a moment, I think he's going to brush it off, deflect the way he always does with pure silence.

He finally lets out a soft exhale, turning towards me, his tortured eyes meeting mine. A slight sheen of tears is dusted on his lash line, and seeing him break, shatters me completely.

"You may," he says.

My stomach drops, nerves twisting tightly in my lower stomach as my heart rate accelerates with pure adrenaline. I can feel each beat pound against my chest.

"I never told you about before," he adds, twirling the paintbrush between his fingers.

"Before?" I ask softly, already afraid of the answer.

He exhales through his nose, and the corner of his mouth lifts into something that isn't a smile, and it fades just as fast.

"Before the bar," he says. "Before all of this."

I shake my head a little. "Reed, I don't—"

"I was in the academy," he cuts in gently, "to become a firefighter."

Firefighter? I blink at him, searching his face for more. "Really?"

He nods once. "Yeah."

My gaze trails over the scars forming on his left side, starting at the peak of his cheekbone, trailing down beneath the collar of his flannel.

I don't know the extent of his burns, but I've also seen

the scars snaking their way down his arms, now that he's shown me more.

"I didn't graduate," he says before I can speak, his voice firm but brittle around the edges. "I was still in it, working my way to earn the badge."

Oh my God.

"Oh," I whisper, because that's all I have.

"I was months in," he continues, his fingers curling tighter around the paintbrush, knuckles whitening. "Early mornings. Long nights. Running drills until my lungs felt like they were on fire. Studying until I couldn't see straight."

I can see it, and it makes my heart swell. Younger. Determined. Hopeful. Standing at the starting line of a life he truly *wanted.*

"I wanted it so bad," he says, quieter now.

My chest aches with a dull pain as I press my lips together, afraid that if I speak, I'll cry, and somehow that feels wrong. This isn't about my tears.

"I thought I was right there," he murmurs. "Right at the beginning."

My heart cracks open.

"I never got the badge," he goes on. His jaw tightens, as if the words hurt to say. "Never got to call myself one. Never got the chance to find out if I was any good."

He finally looks at me then, and the grief in his eyes steals the air from my lungs.

"It ended before it really began."

I swallow hard, my eyes stinging. "Reed..."

He shakes his head slightly. "I don't really talk about it," he says.

The lake is impossibly still as the paint sits untouched between us.

Everything feels suspended in that space between what was and what never got to be.

He drags in a breath, his shoulders rising and falling as he steadies himself.

His gaze drifts back to the water, his voice lowering. "It was supposed to be routine," he says. "A containment drill. We'd done versions of it a dozen times."

The breeze shifts the surface into broken ripples, and he watches the movement, dragging his hand over his jaw.

"Then we heard this hiss." His eyes flick back toward the lake, and I notice the way he tightens his fingers around his knee, gripping the fabric as he relives this horrible memory.

I sit there patiently, watching him take deep breaths before he continues.

"We hit the floor hard, as the fire quickly grew. We couldn't see a damn thing through the black smoke." He pauses, swallowing thickly. "Both our SCBAs were blaring, alerting us we were low on oxygen."

His dog tags clink against each other as he reaches up, enclosing his fist around them.

"Beau, my best friend, tank's went dead first. I tried to give him mine, ripped my mask off, even though the heat was already scalding my skin." His voice roughens, guilt rubbing with every syllable. "He pushed it back. Told me to go."

He looks down at his scarred hand, and suddenly he seems impossibly breakable.

"I grabbed him, I wasn't about to leave him there." His next breath shakes. "But the ceiling collapsed, knocked me back, and when I looked up..."

He closes his eyes, blowing a shaky breath past his lips.

"All I could see was his helmet, burning, then the smoke engulfed the last piece of him I had."

He reaches for his dog tags around his neck, again, twirling the metal chain. "His mother gave me these at his funeral; he served before he joined the academy. She said that he would have wanted me to have them."

I finally set my brush down carefully. My hand moves toward him before I've entirely made the decision, and when my fingertips touch the scarred skin on his left forearm, his entire body becomes still.

The texture surprises me.

"Does it still hurt?" I ask quietly.

He doesn't pull away, and that alone feels monumental.

"Some days," he admits. "Some nights more than days."

His pulse beats strongly beneath his damaged skin. I follow the line upward as my fingers graze just at the edge where the scar disappears beneath his flannel. He watches my hand move, but he doesn't stop me.

"Sometimes," he continues, voice slightly strained, "it feels like the fire never really went out. Not in here." He taps his chest lightly with two fingers. "The guilt burns longer than the heat ever did."

My thumb gently traces the edges of raised skin, a movement not to soothe pain, but to show I'm unafraid of it.

"You shouldn't have been alone with that," I say.

His breathing shifts, growing deeper as if he's fighting an emotion he's not ready for anyone to see. He leans his body closer without touching me, the space between us shrinking into something delicate.

"You're the first person besides my brothers I've ever told the full story," he confesses.

I meet his gaze, and there's no longer any distance between us.

"Thank you for trusting me," I whisper.

The wind shifts again, carrying the faint sound of laughter from the dock across the lake.

His eyes soften, and the tension eases just enough for me to see the man underneath the armor he wears. His hand lifts slightly, as if he's considering reaching for me, then stops, opting to readjust his glasses instead.

We both eventually return to our canvases, but painting feels different now.

His story merges with the colors we spread across the canvas.

Nothing about him seems diminished for having said it aloud. If anything, he's never appeared stronger.

And I suddenly feel terrified by how fast I'm falling for him.

TWENTY-ONE
REED

I glance sideways at Layla curled up in the corner of my couch, her legs tucked underneath her, the hem of her sweatpants brushing the cushion as she shifts.

She leaves tomorrow.

I'd be lying to myself if I didn't want her to go; fuck, I really don't want her to leave. Every time she quietly laughs at something on the screen, I feel the weight of the impending silence grow heavier.

My mind keeps looping back to the exact moment from earlier; her fingertips gently smoothing over my worst scars, not with pity or hesitation, but with a care so soft it shattered something I didn't realize was still fragile.

She touched what I hate most about myself and looked at me as if I were someone worth seeing, as if I were more than just my scars.

I try not to appear obvious by staring at her, but she catches me regardless. Her eyes meet mine in the flickering light, bright and distractingly beautiful.

"I'm boreddd," she declares, dragging out the words with a sigh as she stretches her arms overhead.

I blink, pulled from my spiral. "Bored? We're watching a classic."

"It's a horror movie," she says. "Everything is a classic to you."

I try not to roll my eyes. "It's good."

"It's slow," she counters, nudging my leg with her foot. "And you aren't even watching it."

She's not wrong. I turn down the volume with the remote and place it on the coffee table, resting my arm over the back of the couch. "Alright," I say. "What do you want to do?"

She sits up a little straighter, a mischievous smile forming. "Truth or dare."

My eyebrows raise. "We're not twelve."

She grins wider, leaning in closer until I can smell the faint vanilla of her lotion. "That's not a no."

I let out a laugh because resisting her is becoming impossible. "Fine. You go first."

She taps her chin thoughtfully before asking, "Truth. What's the strangest thing you've seen at Boots & Bourbon?"

I grin and answer easily, "A guy trying to ride the mechanical bull completely naked because he lost a bet."

She winces and laughs simultaneously. "That sounds... unsanitary."

"It was," I say. "We Cloroxed the hell out of it after."

Her laughter dissolves into a soft smile. "Your turn."

I consider her for a moment, then ask, "Truth. Why did you really come back here?"

She looks down at her hands, twisting her bracelet softly. "I needed to breathe somewhere else."

I nod once, accepting the truth without pushing any further. "Your turn."

She pauses for half a second, her eyes locking onto mine with a boldness I didn't expect.

"Dare," she says, choosing for herself.

"You're daring yourself now?"

"Yes," she says, leaning in, the tiny spark of challenge lighting beneath her words. "And I dare you to kiss me."

My heartbeat stumbles so hard it nearly hurts.

The room feels like it's shrinking around us, the air growing thicker, and the distant crickets outside sounding impossibly loud.

She sits quietly, no teasing now, no nervous fidgeting, just patient anticipation, as if she's giving me all the time I need to decide.

My hand still rests on the back of the couch, just inches from her shoulder.

Indulging in her presence, I take in her wide, bright blue eyes, her plump, parted lips, and her slightly unsteady breathing, feeling the same pull toward her as when Catalina introduced us three years ago.

I won't let this moment pass, even if it makes me selfish and the bad guy.

My hand moves from the back of the couch to the cushion beside her hip, seeking something to hold onto before I do something I can't take back.

"Layla," I mumble breathlessly. Her eyes flick to my mouth, and the movement steals the last of my breath. "You're engaged."

"I know, and I don't care," she whispers, as her fingers curl into the fabric of the sofa.

Inhaling sharply, the air tastes like vanilla from her lotion and anxiety I can't swallow down. "This is not a small line to cross." My hand lifts, brushing the hair behind her shoulder so I can see every inch of emotion in her face. "If we do this, I'm not going to pretend it didn't happen."

She leans in closer, pressing her palms flat against my chest, and the warmth of her touch reaches straight through my olive green Henley. "I don't want to pretend," she says. "Not with you."

Her forehead brushes against mine, the slightest, most devastating touch, and everything I've been holding back rises to the surface.

I tilt my head just enough so our noses graze. Her breath comes out in a desperate moan as it fans across my lips.

"You really want this?" I ask, my thumb softly brushing her jaw, the slight tremor in my touch revealing how badly I need her to say yes.

She nods once, her gaze fixed on mine. "Kiss me, Reed," she whispers, her fingers slipping up to the back of my neck, drawing me closer. "I dare you."

Fuck it.

I close the distance.

The first press of our lips starts slow, but the pace quickens instantly in the way she exhales against me, her fingers tightening in my hair. The kiss deepens before either of us can stop it.

I angle her closer, my palm spanning the small of her back as she leans fully into me, her lips parting just slightly, inviting more.

She gasps into the kiss, and every bit of my restraint shatters.

My hand moves up the contours of her back, holding her tightly, ensuring she feels how much this moment I've longed for *wrecks* me.

She pulls back a fraction, her lips brushing mine as she

speaks through unsteady breaths. "Tell me you don't feel the same way," she challenges quietly, her blue eyes searching my face for a lie she knows I can't give.

I shake my head, our noses touching again. "I wish I didn't," I exhale. "God, Layla, I really wish I didn't feel this pull. But I fucking feel everything." I reply as my forehead rests against hers.

Her thumb traces the corner of my mouth. "Then kiss me again."

I lift her fully into my arms, gently settling her onto my lap with the utmost care I've ever felt.

Her hands cradle my jaw as I kiss her deeper, pouring every unspoken truth into the movement of our tongues. Her heartbeat pounds against my chest, in sync with mine, as we hold on to this moment we've been moving toward since the second we met.

She isn't thinking about tomorrow, nor am I.

We pull away again, our lips nearly touch, breaths tangled, hearts pounding.

"Reed," she whispers, her voice trembling with fear and longing, "please don't stop."

I close my eyes just once, not to pull away, but to stay steady, and when I open them again, all the restraint I had is gone.

"I can't stop," I tell her.

She presses her forehead to mine, our breaths mingling in the tiny space neither of us dares to widen. The taste of her still lingers on my lips, and it takes every shred of sense I have to keep my hands from roaming where they shouldn't go.

She's still straddling my lap. Still holding my face as if I'm something worth touching, still gazing at me with a hunger to swallow every fear I've ever had.

Her fingertips drift slowly across my scarred cheek, down my neck, tracing the lines of burned skin.

The lightest touch, but my entire body reacts; I feel my dick hardening beneath my sweats. It's been years since a woman has touched me.

"I'm not scared of your scars," she says softly, voice trembling with emotion.

My throat tightens. I grab her hips instinctively, steadying myself, because if I let myself fall into that line too quickly, I won't find my way back up for air.

"Layla..."

She leans in again, brushing her lips against my map of scarred skin, slow enough that my eyes flutter shut. "You're more than them, I want you to know that," she whispers against my skin.

Her mouth lifts upward, reconnecting with mine; a gentle kiss that quickly turns ravenous, her hands threading into my hair, pulling just hard enough to draw a growl from deep within my chest.

I kiss her back with everything I've been trying not to feel; her lips parting for me, our bodies pressed tightly, a slow grind of her center on the thick line of my cock that's driving me wild.

She breathes against my mouth, "Don't stop."

And God help me, stopping is the last thing I want.

But I force myself to, barely holding back, though every cell in my body screams to keep going. My forehead rests against hers again, chests heaving, trying to catch my breath and regain sanity.

"If we don't slow down..." My voice breaks. I swallow hard. "I'm not gonna be able to."

She cups my jaw as her thumb brushes my lower lip, swollen from her kisses. "Maybe I don't want you to stop."

"Fuck, Layla."

A shiver goes through me, desire and terror clashing.

"You don't get it," I breathe out. "Once I have you... I won't ever fucking let you go."

Her eyes widen at my sheer honesty.

"Reed, don't let me go."

I hold onto the back of the couch because touching her again would break every boundary remaining.

"You leave tomorrow," I remind her, pain weaving through my words.

She swallows, her hands still tangled in my hair. "But tonight..." Her lips ghost mine again. "...I'm here."

My restraint manifests differently; not to take, but to hold.

I wrap my arms around her and pull her into a fierce, bone-deep embrace, my lips pressed against her temple, breathing her in.

She melts into me without resistance, burying her face in my neck. Neither of us moves for a long time.

Her breathing evens out, and her voice vibrates against my skin.

"I don't want this to be goodbye."

I take in a deep breath, closing my eyes.

My heart answers before my mouth does.

"Then don't go."

She doesn't answer, her hands lightly fisted in the fabric of my shirt. I smooth my palms over her hips once and gently tap her thigh.

"Come on," I say, my voice a little rough from everything we just held back.

Her gaze flicks up to meet mine, nerves and hope battling behind her eyes. She nods, the movement small but steady, and I hold her waist as she shifts off my lap.

The warmth she leaves behind is immediate and irritating.

I stand, offering her my hand, and she takes it without hesitation.

We move toward the hallway, still tangled together at the fingers. My bedroom door is just ahead, a simple thing, but suddenly it feels like a line I can't cross.

I stop just outside it.

"Layla..." I turn to her fully this time, our hands still linked. "If you want me back on the couch, I can slee—"

She quickly shakes her head, stepping closer, her free hand sliding up my arm in a slow, steady stroke. "No, stay with me."

I swallow hard and push the door open.

The familiar scent of cedar and laundry detergent greets us, the only things keeping me grounded as the reality of this moment sinks in. I flick on the bedside lamp, warm light softening the room's edges.

I gesture toward the bed, suddenly feeling shy in my own room.

She crawls onto the left side, sinking into the mattress with a sigh that feels like both relief and heartbreak braided together. I join her, lying on the right side.

Her kiss is still everywhere. I'd pulled back when every instinct in me screamed to do the opposite. Even now, my jaw aches from how hard I'm holding myself together.

She turns her head toward me, her eyes finding mine easily in the low light.

"Hey," she says softly.

"Hey," I answer, voice rougher than I want it to be.

She gradually moves closer, her knee touching mine, and I remain still.

The only skin she can see is the left side of my face; the

curve of my cheekbone catching the lamplight, ink tracing from the base of my neck and disappearing beneath my collar.

Roses for my beloved mama, her favorite. Black-and-white ink swirls beneath my neck's base, encased in a mandala, to honor her.

Her gaze catches on the ink across my neck. I feel the weight of her gaze, even before she touches me.

She cranes her neck slightly, adjusting her angle to see better, studying the tattoo with quiet focus.

"That's… really intricate," she murmurs. "I didn't notice how detailed it was before."

I swallow. "You weren't this close before."

A ghost of a smile flickers across her mouth. "Fair point."

She lifts her hand, hesitates for just a beat, then lets her fingers brush across my jaw; not across the scars, but the feel of her touch causes my eyes to flutter shut.

Her touch trails downward, following the ink on my neck with careful reverence. She stops at the collar of my shirt, fingertips resting there, acknowledging the boundary without challenging it.

I exhale slowly, the tension easing just enough to breathe.

She shifts again, closer now, and reaches for my hand where it's curled between us.

Her fingers wrap around mine, and the fucking sensation of butterflies flutters back.

She turns my hand palm-up, studying the lines and ridges. Her thumb drags gently over my knuckles, and then she freezes.

Her eyes drop, narrowing slightly as she takes in the Roman numerals inked there.

XII / XII.

She doesn't say anything at first, as she just holds my hand, analyzing.

"That's a date," she says finally, voice quiet.

"Yeah."

She lifts her gaze to me. "What happened?"

I shake my head once. "Nothing happened." A pause. "It's my mom's birthday, December twelfth."

Her expression changes, not in a dramatic way, just a slow softening, like understanding settling into place.

"Oh," she says.

She looks back down at my hand, her thumb tracing the numbers again, gentler now. "You put it somewhere you'd see it all the time."

"So I wouldn't forget," I say.

She shakes her head. "That's not why."

I glance at her. "No?"

She meets my eyes. "You didn't want to forget *her*."

I don't answer, I can't.

She brings my hand closer, pressing a kiss to my knuckles, right over the ink.

It's brief, tender, and it hits me harder than the kiss we shared earlier.

My arm tightens around her before I can stop it, pulling her against me. She goes willingly, settling into my chest as her cheek rests there through the fabric of my shirt.

I can feel the pattern of her breath, feel the warmth radiating off of her.

Her hand stays in mine as her fingers curl slightly, like she's holding on without gripping too tight.

We don't speak for a long moment.

Settling in closer, she traces a gentle line across my

chest with her fingertip, casually following the seams of my shirt.

"So," she murmurs, "if you could live anywhere... where would you go?"

I glance down at her. "Here's pretty good."

She laughs softly. "C'mon. That's a boring answer."

"It's the truth," I say, brushing a strand of hair away from her lips. "People act like they need a new place to be happy. I think you can build a life worth loving anywhere... if the right person's there."

Her hand stills on my chest, like she's holding her breath.

"That sounds nice," she whispers. "Having someone who truly chooses you."

I tighten my arm around her just a little. I desperately want to pry into her relationship, but if she's out here with me as she's promised to someone else, I can only assume that something is going on.

"I think you deserve that more than anyone."

She stares up at me like she's trying to decide whether to believe it. Her eyes look softer in the low light, open in a way that makes me want to fight every battle she's too tired to fight alone.

"What about you?" I ask quietly. "Where would you go?"

She sighs, thinking. "Somewhere I can paint without worrying how it looks on camera. Somewhere I can just... exist."

I swallow around the ache in my throat.

"What do you like to paint most?"

"People," she replies, voice sleepy. "Faces, hands... moments. I like when you can feel the emotion, not just see it."

"That sounds like you," I murmur. "You don't just look at things. You feel them."

She smiles into my shirt. "Is that your nice way of calling me dramatic?"

"It's my honest way of saying you care deeply," I say. "That's rare."

Her fingers curl into the fabric over my heart, holding on.

She asks, "Okay, your turn. Ask me anything."

I think about it, really think, because there's a million things I want to know, but only one that feels right tonight.

"What makes you feel safe?" I ask.

She blinks up at me, startled by the softness of the question. She chews her lip for a moment before answering.

"...when someone doesn't let go first," she says quietly.

Without a word, I take her hand and lace our fingers together under the blanket, making sure she feels the promise in it.

"I'm not going anywhere," I tell her.

She finally relaxes, settling into me. Her breathing evens out as she presses her face into my chest, like she's trying to hide how much that meant.

"You make it easy to breathe."

I close my eyes and hold her a little tighter, letting my own breath fall in time with hers.

"I'm glad you're here," I reply. "Tonight... I'm really fucking happy you're here."

Her fingers squeeze mine once before sleep claims her, and long after she's gone, still and quiet in my arms, I stay awake thinking one terrifying, undeniable truth.

If love feels like this, I'm already in deep.

TWENTY-TWO
LAYLA

My suitcase finally thunks onto the baggage carousel. The carousel grumbles and shudders as it moves, fluorescent lights flickering overhead. I wrap my fingers around the handle, tugging it free, wheels clattering against the tile.

I reach into my pocket for my phone, because I already know who's waiting.

One new message.

REED

You on the ground?

Warmth floods my chest so fast it almost hurts.

LAYLA

Just grabbed my enormous suitcase 😅

The typing bubbles pop up instantly.

He must still be awake, still thinking of me.

REED

Good.

I miss you already.

I grip the suitcase handle tighter.

LAYLA

I miss you too 😌

I head toward the automatic doors, the late-night chill sweeping in from outside.

My sneakers shuffle against the concrete of the parking garage ramp as I drag my luggage toward P6. The echo of each step bounces back at me, reminding me how alone I am now.

And how alone I was before Reed.

I press the unlock button on my key fob, and my car chirps, its headlights blinking. The sound is too loud in the cavernous garage; I flinch anyway.

Lifting my suitcase into the trunk, my arms straining, as my breath shortens, I finally slide into the driver's seat.

My fingers hesitate before starting the car.

Buzz. Buzz. Buzz.

REED

Text me when you're home.

My heart squeezes.

LAYLA

I will. Promise.

I notice my reflection in the rearview mirror; my eyes are still a little swollen from trying not to cry on the plane, and my makeup is smudged just a bit from sleeping against Reed's chest earlier this morning.

God, he held me.

I swallow the ache rising in my throat.

The engine roars to life as I pull away from the space, winding up the ramp toward fresh air. The exit gate ejects me onto the main road, airport chaos fading into the monotony of the freeway.

Taillights cast red reflections on the wet asphalt. A plane rumbles above, vanishing into clouds I long to follow.

Santa Monica greets me with palm trees swaying in the night breeze, and the ocean's salty breath caressing my windshield, but nothing feels warm about being back home.

Driving into the underground garage of our building, the same spot I've parked at a thousand times, but tonight it feels like I'm driving into a cage.

Taking a deep breath before I get out of my car, I say a silent prayer for myself, hoping Brian is in a good mood. Once I exhale, I get out, slamming the door shut, and grab my suitcase from the trunk before heading up.

The elevator ride up is quiet enough that I hear my pulse in my ears.

Ding. Ding. Ding.

Home, or what once felt like home.

I take a deep breath that doesn't ease my nerves and unlock the front door to my apartment.

Brian stands in the middle of the living room, his posture stiff, arms crossed and jaw clenched so tightly it could crack teeth.

The TV flickers behind him, but he's not watching it; he's watching me.

His eyes scan every inch of me as if he's searching for a lie beneath my skin.

"Well," he says, voice dripping with sour disappointment, "look who finally decided to show up."

My suitcase handle digs painfully into my palm, but I keep my tone steady.

"I told you it was for a brand deal," I say, nudging the door closed with my heel. "Work. You knew that."

He approaches with slow steps, the kind that sends a chill down your spine and makes nerves swirl low in my gut.

"Uh-huh, I'm sure." His lip curls. "*Work. Work. Work,*" his words dripping with sarcasm.

I back up until the entry table presses against my hip, its wood digging into my bone.

"You think I'm stupid?" he asks quietly, which is worse than shouting. "You think I don't notice when my fiancé can't wait to get away from me?"

His hand snaps out, gripping my collar, as his fingers dig into the skin just below my throat. He yanks the fabric down, exposing the faint, healing bruise he left.

A sick smile stretches across his face.

"There she is."

Like he's proud of the mark.

Something inside me recoils so violently that my knees lock to keep me upright.

He finally lets me go and walks away, tossing himself onto the couch as if the conversation bored him.

"Is my baby hungry?" he asks, picking up his phone. "Didn't cook."

Whiplash. Always. Whiplash.

My own phone buzzes in my palm. I quickly look as Brian is distracted.

REED

Sleep well tonight, sunshine.

Tears burn the backs of my eyes. I squeeze my phone in my palm before quickly sliding it into my pocket.

His gaze cuts to me, a questioning look etched on his face. "Who was that?"

"No one," I whisper.

"Layla," he says, "don't forget, you're mine."

I grip the handle of my suitcase and push myself down the hallway toward our bedroom, refusing to show fear even though my legs tremble.

Behind me, he calls out lazily. "You can run all you want, baby. You'll always end up right back here."

The worst part?

He used to be right.

I roll my suitcase into my bedroom and turn on the soft lamp beside the bed.

Lifting my suitcase onto my bed, I stand by, folding a shirt with more care than it deserves, hoping that if I stay quiet enough, he'll leave me alone tonight.

The sounds from the living room fall silent, and all I hear are footsteps echoing off the wooden floors.

He crawls straight into my space, his expensive cologne burning my nostrils, as his fingers already roam my waist.

"So," he murmurs, his lips brushing the back of my neck, "how about you show me how happy you are to see me."

His hand moves lower, cupping my ass, squeezing, as he moans against the back of my neck, making me feel sick.

"No," I say immediately.

He freezes, only for a second, then laughs, a single, mocking puff of air against my skin.

"You've been gone for two days," he scoffs. "And you come home, not wanting to get on your knees for me?"

I push myself away from him and step back. "I said no, Brian. I'm tired."

"Right," he snaps, jaw ticking. "Because you're always tired when I want something."

He stalks closer, pointing his finger straight into my

face. "But God forbid *you* want something, then we gotta pause the world and make Layla happy."

His voice deepens into a sneer, words spitting out like venom. "You think you can leave me horny for days? Are you fucking serious?"

I hold my ground even though my knees wobble.

"You can go f—"

He cuts me off with a harsh laugh and shoves my shoulder, hard enough that I stumble backward into the dresser.

"Spare me," he snaps. "You're useless to me if you can't even—"

He stops just short of saying the word.

But he doesn't need to finish his sentence; I already knew what he was going to say.

He turns his back, pulling his phone out from his back pocket, already scrolling, already over it.

"Forget it. I'll handle it myself," he mutters, dropping onto the bed.

The clacking of his keyboard echoes from our bedroom, punctuated by bursts of laughter through his headset as he yells into the mic at his friends.

He hasn't said a word to me in an hour.

Which is... honestly a relief.

I'm curled up on the living room couch with my laptop balanced on my knees, headphones half-on, half-off. My latest video timeline is open, the one from Boots & Bourbon.

Clips of Reed behind the bar crowd my screen; pouring

drinks with that lazy wrist flick, leaning in whenever a customer laughs, his smile soft, but his eyes sharp.

My audience is going to eat. this. up.

If this video does well, I'll be able to escape, do what I want, and have my own creative freedom with my content without Brian.

Just the thought sends a spark of hope skittering through my chest.

My phone vibrates beside me.

I tap the side button just enough to light up the preview.

REED

What are you doing?

A smile spreads before I can stop it.

I slide fully into the corner of the couch, tucking one leg under me as my fingers dance across the screen.

LAYLA

Working. Trying to make the Boots & Bourbon edit perfect 😌

Three dots appear instantly.

REED

You're perfect.

I stop breathing, just long enough to feel dizzy.

LAYLA

Flattery won't get you anywhere 😉

Okay, Reed wants to play tonight, I see.

REED

Wanna bet?

I bite my lip, glancing toward the bedroom where Brian's voice is booming with laughter and trash talk.

"Bro, I HIT that shot! You're trash!" he yells obnoxiously.

He doesn't even notice I exist.

Good.

I type quickly.

LAYLA

What would you bet?

In an instant, his reply comes.

REED

One kiss wasn't enough.

A rush of heat floods through my core, drenches my pussy, and I squeeze my thighs together, but a light moan escapes my lips.

I let out a breath as my fingertips tremble against the phone.

LAYLA

You sure you can handle another one?

REEED

Pretty sure you're the dangerous one here.

My throat goes dry; we're not even sexting, but I ache for his lips on mine again. I ache for his fingers sliding between my legs and pleasuring me.

LAYLA

Dangerous how?

There's a longer pause this time.

Buzz. Buzz. Buzz.

REED

Because I can't stop thinking about you, and the things I'd do to you.

REED

And I'm trying really hard not to want something I shouldn't want.

My hand flies up to my mouth, letting out a gasp. The last thing I need is for Brian to hear me.

LAYLA

Maybe we both want the same thing.

Oh God, oh God, oh Godddd.

REED

Say it.

I stare at his words, my pussy throbbing, aching to be touched.

LAYLA

I want you, Reed. I haven't stopped thinking about you.

My pulse rockets.

A notification comes through instantly.

REED

Fuck, Layla.

Don't say that, not right now.

LAYLA

Why not? It's the truth.

I hit send and immediately regret how vulnerable it sounds, but it's true.

Our kiss replays relentlessly. Every time I close my eyes, I see my fingers in his hair, the rough scrape of his mustache, and the way he pulled back just enough to rest his forehead against mine and breathe me in like I was something worth memorizing.

Dots appear. Stay. Disappear. Appear again.

REED

I shouldn't have kissed you.

But I don't fucking regret it.

LAYLA

Then why do you sound like you're punishing yourself?

REED

Because I am.

Every time I close my eyes, I see your mouth on mine. I feel the little hitch in your breath when I pulled you closer.

I tell myself it was a mistake. That I should stay the fuck away.

But I keep coming back to it. Keep wanting more.

I let out a shaky breath. Fuck.

LAYLA

I keep thinking about what would've happened if we hadn't stopped.

I would've let you.

REED

Layla…

The screen stays lit on my name while the seconds stretch.

I stare at his message, my chest tight, as my thumb hovers over the call button.

My thighs are still pressed together from that one involuntary squeeze, the ache between them now a steady, insistent pulse.

I don't think as I tap the phone icon next to his name. It rings for less than a second before he answers.

"Layla." His voice is rough and gravelly. I can hear the restraint in his voice from our messages.

I swallow. My mouth suddenly goes dry. "Hey."

A beat of silence, until a soft exhale, almost a laugh, but pained. "Don't make this harder for me than it already is."

"Reed." I shift on the couch, pulling my knees up again, letting my hoodie slip off one shoulder. "I couldn't just... keep typing. I needed to hear you, please."

He lets out a half-groan, half-curse. "Fuck, your voice. It's worse than the texts."

Heat floods my face, spreading everywhere. I let my free hand slide down my stomach, resting it on my lower abdomen. "Tell me why it's worse."

"Because I can hear how turned on you are." His words come more slowly now. "That little hitch in your breath, the way you're trying to stay quiet, is turning me on."

I bite my lip. "Talk to me, Reed, please."

He lets out another rough exhale and a groan that will damn near make me fall to my knees.

I can picture him, probably lying back on his bed with his arm over his eyes, as his phone pressed to his ear, a faint smile stretching across his lips.

"Let go, for me."

Holy shit.

My fingers twitch against the lace of my panties. I part my legs a fraction, sliding my fingers lower. "Reed, I—I want you."

"Fuck." His voice cracks on the word. "Are you wet for me, baby?"

"Soaked." I slide two fingers down, parting myself just enough to feel how wet I am. "From thinking about that night on your couch. About how you kissed me like you were drowning, then just... stopped."

"I stopped because if I hadn't, I wouldn't have let you leave." His breathing is heavier now. "I would've taken you right there, pushed your shorts down, spread you across my lap, and made you ride me until you couldn't remember why you'd ever said yes to him."

A whimper slips out before I can stop it. I press my fingers inside my pussy slowly as my hips lift off the cushion.

"Reed..."

"Touch yourself for me," he says, and I hear the creak in his bed as he shifts. "Tell me exactly what you're doing, sunshine."

I push my fingers deeper, curling them against my sensitive spot. "I'm fingering myself, wishing it was your mouth."

He groans. "Good girl. Keep going. Imagine it's me. My fingers stretching you open."

My breath hitches. I add a third finger, stretching my cunt, quickening the pace. "God, Reed, I'm so close already."

"Fuck, I love hearing you, baby. You sound so pretty when you're about to fall apart for me."

My thumb grinds harder against my clit. "Reed, fuck, I'm gonna—"

"Come for me," he commands. "Let me hear you. But

be quiet, baby, loud enough that I can only hear your pretty moan."

I bury my face in the crook of my elbow, biting down on my hoodie sleeve as my orgasm crashes through me.

My thighs clamp around my hand, hips jerking, wetness flooding my knuckles as I pulse against my fingers.

A muffled, broken moan escapes anyway, his name, barely audible.

"You okay?"

I laugh weakly, still trembling. "Better than okay."

"Good," he says gently. "Get some sleep now, sunshine."

"I will." I pull my fingers free, wiping them with the napkin lying on the coffee table. "And Reed?"

"Yeah?"

"Don't pull away next time, I *dare* you."

He exhales, almost a sigh of relief. "Never again."

I end the call and set the phone face down on the cushion.

Brian bangs his fist on the desk and howls at the game, and I jump instinctively.

I sink into the couch cushions, forcing my breathing to slow, pretending to be asleep.

Across the apartment, the front door buzzes as a food delivery arrives, not for me, not for us, but for him.

He didn't ask if I wanted anything. He didn't look my way as he walked up to the door, grabbed his food, paid for it with the money I've earned, and surely doesn't care about me anymore.

But my mind won't let me think about that right now. I just had phone sex with Reed Hayes.

FUCK.

TWENTY-THREE
REED

What the fuck am I doing?

She's engaged.

She's got his fucking ring on her finger.

And I listened to her cum during a spontaneous phone call last night.

I'm not that guy. I've spent years telling myself I'm not that guy. And why would she want me anyway?

My stomach twists so hard I almost gag.

I shake my head, focusing my attention back to finishing up prep, folding down barstools, wiping a sticky ring left from the earlier shift, when the front door gives a soft jingle.

Derek Reeves steps inside, with Caleb tucked against his side.

Thank God, a distraction.

We met at a grief support group in Opal Springs. Derek's older, sure, but he looked like a man who'd seen fire too, not the kind that leaves scars on the skin, but the kind that burns through your life and leaves you standing in the smoke, wondering what the hell comes next.

We didn't talk much that first night. He just sat beside

me with his arms crossed, jaw clenched, staring at the wall. When the facilitator asked if anyone wanted to share, I felt his tension in my own shoulders.

Different stories. Same kind of loss.

I think that's why he comes here. Not for the drinks, he barely finishes one. It's the company without the pressure to speak. Just another man trying to breathe among the pieces of his past.

And sometimes, knowing someone else is carrying their own ghosts is enough to make yours feel a little lighter.

I shake away my recollection of the time we first met and watch them both saunter up to the bar counter.

He still has that stiff firefighter posture, even in jeans and a T-shirt. Caleb clutches a dinosaur toy under one arm, his small feet scuffing the wood as he tries to imitate his dad's silent swagger.

"You're early," I say, tossing a towel over my shoulder.

Derek tries to answer. His mouth shapes the word *"Yeah"*, but it comes out clipped.

"Y—ah."

He grimaces, his jaw tightening briefly, then raises his hand and signs a simple shrug.

I act like I overlooked his stumble.

Caleb hops onto his favorite stool. "Daddy, let me pick the music in the truck!"

I nod. "Rebellious. I like it."

Derek exhales quietly. His eyes are weary, constantly tired, but they soften when Caleb slams his dinosaur onto the bar with a loud bang.

I grab a Coke from the fridge, pour it into a plastic cup for Caleb, extra napkins because his hands are always sticky, then grab a ginger ale for Derek before he has to ask.

Sliding the ginger ale his way, he grunts with thanks, his lips forming to speak.

"Th... thanks."

His words stumble, the sound stutters on the exit, but he forces it out anyway.

Speech apraxia is cruel; it happened after his accident, which cost him everything.

It doesn't steal your voice; it allows you to hear every syllable clearly in your head, then turns against you when you try to speak.

"You're good," I say, wiping the counter down in steady circles.

Caleb kicks his legs, sipping loudly. "Daddy says he's going back to work soon."

Derek's fingers tighten around his glass. He takes a breath, trying to formulate a whole sentence. "Cap...ta...in... he...want..."

His mouth flutters as his shoulders tighten, his eyes flickering with embarrassment.

He shifts, lifting his fingers and signing. "Captain. Wants. Me. Back."

"Of course he does," I say. "They need you."

Derek chews the inside of his cheek as his gaze drops to the bar top.

He signs more slowly, less confidently.

"My shoulder needs to improve; he'll only take me back if I agree to physical therapy."

His injury, the nightmare that prevents him from holding a hose at full weight, climbing ladders like he used to, or yelling into smoke-filled rooms when seconds matter. His captain isn't worried about his speech as he's in speech therapy, but it's his range of motion and flexibility that need work.

I nod. "It will."

He looks up, like he wants to argue, but Caleb interrupts before he can.

"Daddy's the best firefighter. He saved a puppy once."

Derek tries to hide his cringe.

I let myself smile.

"That's pretty badass," I tell Caleb, leaning in. "Did the puppy thank him?"

"Yeah! He licked his ear."

Derek clears his throat and shoots me a pleading look, like *don't you dare make this a thing.*

I raise my hands in surrender.

Derek's lips twitch, the tiniest laugh hidden behind them.

He looks more alive when Caleb is here.

Caleb finishes his drink with a dramatized slurp. "We're gonna go to the park now, before we head back home."

Derek gives Caleb a gentle nudge, his mismatched eyes —one warm amber-brown, the other piercing storm-blue— softening in a way most people never see. His voice is rough as he pushes out one more word.

"Thanks."

It lands heavily because I understand what it costs him to speak at all.

I nod.

"Anytime, Reeves."

He places a hand on the back of his son's hoodie, and they head for the door. Caleb waves his dinosaur at me, saying goodbye.

SUNLIGHT STRETCHES THROUGH THE BLINDS IN ANGLED stripes, and there is nothing to fill the silence except the faint hum of the refrigerator and the uneven rhythm of my own breath.

I need to move, to do something that feels like living, so I step outside.

The porch boards creak beneath my boots as I head to the mailbox. The neighborhood smells like autumn is near, full of freshly cut grass, honeysuckle, and that gentle warmth that lingers on everything once the sun has been shining long enough.

Someone nearby must be grilling, because the air carries a hint of sweet barbecue smoke too, the scent wrapping around the breeze.

I reach my weathered, rusted mailbox and open the lid; what I find knocks the air from my lungs.

An envelope. Just an off-white envelope with gentle pen strokes spelling out my full name:

Reed Hayes

Her handwriting curves as if she wrote it with a soft smile she couldn't hold back. A small floral sticker seals the flap, and in the top corner is her address in Los Angeles, and I'm floored she even thought to write me at all.

Cherry and vanilla notes waft from the envelope before I even open it; the exact scent of her perfume.

Her presence surrounds me in that simple detail, and for a moment, I stand there, breathing her in.

I take my time breaking the seal. The flap opens with a soft tear, and a Polaroid slips into my hand first, and I catch it carefully.

It's a selfie of Layla as she beams up at me from the glossy surface; her hair tousled by the wind, cheeks flushed from laughter, neon city lights behind her that look wild and alive.

I turn the picture over.

A tiny note in the bottom corner reads:

For your mantle. ;-)

I smile to myself and carefully take out the letter from the envelope. The letter is neatly folded, but the creases look softened, as if she had folded it many times.

Reed,

I promised myself I would wait like a normal person and let you get back to your life without me barging in through the mailbox like I am some drunken pen pal, but apparently, I'm terrible at patience and even worse at pretending I don't think about you every five minutes.

I keep picturing you sitting beside me by the lake, trying to paint tiny yellow suns even though you insisted your flower looked like a sad amoeba, but it was still cute because you made it.

I miss you—the one who let me see the soft parts, even when you hated how exposed it made you feel. I want you to know that those moments mattered to me more than you think, and I keep replaying them like tiny movie scenes in my head.

I hate how much I miss you, and I hate that missing you feels so incredibly good at the same time, which should be illegal because I already have enough emotional confusion. I know this thing between us is messy, probably ill-advised, and something my therapist will eventually raise her eyebrows at, but I can't bring myself to regret a single second.

If you want to reply, you should, because I am checking the mailbox like a raccoon hunting for shiny things, and I'm pretty sure my neighbors think I'm in love with a mailman.

Keep my seat warm, okay?

xoxo, Layla

Her words blur for a second, not because they are unclear, but because they land somewhere within my heart that has been hers all along.

I sit on the porch step because my knees need support, and I run my thumb along the Polaroid again, unable to ignore the heat building behind my ribs.

Folding the letter carefully, avoiding any creases on its softer edges where her hand rested longest, I hold it open in my palm for a moment longer, letting every last trace of her scent and warmth seep into my skin before I rise again.

She is out there, missing *me*.

And for the first time since she left, my heart no longer feels like it's bracing for impact.

I fold the letter one more time, mostly because I'm afraid that if I don't, I'll keep reading it until the ink fades from how hard my eyes cling to every word.

Carefully tucking the envelope into my pocket, I take more than two steps toward the front door as gravel crunches loudly in my driveway.

Two vehicles pull up, totally disregarding the noise ordinance that likely exists somewhere in this town.

Maverick arrives first in his unnecessarily massive Bronco, its engine rumbling.

He swings the door open with too much enthusiasm, and Leo immediately starts screeching from the backseat, his black vans kicking against the seat as he reaches for his dad.

Amelia follows behind Maverick, smoothing a hand over Leo's bright, blonde curls while giving my house a curious once-over.

Carter's black truck pulls in behind them with a bit more grace, although the man driving it still looks like he could bench-press the entire vehicle just to prove a point.

Catalina jumps out first, already mid-sentence about something Carter apparently did wrong five minutes ago.

Carter looks at her as if he would gladly spend eternity being scolded if it meant she kept talking to him.

They didn't call.

They arrived assuming I was home. Apparently, no one in this family believes in knocking or decency.

"Did you seriously say 'we'll see' after I planned the entire—oh, hi, Reed!" Catalina's irritation flips into a bright smile the second she spots me.

"Hey, Cat," I say, leaning on the porch railing as they approach.

Maverick lifts Leo higher onto his hip and squints at me, eyeing me up and down with his infamous shit-eating grin.

"What's that in your pocket, bro?"

"Nothing," I counter. "Worry about your son."

Amelia snorts.

Maverick's gaze drops again on the envelope shape pressed against my pocket. His brows lift, subtle but curious.

"Who's writing you letters, man?"

Carter's eyes follow as Catalina tries to hide her interest and fails immediately.

I shift my stance, casual even though my pulse decides to misbehave.

"Just mail."

"Bills don't smell like perfume," Maverick says under his breath.

I clear my throat, keeping my voice measured. "It's personal."

Maverick nods once, though curiosity remains in his eyes.

"Fair enough," he mumbles, adjusting Leo, who has begun shoving his fingers in Mav's mouth.

"You all planning on invading my house again?"

Amelia gives a slight shrug. "You can say no if you want."

I should, I could.

But they already made me feel better just by showing up.

"Door's open," I reply, pushing off the railing.

Maverick grins and heads toward the porch, holding on to Leo as he gnaws on his plastic football.

The laughter of my family fills the porch as they file inside, and the envelope in my pocket stays there like a spark I'm still afraid to protect out loud.

I just know, the next time I see her, my hesitation, pull-back, and guilt about her being engaged will be gone; I don't give a fuck anymore.

I *need* her.

TWENTY-FOUR
LAYLA

I'm lying on my bed staring at a paused video frame of Reed Hayes like an obsessed woman.

He's behind his bar in the clip; shoulders flexing under his flannel, forearms moving smoothly in circles across the polished wood, jaw clenched with focus.

The warm amber lights soak into every line of his body, turning him into trouble carved out of shadow and bourbon.

He glances up toward the camera, toward me.

The memory of his hand curling in my hair, the heat of our kiss, hits me with full force.

I snap the laptop shut before I do anything embarrassing, like lick the screen.

My phone buzzes.

Buzz. Buzz. Buzz.

Snatching my phone off my comforter, I press the side button to preview the incoming message.

REED

Every mile between us is pissing me off, because I can still taste your lips and I'm nowhere near finished with you.

The way you broke that kiss like you needed air? I want to steal every breath you take when you get back here.

My brain short-circuits. My soul leaves my body. My toes curl so tightly I might never walk upright again.

It's so bold of him to message me like this. I mean, I initiated it last time, AND we did have phone sex.

Layla? What are you babbling about?

LAYLA

So you admit you're thinking about my mouth right now? 😇

The typing bubbles appear without hesitation, like he didn't even put the phone down.

REED

I haven't stopped thinking about your mouth since the second I walked away from it.

And I'm done pretending I didn't want more.

That phone call shattered every shred of restraint I had left.

Heat surges through my veins, and like clockwork, my pussy throbs, and I can feel myself getting wet.

Before I can respond, Catalina blows up my phone, her messages flooding in.

CATALINA

FAMILY DINNER NEXT SATURDAY HOE

I have a HUGE announcement

Like you're going to freak out

I want EVERYONE there, including you, because you're family

Book the damn flight BITCH

LAYLA

What kind of announcement?? 👀

CATALINA

If I told you, you'd faint and maybe die and I don't want to bury you, so BOOK.

Reed's text interrupts, and oh boyyyy.

REED

I need another taste of you, sunshine.

My pulse becomes a drumline.

LAYLA

Bold of you to assume I'd let you kiss me again. 😇

REED

I'm not assuming anything.

I'm telling you that the next time I get you under my hands, I'm not stopping until you're making every sound you tried to bite back the first time.

I bury my face in a pillow and squeal into it like a feral animal.

LAYLA

So, hypothetically, if I got a red-eye and came tonight...

You'd want that?

REED

There's nothing hypothetical about it.

Come early.

I want time alone with you.

I'll pay for your flight. Come back to me.

I make a squeaky sound and immediately shove my fist into my mouth to keep from full-on shrieking.

My legs kick out on instinct, heels thumping against the bed as I roll onto my back, then onto my side, then back again because there is simply too much feeling in my body to stay still.

"Oh my God," I whisper, my eyes burning, my smile so wide my cheeks ache. "Oh my God."

My chest feels fizzy, sparkling, like I just downed champagne on an empty stomach.

I hug my phone to my sternum and squeeze, breathing him in through his words, as if that's enough to hold me together.

My phone buzzes again, and I suck in a sharp breath, sitting upright as my hair falls into my face and I swipe the screen.

A screenshot of my flight details.

"He—" My voice cracks, barely louder than air. "He booked it?"

I read it again. And again. And again, because there's no way this is real, and also because it very much is.

My hands start fluttering in front of me like they've lost all structural integrity, and I squeal, burying my face in my pillow so I don't wake the entire building.

LAYLA

Reed, you didn't have to pay for my flight 🙂

REED

I wanted to. I'll pick you up from the airport.

And I'm going to spend the entire 7 days reminding you exactly how you tasted when I had your lip between my teeth.

I gasp. I flop back onto the bed, kicking my feet like a psycho.

Dropping my phone in shock and arousal, I immediately retrieve it, remembering to message Brian, right? My fiancé. The one who hasn't kissed me in... weeks? Months?

LAYLA

I'm going to Tennessee for a work trip. I'm leaving tonight.

The "Read" receipt pops up almost instantly.

BRIAN

Heyyy girlie, it's Rebecca 😘

Brian's busy right now, but I'll let him know, okay?

My stomach doesn't drop; it doesn't even twitch. But the sheer audacity, I scoff, choosing not to answer because what the actual fuck.

My phone buzzes again, and anger seeps through me, assuming it's Brian, but it isn't.

REED

I can't wait to see you, sunshine 😊

Oh my God, he used an emoji.

AHHHHHHHHH. I mentally scream to myself, because if I were to scream out loud, my neighbors would call the cops.

My skin warms with excitement, as my heart steadies. I buzz with anticipation, excitement, nerves, and giddiness for another man.

LAYLA

Start counting down the hours

Throwing my phone onto my bed, I squeal with excitement. Before I can pack my backpack, I need to check my mail.

I clamp a hand over my mouth, my heart racing. The air still smells faintly of the coffee I left unfinished this morning, and the hum of the fridge is the only thing that answers me. My cheeks hurt from smiling.

I've never genuinely smiled this much in my life. My smiles for my content are always fake, performed. But with Reed? They come naturally.

I slip on my shoes, the rubber soles squeaking faintly against the wood, and grab my keys.

The hallway outside my apartment is quiet, with sunlight slanting through the high windows and dust motes floating lazily in the air.

I jog down the stairs, my excitement buzzing under my skin.

My footsteps echo as I head toward the mailroom, my pulse quickening with every step.

The wall of mailboxes comes into view; rows and rows of small metal doors, each dented or scratched, each holding someone's life in envelopes.

I find mine, sticking the key in.

Jiggling it once, twice, I twist harder until the lock finally gives with a dull click. The door creaks open, metal scraping softly, and I lean in, peering inside.

A stack of mail waits for me, its edges uneven. I pull it out and rest it against my hip, flipping through it one piece at a time.

Electric bill, gross.

Health insurance bill, scam.

A grocery flyer I absolutely didn't ask for.

My chest tightens just a little as the next envelope comes into view.

I slide it out carefully, my fingers catching on the edge for a second before it comes free. It's heavier than the others, thicker somehow, and my thumb drifts over the ink without thinking.

The handwriting stops me cold. I know it. I've watched that hand wrap around a mug, grip a paintbrush, and rest against my hip.

Reed.

He wrote me back.

I press the envelope to my chest without thinking, my heart slamming so hard it makes me dizzy.

For a second, I stand there in the mailroom, surrounded by metal, concrete, and other people's junk mail, trying to remember how to breathe.

Shoving the rest of the mail back into the box, I close it with a soft clang and float back upstairs.

Once inside my apartment, I lock the door, and the click echoes through the quiet. I lean back against it, staring down at the envelope in my hands, finally letting myself feel it.

I push off the door and cross the room slowly, heading into my bedroom. I sit on the edge of my bed and smooth the envelope against my thigh before turning it over in my hands.

Carefully, I break the seal.

First, a pressed sunflower falls out, and I instantly tear up. My fingers trace the dried flower, admiring its beauty.

Next, the paper inside slides out with a whisper, folded once. I unfold it, holding my breath, my heart pounding loud enough to feel in my ears.

Sunshine,

I don't know when you'll read this. I thought about waiting until I saw you again, but I didn't want to.

I keep thinking about you. About the way you laughed that night. About the kiss. I don't think I realized how much it would stay with me.

I miss you more than I expected to.

I'm not great at putting things into words, especially on paper, but I wanted you to know that I'm really looking forward to seeing you again.

I'll be here when you get back.

– Reed

I read it again, slower this time.

The words don't change, but the way they land does. They sink in, settling low in my chest. There's no rush to them. No pressure. Just Reed, exactly as he is; honest, careful, choosing me in the quietest way possible.

I miss you more than I expected to.

Pressing the letter flat against my thigh, I stare at the far wall of my apartment.

I've had big feelings before—loud ones, messy ones that burned hot, fast, and left me dizzy.

This feels different. This feels like something that doesn't need to announce itself to be real.

He isn't asking me to promise anything. He isn't demanding space in my life. He's just... there. Waiting.

This is what it feels like to be missed without being needed. To be wanted without being chased.

I fold the letter carefully, smoothing the crease with my thumb, and tucking it back into the envelope.

Opening my closet, I carefully hid the letter in a box, pushing it behind my winter coats.

"Okay," I whisper, turning to my empty room, my voice steady.

I grab my backpack and finally start packing, throwing whatever I grab from my drawers, not thinking because excitement is eating me away.

For the first time, I'm not nervous about what comes next.

I'm just ready to see him.

Crisp autumn air lingers on my skin as the faint rumble of cars moves along the interstate.

The outdoor lights cast long streaks of gold across the pavement, illuminating dust motes drifting lazily through the air.

I'm tugging on my backpack straps as I scan the passenger pickup zone. Reed said he'd be here.

I check each car for his truck until I spot Reed standing

next to his matte black motorcycle.

His tall, broad shadow is carved beneath the moonlight. He's leaning against a steel pillar, his boot crossed over the other, with both arms folded across his chest.

I take him in from a distance, admiring him just for a moment.

Worn black jeans molded to the strong contours of his legs, and a black T-shirt replacing his usual flannel. The fabric stretches over his muscular frame, broad across his shoulders and tapering to a lean waist.

The lamplight highlights the edges of his glasses, the lenses shimmering with reflections of the moon overhead. The shadows shift to reveal the burn scars scattered along his arms and the dark ink of his tattoos wrapping around them.

He wore a shirt for *me*.

His dog tags hang against his chest, brushed silver in the glow, swaying slightly with each breeze through the corridor —his hair curls at the nape of his neck, softening the severity of the rest of him.

Every delicate curl.

Every scar.

Every line and bend of muscle.

I'm in such awe of him until he lifts his eyes from his phone and they land on me.

He pushes off the metal beam and makes his way toward me, and my heart thumps against the straps of my backpack.

In one hand, he holds a scuffed matte-black helmet I've worn before. In the other, he holds a second helmet. Also black, but its surface is alive with hand-painted sunflowers, their petals imperfect, golden, and tender in a way that only matters when someone paints them with their heart rather than their skill.

A tiny breath slips out of me.

He painted sunflowers. For *me*.

Reed finally reaches me and stops inches in front of me, close enough that his warmth brushes against my lips.

"Sunshine."

I attempt to smile as I gaze up at him. "You came."

"Of course I was going to come," he says, his fingers twitching at his side, like he wants to reach for me.

Before I can speak again, he leans slightly and gently sets both helmets on the pavement.

His hands rise slowly from his sides, almost hesitant as his palm slides behind my head, his fingers parting through my hair at the nape, gently guiding me as his other hand finds the side of my jaw, his thumb tracing along my cheekbone in a slow stroke that sends a shiver down to my knees.

My breath stutters. "You wrote me back."

"Of course I did, baby, I missed you," he mumbles, as his thumb caresses my jaw.

And without warning, he leans his massive frame lower, and he kisses me.

His lips press against mine with warm certainty, as if he's already memorized exactly how we connect.

The cool night air swirls around us, replaced by the heat radiating from his mouth.

My fingers instinctively find the front of his shirt, gripping the soft, worn cotton and tugging him impossibly closer to me.

His hand gently tightens at the back of my head, guiding my face as his mouth presses to mine, deepening the kiss. His lips softly drag over my lower lip before he gently nicks it between his teeth; a careful scrape that causes a slight, desperate moan to escape from my throat.

He hears it, he *feels* it, because a low growl hums through his chest and spills into my mouth, with the sound vibrating heat directly between my legs.

His tongue brushes my bottom lip, teasing, coaxing, asking for permission without asking.

I part my lips for him, and the kiss shifts, becoming something driven by hunger, carefully restrained in every slow stroke.

Our breaths intertwine as his thumb glides over the hinge of my jaw, urging me closer, deeper.

The taste of him, a hint of mint and whiskey, washes over me until the world slips away completely.

I tilt my head, following every subtle nudge from his mouth, as his tongue meets mine again.

My knees threaten to give out, so I tighten my grip on his shirt, fingers curling around the hard muscle beneath.

He kisses me as if he's trying to learn every reaction from me, every shiver, every breathless sound, and keep them for himself.

A car passes somewhere beyond us, but the whole world narrows to the press of his thumb against my jawline and the quiet catch of my breath as his mouth angles just right.

He finally pulls away, his forehead nearly touching mine, his hand staying at the back of my head, as his thumb still traces a warm path along my cheek.

"I needed that the second you walked toward me."

My pulse struggles. "Me too," I whisper.

He draws another slow stroke through my hair before letting his hand fall, reluctantly. He crouches to grab the helmets, lifting the sunflower-painted one into the glow of lamplight.

"This one's yours," he says, straightening his posture to his full, impossible height. "It felt wrong for you to wear mine again. So I did something about it."

I run my fingertips over a sunflower's petal, the textured brushstroke brushing against my skin. Warmth flows into every part of me, not from adrenaline or nerves, but something softer.

"I love it," I say, barely a breath. "I love that you made it for me."

His eyes flick to mine, filled with something that could undo me if I stare too long.

"Good," he murmurs. "Because I made it knowing exactly who would wear it."

I smile in response, gazing up at him.

He pulls back, eyeing my backpack. "Just a backpack, sunshine? You'll be here for seven days."

I tug on the straps, smiling to myself. "I was so excited to get here, I just threw whatever in there, wanted to pack light."

He smiles, leaning down to kiss my forehead.

My eyes flutter shut with the contact. His motorcycle engine idles in the distance.

Pulling back again, he offers me his free hand. "Come on," he says softly. "Let's get you out of here."

TWENTY-FIVE
REED

How am I supposed to handle seven days alone with her if I'm already losing my edge after just one night?

I'm finishing up closing the bar, and she's here, driving me wild.

She laughs, making my situation worse, as she straddles the mechanical bull.

"I've never actually been on one of these," she says as her fingers curl into the leather strap.

God help me.

I switch the control to its easiest setting, but my pulse still races when the machine moves under her. She sinks deeper into the seat, the movement pulling her dress higher on her thighs. My throat tightens.

"You're supposed to hold on," I murmur, stepping closer than I should.

"Maybe I want to fall."

Fuck.

I place my hand over hers, steadying her grip on the strap. My other hand hovers near the small of her back, but doesn't quite touch.

"You fall," I tell her, gently caressing her fingers with my thumb. "I'll catch you."

She bites her lip like she knows exactly what she's doing to me.

The bull rocks again, and she rolls her hips to match the movement, an involuntary sound slipping from her throat.

It's quiet, but it wrecks me.

My cock hardens under my jeans, pressing against the zipper.

"Like that?" I manage to ask.

She nods, her breath shallow, and her cheeks flushed a rosy pink.

"Faster."

I increase the speed slightly, and her body moves with the rhythm as her thighs flex, her dress slipping dangerously high, revealing more of her ivory skin.

She's clutching the strap with one hand now, as the other rests on my shoulder to steady herself.

"You okay?" I ask.

"No," she whispers, leaning in, lips inches from mine. "I've been losing my mind around you for years."

Years?

Her honesty and bluntness catch me off guard.

"Years?" I ask.

She nods, a soft, almost an embarrassed smile tugging at her lips, as if she can't believe she's finally saying it out loud.

"Yeah," she says quietly. "Years."

My chest tightens.

I remember that night.

Catalina burst through the door like she owned the place already. Carter was behind her, glaring, pretending to hate her, but I knew he didn't. I saw the way his face brightened every time she glanced his way.

Amelia was quiet, defensive, glaring at Maverick.

And then there was Layla, half a step behind them, her smile so wide it brought light into my bar like sunshine incarnate.

One look at her, and I was done for.

My sunshine, my weakness, my reason to stay.

"You were behind the bar," she says, her voice softer now. "Quiet. Focused. Not trying to impress anyone. You looked at me like you already knew me, and it threw me completely."

My throat goes dry.

I remember introducing myself to her and thinking I needed to be careful. Whatever that pull was, it wasn't something I could afford to misread.

"I told myself it was nothing," she admits. "Just a stupid crush. One I'd get over."

She doesn't look away when she says the next part.

"But every day, I thought about you. Even though it's wrong, I don't care. I've wanted you, Reed; it's always been you."

My restraint dies a quick death.

I kill the machine and grab her waist, lifting her off the bull. As soon as her feet touch the floor, her hands go into my shirt, pulling me close.

Her lips meet mine in a frantic motion as her fingers weave through my hair.

It's messy at first as our tongues swirl together, teasing and tasting, like she's been starving and has finally found her favorite meal.

I groan into her mouth as my hand slides up her thigh, gripping tight.

"Layla," I warn, breathing hard, "I'm not going to stop this time, your fianc-"

She fists my shirt, pulling me closer, as her lips brush mine, cutting me off. Before she pulls away, her breath ragged as she finally speaks.

"Fuck him."

That's it, fuck him, she's mine to have, mine to take care of, mine to cherish.

I gently push her back against the mechanical bull, kissing her more passionately, swallowing every moan she gives me. Her legs curl around my hips, dragging me impossibly closer.

She whimpers when I grind against her, the contact too good, too much, and my brain shorts out.

"Tell me to stop," I breathe against her jaw. "Tell me you don't want this."

Her nails rake my shoulders, voice breaking. "I want you."

I curse under my breath as I press my forehead to hers. "You have no idea what you're asking for."

She smiles and whispers. "Show me then, I *dare* you."

Her breath trembles against my lips as I cup her jaw, my thumb grazing the corner of her lips.

"You scare me," I admit, voice so raw it hurts.

Her fingers slide up my throat, resting just below my jaw, her pulse racing against mine.

"Why?"

"Because I want you," I breathe, "more than I've wanted anything since the fire."

And I don't get to want things anymore.

Her expression softens as she sees right through the steel plates I've welded over my chest, and without hesitation, she presses her lips to the scar climbing my cheek.

"You deserve things you want," she whispers.

Fuck. I'm ruined.

My hands go to her hips as I lift her, placing her back onto the bull, her legs swinging idly on the bull's side.

Not to increase the distance between us... but to admire. To breathe. To memorize.

She's sitting there, her legs parted just enough for me to stand between them, her dress riding high, giving me a peek of her white lace thong.

"Reed... touch me."

My self–control shatters completely.

I run my hands up the front of her thighs as my fingers trace reverent paths on her skin.

She trembles, not from cold, but because of me. Every tiny sound she makes burns into my bloodstream.

"You're shaking," I say quietly.

"I'm excited," she counters as she leans her forehead into mine. "And you're looking at me like I'm yours."

Trailing my lips along her cheek, down her throat, I taste her pulse pounding under my tongue.

"You think I don't already feel like you are?"

A ragged breath escapes her as she arches her back, pressing her chest against me, desperate for friction.

I nip at her hardened nipple beneath her dress, grasp her hips, and pull her closer until her body molds perfectly to mine.

A soft, breathy moan slips out of her as she reaches down and palms my cock through my jeans. Fuck, I'm shaking now, too.

My hands move downward until they meet the soft lace again. I run my finger over her swollen clit, before slipping my fingers under the lace, gently pulling them aside.

I slide my finger up her tight heat, feeling how wet she

is, which makes me groan. "You're so wet for me," I choke out, my forehead pressed to her collarbone.

"Touch me," she pleads as she grips the collar of my flannel. "Please, Reed—"

I kiss her neck gently before I push two fingers into her tight, wet cunt, feeling her walls tighten around me. I curl them just right, feeling the way her thighs tremble with every stroke.

She moans in response, and it's a sound so sweet that it shoots straight to my throbbing cock.

I pump my fingers faster, in, out, in, out, her moans growing louder within the bar.

Quickly, I stop, but only briefly to glance up at her.

"Layla..." My voice cracks. "I don't want to be a mistake you regret."

Her hands cradle my face, keeping me steady. "You're the first thing in a long time that feels like hope," she says. "Don't take that from me."

Hope.

No one has ever used that word with me, not without flinching.

I slide my hand between us again, moving my finger in slow, gentle circles over her clit. She gasps, a desperate little sound that hits me hard, as she grips my shoulders.

"Tell me what you need, baby," I murmur, my lips brushing her ear. "I'll give you every damn bit of it."

Her hips buck upward, telling me what she wants.

"You," she whispers. "I just need you."

Fuck consequences.

I press my forehead to hers as my hand slides beneath the lace, my fingers feeling the heat and slickness that make my knees weak.

Her eyes flutter shut, a sigh falling from her lips like she's letting go of everything but us.

"That's it, baby," I whisper, kissing the corner of her mouth. "Let me take care of you."

She arches her body with my touch, her moans tremble with each stroke as I fuck her cunt with my fingers.

Her breath stutters when I push three fingers deeper into her pussy, and Jesus Christ, she's perfect.

The way she clenches around my fingers, like she was made for me.

Her forehead drops to mine, her swollen lips parted, catching her breath. "Reed..."

Fuck, my name sounds so good leaving her pretty lips.

I curl my fingers inside her, pleasuring her G-spot, and her whole body bucks into my palm. I anchor my other hand at the small of her back, holding her steady so she doesn't slip.

So she knows I've got her. Always.

"There you go, baby," I murmur, peppering kisses along her jaw. "Let me feel how much you want this, make a mess for me."

Her nails dig into my shoulders, a plea ripped straight from her chest. Every tiny sound she makes goes straight to my aching cock, what I'd do to feel her wrapped around me, but not yet.

"You're so fucking wet," I breathe, voice rough and low. "All for me, baby?"

She nods, eyes fluttering shut as her thighs tremble around my hips.

"Yes," she gasps. "All for you."

A rough, hungry sound escapes me as I kiss her forehead once, softly, before letting my lips slide down the curve of her throat.

I latch onto the spot that makes her tremble, sucking until I feel her fingers clutch at me, marking her because I don't give a fuck.

Pulling back, I look into her pretty blue eyes before kissing her again, while my fingers work deeper, stroking that sweet spot that makes her gasp into my mouth.

Her hips grind forward, chasing every move, helpless against the way I'm unraveling her.

"Layla," I groan, biting her lower lip. "Feel what you do to me."

I rock my hips into her thigh, letting her feel exactly how hard I am, how close I am to losing myself completely.

She whimpers, clutching my hair. "I-I'm not gonna last—"

"Don't," I tell her, my thumb circling her clit with firm, teasing sweeps that make her whole body jerk. "Make a mess, baby, let me finally see how pretty you look when you fall apart."

Her breathing turns frantic as her thighs clench around my arm as she rides my hand, chasing her release. Her lips press against mine, and she moans into my mouth, the sound of a woman breaking open.

My fingers keep moving through her, through the waves, kissing every sound she gives me, drowning in the way she feels around me.

She clings to me, trembling, and I've never seen anything more devastatingly beautiful.

"Reed!" She yells, as her orgasm crashes through her, she squirts all over my hand, leaving my jeans damp.

My breath comes in ragged pulls as I gently withdraw my fingers from inside her, not wanting to overwhelm her.

She whimpers at the loss as she's still trembling, her

breathing quick, and I can't look away from the way she glistens for me, proof of how incredible she just felt.

Lifting her head, she watches me with dilated pupils.

I bring one slick finger to my mouth, holding her gaze as I taste her. The soft moan that slips from her lips nearly undoes me.

"Fuck, Layla..." My voice comes out lower than I intend. "You taste so fucking sweet."

Her cheeks flush deeper, but she doesn't look away. I lift my other two fingers, coated in her release, holding them close to her lips.

"Here," I murmur, a little rougher now. "Taste yourself, baby."

She bites her lip, then wraps her hand around my wrist as she guides my fingers into her mouth, curling her tongue around me while she sucks and licks herself clean.

It's the single hottest thing I've ever seen.

She collapses against me, panting.

I hold her through the aftershocks, my hand still between her thighs, my lips soft against her temple.

"Oh my God, that's never happened to me before."

I let out a huff, kissing the corner of her mouth. "That was so sexy."

A faint blush colors her cheeks as she whispers. "Really?"

I rest my forehead against hers, fighting the urge to take her against the bull, consequences be damned.

"Yeah, baby," I say, my thumb sweeping the inside of her knee as I catch her gaze, "You're fucking stunning without even trying."

She blushes again, hiding behind her fingers.

"We probably shouldn't have done that," she finally whispers.

"Probably not," I admit, kissing the corner of her lips. "But you're gonna have to drag me away from you if you want me to stop."

TWENTY-SIX
REED

Catalina had said she wanted a family dinner on Saturday, but since she's impatient and wants things her way, here we are, a day later, after I fingered Layla in my bar.

Surprisingly, she hasn't asked why Layla is here early, which is good because once Catalina prys, she doesn't stop and will scream at you until she gets answers.

I don't know how I'm going to focus the whole time without thinking about Layla squirting all over my hand.

Christ, she's poured her sunshine into my veins, and I can't get enough.

Shaking my head, I take in my surroundings so I don't look like a lunatic, thinking to myself.

Carter and Catalina's house smells like rosemary and butter, the walls vibrate with everyone's laughter, and every inch of the table is covered; half-empty plates, wine glasses, crumpled napkins, and Leo's baby bottle sitting close to a bowl of mashed potatoes.

Maverick's in full dad mode.

He's got Leo strapped to his chest, bouncing him while

his other hand shovels food into his mouth, his other hand gesturing wildly as he tells a story that's way too animated.

"So there I am, three a.m., no sleep, no clue what's happening, and this tiny dude—" he looks down at Leo with utter adoration, "—decides to unleash hell all over my shirt. I thought I'd seen horror, but this, this was next level."

Amelia groans as she buries her face in her hands. "He's exaggerating."

"I am not!" Maverick says, his voice full of fake outrage. "I'm traumatized! I went to change him, and he—he giggled, or farted. He knew exactly what he did."

"Babe," Amelia says, trying not to laugh, "he's three months old."

Maverick points dramatically. "So!"

The table erupts into laughter.

Catalina lets out a huff, turning her attention towards Layla, who's sitting right next to me.

She tilts her head, squinting across the table, as she leans forward, analyzing.

"Oh my God." Catalina's finger lifts, pointing right at Layla. "Layla LeBlanc," she says slowly, reverently, "you dirty girl."

Heat crawls up my neck, burning its way across my cheeks, and I smother myself in my bourbon glass to hide it.

My stomach, though, drops straight out of my ass.

"What?" Layla says, already panicking, but trying to hide the shakiness in her voice.

Catalina practically vibrates. "Brian gave you a nice hickey on your neck."

Layla spits her water clear across the table, choking, coughing, and slapping her hand down on the table. "I—WHAT—CATALINA—"

I stare at my plate.

Relax, Reed, there's no way they'd suspect anything.

My ears are on fucking fire. My jaw tightens. I consider, briefly, whether I can still disappear into the woods and never be seen again.

Maverick loses his damn mind, laughing so hard, all while Leo is strapped to his chest. "NO FUCKING WAYYY," he shouts.

Carter groans, and Amelia drops her head onto the table, letting out a long sigh before glaring at her husband.

Catalina is squealing. "Oh, babe, that's not subtle at all," she continues. "That man said 'this one's mine' and signed it in purple."

She's not his. She's *mine*.

Layla slaps at her neck, mortified, covering the hickey *I* gave her. "It's not even that bad!"

Catalina squints harder. "Baby, it's purple."

I clear my throat, which does absolutely nothing to help. I keep my eyes down, gripping my glass.

Maverick leans back, a feral grin forming across his lips. "Amelia has a ton of those. Show em', baby.

Amelia squints at Maverick. "Really, Maverick? In front of our son?"

Maverick gently covers Leo's ears. "My wife loves to be fuc—"

I choke on absolutely nothing.

"Enough," I mutter, finally looking up and shooting him a warning glare. "You're done."

Maverick only grins wider. "Am I?"

Carter groans, pinching his brows together. "You're all done before I flip this table."

Catalina's laughing so hard she almost spills her water, leaning into Carter's shoulder.

Carter shakes his head, smiling, his hand resting on hers on the table.

Every time she looks at him, he softens, his tough exterior melting away into something that still surprises me at times.

They look happy. Effortlessly happy.

Catalina tucks her hair behind her ear, her eyes flicking toward everyone with a glow that feels different. Softer. Nervous, maybe.

Her cheeks are flushed, as her hand tightens around Carter's atop the table.

"Alright, settle down, you fucks" she says suddenly, her voice bright but trembling. "Can I have everyone's attention for a sec?"

The room quiets instantly, or as quiet as it can get with Maverick in it.

Carter glances at her, brow furrowed. "What's going on, darlin'?"

She turns to him first, and that's when I notice the way her eyes glisten, the shimmer that no longer looks like laughter. "So..." she begins, voice trembling slightly. "I wasn't sure how to say this. I've been keeping a big secret."

Carter freezes. "What kind of secret?"

She takes a deep breath, her lips parting in a nervous smile as her gaze softens. "You're going to be a dad."

For a heartbeat, everything stops.

Carter blinks, still holding her hand like he's not sure he heard right. "What?"

Catalina's smile widens, tears streaming freely now. "Baby, I'm pregnant."

His chair scrapes back as he stands, blue eyes widening in disbelief. "You're serious?"

She nods, laughing through tears. "Yeah. I found out weeks ago. I wanted to be sure before I told you."

He covers his mouth with his hand, his throat working, trying to hold back the tears, but it doesn't last.

A choked sound escapes him, half laughter, half sob. He pulls her from the chair, pulling her against his chest, his arms wrapping around her so tightly.

"Baby," he breathes into her hair. "You—God, you're—" He laughs again, tears streaming down his face. "You're gonna make me a dad."

Catalina nods, her hands clutching the back of his shirt, both of them shaking, crying, and smiling all at once.

The rest of the table erupts. Maverick yells loudly enough to startle Leo, standing with his hands in the air. "UNCLE OF THE YEAR, BABY!"

Amelia's crying now, too, clapping her hands together. "Oh my God, Catalina!"

Layla squeals, practically bouncing in her chair, already rushing over to hug Catalina. "You're gonna be the cutest mom in the world!"

Carter's still holding her, still in disbelief, tears wet on his cheeks as he presses his forehead to hers.

He whispers something only she can hear; her hand moves up to cup his jaw, and both of them smile through it.

And I can't look away.

Because in this room, surrounded by warmth, laughter, and love that feels alive in every corner, I've never felt more like I'm on the outside looking in.

I want that.

That kind of love. That kind of life. Someone to look at me like I'm the only person in the room. Someone to cry with me over something this beautiful.

But I can't even imagine it.

Not with this skin. Not with these scars. Not with the face people still flinch at if they catch me from the wrong angle.

I take a slow sip of whiskey, letting it burn down my throat, eyes fixed on my glass instead of the scene before me.

The sound of Catalina's laughter echoes through the house, followed by Carter's low voice, the kind he only uses with her.

Layla's hugging them both now, her hair catching the light as she smiles.

I tell myself I'm fine. That this is enough, that being here, part of their world, even from the sidelines, is something I should be thankful for.

But deep down, it feels like standing in a room full of light and realizing you'll always be the shadow.

So I raise my glass, pretend the tears in my eyes are just from the bourbon, and force a smile when Carter looks up, laughing through his own.

"To family," he says, his voice thick with emotion.

Everyone cheers. Everyone smiles. Everyone glows.

And I sit there quietly, holding my glass to my lips—wishing, just once, that I could believe I deserved to be part of it, too.

Hours pass, and the table's a mess—plates piled on one side, napkins crumpled in wine glasses, crumbs scattered everywhere.

Carter hasn't stopped looking at her.

He's sitting close, his arm still wrapped around her shoulders, his other hand absently tracing small circles on her thigh. His eyes are red-rimmed, but there's a light in them I've never seen before; soft and raw all at once.

She's glowing. He's undone.

It's the kind of love that fills a room and makes everyone else disappear.

I sit at the far end of the table, silent. My hand rests on the base of my glass as my index finger slowly drags along the rim.

I can still hear Carter whispering to her—half-laughing, half-choked up.

"Can't believe it," he murmurs. "You're gonna make me a dad, baby."

Catalina wipes at his cheek, smiling through her own tears. "I love you so much."

A dull, lingering ache hits me in the chest, one that never fully goes away.

Across the room, Maverick still has Leo strapped to his chest, pacing. Amelia trails behind him, trying to coax him into sitting down.

"Baby, he's fine," she says, laughing.

"He's too quiet," Maverick says, peering down at Leo. "That's suspicious."

Amelia raises a brow. "He's sleeping."

"Exactly," Maverick says grimly. "He's planning something. Probably another blowout."

Catalina bursts into laughter, and Carter groans. "Christ, Mav, sit down before you drop him."

"I got this," Maverick says, confidently, right before Leo starts fussing.

This putrid smell hits, making Catalina gag.

"Oh my God!" Catalina squeals, pinching her nose.

"Oh, no," Maverick says, going pale. "Not again."

Amelia groans, already rolling up her sleeves. "I told you he was fine."

"He's not fine!" Maverick's voice cracks. "He's leaking! Oh my God—Catalina, do something!"

Catalina's doubled over laughing. "Hell no! Auntie duties are closed for tonight."

Amelia unstraps Leo from Mavs chest, picking him up, muttering, "Babe, I swear!" as she heads down the hall.

Maverick calls after her, dramatically clutching his chest, as he follows suit. "Hold on, dollface! You're so hot when you yell at me."

I sit there, smiling faintly, but it doesn't quite reach. My chest feels heavy, full of everything I won't say. It all becomes too much, and I excuse myself, hiding out in the kitchen.

Ducking into the kitchen, I brace my hands on the counter, trying to breathe in through my nose and out through my mouth, attempting to swallow the sting crawling up my throat.

I'm still catching my breath when I hear soft steps behind me, already knowing it's Layla.

"You disappeared," she says softly, edging a little closer.

"Crowded room," I mutter, turning towards her. "Needed a minute."

"You sure?" she asks, voice low, eyes searching my face as if she's worried she might find the truth.

I laugh under my breath, humorless. "I'm fine."

She moves closer. "Reed... you don't have to be okay with me."

Her words hit harder than they should because she's the last person I should let in.

After what happened between us last night, her trembling against me, my name slipping from her lips, I've been terrified that seeing her in daylight would make everything too real.

It does, and God, I wish I could call her mine, even if it were only for one damn day.

She wets her lips as her hands twist nervously at her sides. "Are you... regretting it?" she asks, her voice small.

My head jerks up. "What? No. Fuck, no."

"Then why are you hiding from me?"

That hits right where I try to bury it every damn day.

I reach up and tuck a strand of hair behind her ear, my fingertips brush the side of her neck, caressing over the hickey I left there.

"I'm not hiding from you," I say softly. "I'm hiding from the part of me that wants more."

"More... what?" she whispers.

I swallow hard.

"More mornings," I confess. "More... us."

Her eyes widen, every hint of playful confidence fading into something raw and fragile.

"Reed..."

"I know I shouldn't want you like that," I continue, still caressing the side of her neck. "Not while you're still tied to someone, but you..." I pull in a shaky breath. "You feel like a life I never thought I could have again."

She moves closer to me, her hands rising to rest on my chest. My heartbeat falters beneath her palms.

"I didn't know you felt that way," she admits. "About... anything. About me."

I huff out a rough laugh. "No one does. I don't let them."

Her fingers curl into my shirt. "You let me," she whispers.

Fuck. I do.

I tilt her chin up so she's looking at me; nowhere to run, nowhere to hide.

"You scared the hell out of me last night," I tell her.

"Because when I touched you, it didn't feel like something I should forget in the morning."

She sucks in a breath, exhaling as she stands on her tippy toes, looping her hands around my neck. "I don't want to forget it either."

I lean in, not quite kissing her as my lips brush her cheek, then the corner of her lips.

Her breath comes fast, matching mine. She tilts toward me instinctively, as if we've done this a thousand times.

I mumble against her lips. "Tell me you want more."

Her fingers slide up, threading into my hair, a whisper of a tug that nearly buckles my knees.

"Yes," she exhales. "I want... everything we're not supposed to want."

I close my eyes for a beat.

Hope hurts, but she's worth the pain.

Before I can steal the kiss I'm craving, voices draw nearer from the living room; laughter and footsteps heading our way.

We break apart just enough to look innocent, just enough to *lie*. But her hand stays in mine, hidden between our bodies, as if she can't bring herself to let go.

Neither can I.

TWENTY-SEVEN
LAYLA

My laptop is warm against my thighs, and the fan hums like it's working overtime right along with my brain.

The timeline stretches across the screen; tiny clips stacked together like proof that the last months actually happened.

Ruby Ridge in golden light. Storefronts glowing underneath the twinkling twilight. The bar sign swinging gently in the breeze.

I scrub through footage of Reed's bar, pausing again—because of course I do—on a shot of him behind the counter with his sleeves rolled, completely unbothered by the fact that he looks like literal sin.

"Okay, don't panic," I whisper to myself. "This is very professional. I am a professional."

I immediately zoom in, clip certain scenes, and make sure the length is right.

The sunflowers come next. The footage wobbles because I'm laughing off-camera breathlessly, tugging him along. I leave the laugh in. It's messy, real, and very *me*.

A creak pulls me out of my trance, and I instinctively jump at the small sound.

"I swear," I call, way too fast, "I was just about to take a break. Like, literally right now. This exact second."

Reed's voice is calm and amused. "Good. I come bearing bribes." The bed dips as he sits carefully, and something cold touches my arm.

I glance over. A berry smoothie, already sweating down the glass.

"Oh," I say. "You're an actual angel."

He averts his gaze, clearing his throat. "You needed a snack," he replies.

I snort, taking a sip as I ramble. "Okay, but this is really good. Like, unfairly good. Did you eyeball the ratios? I never get them right, and then it tastes like sadness, but this is spectacular!"

He leans in and kisses my shoulder, his mustache tickling my skin.

My brain promptly exits the building.

"For energy," he murmurs.

"Right," I say quickly. "Yes. Energy. Very important. I have... timelines. And feelings."

He chuckles, and it makes my chest feel fizzy.

"Do you want company?" he asks. "Or am I distracting you?"

I nod too quickly. "No—yes—I mean, company. Definitely company. You're not distracting. I'm just... easily distractible."

"Noted."

He shifts behind me, settling against the headboard, and tugs me gently so I end up between his legs.

His arm comes around my waist, loose, like he's not trying to cage me, just... be there.

I immediately start talking again, because he is somehow the only person who can make me nervous.

Have you seen him? Six-seven of pure muscle, I literally don't know what these Hayes men eat.

Anyways.

"Okay, so this clip is the first night. Here's me showing off the bull and the decor, and then there's you pretending not to notice me, rude by the way."

"I noticed," he says quietly, his lips brushing my temple.

I freeze. "You did?"

"Yeah."

"Oh." I laugh nervously. "Cool. Love that for me."

His lips curve against my skin. "You get cute when you're flustered."

"I do not," I protest immediately. "I get verbose. There's a difference."

He kisses just below my ear, and my words scatter.

"You make everything look like it matters," he whispers.

My fingers falter on the trackpad. "It does. I... sometimes I get scared I'll miss something. Like if I don't capture it, it'll disappear."

His arm tightens slightly. "I'm not disappearing," he murmurs.

I lean back into him without thinking as my head rests against his shoulder. "Good. Because I already put you in like... three different clips."

"Guess I'm committed now."

"Deeply," I say, then add quickly, "Artistically. I mean. Unless—" I stop myself, laughing. "Wow, okay. I'm spiraling."

"I've got you," he says softly, kissing my shoulder again. "Babble all you want."

The footage keeps rolling, sunflowers, laughter, light,

but now there's warmth at my back, and a quiet promise in his voice.

I hit play again, smiling. And for once, my nerves don't feel like a warning.

They feel like *hope*.

The timeline inches forward as my fingers hover, indecisive, over the trackpad. I nudge a clip half a second to the left. Pause. Nudge it back. The sunflower field sways on the screen, yellow blurring into gold, and my chest tightens in that familiar way, like I'm holding something fragile and don't want to drop it.

"I'm being annoying about this part," I murmur, my words tumbling out before I can stop them. "I know I am. I just—if the cut is wrong, it changes the whole feeling, and I don't want it to feel rushed, because it didn't feel rushed when we were there. It felt—"

Reed's lips brush my shoulder again.

My sentence dissolves.

"You're not being annoying," he whispers, his lips warm against my skin. "You're careful."

I swallow, nodding even though my eyes are glued to the screen.

His hand rests at my waist, not gripping, just there as his thumb moves in the smallest circle, slow enough that I almost miss it, except my whole body notices.

I keep editing because if I don't, I'll lose it.

A clip of the bar fades in; low light, wood grain, the quiet clink of glass. I let the ambient sound breathe rather than cutting it clean, and something in my chest eases as I finally let out an exhale.

"That," I say quickly, babbling again. "That sound. It feels important. Like... like a heartbeat."

"It is," he murmurs.

His lips drift again, this time along the slope of my shoulder to the delicate spot where my shoulder meets my neck.

He presses slow kisses, taking his time, a groan escaping between each kiss.

My shoulders drop, tension melting out of places I didn't realize were clenched.

I scrub forward, trimming, aligning, telling myself to focus—only for Reed to lift my hand gently from the keyboard.

He turns it palm-up, studies it for half a second, then presses a kiss to the center of my palm.

My breath hitches. "Reed," I whisper, not a warning, just his name.

"I know," he says softly, kissing the base of my thumb, then my knuckles, one at a time.

I laugh under my breath, a nervous little sound. "You're distracting me."

He smiles against my skin, feeling it as his lips brush my shoulder again, the coarse hair of his mustache tickling me once again. "You can tell me to stop."

Clearly, I don't.

I lean back into him, my spine fitting against his chest as it always has.

He adjusts instantly, his arm tightening just enough to hold me steady, his chin dipping toward my hair.

"I'm right here," he murmurs near my ear. "Take your time."

The footage returns to the sunflower field. My laugh slips through the speakers. I hesitate as my fingers hover.

"I almost cut that," I admit quietly. "My laugh. I thought it was too much."

His lips brush the back of my shoulder blade, barely there. "It's perfect, I love your laugh."

Something warm pools behind my eyes. I blink, refocusing, keeping the momentum going.

He continues kissing a soft trail along my shoulder and upper back, never lingering too long in one place.

My hands pause, and his fingers lace with mine for a moment, just enough pressure to remind me I'm not alone, before he releases me so I can keep working.

"You don't rush beauty," he whispers. "You let it arrive."

A small, but reluctant smile dances across my lips before I press play.

The edit flows, Ruby Ridge glowing, the bar alive with quiet moments, sunflowers bending toward the light, and Reed stays wrapped around me, kissing my fingers when they rest, my shoulder when I sigh, and my back when I lean into him.

For the first time all day, my nerves settle, not because they're gone but because they're being held.

"You're doing that thing," he murmurs.

I glance back at him. "What thing?"

"That little smile," he says. "The one you get when you're happy with it but pretending you're not."

I laugh softly, nerves bubbling up again. "I don't pretend."

"You absolutely do."

I roll my eyes, but I'm smiling as I turn back to the screen. His lips trail gently along the curve of my neck.

"I'm proud of you," he whispers near my ear. "You know that, right?"

My chest tightens. "You don't even know what the final cut looks like yet."

"Doesn't matter," he says easily. "I know you."

I lean back into him, letting myself be held for a moment longer than necessary. He presses a kiss to the top of my shoulder, then another atop my head.

"I'm gonna use the bathroom," he murmurs. "Don't let the footage bully you while I'm away."

"I make no promises," I tease.

He chuckles, kissing my shoulder one last time, and slips into the ensuite bathroom, the door clicking softly behind him.

I exhale, reach for my smoothie, then, without really thinking, grab my phone from the nightstand.

A flurry of notifications.

My stomach dips, just a little.

The first message was from earlier. Sweet, almost normal.

BRIAN

Hope your trip's going well.

Miss you.

I stare at it, my thumb hovering. My chest tightens; not with longing, but with muscle memory. I know he's going to flip.

More messages an hour ago.

BRIAN

You haven't answered.

Guess you're busy fucking someone out there.

My throat goes dry.

Another fucking buzz.

BRIAN

I'll take care of it when you're back.

You act like anyone else would want you.

I swallow hard, the warmth Reed left behind cooling fast.

BRIAN

You're nothing without me.

You never will be; all those followers are from me.

My fingers curl around my phone, knuckles whitening.

I quickly lock the screen, pressing my phone face down on the nightstand just as the bathroom door opens again.

Reed steps back in, a soft smile already there, unaware.

He crosses the room and settles behind me again, his arm sliding back around my waist like it never left.

"You win," he murmurs, kissing my shoulder. "I was gone for two minutes, and I already missed you."

I nod, forcing a smile, and lean back into him anyway, because his warmth still feels like safety, and right now I need that more than answers.

His lips brush my temple. "You okay?"

"Yeah," I say quietly. "Just editing."

He hums, satisfied, then presses a slow, sweet kiss to my shoulder again.

And I let him, holding on to the softness even as something sharp lingers just beneath it.

It's late afternoon, and I'm fucking spiraling.

I'm kneeling by the edge of his bed, rummaging through my backpack.

Golden light slants through the wide windows, casting long stripes across the hardwood floor and my open backpack that's practically mocking me right now.

Seven pairs of underwear, thank God. Two T-shirts, not enough, and a single pair of jeans.

I was in such a rush packing to get here, the excitement of being in Reed's arms again, that I basically grabbed whatever was in my dresser drawers and bolted.

Now I'm sitting here realizing I forgot most of my clothes, like an actual moron.

My chest feels rigid, not from panic exactly, but from the stupid, embarrassing wave of shame that hits when I imagine having to ask him to drive me somewhere.

I hate asking.

I've never been the girl who needs to be taken care of. I've always been the one who figures it out, who makes do, who pretends she's fine even when she's not. I take care of myself, I always have.

The floorboard squeaks as heavy footsteps come into earshot.

I don't turn around yet, as I keep staring at my backpack, like it might magically refill itself if I glare hard enough.

The sound of his footsteps halts in the doorway, and I softly hear the gentle clink of ice against a plastic, followed by the gentle thud of a cup set down on his dresser.

"Hey, sunshine," he says, walking closer towards me. "What's wrong?"

A wave of humiliation washes over me, my throat working as I try to swallow the emotions down.

Choosing not to look up, I stare at my hands in my lap. "I... I fucked up packing."

Nothing on his end, as his footsteps still, a tell he's waiting for me to continue.

I force my words out, quieter than I mean to. "I was so excited to get here that I just threw shit in my bag and left. I forgot almost everything. I've got like... three days' worth of clothes if I'm lucky."

It's silent for a beat before his footsteps move closer until my gaze lands on his tobacco brown, *Thorogood* leather boots.

He kneels in front of me slowly, as one knee hits the floor, followed by the other.

I finally lift my gaze, and there he is, kneeling in front of me, wearing a faded black T-shirt stretching across his shoulders, his burn scars on full display for *me*.

His hair is still a little messy from earlier, with that soft half-smile he only ever shows when it's just us.

He gently reaches out as his fingers brush my cheek first, tucking a strand of hair behind my ear.

"Come on," he says softly.

I blink, confused. "What? Why?"

He doesn't answer right away, as he keeps looking at me with this simple adoration that takes my breath away.

I never knew a man could look at me this way, not when I've been conditioned with anything but this.

He leans in, pressing a slow kiss to my forehead, before resting his forehead against mine. "I'll take you shopping, baby."

He'll what?

My eyes flutter shut, feeling the intense sting of tears rushing through.

No one has ever done this for me. Some may think, *"Well, Layla, it's just shopping."*

Well, it's never been as simple as just someone taking me somewhere because they want to. It's always Brian making me feel foolish for even asking, adding a sigh or an eye roll to make me feel small.

Brian would've laughed, then told me to figure it out on my own. My mom would've sighed and reminded me how scatterbrained I've always been.

But Reed... He kneels here, offering to take me like it's the most natural thing in the world to drop everything and fix something that's upsetting me.

A tear slips free before I can stop it, and I let out a shaky laugh, trying to play it off.

"You don't have to—"

"I want to," he says, pulling back to make eye contact, not giving me a chance to argue.

He reaches out, his thumb brushing beneath my eye, wiping away a tear.

I blink at him, watching his movements. Still in shock and awe, he's on his knees for me.

He shifts a little closer as his hand rests lightly against my knee while the other tucks that same piece of hair back behind my ear again.

"I want to take you to a boutique," he continues softly as his thumb traces an absent little circle against my knee, "or wherever the hell you want to go."

My chest constricts, my heart rate picking up rapidly.

"I want to carry your bags," he says, glancing at my backpack before looking back up at me, the corner of his mouth lifting just a little. "Watch you try on clothes."

My lip trembles, I can't fucking help it.

"No one's ever..." I start, having to stop because my

voice stutters. "No one's ever just... taken care of me like that. Without making me feel insignificant first."

His eyes soften even more, if that's possible, as he leans forward pressing his forehead to mine.

"You don't ever have to feel small with me," he whispers, lifting his hand to cup my face, gently stroking his thumb across my cheek. "Not once. Not ever. You're allowed to forget things. You're allowed to be messy. You're allowed to need something and... ask. Or don't even ask. I'll see it, and I'll give it to you."

Another tear trickles down my cheeks as I silently laugh through them.

"Okay," I whisper, covering my hand with his.

He gives me a genuine smile, causing his eyes to crinkle at the corners.

"Okay."

He stands, offering me his hand.

I look up at him before I take his hand as his fingers weave through mine.

Pulling me up gently, he presses a soft peck on my lips before retreating to the dresser.

He grabs the iced coffee from the dresser, the one he made me just because, and presses it into my palm.

"First things first," he says, his thumb brushing my knuckles. "Caffeine, clothes, then dinner.

A laugh escapes me as I get on my tippy toes and give him another gentle peck on the lips.

"Thank you," I whisper against his lips.

He kisses me back slowly, like he's saying you're welcome without words.

"Let's go, sunshine."

TWENTY-EIGHT
REED

Shopping with her went by in a fucking blur yesterday. She looked incredible in everything she tried on, and I can't take it anymore.

I should've taken her somewhere else to dim the urge to touch her, to kiss her more, but, if I'm being honest, my restraint died a quick, violent death the moment she walked back into my bar looking like a ray of beautiful sunshine.

She's straddling my lap on the couch, her knees hugging my hips like she belongs there.

My hands stay anchored to her waist, greedy for the feel of her warm skin beneath the thin shirt she stole from me.

Every kiss she gives me comes with a tiny sound in her throat she can't hide, and each one punches my control clean out of me.

I pull her closer, my hands tentative at first, tracing the curve of her waist.

My burn scars itch beneath my shirt; the twisted skin on my body is a constant reminder of the grief I carry, of how they changed my image and made me hate myself.

I fucking hate them, but with Layla, I don't hide them anymore.

She tilts her head as her lips brush mine in a soft kiss.

I cup her face, deepening the kiss as my tongue slides past her lips to intertwine with hers.

She moans softly, a sound that shoots straight to my cock, hardening beneath my sweats.

My hands roam lower, slipping under her shirt to feel the smooth heat of her skin. She arches into me, her fingers threading through my hair and pulling me closer.

She shifts her hips once, a careful roll that makes me moan into our kiss.

"Layla..."

"Reed," she whispers against my lips, breathless, her cheeks flushed pink.

I pull back just enough to look at her, my heart pounding.

She's so damn beautiful that I could stare at her for the rest of my days and be a happy man.

That's all I want, *life*, with her in it.

"Is this too much?" I mumble, my voice rough but steady. I'm not the talkative type, but with her, words came easier. "We can stop if—"

"No," she says quickly, her hand pressing against my chest, right over the scars hidden beneath. "I want this. I want you."

Her lips find the edge of my jaw, kissing lower, slower, as she gently nips at my neck.

My hands slide up her back as my fingers tangle in her hair so I can feel every shaky breath she exhales against my throat.

She pulls back again, looking at me with her pretty blue

eyes, honey and amber threads woven through them, as she stares, her pupils dilating.

"I want more, Reed."

The world narrows to her. To now. To us.

But she still has one foot tangled in another life in LA. And me? I still don't know if my scars are something she truly wants to see.

I murmur her name, a plea and a stall, "Layla..."

She lifts her hands to my face, forcing my gaze to meet hers. Her voice softens into something that strips me bare. "I want to see you. All of you."

Fuck. No one has ever asked me that.

For a beat, fear claws at my ribs.

She must sense the hesitation, because she rests her forehead against mine and whispers, "I'm not going anywhere."

I nod, trusting her.

Together, we reach for the hems of our shirts. Cotton slides over our skin as the fabric falls to the floor in two careless piles.

We stare, admiring each other's bare skin.

Her eyes sweep over the scars etched across my neck, chest, arms, ribs, and side—raised, jagged reminders of everything I lost.

I brace for pity, expecting her to be disgusted and walk away.

She extends her hand as her fingertip traces a long scar near my collarbone, leaning in and pressing her lips to the beginning.

She maps me with her lips, every mark the fire left behind, giving back something I didn't know I was missing.

"You survived this," she says quietly against my skin. "Every inch of you is proof."

I look away because the emotion hits quickly.

She takes my face in her hands again, grounding me with her stare. "You're beautiful," she whispers, so sure that it destroys every argument I've ever had about myself.

My touch trails up her sides again, watching goosebumps erupt across her skin, feeling each breath she takes.

I cup her jaw, guiding her mouth back to mine, kissing her unhurriedly, as if I'm finally letting myself believe her.

"You have no idea what you do to me," I mumble against her lips. "Every part of you... I could spend a lifetime admiring."

Her eyelashes flutter, her breath catching, and it's the prettiest thing I've ever seen.

She settles completely into my lap, her bare chest pressed against mine.

The sun spills over her bare shoulders, illuminating her as if she's meant to be seen.

I let my hands follow the lines of her, the curve of her waist, the delicate strength of her back, worshipping quietly with every touch.

"You're art," I tell her. "And I'm not sure I deserve to look."

She shakes her head as her thumb grazes my cheek. "You deserve someone who sees you. I do."

Fuck.

My fingers move up, tracing along the delicate curve of her breasts.

Her nipples pebble in the cool air, fuck me.

I lean down, taking one into my mouth, gently sucking while my tongue flicks over the tip.

She gasps, her back arching as she clutches my shoulders.

I palm both her breasts, putting my face between them,

alternating sides, sucking, nipping, and soothing her nipples with licks until she's squirming in my lap as her hips grind against the bulge in my sweats.

My cock's throbbing, aching to be free, but I want to take my time with her.

Guiding my lips back up to hers, I kiss her slowly, our tongues intertwining, allowing us to feel every pull and drag of our connection.

I pull her closer, as if she's the only air I'll ever need.

Her lips part as she whispers against mine, "I want you, Reed. Take me, please."

I rest my forehead against hers, breathing her in."If you want all of me," I whisper, voice wrecked and honest, "you've got it, baby."

Lifting her effortlessly, I give her ass a subtle squeeze as I carry her to the bedroom, laying her down on the rumpled sheets.

I watch her as she undresses completely, slipping off her pants and lace thong in one quick swoop, teasing me with her fingers as she rubs her clit in slow, sensual circles.

Swallowing hard, I make my way to her, covering her hand with mine, kissing her deeply, expressing my gratitude through touch.

Pulling back again, I admire her bare body; soft curves, smooth skin, her pussy already glistening with arousal as I part her thighs.

I pebble kisses along her throat, her tits, her tight stomach, before settling between her legs, my breath hot against her inner thigh. "I'm gonna taste you now, Layla," I say, looking up to meet her gaze. "Is that okay?"

"Reed, wait," she hesitates, running her fingers through my hair.

I'm just a breath away from her clit, drooling to get a

taste, but I pull back, meeting her worried stare. "What is it, sunshine?"

"N—no one has ever gone down on me."

What the fuck?

I stare at her, puzzled. What do you mean, a man hasn't taken the time to pleasure her? Has her fiancé never done this?

I press a kiss to her lower abdomen, "Let me take care of you, baby."

Her pulse jumps beneath my lips as I work my way lower, dragging my lips along the inside of her thigh.

She tastes faintly of honey, and I wouldn't mind suffocating between her thighs.

A soft whimper escapes her as she slides her fingers through my hair, holding me there like she's terrified I'll change my mind.

"Easy, baby," I murmur, kissing just above her sensitive spot. "I'm going to make you feel good."

Her thighs tense around my shoulders as she draws a sharp breath.

Looking up at her, I meet her eyes over the curve of her body.

"You sure you trust me with this?" I ask.

"I trust you with everything."

"If anything feels wrong, you tell me. We stop. No hesitation."

She nods, breath shaking. "Yes... I promise."

"Good girl," I say before I can think better of it.

I press another kiss just above where her thighs meet, my breath a warm brush across her sensitive skin. My thumbs massage slow circles into her hips as I spread her open for me, watching her chest rise too fast.

She bites her lip, but I catch her chin, guiding her gaze

back to mine. "No hiding from me," I whisper. "I want to watch you enjoy this."

She exhales, a light moan escaping past her lips.

Taking my glasses off and setting them on the floor, I bury my face between her thighs.

I start slow as my tongue licks up her sweet cunt, savoring her decadent taste.

She whimpers as her thighs tense, and I hook my arms under her knees, holding her open. "Breathe, baby," I coax, my voice muffled against her sweet pussy. "Open up for me, sunshine."

My tongue delves deeper, circling her clit with light flicks before gently sucking it between my lips.

Her hips buck, a cry escaping her, and I hum in approval, the vibration making her shiver.

"That's it," I murmur, pulling back just enough to speak. "Your pussy's so responsive for me, baby. So wet and eager to be tasted." I plunge my tongue inside her, fucking her with shallow thrusts, then return to her clit, lapping at it relentlessly.

I watch her face, adjusting my pace, sucking harder when she arches, easing off when she trembles too much. "Feel that?" I ask, sliding a finger along her entrance, teasing. "Gonna add a finger now. Push back against it, baby."

Sliding one finger inside her tight cunt, her walls already clench around me.

She's soaked, her juices coating my hand as I pump slowly, curling to hit her sweet spot that make her eyes roll back.

"Reed... oh God," she pants, her grip in my hair tightening.

"You're doing so well, baby," I praise, adding a second finger. My mouth returns to her clit, sucking in time with my thrusts. Her thighs quiver around my head, her breath coming in short bursts. "Come for me, sunshine. Let go."

"Reed!" she screams, arching her back off the bed, trembling under my hold.

Fuck, I love the way she says my name. I could listen to that sound forever.

Her pussy spasms around my fingers, flooding my mouth with her release as she cries out my name, her body trembling with each wave.

I don't stop until she tugs at my hair, oversensitive and gasping.

Withdrawing, I kiss my way up her body, tasting her release on her skin as I capture her lips. She kisses me hungrily, with no hesitation, her hands exploring my back.

My cock's rock-hard, leaking pre-cum against my sweats.

"Take it off, Reed."

I stare at her until I slowly peel off my sweats and boxers, tossing them aside as I wrap my fingers around the shaft and pump my cock, moaning with pleasure.

She lets out a gasp, staring at my hard cock leaking precum, watching me jerk off.

I reach for a condom in the nightstand, my hand brushing past the drawer's edge before her fingers circle my wrist, halting me.

"Reed," she whispers, her voice trembling. "I want to feel you." Her eyes meet mine, wide and glassy from the orgasm I just gave her. "I haven't slept with Brian in months," she adds, her breath shaky. "And I've been tested."

My throat tightens as I study her, every inch of trust she's offering.

"Layla..." My voice comes out rough. "Are you sure you want this?"

She nods, but I keep my hand on her cheek, needing her to see the truth in my eyes.

"I haven't been with anyone in years," I admit quietly. "Not since the accident."

Her eyes soften as her fingers trace the burn scars along my jaw and down my neck, sending goosebumps across my skin.

"I'm sure," she whispers.

I kiss her softly, positioning myself between her legs, lining up at her entrance.

Her eyes widen as she feels the head of my cock nudge her lips. "Reed... you're so big," she whispers, a hint of worry in her voice, yet her legs wrap around me, pulling me closer.

"Take a breath, baby. It'll fit," I coo, my voice low and reassuring as I rub the tip along her slickness. "Be a good girl and open up for me."

Inch by inch, I push inside, her heat enveloping me like velvet fire.

She's tight, so fucking tight, but wet enough that I slide deeper with each careful thrust. "There's my girl," I groan, bottoming out, my balls pressed against her ass. "Feel how perfect you fit around my cock?"

She nods, moaning, as her nails dig into my shoulders.

I begin to move, slow rolls of my hips building the rhythm. We find our pace together, her sunshine blending into my shadows, our bodies locked in the most intimate dance.

I hold still for a moment, buried deep inside her, letting her adjust to the stretch of my cock filling her. Her pussy clenches around me, pulling me in as if she never wants to let go.

Her eyes are half-lidded, her lips parted in a soft moan,

and I can't tear my gaze away from her stunning face—flushed, glowing, utterly wrecked in the best way.

I'm going to make her my wife, one way or another. She's going to be mine. I can't live without her, I can't breathe without her, and in this moment of our connection, I'm ruined for anyone else.

"Fuck, Layla," I groan, my voice gravelly as I start moving again, pulling out halfway before sliding back in with a slow, deliberate thrust. "You feel incredible. So tight, gripping my cock like you were made for me."

She whimpers, lifting her hips to meet mine as her hands glide down my back. "Reed... it feels so good. Please, don't stop."

Picking up the pace, my hips snap forward in a steady rhythm, each thrust bottoming out and grinding against her clit.

The bed creaks under us, its sound blending with the wet slap of our bodies meeting.

I lean down, capturing her mouth in a messy kiss, our tongues sliding together as I fuck her harder.

"You're perfect, baby," I mumble against her lips, breaking away to trail kisses along her jaw and neck. "Every inch of you."

She laughs, a breathless sound that turns into a gasp as I angle my hips, hitting that spot inside her that makes her eyes flutter.

"Reed! Yes, right there. You're... you're making me feel things I've never..."

"That's because you're mine now," I say, smirking down at her as sweat beads on my forehead.

My scars pull taut with each movement, but her hands roam over them freely, tracing the rough edges. It fuels me, making me thrust deeper, faster. "Gonna worship your body every chance I get. Lick it, fuck it, make you come over and over."

She moans louder, her legs wrapping tighter around my waist as her heels dig into my back. "Promise?" she says, her eyes sparkling even through the haze of pleasure.

"I promise, baby," I say, shifting to hook one of her legs over my shoulder, opening her up further. The new angle lets me drive in even deeper, my cock dragging along her walls with each plunge.

She cries out, her pussy fluttering around me, and I feel her building again, her breathing coming in pants.

"Look at you, taking my cock so well. You love it, don't you? Love how I stretch this pretty pussy?" I ask, gripping her ankle as I pound deeper into her.

"Yes, baby," she admits, biting her lip, her cheeks flushing bright red. "Give me more."

Her words send a shock through me, my balls tightening as I pound into her without mercy.

I worship her with my body and my praise as I lean down to suck on her neck, leaving more marks because I don't give a fuck.

"Your thighs," I rasp, gripping one and squeezing as I thrust, "wrapping around me." "This ass—" My free hand slips under her, cupping the soft curve, pulling her into each stroke—"so grabable, and your face when you come... gonna see it again, baby. Come with me."

The tension coils tight in my gut, her pussy squeezing me, milking my cock with every withdrawal.

She's close. I can feel it in the way her nails rake my shoulders, her moans turning desperate.

"Reed... I'm—oh God, I'm gonna—"

"Not yet," I command softly, slowing just enough to tease, circling my hips. "Wait for me, sunshine."

She nods frantically, her body trembling beneath me. "Please... I need it. I need you."

I ramp up again, fucking her with everything I have, the room filling with our gasps and the obscene sounds of her wetness coating my shaft.

My thumb finds her clit, rubbing firm circles to push her over. "That's it, baby. Let go. Where do you want it, Layla? Tell me."

Her eyes lock onto mine, wild and pleading. "Inside me. Please, give it to me."

I thrust deep one last time, my cock pulsing as I come, hot spurts flooding her pussy.

She clenches around me, her orgasm crashing over mine in waves, crying out my name as her body convulses, her slick mixing with my cum.

We ride it together as my forehead presses to hers, and aftershocks ripple through us both.

I collapse beside her, pulling her into my arms, our sweat-slicked bodies tangled together.

She kisses my chest, her gaze meeting mine. "I never knew it could feel like that."

I smile, caressing her jaw, leaning up to press a soft kiss to her forehead. "There's a lot you haven't been given, baby. I plan to fix that."

TWENTY-NINE
LAYLA

Today, I finally post what I've been working on.

This is it.

You've got this, girl.

I'm sitting cross-legged on Reed's bed, his sheets still wrapped around my hips as my laptop sits in front of me, the cursor blinking as if it knows how important this moment is.

He's half-asleep beside me, his hair a messy tangle, his mustache rasping against my skin as he nudges his head into my thigh.

He presses lazy kisses on my thigh, making it impossible to focus.

Shifting next to me, he reaches up, gently gripping my chin, guiding my mouth to his, giving me a soft kiss, mumbling. "Mornin', sunshine."

I can't help but smile as my hand automatically threads through his soft curls at the nape of his neck.

He exhales, as if that tiny touch is the best part of his day, and places another kiss on my thigh.

His arm wraps around my legs, pulling me closer as he

rests his head on my thigh, perfectly content. My heart does that stupid fluttering thing again, mixed with affection and guilt.

My finger hovers over the screen. All the footage from Boots & Bourbon and Ruby Ridge is coming together into a story I've been too afraid to tell.

But I promised myself I need to do this, to try this new content and see if it works, so I can finally pack my shit and leave Brian.

I take a deep breath through my nose, holding it for three seconds before letting it out slowly, my finger hovering for a second before I click upload.

The loading bar moves at a glacial pace until it finally uploads, and I swell with pride, but uneasiness fills my chest, making me skittish as pins and needles flood my fingertips.

"It's up," I whisper.

He lifts his head just enough to look at me, his sleepy green eyes locked on mine. "Yeah?" he asks, the corners of his mouth lifting into a small smile. "That's huge, Layla."

The nerves hit all at once. My hands grow slick with a clammy feeling, my heart races, and I suddenly feel like I'm going to get tunnel vision.

My throat tightens. "I'm terrified," I admit, my voice cracking as I face the truth I've been avoiding. "What if no one cares? Or what if they do and hate it? What if this is just another thing that falls apart and doesn't work out for me?"

His brows furrow, the protective edge emerging before he fully wakes. He shifts up to sit behind me, wrapping his arms securely around my waist as his chin rests on my shoulder.

"You're allowed to be scared," he mumbles against my shoulder. "Doesn't mean you don't do it anyway."

I lean back into him, letting the worry seep into the warmth of his touch.

His lips trail kisses on the side of my neck next. "I'm right here," he murmurs. "No matter what happens next."

And just like that, the fear doesn't go away... but it feels a lot smaller with him holding me.

I refresh the page once, twice, and three times.

Zero likes. Zero comments. Zero views.

Each zero punches a new hole through my confidence.

I cover my eyes with the heels of my hands, letting out another exhale.

"Hey," he says, brushing his nose against my shoulder. "That computer's not gonna bite."

I huff out a shaky breath, my fingers already poised to refresh again. "I just need to che—"

"Nope," he interrupts, as his lips find the spot right beneath my ear. The one that scrambles coherent thought. "You need to breathe."

His hands slide down my arms as his thumbs trace lazy circles on my wrists. He gently nudges my laptop shut with his knuckle.

I make a weak protest noise, since he's already kissing my neck, and it's maddening. "Reed..."

"Mmhmm?" he hums against the crook of my neck. "You know what'll happen? It'll do whatever it's supposed to. With or without you staring at it."

He turns me in his arms so I face him, my legs still crossed, his knees framing my hips as his palms rest at my waist.

My eyes trail along his clothed chest, the scars trailing

up his arms and around his neck, until I meet his gaze, a look of pure devotion in his eyes.

"But what if—"

He shuts me up with another kiss on my shoulder, one on my collarbone, then my lips.

"You did something brave this morning," he whispers.

My pulse leaps beneath his lips.

He leans back slightly, giving me that boyish half-smile that always feels like a secret shared just between us.

"You refreshing that page won't make the world spin any faster," he says quietly, kissing the underside of my jaw. "But this? I can make this morning a hell of a lot better."

He presses his forehead against mine, his breath warm, his voice softer than I've ever heard it. "Be here with me, just for a minute."

His fingers glide up my spine in a slow, unhurried path, sending warmth from my chest down to my toes. My anxiety loosens its grip.

Because he's right. Because he's here.

I curl my fingers into the front of his shirt, tugging him closer, and he smiles.

His hands slide up my hips, his fingertips tracing the line of my ribs as if he's memorizing me all over again, before he leans in, pressing a gentle kiss to the curve of my cheek.

"I'm proud of you," he murmurs, like it's the easiest truth he's ever said.

Another kiss, just below my ear. "And I'm honored you trusted me enough to share it."

His words sink deeper than any compliment ever could. My breath stutters, and he notices, continuing to trail kisses down the column of my throat, each kiss patient.

"You don't have to perform for the world today," he says quietly against my skin. "Just be here, with me."

His voice remains husky from sleep as he slips his arm around my waist, pulling me close to his chest until our heartbeats sync.

I feel him smile against my neck.

"You're enough without the views, without the numbers, without the followers, without any of it."

My eyes sting, just a tiny burn of emotion that catches me off guard.

He lifts his head and rests his forehead against mine as his thumb brushes the corner of my eye, keeping anything from falling.

"Look at me, baby."

I do. And it destroys me, the tenderness there, the confidence.

"You're brilliant," he says, his fingers tracing a gentle line along my jaw. "You're brave. You didn't need anyone's permission to prove it."

His lips meet the spot just below my collarbone, a delicate press that sends warmth blooming through my chest.

"I've got you," he whispers against my skin. "Every step. Every risk. Every scared part of you. I've got it all."

He pulls back just enough to see my face, his hand cupping my cheek, as his thumb strokes with slow reassurance. "So let the world do what it's gonna do," he finishes. "You just *breathe*."

My voice comes out barely there, but I manage, "Okay."

He smiles in relief and wraps both arms around me, pressing his face into my shoulder.

I melt into him, letting his steady warmth drown out the anxious noise in my mind.

For the first time in a long time, I feel safe choosing myself.

He repositions himself, holding me from behind, wrapping around me with his chest warm against my back.

For a while, I breathe him in; cedar, oakmoss, and a hint of smoke that clings to his clothes no matter how often he washes them.

It's comforting; it's something I look forward to every time I'm here and miss when I'm away.

My nerves creep back, tapping at the edge of my mind.

"What if..." I start, not sure how to finish.

He keeps a firm hold as he nuzzles into the curve of my neck, his voice soft. "Check it," he says. "I'm right here."

My laptop is only within arm's reach, yet lifting it feels like holding something that could explode in my hands. My fingers tremble as I open it, find the refresh button, and click it hesitantly.

My breath leaves me in a silent rush.

Thousands of views. Hundreds of comments. Notifications are flooding in faster than I can blink.

"O... oh."

His arms tighten around my waist as he settles his chin on my shoulder, looking at the screen with me.

Comments rush upward on the screen as I scroll through.

Omg, Layla, I LOVE THIS!!!

You look so happy???

Wait, who is that HOT bartender?? 👀🔥

This is the best content you've ever posted. Do MORE

Your energy is back, girl, keep going!!

Thank god Brian isn't in it; he's so boring.

My hand flies to my mouth. A sharp breath escapes,

half shock, half relief, and then a tear slides down before I can stop it.

"Hey..." He turns me slightly so he can see my face, his thumb already catching a tear. "What's that for?"

I shake my head, a watery laugh bubbling up. "I just... I've never had this kind of response before. Not this fast. Not...like this."

Not when Brian was in the video. Not when I was pretending to be happy. Not when I was acting like my life was perfect, or for some silly brand deal video.

My chest tenses, not from fear. For the first time... It's *hope.*

"They like me," I whisper, my voice trembling. "Just me. Not this version, I curated online, or the ones the brands prefer. I'm me, my true self, and they love it."

He brushes a strand of hair behind my ear, his touch gentle. "You are enough as you are," he reminds me. "You always were."

Another tear slips free, but this one feels like the release I've been holding back for years.

Maybe I can do this. Maybe I can leave. Maybe I don't have to stay with someone who treats me like nothing and only uses me for money.

My heart flips, and suddenly I become painfully aware of the man holding me, of how safe I feel, and of the future that doesn't include Brian.

He presses a slow kiss to my temple. "You don't have to decide anything today," he murmurs. "Just... don't sell yourself short. Not anymore."

I nod, swallowing hard, and lean into his chest like it's the only place I've ever belonged.

Because deep down I already knew the truth, I left Brian the moment I stepped into Reed's bar.

I just need the courage to bring it to life.

He shifts beside me, letting go of me, as a rush of cool air replaces his warm touch.

The mattress dips under his weight as he props himself up. The sheet slips from his chest, exposing the warm stretch of solid muscle along with the tattoos and scars that run across his arms, the ones he no longer hides as much.

Morning sun rushes in to find him, tracing the raised lines of his skin.

He rakes a hand through his hair, shaking off the sleep, that slight curl behind his ear refusing to behave, and something in my chest sighs softly.

Grabbing his glasses from the nightstand, he slides them onto his face with a practiced push on the bridge of his nose.

The lenses catch the light for a second, making him look like the world's hottest professor who moonlights as a brooding hero.

His thumb brushes across his mustache, smoothing it into place.

A tiny, unconscious motion... and I swear my bones turn to liquid. My mouth goes dry. My brain? Gone. Completely gone.

I try to be subtle about staring, but I fail spectacularly.

He doesn't look back when he says, voice still raspy with sleep, "Stop looking at me like that."

My pulse trips.

"I'm literally just sitting here," I whisper, but it sounds breathless, guilty, and not even close to convincing.

He pauses in the doorway, finally glancing over his shoulder, his eyebrow raised in clear amusement.

"Layla," he drawls, "if you keep staring at me like I'm something you want for breakfast, we're not gonna make it to the kitchen."

My whole face burns with desire, a rush of heat surging between my thighs, leaving me soaked.

I remember the intimate times we shared, how his mustache felt between my legs when he was kissing, sucking, fuck—.

Okay, Layla, reel it in.

He smirks, one he shows me only, his eyes glinting with that flirt he never explicitly says but always means. He turns again, disappearing into the hall, the scars on his arms shifting as he walks. He's shown me all of his scars, and that alone means everything to me.

From the kitchen, I hear the gentle clink of pans and the soft hum of a country tune slipping from his lips, rugged and sweet all at once.

The smell of coffee drifts down the hall, wrapping itself around the anxiety still buzzing in my veins.

I glance back at my laptop. The screen is a cascade of notifications; hearts, comments, excitement pouring in too fast to follow.

This is the Layla we love.

Girl, you're glowing.

More videos like THIS pleaseee.

My throat tightens, but this time it feels like relief. Like a new beginning.

I wipe under my eye before anything falls.

Reed hums louder, off-key in the cutest way, as the cabinet doors open and shut like someone who genuinely enjoys cooking breakfast for two.

For *us*.

I close my laptop slowly.

He's giving me space to breathe, while offering reasons to choose a different life.

One where I'm not invisible. One where being myself

isn't something I have to apologize for. One where a man looks at me like I could be home.

I pull the sheet tighter around me, steadying my heartbeat, before pushing myself up to stand. My feet hit his cool hardwood floors, and I follow the sound of him into the light.

Because I want to. Because I choose to.

Because Reed Hayes is starting to feel like a future I'm not afraid to want.

THIRTY
LAYLA

If happiness had a weight, I think it would feel like Reed's arm draped over my waist, his nose buried in my hair, and his sleepy breaths warming the back of my neck. I haven't stopped smiling since I opened my eyes.

Honestly? I'm not sure I had a genuine smile before him.

He moves behind me, his lips brushing the tip of my shoulder like a sleepy habit he's had forever.

I turn into his arms, and there he is, already staring at me with his messy hair and tired green eyes, smiling at me like I'm his favorite sight.

"Morning," he murmurs, sleep woven into his gravelly voice.

A smile touches my lips as I lean in and kiss him slowly.

I kiss him first on the lips, then trail kisses down the side of his neck, riddled with scars, until I trail them back up to meet his mouth again.

He lets out a low groan as I kiss him, sending a wave of butterflies through my body.

We must stay like that for twenty minutes, tangled up, exchanging lazy kisses, neither of us willing to break the spell.

My fingertips trace the strong line of his jaw, down his throat, and over the warmth of his chest.

He shivers and laughs softly. "I could wake up like this every morning, sunshine," he says, brushing my hair out of my face.

"Me too," I reply, pressing a kiss to the corner of his smirk.

His arm tightens around me as he presses his face into the crook of my neck, remaining silent.

We eventually drag ourselves out of bed because he apparently has plans for us. He tells me to get dressed and meet him out back, no hints, just that boyish grin he reserves for me.

He leaves the room once he's dressed. I quickly follow suit, throwing on black leggings and grabbing Reed's muted yellow flannel, my favorite.

I scuffle down the hall, barefoot, flying toward the screen door like an ape, and open it with such force that I'm shocked it didn't fly off the railing.

When I step outside, I stop dead, instantly feeling tears swell at my lower lash line.

He's set up a picnic blanket under a large oak tree, with a spread of food that feels like a brunch daydream.

Fresh fruit, croissants, sandwiches, and small pastries that smell divine. Two iced coffees cool in the sun, mine with vanilla, his with caramel.

And beside them?

Two blank canvases on small easels, and a complete set of paints, with colors ranging from neutrals to bright.

He stands there with his hands in his pockets, his glasses catching the sun, a shy smile tugging at his lips, as if he's unsure whether this is too much.

My heart somersaults and stops right here in this beautiful moment, with this gentle man watching me like I'm his whole world.

"Reed..." I breathe, already walking towards him.

"I know you fly back in soon," he says, voice softer now. "And I just wanted to spend today doing something that makes you happy."

I throw my arms around his neck because words aren't enough.

He laughs into my hair, his arms rising to hold me tight, squeezing gently as he kisses the top of my head.

"It's perfect," I whisper against his skin. "You're perfect."

He groans as his forehead rests against mine. "You keep saying things like that, I'll never let you leave."

Maybe that's the point, maybe I don't want to leave.

We settle onto the blanket, our knees brushing, our shoulders touching.

He hands me my iced coffee, and his thumb brushes the back of my hand as I take it.

"I'm soooooo excited!" I screech, staring at the blank canvas.

He dips a brush into the yellow paint and sketches a small sunflower in the corner of mine, a simple thing that shows he's been paying attention.

"Well, get to it, sunshine," he teases, leaning in to press a kiss to my cheek.

I just stare at him for a second, this quiet, gentle man who built a world in his backyard to keep me here a little longer.

The thought comes tumbling into my mind in this small, quiet moment.

If love looks like this?

If home feels like this?

I *never* want to leave.

Swirling my brush in pastel yellow, I try to pretend I'm focusing on the canvas rather than on how Reed sits beside me, his legs spread, shoulders relaxed, his arm warm against mine every time he moves.

He squints at his canvas as he paints.

"What are you painting?" I ask, sipping my iced coffee.

"A surprise," he answers, which... suspicious.

"Reed Hayes," I warn. "If that's a stick figure with a cowboy hat—"

He smirks but doesn't deny it.

"It's abstract," he says, seriously. "You wouldn't get it."

I gasp dramatically, smirking. "You're starting to sound like Catalina."

He chuckles, a deep, warm sound that sends vibrations down my spine, before dipping his brush into bright green paint, suspiciously.

I narrow my eyes. "Don't even think about—"

His brush taps the tip of my nose with a perfect neon dot.

I freeze.

He freezes.

Then he laughs, this deep baritone laugh that's so unfiltered, raw, and real, and it's something I could listen to forever. This man has burrowed his way into my heart, and I never want to let him go.

"Oh!" I say sweetly. "War!"

Before he can react, I swipe my brush across his forearm, leaving a streak of sky blue on his warm skin and over his scar-ridden tattoos.

His eyes go wide. "You did not just—"

I'm already scrambling back, giggling, because yes, yes, I did.

He lunges playfully, and I scream-laugh, waving my paintbrush as he gently tackles me onto the blanket.

"Say you're sorry," he demands, waving his brush over my cheek.

"Never," I reply.

He lines a streak of yellow along my jaw. I leave a pink handprint on his chest. He strikes my upper arm with turquoise. I smear lavender across his jaw.

We're a mess. A colorful, giggling, gorgeous mess.

I can't breathe from laughing, my cheeks flushed, heart so full it might burst.

He's still leaning over me, both of us breathless, staring at each other, paint smeared all over, grinning like idiots.

"You started that," he says, brushing his nose against mine.

"You asked for it," I whisper back.

His smile softens as his eyes dip to my lips, then back up.

"You're dangerous," he murmurs.

"Dangerously hot," I shoot back.

"Yeah, you are, baby," he answers immediately.

My laugh softens into something quieter yet more expansive.

He's still hovering over me, his hand resting on my hip, his thumb idly stroking paint across my skin.

I reach up and trace the edge of his glasses, slightly crooked from our chaos, nudging them straight again.

He watches me like no one else exists.

He looks at me like I'm his whole future.

And for the first time in so long, I want a future too.

He flops beside me on the blanket, laughing—really laughing—like his whole chest is finally free to breathe again.

We're both covered in paint. The canvases are a joke, and breakfast is probably warm by now, but none of it matters.

I can't stop touching him as my fingers trail from his arms, feeling his ridged skin, to his jaw, the subtle shadow of his trim beard. I swirl my fingers through his mustache before caressing his lower lip.

"I'm gonna go wash up real quick," I tell him, still grinning like an idiot.

He catches my wrist and pulls me into a soft kiss that steals the edges of my smile. "Hurry back," he murmurs, his thumb brushing my cheek.

My stomach does this wild swoop I'm still not used to.

I slip inside and close the bathroom door behind me, my heart doing cartwheels.

Placing my phone on top of the toilet, I lean over the sink, trying to scrub paint from my cheek, when my phone lights up and keeps lighting up.

Buzz. Buzz. Buzz.

Buzzbuzzbuzzbuzzbuzz—

My smile fades.

Brian has left me forty-six texts. I haven't really heard from him, and now, he's spiraling.

I wince as I grab my phone, my nerves racing, making my breathing come in shallow bursts.

BRIAN

So this is what you call work now?

Another arrives before I can breathe.

BRIAN

Filming trash in some small town?

Trying to look relevant?

I swallow the knot in my throat, tremors running through my body.

BRIAN

I saw your stupid video.

You fucking him?

My stomach turns into an endless pit of nerves.

BRIAN

He's a freak, and those scars make him look fucking disgusting.

That's your new content?

You're ruining what we built.

Waves of pins and needles radiate throughout my body, making my hands tremble with anger, fear, and *guilt*.

BRIAN

You wouldn't have a platform without me.

Don't start thinking you can do this alone.

A lone tear escapes before I can stop it.

Ping. Ping. Ping.

BRIAN

Delete it.

Now.

I finally break. A quiet sob escapes my lips, but just as quickly, my palm shoots up, covering my mouth, so Reed doesn't hear me in case he walks back inside.

BRIAN

You're mine.

We'll fix this when you get home.

He tries to call me, but I decline his call as another text pings through.

BRIAN

Answer your fucking phone when I call you.

My phone vibrates violently in my palm again.

Incoming call from Brian.

I hit decline, again.

I suddenly feel insignificant again, shrunken into the tiny version of myself he created, maintained, and prodded around when it suited him.

A soft knock breaks through the panic.

"Layla?" he says softly. "You okay in there, baby?"

I squeeze my eyes shut, my breath fractured. "Yes," I force out, my voice barely working. "Just... one second."

"Alright," he says quietly. "I'm right out here."

He's not asking questions; he's not pushing. He just waits patiently, as he always does.

My phone buzzes again, with more vicious messages sliding across the screen, and something inside me buckles under the weight of my two worlds colliding.

One life shaped by lies and fear, and another by hope and genuine love.

My gaze lifts to the mirror as I stare into my reflection.

Paint still smears my cheek where Reed touched me. My lips are swollen from his kisses. My eyes are soft, happy, and alive in a way Brian has never seen.

And for the first time… I'm not terrified of losing him. I'm afraid of going back.

THIRTY-ONE
REED

She leaves in two days, and I wanted to take her out on that "date" she declared when we were out by the wild sunflower patch.

"You gotta trust me," I say, keeping my eyes on the road even as I feel her watching me.

She narrows her eyes anyway. I can hear it in her voice. "I don't like that tone."

"It's a good tone," I argue. "A trustworthy one."

She laughs nervously. "That's exactly what someone says before a surprise I'm not emotionally prepared for."

I reach over and rest my hand on her thigh, grounding us both. Her skin is warm beneath my palm, familiar already in a way that still catches me off guard.

She studies my face, glancing down as my hand settles on her thigh.

Her hand moves to mine, instantly warming my skin as her fingers curl around mine.

"Okay," she says, smiling to herself. "I trust you, which feels bold of me."

I huff a quiet laugh. "It's earned."

"Debatable," she murmurs, but her thumb begins tracing slow lines over my knuckles.

The road stretches out as I keep driving.

I keep pretending my chest isn't doing that thing it does when she touches me like this, like she's chosen me without making a big deal of it.

"Is this a close-your-eyes surprise?" she asks.

"No," I say immediately.

She looks relieved. "Good. I hate those."

"Yeah," I agree.

She laughs and squeezes my hand again. It does something to me. Settles me and wrecks me all in the same breath.

"You okay?" she asks, glancing over, like she can feel the shift.

"Yeah," I say, honestly. "Just glad you're here."

Her smile softens as she leans back into the seat, still holding my hand.

I guide us down the road, heart full and steady, already knowing—whatever's waiting up ahead, the best part is right here.

She keeps her hand wrapped around mine as we drive, her thumb continuing to trace those slow, absent lines over my knuckles.

The road narrows, trees closing in just enough that the world feels smaller and quieter.

She tilts her head toward the window, watching the dark roll by. "You're being very calm for someone who has a surprise."

"That's because I've already seen your face when you're happy," I say. "I'm not worried."

She snorts softly. "That's unfairly confident."

I glance over at her, the dash lights catching the curve of

her smile and the way her eyes flicker when she's trying not to overthink.

She squeezes my hand, and my heart squeezes in that quiet way it's been lately.

We crest a small hill, and I feel her notice the change before she sees it.

Her grip tightens just a little. "Reed," she says softly.

I ease my truck forward, the old theater sign coming into view, washed in that faint, nostalgic glow.

"Oh," she says quietly. "You remembered."

"Of course I did."

I pull into a parking spot and cut the engine.

The night settles around us as crickets chirp, distant murmurs, and the low crackle of a speaker warming up nearby.

I don't move my hand from her thigh, not yet.

She turns to look at me, really looks at me, her eyes bright in that way that makes me feel like I've done something right.

"I didn't think—" She stops, shaking her head as she laughs under her breath. "I didn't think you'd actually do it."

"You asked."

Her fingers lace tighter with mine, and she leans slightly toward me, her shoulder brushing my arm.

"I like that about you," she says. "You listen."

I squeeze her hand back gently. "I like that you notice things."

She smiles, resting her head against my shoulder before we get out of the car and head inside.

The theater is emptying around us; murmurs, footsteps, the occasional cough.

We stay in our seats, shoulders brushing, her pinky hooked loosely around mine under the armrest, as if neither of us wants to be the first to break contact.

Eventually, she turns her head just enough for me to catch the small, private smile she's trying to hide.

"Ready?" she asks quietly.

I nod. "Yeah."

We walk out together, taking our time as my hand finds the small of her back again. She leans into it just enough that I feel her warmth through the thin cotton of her sundress.

Outside, the sky is clear, and the moon is full, spilling silver across the asphalt.

My truck is parked at the far edge of the lot, away from the lights. We make our way there, and I open the passenger door for her.

She climbs in, the hem of her dress riding up her thighs as she settles. I shut the door, circle around, and slide behind the wheel.

I don't reach to press the button to start the engine, not yet.

Moonlight pours through the windshield, catching on the dashboard, the steering wheel, and her.

She's already half-turned toward me with her leg tucked under her as moonlight slides across her cheekbones, pooling in the hollow of her throat, and turning her eyelashes into soft shadows.

Her lips are still a little swollen from how she kept biting them during the quiet scenes. Her hair is messy from how she kept pushing it behind her ear every time, a nervous cue I've come to love.

I can't look away.

She catches me staring, of course she does.

"What is it?" she asks, her voice soft and teasing, but there's a tremor beneath it as she lifts her eyebrow.

"Nothing," I lie.

"Bullshit." She tilts her head, moonlight slipping down the side of her neck. "What's going on in there?" She taps her temple, then points at mine.

I let out a breath that's more shudder than exhale. "You really want to know?"

"Yeah." Her voice drops. "I really do."

I reach over to her as my fingers find the side of her face, and my thumb brushes the corner of her lips.

Her breath seizes as her eyes flutter half-closed.

I lean in, and our mouths meet like we've done it a thousand times, because with her, everything feels so familiar. With her, I feel complete. With her, I feel like we're on the same frequency, and fuck, I can't get enough.

My heart beats with hers, always hers.

She opens for me immediately, tasting of buttered popcorn, cherry ChapStick, and want.

I groan low in my throat; the sound vibrates between us, and she answers with a small, broken whimper that goes straight through me.

My other hand slides to the back of her neck, as my fingers thread through her hair, tilting her head so I can take more.

I pull back just enough to breathe as I press my forehead to hers, our noses brushing.

Our lips are so close I can feel every shaky exhale we both take.

"I don't want you to go." I rasp.

Her fingers curl into my shirt, right over my heart. "Then, keep kissing me."

I kiss her again, harder, more desperate.

She makes a needy little sound and climbs halfway into my lap without breaking contact, as her knee is braced on the seat between my thighs.

Her hands slide up my chest, as her nails scrape lightly through my flannel, then into my hair, tugging just enough to make my scalp sting.

I growl and nip her bottom lip, sharp enough to make her gasp, soft enough to make her arch closer.

"Fuck, Layla," I mutter against her lips. "You have no idea how long I've wanted you."

"Since our hot kiss on the couch?" she whispers, voice trembling but sure.

"Before that," I whisper, peppering kisses along her jaw and down her throat. "Since the first night you walked into Boots & Bourbon."

She stills, just a little, enough for me to feel it.

I pull back, looking at her as rays of moonlight catch the sheen of tears in her eyes.

Glancing down at the little flower pattern on her sundress, bunched between us, my gaze travels back up to her face, brushing a strand of her blonde hair behind her ear.

"You were laughing, your hair was styled in a high ponytail that I fucking love, wearing that sundress that hugged you just right." I continue, swallowing hard, as my palm slides to the small of her back, my thumb tracing slow circles. "I was behind the bar, wiping glasses I didn't need to, and I couldn't tear my gaze away from you."

My forehead drops to hers, my glasses nudging her cheek as I breathe her in, vanilla frosting and cherry sweetness wrapped up in one woman who feels like sunlight in my hands.

"I kept telling myself not to stare," I mumble, my fingers curling into the fabric at her hips when she shifts closer. "Told myself you were just Catalina's friend." I let out a shaky laugh, my nose brushing hers. "But then you smiled at me, baby, and I was gone for you."

I tilt my head, pressing a slow kiss to the corner of her mouth before pulling back just enough to look at her, as my thumb strokes the soft skin under her lip.

"I think... I've been yours since that night," I whisper, my hand sliding up her back to cradle the nape of her neck, holding her gently. "I just didn't know how to admit it."

Her breath comes in quick, shallow beats as her fingers tighten in my hair.

"I watched you all night," I keep going, my hands resting warm on her thighs. "Every time you laughed. Every time you tucked your hair behind your ear. Every time you licked a drop of tequila from your lip."

My breath shakes as I lean back against the seat, looking at her like she hung the fucking stars outside my windshield. "I hated every second you weren't looking at me, and when you finally did, when your eyes found mine across the bar, and you smiled, I felt it here."

I take her hand gently, guiding it to my chest, pressing her palm flat against my heart, where it's pounding too hard. "Like a hook, like you'd already caught me, and I didn't even fight it."

She's crying now, her tears cascading slowly down her cheeks, catching the moonlight spilling through the truck window, and my chest caves in at the sight.

"Then I found out you were engaged," I say quietly, lifting my hand to her face as my thumb brushes beneath her eye, wiping the tear before it falls, my knuckles grazing her cheek as I cup her jaw.

She inhales sharply, her lips trembling, and I keep my touch there.

"I saw the ring," I continue, my jaw tightening as my thumb traces the faint imprint it left on her skin. My fingers hover for a second, drifting down to lace with hers, squeezing her hand. "Saw the way you twisted it when you were nervous."

My free hand drops to hers instinctively as my fingers close around her knuckles, pulling them to my mouth so I can press a quiet kiss there, needing the contact more than air.

"It fucking killed me, Layla." My voice roughens, the words dragged from my chest while my other hand slides up her back, spreading warmth.

"Every single day since then has felt like breathing around a knife, knowing you were promised to someone else, knowing I had no right to want you like this, knowing I should stay away." I shake my head once, pressing my forehead to her collarbone, my glasses nudging her skin as I let out a broken breath. "And failing at that every time I looked at you."

I pull back, leaning in again to brush my lips along the tear track on her cheek as my hand cradles the back of her neck to keep her close.

"But I couldn't," I whisper against her skin, my nose grazing hers when she tilts toward me. "I still can't. You're in my head every time I close my eyes. You're the first thing I think of when I wake up."

My thumb strokes her jaw gently. "You're my light, baby. The only bright thing in all this gray. And yeah, it fucking tears me apart that you're wearing his ring, that you go home to him, that he gets to wake up next to you."

My hand tightens in the fabric at her waist, holding her like she's already slipping away. "But I'll wait. I'll wait as long as it takes."

I pull back just enough to look at her, brushing her tears away with both thumbs, my voice softer now, steadier, even though my heart's breaking open in my chest.

"Because even if it's just stolen nights, stolen kisses in my truck, stolen days when you're mine"—my forehead drops to hers as my breath mixes with hers—"I'll take them. I'll take whatever you can give me. Because you're worth every second of the ache."

Her sob is soft, muffled against my shoulder as she buries her face there. Her arms wrap tightly around my neck.

"I don't want you to wait forever," she whispers, voice cracking. "I don't want to keep hurting you."

I pull her closer, as my hand cradles the back of her head, the other splayed across her lower back.

"Then don't," I murmur into her hair. "Whenever you're ready, whenever you choose, come to me. And I swear, Layla, I'll spend every day making sure you feel loved, appreciated, fuck, I'll give you everything I have."

She lifts her head. Her eyes are red-rimmed and shining, yet there's a fierce look in them now.

"I'm scared," she admits, barely audible.

"I know, baby." I brush my thumb under her eye, catching another tear. "Me too, but I'm more scared of never fucking having this; of never knowing what it feels like to love you out loud."

She searches my face for a long moment before she leans in and kisses me, her lips trembling against mine.

Pulling back just enough to speak, she brushes her lips against mine with each word.

"I don't know how to do this yet," she breathes. "But I want you. I've always wanted you, and I'm tired of pretending I don't."

I cup her face with both hands, as both of my thumbs stroke her cheekbones.

"Then don't pretend," I say against her mouth. "Not with me. Not anymore."

She nods.

I kiss her again, longer this time, savoring every slide of her tongue against mine, every soft sound she makes when I nip her bottom lip, every time her hips shift and press closer.

My hands roam down her back, over her hips, up her sides, learning the shape of her body like I've been starving for years.

Because I fucking have been.

THIRTY-TWO
REED

The front porch light casts a honey glow over Layla as she slides her sunflower helmet into place, blonde waves escaping in wild little tendrils around her cheeks.

God, she's radiant. There isn't a word to describe Layla LeBlanc's beauty; she's a unique kind.

I take a moment to breathe in my surroundings—her smile, the only thing that brings light into my life.

Her eyes reflect the dark sky behind me like it's full of constellations just for her.

It takes effort to look away long enough to wheel my BMW S1000RR out of the garage. Its matte-black body gleams under the moonlight.

The engine comes alive with a deep growl that vibrates beneath my hands.

She inhales sharply behind me, running over as she lets out a small, almost-squeal, her excitement impossible to hide.

Her hand slides down my lower back as she settles into the seat, her legs hugging my hips. She molds to my spine, like we are two puzzle pieces made for each other.

She leans in, speaking through the helmet's Bluetooth. "Take me somewhere the world can't find us."

I don't even respond as I twist the throttle.

We glide down the driveway, gravel crunching under the tires, hitting the pavement as the wind glides past us.

It howls past our helmets, carrying the scent of pine, wildflowers, and a hint of smoke from someone's distant bonfire.

The deep blue sky folds around us as endless, freckles of starlight scatter amongst it.

Her laughter bursts free, wild and genuine.

A sound I'd chase anywhere.

The engine hums steadily beneath us, seven thousand RPMs and rising, its vibrations traveling through my hands, up my arms, into my chest. I shift gears, and the bike roars.

Her arms tighten around me, gripping with excitement.

She swivels her head, taking in our surroundings, her visor reflecting passing headlights, quick flashes of silver across sunflower fields.

We carve through the curves of back roads, the world just the line of asphalt lit by our headlights and the warm press of her body.

A pure, unfiltered scream escapes her as she laughs even louder.

I swear, just hearing her laugh can erase any negative thought I've had about myself.

She's not thinking about anything else.

Right now, she's just here with *me.*

I take a turn that opens into a long straightaway, a stretch of road where I know it's safe to give us a little more.

Leaning into the throttle, I accelerate, going faster, feeling the speed increase, my adrenaline rising every time the speedometer increases.

She gasps, tightening her arms around my waist as her hips press closer to my back. Her helmet softly knocks against mine as she presses herself between my shoulder blades.

I know she's smiling beneath her helmet, I can feel it.

We are speed, night, and two hearts syncing to the same wild rhythm. And as the wind carries her laughter into the stars, a truth hits me deeper than any spark, kiss, or touch ever could.

This woman is the first breath I've taken in years that truly feels like air.

With one hand steady on the throttle, I reach behind with the other, sliding my palm along her thigh as my thumb gently brushes against the denim of her jeans, a silent promise that I'm here, that she's safe.

She responds instantly, tightening her arms around my waist and pressing her chest even closer.

For a moment, everything else disappears.

"You good back there, baby?" I ask through our helmets' Bluetooth.

Her helmet dips toward me, answering me with a nod as she taps twice on my hip, our code; more.

I smile into the night and angle my wrist, my hand gliding along the curve of her leg again before settling back on the bars as I shift down into the turn.

Her fingers tighten in the back of my shirt, like that small touch just rewrote her entire world.

And maybe... maybe it rewrote mine, too. Because damn, I don't want to stop touching her, hearing her laugh, or feeling her pulse against me like this.

I want more, damn it. I want everything with her. But she needs to leave him when she's ready, and I'll be here, waiting for her like the next sunrise, because she's my light, my next breath, *mine.*

The night surrounds us, its cool breeze enveloping our bodies.

Opal Springs sign comes into view, and I turn left, making my way to the lake.

Sapphire Lake remains still, reflecting the kind of sky only visible this far from the city. Crickets sing softly from the tree line, while the air smells of pine, cool water, and the faint sweetness of primrose surrounding the lake.

I park my bike and stabilize it with the kickstand. Swinging my leg over, I reach for her, helping her down as my other hand rests on her waist.

Once she's off the bike, we remove our helmets and walk hand in hand toward the water.

She sits cross-legged beside me on the blanket I laid out, kicking off her shoes, her hair still a little tangled from the ride. She's painting something invisible across her knee with her fingertip; a habit I've come to learn when she's thinking too hard.

"What's going on in your head, sunshine?" I ask.

She glances over, smiling faintly. "You wouldn't want to know."

"Try me."

Her shoulders lift in a gentle shrug. "Just thinking about how some people feel... familiar. Like you've known them forever, even when you haven't."

I do, and you're my person.

Something shifts in my chest, just a steady tug that's been there since the first night she tumbled into my bar with Catalina, laughing too loud.

"I know what you mean," I respond. "Feels like this click, this pull, where you just know."

That earns me a small smile as she tucks her hair behind her ear, and I can't stop watching her, the way moonlight paints her ivory skin, giving me a glimpse of the small beauty mark on her neck that I've come to love.

I move closer, at a pace slow enough for her to stop me if she wants to. She doesn't.

"You ever think," I murmur, "that some people are just meant to find each other? No matter how many wrong turns they take?"

Her gaze shifts to mine. "You mean like soulmates?"

Yes.

I nod once. "Yeah. I believe there's always that one person for someone."

Her lips part, but she doesn't speak, continuing to look at me like I've said something she's been waiting her whole life to hear.

I reach out, my fingers tracing the curve of her jaw and the soft skin at her throat. She leans into my touch instinctively, her eyes fluttering shut.

"Layla," I whisper.

I kiss her slowly, as if I'm trying to memorize the shape of every breath between us. Her lips are warm, trembling, with a faint taste of vanilla.

She exhales into me, her hand sliding into my hair, the slight scrape of her nails sending a shiver down my spine.

We break apart, she laughs softly, not out of humor, but from disbelief.

"What?" I ask, brushing my thumb over her bottom lip.

"I didn't know it could feel like this," she says, her voice barely above a whisper. "Like we've done this before."

I rest my forehead against hers, our noses touching as our breath mingles. "Maybe we have," I murmur. "Just took a while to find each other again."

Her smile jitters, and I kiss her again, deeper this time, until everything else fades away—the lake, the crickets, even the air.

There's only her, pressed close as her hands slide up my chest until she's holding my face.

We stop kissing, catching our breath, and she doesn't pull away.

She remains right there, pressing her forehead against mine, breathing steady against my lips.

"I think I believe you," she whispers.

"About what?"

"Soulmates."

I grin. "Good."

She laughs softly against my lips, then kisses me again under the kind of moonlight that makes a man believe in fate.

THIRTY-THREE
REED

She's buzzing with adrenaline; I can feel it in the way her fingers curl into my flannel, the way her breath comes hot against my neck when she leans in close.

I swing off my bike first, pulling the helmet from her head, and watch her shake out her blonde waves until it falls wild around her shoulders.

Her cheeks are flushed pink, eyes bright and reckless in the moonlight.

"Get inside, baby," I growl, voice rough from the wind. "Before I lose my patience and take you right here on the bike."

She bites her lip, that little smile tugging at the corners, but she slides off, her legs a little unsteady, and I grab her hand, pulling her up the steps to the front door.

My keys fumble in the lock as her body presses against my back, her hands already slipping under my flannel as her nails scrape lightly over my abs through my shirt.

I push the door open as we stumble into the hallway, lit only by the faint glow from the kitchen light I left on.

Kicking the door shut behind us, I spin her around and pin her against the wall with my hips.

Her gasp turns into a moan as I crush my mouth to hers, our tongues tangle as if we've been starving for this all night.

"God, Reed," she whispers against my lips as her fingers yank at my flannel buttons. "Baby, I want you so bad, I'm wet already."

A low groan vibrates in my throat as I continue shrugging off my flannel, letting it hit the floor. "Good, means you're ready for what I'm about to do to you, sunshine."

Her hands tug at the hem of my shirt, pulling it up over my head in one swift motion.

I help, tossing it aside, my fingers reaching aimlessly for her top, a thin tank that's been teasing me with glimpses of her lace bra all night.

Peeling it off slowly, I savor the way goosebumps erupt across her skin, the way her nipples harden through the white lace before I even touch them.

"Fuck, you're beautiful," I mutter, palming one breast as my thumb circles the peak until she arches into me. "Been thinking about stripping you down since you climbed on behind me."

She laughs and reaches for my belt. "Then stop talking about it, and do it."

We move down the hall, kissing, groping, shedding clothes in a trail behind us.

Her bra unclasps easily under my fingers; I drag the straps down her arms, as my lips follow the contour of her neck, sucking to leave a mark just above her collarbone.

She unbuckles my belt, yanks the zipper down, shoving my jeans and boxers low enough that my cock springs free; hard, aching, already leaking for her.

"Jesus, Reed," she breathes, wrapping her hand around

me, stroking once from base to tip. "You're so fucking hard. Did the adrenaline get you, too?"

I hiss through my teeth, thrusting into her fist. "You think? Been fighting myself not to pull over and bend you over the bike."

Her jeans button pops under my fingers until the denim pools at her ankles. Pushing the lace aside, I slide two fingers between her thighs, finding her soaked, her clit swollen, and begging for attention.

She moans, her head falling back against the wall. "Then why didn't you?"

"Because I want you in my bed," I say, curling my fingers inside her, my thumb pressing circles on her clit until her hips buck. "I want to spread you out and take my time."

She kisses me, not saying a word, as she threads her fingers in my hair, continuing down the hallway.

Barely making it to the bedroom door somehow, her hand still strokes my cock, my fingers still buried in her pussy.

I shove the door open with my shoulder, backing her toward the bed.

She lets go of me, sitting on the edge of the bed as she quickly throws her panties off.

Spreading her legs, her eyes are dark and hungry as she watches me kick off my boots and jeans completely.

"Glasses," she says, voice husky, reaching up to slide them off my nose. "Don't want them fogging up."

Leaning in, I let her take them off before she sets them on the nightstand.

I gently push her back onto the mattress. She scoots up, her head hitting the pillows as her thighs part wider in invitation.

"Fuck, look at you," I say, kneeling between her legs as my hands slide up her thighs, spreading her open. "So wet for me, baby. You ready for me?"

She nods, threading her fingers through my hair.

Fuck me.

I lower my head, my breath hot against her clit. "Spread wider, baby."

She spreads wider, her laugh turning into a gasp as I slowly lick her from entrance to clit. She tastes so fucking sweet.

I do it again, savoring as I circle her clit with the tip of my tongue.

"Fuck!"

I suck gently, then harder, feeling her thighs tremor against my ears. "You taste so fucking good, baby. I could never tire of having my face between your legs."

She tugs my hair, her hips lifting off the bed. "Don't stop, baby. Please, your mouth—"

I slide two fingers inside her, curling them against her sweet spot, making her back arch. My tongue flicks faster, relentless, as I pump my fingers deep inside her.

"You gonna come for me like this?" I mumble against her clit, the vibration making her whimper. "Gonna soak my mustache before I even fuck you?"

"Yes, Reed, fuck, yes—"

I add a third finger, stretching her, as I suck her clit hard. She shatters, her body seizing, as her pussy clenches around my fingers in rhythmic pulses, her arousal coating my tongue.

Her cry echoes off the walls, my name coming out in broken gasps.

I lick her through it, gently now, until she's twitching

and oversensitive, pushing at my head with a breathless laugh.

"Too much, come here."

I crawl up her body, pebbling kisses as I drag my hard cock against her thigh.

"Don't you dare think we're finished," I murmur, nipping at the delicate column of her throat. "That was the first one, baby. I'm not stopping until you can't say my name without shaking."

She gives me a weak nod while trembling beneath me, her thighs spread wide, pussy still fluttering.

I notch myself at her entrance, but I don't push in yet, letting her feel the blunt pressure.

"Look at me, sunshine," I murmur.

Her eyes snap to mine, pupils blown wide as she sucks in a breath.

"I'm gonna go slow," I tell her, caressing her lower lip. "I want you to feel every inch. I want you to count them for me, out loud. Can you do that, baby?"

She nods fast, biting her lip. "Yes, please—"

I flex my hips, pushing just the tip inside.

"One," she gasps, her voice high and shaky as she digs her nails into my shoulders.

I groan, fighting the urge to push all the way in. "Good girl. Feel that? That's just the tip stretching you."

I ease in another inch slowly, watching her face the whole time. Her mouth falls open, her eyes fluttering.

"Two," she breathes.

"Fuck." I rock gently, letting her adjust. "Look how pretty you open up for me, taking me so sweet already."

Pushing another inch slowly, she whimpers as her walls flutter hard around me.

"Three," she manages, her voice cracking, her hips canting forward, begging for another inch.

I lean down, kiss her slowly as my tongue slides against hers while I feed her another inch.

"Four," she moans into my mouth. "Reed, fuck, you're so—"

"Shhh," I whisper against her lips. "You're doing so well, love."

Pushing another inch, her pussy grips me tightly; she's so wet I can hear it every time I move.

I pause, grinding in a slow circle, letting her feel me press against her sweet spot deep inside.

"Five," she sobs softly. "Five, fuck, I can feel you everywhere—"

I kiss her temple, her cheek, and the corner of her eye where a tear slipped free. "You're perfect. So fucking perfect. Almost there, baby."

With just a fraction of a pull back, I sink deeper inside her. Her back arches off the mattress, her thighs trembling against my hips.

"Six," she chokes out. "Reed, please, I need—"

"I know what you need, baby," I murmur, brushing a stray hair from her forehead. "One more. Give me one more, and I'll fuck you the way you've been begging for."

I roll my hips slowly, feeding her the last inch until I'm buried deep, my balls pressed tight against her ass, every inch of me inside her.

"Seven," she cries, voice breaking on the word. "Seven, oh my God—"

I rest my forehead against hers, breathing hard, shaking from how good she feels. "There's my pretty girl," I say, kissing the slope of her neck.

"You did so well, baby." I continue, moving in slow

strokes. "That's it. All of me. Every fucking inch stretching this perfect little pussy. Feel how full you are of me?"

She nods frantically, tears slipping down her temples. "So full. Ca-can't think–"

"You don't have to think," I whisper, pulling out, then back in, letting her feel every inch. "Just feel me, baby. My cock has been aching for you all night."

She moans as her hips rock up to meet me on the next thrust.

"Fuck, you feel so good, baby," I tell her, pressing my forehead against hers.

Her walls clamp down hard with my praise.

She sobs my name as her nails rake down my back. "Reed, please, harder–"

I kiss her deeply, swallowing the sound she makes as I pick up the pace, just enough to make the headboard tap the wall, just enough to make her feel every thick inch claiming her.

"Let me hear you," I growl against her mouth.

"Reed, I-"

She's already shaking again, and I know she's close again. I memorized the way her body weeps for me.

"Come for me," I rasp, burying myself deeper, my cock twitching inside of her. "Let me feel you soak me, baby. Let me feel how much you love being stretched full of me."

She breaks as her whole body seizes, her pussy pulsing and fluttering around every inch, milking me in frantic waves.

I groan her name, holding still while she rides it out, letting her feel me throb deep inside her.

Her arms loop around my neck, as her nails rake into the back of my shoulders.

Every time I bottom out, she whimpers, like she can't believe how full she is, how completely I'm claiming her.

I lower my mouth to her ear, whispering.

"This" *Thrust.* "Cock" *Thrust.* "Is" *Thrust.* "Yours" *Thrust* "Baby."

Punctuating my words with a slow, intentional thrust, I lean down, kissing her passionately before nipping her lower lip. "Every fucking inch belongs to this perfect little pussy. No one else gets to feel me like this, just you."

She whimpers, her thighs trembling against my hips.

"Say it," I murmur, nipping the shell of her ear. "Tell me who this cock belongs to."

"It's mine," she gasps, "Mine."

I slide my hand up between us, wrapping it gently around the delicate column of her throat, not squeezing, just holding.

My palm covers most of her throat as my fingers rest along the sides, my thumb brushing the frantic flutter of her pulse.

"Look at you, taking my cock so well, baby," I growl, squeezing just a little to make her gasp. "My hands around your throat as my name leaves your pretty little mouth."

"Reed," she stammers, gripping my forearms.

I ease my grip, leaning down to give her a tender kiss as she meets each thrust.

Guilt begins to creep in, knowing she's promised to someone else, but it dissolves as she tightens around me, moaning my name.

"Reed, baby, please—"

I tighten my grip just enough, letting her feel the weight of my hand.

"Look at me, baby," I command, my fingers caressing her throat. "Look at me while I fuck what's mine."

Her lashes flutter open as tears cling to them, her pupils dilated.

"Seven inches of cock that's yours," I rasp, rubbing my thumb across her swollen lip. "Gonna fill you up with it. Gonna make you come so hard you soak me again. You ready to come with me, baby?"

She nods frantically, while simultaneously caressing my scarred face.

"Look at me while you come, baby. C'mon, give me one more."

I angle my hips just right, grinding against her clit with every deep thrust, as I grip her chin, keeping her eyes on mine.

"Come on this cock that's yours," I say, caressing her lower lip, keeping the pace steady. Let me feel you."

Her whole body locks up again as her thighs clamp around my waist, her pussy spasming violently around me.

She screams my name, her walls pulsing in frantic waves, flooding around my shaft as she comes undone for a third time.

The sight of her, the feel of her, the sound of her moaning snaps the last thread of my control.

I bury myself deep and come with a guttural groan.

My hand flexes on her throat, holding her through it while I empty everything I have inside her.

We shudder together, breathing raggedly, resting my forehead into the crook of her neck.

I don't pull out, not yet.

Keeping my hand around her neck, soft now, I stroke my thumb across her pulse point, as I kiss her, tasting the salt of her tears.

"Mine," I whisper against her lips.

She smiles, tugging my lower lip with her teeth. "Yours," she breathes, tangling her hands in my hair.

As I pull out, I collapse beside her, pulling her close as the moonlight fades and our breaths sync.

"You okay, sunshine?" I murmur, the words catching in my throat.

She nods, smiling faintly against my chest. "More than okay."

I press a kiss to the top of her head, breathing her in. "Good," I whisper. "'Cause I don't think I could let you go right now."

For now, she's mine, and that's all that matters.

THIRTY-FOUR
LAYLA

Reed sits next to me on the porch steps, his shoulders slumped, as his fingers trace the condensation on a glass of sweet tea.

He hasn't said much tonight, and neither have I. Everything between us already feels like a ghost.

Tomorrow, I'm gone.

I whisper, "Say something."

He looks at me, his eyes shadowed in the porch light. "What do you want me to say, Layla? That I hate this? That I'd stop time if I could?" His voice breaks halfway through. "You already know that."

I stand before I can lose my nerve. "Dance with me."

He looks at me for a long moment, his jaw clenched, throat working.

Before he can think better of it, he nods once, setting the glass down, and goes inside.

A minute later, music flows through the screen door as the opening chords of *Fade Into You by Mazzy Star* drift into the night.

He steps back out, walking towards me, his eyes never leaving mine.

When he reaches me, he slides his hand to the small of my back and the other to mine.

I press my palm flat against his chest, right over his heart, feeling it beat beneath my touch.

We begin to move, barely, just enough to call it dancing. The grass feels cool beneath my feet as the wind tickles my bare ankles beneath my jeans.

Rain begins to trickle on us, soaking us in the night, but we don't care as we continue to sway to the beat.

"I don't know what I'm doing," I whisper.

"Me neither,' he says, "I keep thinking maybe if I hold you tight enough, the universe will take a hint."

I laugh, the tiniest, most broken sound, and it turns into a sob before I can stop it. "Don't make it harder."

He cradles my face in his hands, pressing his forehead to mine. "Then stop looking at me like that."

"Like what?"

"Like you might stay."

My throat burns. "Maybe I would if you asked me to."

"Layla, I can't ask you to stay when I only have parts of you," he says, his voice trembling as his hand continues to hold my cheek.

His calloused thumb traces the curve of my jaw, and I feel the rough edge of his palm trembling against my skin. "I want every part of you," he breathes. "I want mornings with you. I want more dates." His voice breaks, and a tear slips free before he can stop it. "I. Want. Everything."

The tears come quickly, and I reach up to cradle his face as he holds mine. "You're not supposed to make it easy to leave."

"I'm not trying to." His breath stutters as his hands fall to his sides. "I'm just trying not to fall apart before you do."

I meet his eyes, wet not from the rain but from him holding back tears.

He's blinking quickly, trying to hide it, but I notice everything—the tremor in his jaw, the way his mouth keeps forming words he can't speak.

"Reed..."

He tilts my chin with a shaky hand as his thumb traces my bottom lip. "Every time you see the moon," he whispers, "I'm looking at it, too. Waiting for you, love."

The sound I make isn't human. It's grief and want, tangled into one.

I place my hand on his chest, feeling his heartbeat sync with mine. "Don't say that," I beg. "Please don't."

He leans in closer, his thumb brushing my knuckles. "I need you to know it," he says, his eyes flickering between mine.

His chest rises with a shaky breath, then he adds, "I'll wait for you until you're ready to leave him so you can come home to me. I'll wait years if I have to." His jaw tightens, but his tone stays soft. "So when it gets hard out there, you'll remember someone's still here, loving you quietly, even when you can't hear it."

I kiss him desperately before he can say more.

Every tear, breath, and unformed memory burns between us.

When we part, our foreheads stay pressed together, the world spinning too fast to catch up.

"I don't want to go," I whisper.

He shakes his head, his eyes red from tears. "I don't want you to go, either."

I don't answer. I can't. I sob into his chest, trembling from tears, cold wind, and rain.

We stand there, his arms around me, the night heavy with everything we didn't say, but I desperately wanted to.

He presses his face against the crook of my neck, his shoulders trembling with every breath.

I press a kiss into his hair. "Come on," I murmur. "It's getting cold."

He nods as he wraps his fingers around mine.

The door creaks open behind us as we walk hand in hand down the dark hallway, the boards creaking under our steps, every sound too loud in his quiet house.

I reach his room, and we both sit gently on the edge of his bed.

Moonlight spills through the window, cutting silver across his face and illuminating the scars on the left side.

He looks at me, his eyes red-rimmed, his mouth trembling, and the sight of him makes it damn near impossible for me not to leave.

I brush the hair from his face, my fingertips trailing down his jaw. "You look at me like this is the last time," I whisper.

His voice cracks. "Isn't it?"

I shake my head as my thumb traces his lower lip. "I'll be back. I promise."

For a heartbeat, neither of us breathes.

The rain has quieted to a soft, steady murmur outside, but inside his home, everything feels suspended; time, sound, and the ache that's been living in my heart for *years*.

His eyes are locked on mine, brimming with a longing so raw it makes my chest ache. His hands rest on my waist, thumbs tracing slow, absent arcs over the wet denim of my jeans.

He leans in first, brushing his nose with mine before kissing me.

The kiss begins so softly it barely registers; just the warm press of his lips to mine, a question wrapped in tenderness.

He then deepens it slowly, as our tongues meet in a gentle, searching rhythm that tastes like rain, salt, and everything we're trying not to say goodbye to yet.

My fingers slide into his damp hair as his hands tighten on my waist, pulling me forward until I'm straddling him on the edge of the bed.

We finally part, pressing our foreheads together, breathing each other's air.

He doesn't speak right away as he just looks at me, until I feel the weight of his gaze settle deep behind my ribs.

So quietly, I almost miss it over the sound of the rain.

"I'm going to miss touching you like this."

His hands slide up my sides as his thumbs brush the wet fabric over my ribs.

He lifts my tube top, slipping it off my shoulders one at a time, then loops it off my neck.

The soaked cotton clings stubbornly for a second, reluctant to let go, but he peels it down gently, exposing the swell of my breasts.

He exhales, shaky, almost pained.

"God, Layla..." His voice cracks on my name. "Look at you."

His palms glide up my arms, over my shoulders, down the sides of my breasts, never squeezing, just tracing, memorizing as his thumbs brush the undersides, circling the tight peaks of my nipples with the lightest pressure.

Goosebumps race across my skin despite the warmth of his house.

"You're so beautiful," he whispers, eyes tracing every inch he's uncovered. "Every single part of you. I still can't believe you're real sometimes."

Tears prick my eyes again. I reach for him as my fingers tremble, tugging at the hem of his soaked T-shirt.

He helps me lift it over his head, his arms flexing, his muscles shifting under skin marked by the years he's lived before me.

His shirt lands beside my tube top.

I trace the old scars across his chest, my fingertips following them slowly, reverently.

"You're beautiful as well," I whisper, my voice carrying emotion. "Every scar, every mark, they're evidence of you surviving everything that once threatened to take you from me before I even knew you existed."

He swallows hard as his hands come up to cup my face, his thumbs brushing the tears that have slipped free.

"I've got a lot of scars," he says softly. "But none of them hurt anymore, not when you touch them like that."

He helps me out of my jeans, as he steps out of his, kicking them aside until he's as bare as I am.

As he presses his lips to my temple, he whispers into my hair, "I'll love you quietly, even when you're gone."

Love?

That word doesn't scare me because he said it.

I won't say it back; I want to save it for when I finally leave Brian, when I can claim it without the weight of secrets pulling me down. But hearing it from Reed, like a promise he's kept buried too long, wraps around my heart.

"Come here," he murmurs.

He leads me into the ensuite bathroom, turning on the shower until steam curls out of the glass doors. He steps inside with me, pulling me under the spray.

Warm water hits us both, cascading over my back, shoulders, and hair.

It streams down his face, catching in his lashes, and runs in rivulets over the scars I just traced.

He turns me so my back faces his chest, his arms wrapping around me from behind as his chin rests on my shoulder.

His hands slide up my arms and down my sides, cradling my breasts once more.

"I'm going to miss the way your skin feels under my hands," he whispers into my ear. "The way you shiver when I kiss the back of your neck. The little sigh you make when I hold you like this. I'm going to miss waking up to feel your heartbeat against my palm when I rest it right here—" His hand flattens over my chest, covering my heart. "—just to make sure you're still real."

A sob catches in my throat.

He turns me in his arms until I'm gazing up at him again.

His hands slide up to cradle my face, his thumbs stroking slowly along my cheekbones as he searches my eyes. "I'm going to keep every promise," he continues, his voice cracking just a little, the words almost lost beneath the hiss of the shower.

He leans down, pressing his forehead to mine so our noses brush. "I'm going to be patient." His thumbs keep moving in gentle arcs, wiping away water, or maybe tears, I can't tell anymore.

"I'll be here waiting for you, baby." He says, as his hand slips to the nape of my neck, his fingers thread through my wet hair, holding me close.

My sweet Reed.

"I'm going to be the place you come home to, no matter

how long it takes." His other arm wraps tighter around my lower back, pulling our bodies flush.

"And when you're ready..." He pulls back just enough to look at me again, eyes shining, voice dropping to a raw whisper. "...I'll be right here, exactly where you left me, with open arms..."

He lifts both hands now, palms open toward me, then slowly brings them back to cup my face again. "...and the same stupid heart that's been yours for years." His thumbs tremor the tiniest bit against my cheeks.

A quiet, broken laugh escapes him, and he presses his lips to my forehead.

Tears mix with the shower water on my cheeks.

We stand there for a brief moment, holding each other as the warm water begins to cool, but neither of us moves to turn it off.

My forehead rests against his sternum as his arms wrap around me, as if he's trying to memorize the exact shape of my spine and the exact weight of me against him.

I swallow the lump in my throat.

"I'm going to miss you so much," I admit quietly, my heart whole yet heavy with what's coming.

He tilts my chin, guiding my gaze back to his. His eyes are warm beneath the shower, and as droplets fall from his lashes, I see so clearly every flicker of pain, love, and resignation in them.

"You haven't even left yet," he says, voice low and rough, "and I'm already missing you."

He doesn't say anything else as he looks at me, like he's trying to burn every detail of this moment into his memory: the way my wet lashes stick together, the flush still high on my cheeks, the tiny freckle on my collarbone he always kisses when we're falling asleep.

His hands slide up to cradle my face again as his thumbs stroke slowly along my cheekbones.

"Fuck, I don't want you to go," he says finally, so softly it almost disappears under the sound of the water.

I rest my palms against his chest, feeling the warmth of his skin beneath the spray, holding myself together with a strangled sob trapped in my throat.

"I hate that you have to," he mumbles, his voice rough against my ear. His hand slides slowly up my arm as his thumb brushes back and forth. "I hate that you're going back there, back to him, to figure things out."

His forehead dips to mine, our noses barely touching, and I feel the roughness of his mustache. "I hate the thought of you sleeping in your apartment again."

My fingers curl into his shoulders, holding him as the water cascades over us.

Water trails down his lashes, and I swipe it away gently with the pad of my thumb, my heart breaking at how vulnerable he looks right now.

"I hate that tomorrow morning I'm going to wake up, and you won't be here to steal the covers," he continues, his hand sliding to my waist. "Elbow me in your sleep, or smell like my shampoo because you used it all."

A shaky laugh leaves me before I can stop it, and I step on my tippy toes, leaning in closer, brushing my cheek against his.

I tilt my head, pressing a soft kiss just beneath his scarred jaw, my hands move slowly up his back in quiet reassurance, wishing I could stay exactly like this forever.

"But I understand," he whispers.

A fresh tear slips down my cheek, and he catches it with his lips.

"I can't live without you," he says against my skin. "I already know that."

He kisses me slowly, caressing the peak of my cheekbone.

"I'll be right here," he murmurs, kissing me again, slower, softer, as if every promise he's ever made is tucked into his touch. His forehead rests against mine as the water runs over us. "Same bar..." He kisses my temple, his thumb catching a tear before it slides away. "...same small town."

The ache in my chest sends a consistent dull pulse, so hard it hurts, and I clutch him closer, burying my face in his neck, breathing him in.

"My heart is yours, Layla; it's always been yours." He kisses me again, trembling, his hand cradling the back of my neck. "...It's always been you." Another kiss, softer this time, lingering. "Baby."

I shatter completely, because this man has been it for me the moment I offered to film his bar.

My hands slide up to cup his face as my thumbs brush water from his glasses, trying to see him clearly through the blur of my tears.

Pressing my forehead against his, my voice comes out wrecked and shaking. "I wish I had never met him," I whisper, kissing him between my words, my lips barely brushing his.

He kisses me back like he's scared too, like he's been waiting years just to breathe me in.

"I'm going to leave him," I say, quieter now. "I can't keep living like this. I'm going to leave him, Reed." I hide my face in his shoulder, sobbing into his skin while the water runs over us.

His arms tighten around me instantly as his hand slides up my spine while the other cradles my head, pressing soft kisses into my hair, my temple, and the wet corner of my mouth.

"I'll be right here," he whispers again, kissing me between each word. "Waiting for you, sunshine."

I cling to him harder, shaking, letting him hold me as the steam curls around us, his lips brushing mine, my cheeks, my forehead, as if he's trying to stitch me back together one kiss at a time.

"I'm scared I won't be brave enough," I whisper into his neck.

"You already are," he says quietly. "You're the bravest person I know. And I'm going to be proud of you every single day you're gone. Every single day you choose yourself."

He reaches behind me and finally turns the water off.

The sudden silence is loud.

Tomorrow I leave.

But tonight, tonight, he's still holding me like I'm the only thing that's ever mattered.

I'm coming back to him. I always do.

THIRTY-FIVE
REED/LAYLA

The morning light filters through the curtains, gentle yet harsh.

My bed feels cold. The sheets carry her scent, cherry and vanilla, and I swear if I breathe too deeply, I'll fall apart.

I sit at the edge of my bed, running my fingers through my hair, feeling the sting of tears welling in my eyes.

My throat burns as I drag my hand over my face, trying to steady the breath that won't come. "Damn it, Layla..."

The house feels foreign without her.

Her iced coffee glass sits on the counter, the unfinished canvas leans against the wall, and her hair tie lies on the nightstand.

Little ghosts of her everywhere.

I grab my keys from the hook and shove my jacket on. My helmet sits next to hers, where she left it on the bench.

Picking up my helmet and tossing it on, I trace the paint on hers with my thumb. The breath that leaves me isn't steady.

I finally push open the door, and the cool autumn

breeze hits sharply. The sun's barely up, burning gold over the horizon. Dew clings to the grass, glimmering as if the world is trying to look beautiful just to spite me.

My motorcycle sits where I left it, its black metal catching the light. I swing my leg over, and for a second, I sit there, gripping the bars, staring at the open road stretching out ahead.

I miss her.

The engine roars to life beneath me, rattling through my bones as its vibration hums up my spine as I ease it onto the road.

A cool gust of wind hits my face through the visor the moment I pick up speed.

The fields blur past in streaks of green and gold, and the smell of wet dirt and honeysuckle cuts through the ache.

She's everywhere out here.

In the way the light hits the trees, in the stretch of sky that still looks half-asleep, and in the damn song that keeps looping in my head.

I blink hard, swallowing the lump in my throat. She's embedded herself in my veins, and I don't want to wake up to another sunrise without her.

Blue Moon Ranch comes into view, the wind's dried the tears I wouldn't let fall. I turn onto the gravel road toward Carter and Catalina's, the hum of my bike slowing as I pull into their driveway.

Their farmhouse looks just the same, their porch swing swaying, the faint sound of music inside, and the smell of coffee strong enough to pull you in.

I kill the engine.

For a second, I almost turn back.

Almost.

The front door creaks open, and Carter steps out,

wearing his worn wranglers, black boots, black Henley, and his infamous black cowboy hat, holding a coffee mug, squinting against the light.

He takes one look at me and frowns. "You look like shit," he says.

"Good morning to you, too," I mutter, pulling off my helmet.

"Didn't realize you were up this early," he says. "Something wrong with the bar?"

"No," I say quietly. "Just needed something."

He studies me for a long beat, then nods toward the door. "Cat's making breakfast. Come in before she starts yelling about bugs coming in."

I follow him inside, the smell of coffee and cinnamon wrapping around me like warmth I don't deserve.

Catalina is standing at the stove, wearing Carter's oversized tee, a small ghost of her baby bump showing, and her hair tied up as soft morning light hits her face.

She turns and beams when she sees me.

"Reed!" she says, voice bright. "You never come this early unless something's wrong."

Everything's wrong.

She says it like a joke, but her smile falters when she really looks at me.

Carter hands me a mug, the steam curling between us. I wrap my fingers around it just to feel something.

"I met someone," I say, the words falling out before I can stop them.

That gets Catalina's attention immediately.

Her eyes widen, her grin blooming. "You what? Who? When? Tell me everything!"

"Darlin'," Carter warns, but there's a faint smirk on his face.

I take a slow sip of coffee, the heat burning down my throat. "It's complicated."

"It's always complicated with you, " she says. "But you're going to tell me anyway."

"She's engaged," I say quietly.

That kills the sound in the room.

Catalina's lips part as she drops the wooden spoon she was holding. "Oh!"

"Yeah," I say, "and she's been seeing me anyway."

Carter raises a brow but doesn't say anything as Catalina leans forward on the counter, her eyes full of questions she doesn't ask yet.

Catalina's voice gentles. "And you love her?"

I nod once. "Yeah, I do."

She reaches across the counter, her hand brushing mine. "Does she make you smile, Reed?"

I stare into my coffee, my throat tight. "Fuck, does she. Just looking at her makes me forget about all the pain I've ever gone through."

Her eyes glisten, not pity, just understanding. "Reed, you can't just talk like that, you're going to make me sob."

I give her a ghost of a smile, taking another sip of my coffee.

Carter sets his mug down beside mine. "You want advice, or you just need to bleed it out?"

"Bleed it out," I murmur.

He nods once, signaling quiet approval as he squeezes my shoulder.

Catalina squeezes my hand again before pulling away, then turns back to the stove with a sniff.

"Well," she says softly, "if she's meant for you, she'll find her way back. The ones that matter always do."

I stare down into the dark swirl of coffee, her words

echoing somewhere deep in the hollow space she left behind.

Maybe she's right. Maybe she will.

But for now, I sit here in my brother's kitchen, the sun pouring through the window, the smell of cinnamon and coffee in the air, trying to believe that love this quiet can still find its way home.

That two souls who are meant to be will always find a way back to each other. No matter the distance or the situation, what's meant to be will be. And I pray to whatever God that my sweet girl, Layla, will be able to leave and come back to me.

Catalina looks back at me, resting her chin on her hand as she studies me with those sharp yet gentle eyes that see too much.

"I can tell you love her," she says quietly. "Even if you won't tell me who she is."

I huff out a quiet sound that might be a laugh if it didn't ache. "You always this nosy?"

"I'm pregnant, and I'm a chismosa," she says dryly, her hand resting on her small bump. "It's literally my job to know everything."

That earns a half-smile from me, but it fades quickly. The kitchen hums softly around us, gentle morning light, the kettle hissing faintly on the stove.

My throat tightens up as I drag a hand down my face. "When she's gone, Cat, it feels like the lights go out. And when it's quiet, really quiet, it gets hard to be here with my own thoughts."

Her expression softens instantly. "Reed..."

I shake my head, staring at my hands, avoiding her gaze. "These thoughts come lingering back, and sometimes I—"

Choking up on that thought, I remember when the darkness became too much, and I attempted.

My brothers found me, and they each swore they'd never let me go through this again, but it's easier said than done when you have these demons living in your head.

The constant gaze directed at me, the whispers of 'freak' thrown my way, and the persistent loneliness I endure.

Given what I've experienced—the accident and the grief from my mama and Beau—it weighs heavily on me most days.

But Layla, fuck, she brought color into my life.

I shouldn't say it, but I do. "Sometimes it feels easier to disappear."

Before I can blink, Catalina is already on her feet, crossing the space between us, and she slaps my arm.

"Don't say that," she snaps, voice cracking at the edges. "Don't you ever say that again."

I look up, startled.

She's glaring at me with tears shimmering in her eyes. "You think we wouldn't notice if you were gone?" she says, her voice trembling but fierce. "You think Carter wouldn't break? You think Maverick wouldn't fall apart? You think *I* wouldn't?"

I try to look away, but she won't let me.

She steps closer, eyes shining. "You were there, Reed," she says, softer now. "You saw me in that hospital. You remember what it looked like when I thought I had nothing left to live for."

"I do," I whisper.

The memory hits hard; the sterile light, Carter's cracked voice, Catalina pale against the white sheets, the quiet horror in all of us.

She nods, her voice trembling. "And you were the one

who sat by my bed when Carter couldn't even breathe. You held my hand and told me that sometimes we just need one more sunrise. That's what you said. One more sunrise."

I close my eyes, my throat tight. "Yeah."

"So don't you dare forget that now," she says, her voice breaking. "Don't you dare let the dark convince you that it's easier to stop trying. You matter here. You matter to *us*."

I swallow hard, my voice barely audible. "It just gets quiet sometimes."

"I know," she whispers. "But the quiet doesn't mean you're alone."

I look up, meeting her gaze as she takes my hand, squeezing it.

"You've carried so much for so long," she says softly. "Grief, guilt, silence. You wear it like armor, but it's just weight, Reed. You can set it down now."

I let out a shaky breath. "I don't know how."

She offers a faint, tearful smile. "Then let us help you. Let me help you. You're family, and family doesn't let each other disappear."

Something inside me fractures as I place my hand over hers, anchoring myself in the warmth of her skin.

"You're too good, Cat," I murmur.

She sniffs, her eyes wet but steady. "No. I'm just someone who understands what it's like to almost lose yourself."

I look down, blink quickly, and she squeezes my hand again.

"You'll find your way through this," she says. "And when she comes back, and she will, you'll be ready to love her without losing yourself in the dark again."

I nod slowly, the air thick between us, each breath feeling heavier yet somehow lighter too.

She finally releases, wiping her cheek, as she walks over to me, hugging me. "You're loved here, Reed. I'm always here for you."

I let out a breath against her shoulder, feeling the tear fall down my cheek.

For the first time since Layla left, I don't feel like I'm suffocating.

I'm just breathing through this ache, one sunrise at a time.

Layla

Brian's pacing across our living room like a wild animal. He's holding his phone as the screen is replaying the video on a relentless loop.

That video.

"You really thought this was smart?" he says, shoving his phone to my face.

I cross my arms, pushing his arm. "It's just content, Brian."

He laughs, straightening his sleeve as he shoves his phone into his pocket. "Content? Six million views of you parading around some hick town, letting people think you've moved on? That's not content, Layla, that's suicide for our brand!"

"I'm not our brand!" I snap, louder than I intend. "I'm me!"

His expression hardens. "You're what *I* built."

"You didn't build me," I say, turning to walk away. "You just took credit every time I breathed."

He stops pacing, grabbing my arm quickly, squeezing hard. "What did you say?"

I feel my pulse thumping erratically. "You heard me."

"Careful," he warns, letting go of me. "You wouldn't have half of what you do if it weren't for me. The brand deals, the followers, people love me; you think any of that happened because you're special?"

"I think it happened because I worked for it!" I fire back. "Because people actually like me, Brian. Because for once, I was *happy!*"

He laughs again, but there's no humor left in it. "Happy?" His free hand moves, gripping my shoulder. "You call this happiness? Running around barefoot, letting some nobody touch you on camera?"

"Don't," I say through clenched teeth, getting out of his hold.

He steps closer. "Don't what?"

"Don't talk about him."

Something flashes in his eyes. "So you are fucking him?"

"Brian, I—."

He cuts me off by slapping his hand over my mouth, exhaling slowly, and shaking his head. "You really are ungrateful."

Releasing his grip, he begins gathering items from the coffee table—my notebooks, my makeup bag, my camera—and slams them onto the floor.

He rips up the paper, stomps all over my makeup brushes, and finally destroys my camera.

"This is what you wanted, right? Attention? Congratulations!"

"Stop it!" I say, my voice shaking. "You're scaring me!"

He turns to me, face flushed, jaw clenched. "Don't you raise your voice at me."

"I'm not—"

"You are." His voice drops low and dangerous. "And you forget who you're talking to."

My heart pounds so loud I can hear it in my ears. He moves closer, his cologne sharp enough to sting.

He lifts his clenched fist toward my face, hesitating; thankfully, he lowers his hand, but what he does next is worse.

Gripping my shoulders, he slams me onto the coffee table, where all my belongings are broken.

He's yelling at me, but I can't hear anything over my heartbeat pounding in my ears. He kicks me in the side, spits on me, all while saying these terrible things.

"You don't walk out on me, Layla! You're not going to leave me!"

I freeze, every muscle taut. My breaths come in shallow pulls, pain spreading in my side, where he touched me.

The hands that once cared for me, savoring the feel of my skin with his, are the same hands that just hurt me.

He scoffs, muttering obscenities under his breath, and leaves without looking back.

I lay there in the aftermath; makeup scattered across the rug, the notebook open on the floor, its pages torn. My hands won't stop trembling.

It takes me a full minute to realize I'm crying.

A silent cry forces its way out of me, my lungs burning as I try—and fail—to breathe.

I curl into a ball, staring at the mess, trembling. A smear of paint stains my wrist, glowing faintly under the harsh apartment light.

The ache in my chest sharpens. I wipe my face and whisper to the empty room, "You said you'd be looking at the moon."

"I'm coming back," I whisper. "I just have to figure out how."

THIRTY-SIX
LAYLA

Brian hasn't come home in days.

Thank fucking God, because I'm still trembling from the way he put his hands on me. The bruise on my side is tender, and it throbs when I move too fast.

I'm curled up in bed, with only the glow of my phone lighting the room, as I scroll through the comments on the video I posted of Reed's bar and the footage of Ruby Ridge.

It's blowing up; it's my most-viewed video ever.

People keep mentioning how cozy it looks, how they can almost smell the whiskey through the screen.

I smile softly, feeling a pride I haven't felt in a long time.

A notification chimes in; I swipe down to see it's Reed.

My heart aches and swells in one breath.

REED

You still awake, sunshine?

LAYLA

Yeah, I can't sleep. Are you looking at the moon like me?

REED

Yeah, baby. I miss you.

LAYLA

I miss you too 🥺

REED

When can I see you again?

LAYLA

I have some brand deals and events out here. I'm hoping once that's done, I can fly back out there. 🤍

REED

I'll be waiting, sunshine.

I bite back a smile that barely reaches my eyes, rolling onto my back, my heart fluttering like it forgot it was allowed to feel something good.

I wipe my thumb across the screen, rereading his words until my vision blurs.

For a moment, I almost forget the bruise, the silence in my apartment, the dread lurking in every shadow.

The click of the lock comes within my hearing, and I clench my jaw, feeling my stomach flutter with nerves, nausea, and worry.

My phone slips from my hand and falls face down onto the blanket just as Brian walks in, carrying a bouquet of sunflowers and an iced coffee.

His expression is gentle, almost pleading.

"Baby," he says gently, stepping closer. "I'm so sorry."

The words 'taste sweet in his mouth,' but all I feel is the sting of his palms and the weight of a man I wish I didn't have to fear.

He places the coffee on the nightstand, the clink of ice

echoing loudly in the silence. The bouquet follows, petals brushing the wood.

"Look at me, baby," he says, his voice trembling just enough to sound human. "Please."

I don't look at him as he begs.

Keeping my eyes on the wall, I trace the faint shadow of moonlight slipping through the windows.

My chest feels taut, I feel the pace of my breaths quickening, and this dread curling low in my stomach.

He moves closer, the mattress sagging beneath him. I flinch before I can stop myself. His hand halts halfway to mine.

"Layla..." His voice cracks, and he drops his gaze, as if he's the one hurt. "I don't know what got into me. I just—" He exhales shakily, running his thumb over his lower lip. "You're everything to me."

I've heard them before. Every time he crosses a line, every time he swears, it won't happen again. And for a moment, I almost let myself believe it, because that's what I always do.

He reaches out again, his fingertips brushing my wrist. "Please, baby. Just look at me."

Brushing my hair out of my face, I tilt my head slowly until I meet his blue eyes.

He looks exactly the same as he did when he laid his hands on me; same tousled hair, same tired eyes, but all I see is a flash of anger, the way his jaw tightens before everything goes black around the edges.

"Brian," I whisper, my voice barely there. "You can't do this again."

He smiles, small and shaky. "I know. I know, baby. I'm fixing it. I swear." He leans in, pressing a kiss to my forehead before I can pull away. "You'll see."

The coffee sweats on the nightstand, dripping condensation onto the wood.

I stare at it, at the brown ring it leaves behind, at the tiny mess that will stain if I don't wipe it up.

My phone buzzes again under the blanket. I don't need to look to know it's Reed again.

I don't feel guilty about wishing I were somewhere else; somewhere warm, quiet, and safe, with a man who doesn't make me fear my own heartbeat.

He notices the vibration, his eyes flicking toward the phone, and his smile falters.

"Who's that?" he asks, his voice calm yet tense, a storm brewing beneath.

My pulse stutters. "Probably just Amelia," I lie, forcing a small shrug. "She's been talking about Leo."

He hums. "At midnight?"

He starts pacing, running a hand through his hair as if trying to compose himself.

The gesture seems rehearsed. I remain perfectly still, my fingers clutching the blanket.

"Brian—"

"I said I'm sorry," he interrupts. "I'm standing here trying to fix us, and you're sitting there texting someone else?"

The sweetness in his voice fades. The fake-ass apology, the flowers, the coffee, all of it fades away.

My throat tightens. "You don't understand—"

"Don't lie to me, Layla!" he snaps, stepping closer.

His eyes flick to my phone again, the blue glow from the screen reflecting off the anger already building in his face.

He grabs the edge of the blanket and yanks it back before I can stop him.

My phone falls onto the mattress, lighting up once more with Reed's name.

"Reed?" he says slowly, venom dripping from each syllable. "That freak bartender from your video?"

I scramble up, heart pounding so hard I can hear it in my ears. "No, it's n—"

He lets out a low, humorless laugh. "What is it then?" His gaze darkens, his mouth twisting into something cruel. "You think you can play me, huh?"

"Brian, please—"

He moves closer until I can smell the mix of whiskey and cologne on his breath. His hand shoots out, gripping my chin, forcing me to meet his gaze. "You forget who I am sometimes," he murmurs, his voice dropping to a quiet, dangerous rasp. "Only I get to cheat on you."

My stomach twists, nausea clawing its way up my throat.

"Brian, stop—"

He tilts his head, smiling. "Relax, baby. I'm just saying, don't embarrass me. You know how much I love you. Don't make me prove it again."

His fingers press into my jaw again before he releases, stepping back with a sigh that feels almost satisfied. "See? You're okay. We're fine."

He tosses the flowers onto the dresser, petals scattering like debris, and heads toward the bathroom. "I'm gonna shower," he says lightly, as if nothing just happened.

The sound of running water fills the silence.

I sit frozen with my heart still racing, staring at the bouquet wilting on the dresser.

THIRTY-SEVEN
REED

I should've gone home hours ago, but walking into my empty house doesn't feel right when all I can think about is her.

Layla's been gone for twenty-eight days.

Four weeks have passed since she hugged me at the airport, whispered that she'd come soon, and then vanished into the crowd with her gorgeous smile.

She's been texting whenever she can—quick updates, photos of coffee cups and L.A. sunsets, but I can see the exhaustion behind her words.

She says she's fine, but I know she's not.

I'm buried in receipts when my phone rings with a FaceTime from Layla.

I feel a tight sensation in my chest, and butterflies swarm inside me, fluttering with nerves and giddiness—a feeling she only brings out of me.

I answer before it even rings twice.

She's lying on a pile of crisp, white sheets, her blonde hair tousled, eyes sleepy but smiling. "Well, if it isn't my favorite person," she says softly, voice warm. "You miss me yet?"

"Didn't even try not to," I tell her, leaning back in my chair. "You finally figure out how time zones work, or just feel like torturing me again?"

She laughs. "It's not that late."

"It's midnight, sunshine."

She yawns, stretching. "Oh yeah, I'm two hours behind. I'm home alone, bored, and couldn't sleep. Figured you'd still be up doing something exciting."

"Oh yeah," I respond. "Livin' wild, organizing receipts and going through inventory."

She giggles, her eyes crinkling with amusement. "You're such an old man sometimes."

"Yeah, but you love that about me."

"Excuse me?" she raises a brow. "I do not." A pause. "Okay, maybe a little."

I chuckle, noticing what her smile can't hide—the faint shadows beneath her eyes and her skin paler than usual. Even through the pixelation, she looks exhausted. "You look tired, sweetheart. Did you sleep at all this week?"

She sighs, pushing hair from her face. "Barely. It's been... a lot. Shoots, meetings, events. I don't know, I haven't been feeling great."

"You sick?" I ask, frowning.

She shakes her head, her lips looking a little too pale. "No, just tired. Probably from stress."

"Or maybe 'cause you've been runnin' yourself into the ground," I mutter. "You eat today?"

Her guilty silence answers for her.

"Layla," I warn.

She scrunches her nose. "Half a protein bar and an iced Dunkalatte."

"Jesus Christ." I drag my fingers down my mustache. "You're gonna make me drive to L.A. just to make sure you eat something that didn't come from a vending machine."

"I wouldn't hate that," she says softly. "You could cook for me, and we can watch your nasty horror movies."

"They're not nasty."

"Yes, they are." She gives me a lazy grin, her eyes barely staying open.

I choose not to say anything, just watching how her golden hair spills across her pillow, wishing I were there to hold her, wishing I were there to kiss the soft slope of her neck, telling her how much I miss her, how much I need her.

She lets out a yawn, speaking again. "You've been counting the days, haven't you?"

"Every damn one."

Her eyes flicker, emotion replacing the teasing. "I miss you, Reed."

"Yeah," I say quietly. "Miss you too, sunshine."

She smiles then, her eyes fluttering shut.

"Get some rest, baby. Call me soon, okay?"

"Promise," she murmurs, blowing a kiss before the screen goes dark.

I shut down the computer, and the quiet of the office settles around me, already counting the hours until I hear her voice again.

Maverick's house always smells like breakfast, and there's always some havoc ensuing—coffee brewing, music playing, somebody laughing too loudly, their pets running around like bufoons.

Today's no different.

Amelia's sitting on the counter with a cold brew in hand, her bare legs swinging as she watches Maverick dance around the kitchen, shirtless, and half-awake with his hair twisted in different directions.

He's got Leo tucked against his chest, as his tiny fists are clutching at his dad's chain while Maverick flips a pancake one-handed.

"Look, buddy!" he says, voice booming. "Daddy's got skills."

Amelia groans, but she's smiling. "You're going to drop our child and the spatula."

"Impossible, dollface," he says, grinning. "I was born for this."

Maverick hands Leo over to me as he kicks, squealing, and I can't help but laugh under my breath.

I drop onto the floor beside his bouncer and place him in it, rolling his rattle to him. He tries to grab it with both hands, blue eyes shining.

When he can't, he screeches anyway.

The front door swings open, and Carter's voice cuts through the madness.

"Jesus Christ. Every time I come here, it's always so damn loud."

Catalina trails behind him, her hand gently resting on her small bump.

Her glow illuminates the room; she's always been beautiful, and the way Carter looks at her now makes my heart crack a little.

Carter's glued to her side, his arm protective around her

waist. He presses a kiss to her temple before she hobbles over to the kitchen.

Maverick groans dramatically. "God, can you two not be nasty in my kitchen, or I will gag."

Catalina smirks. "You're just jealous because Amelia's the only woman who threatens to stab you daily."

"We're kinky in this house," he fires back.

Amelia lifts her coffee in salute. "Can't argue there."

Carter sighs and leans against the counter, watching his wife with a smile that's damn near worshipful.

Catalina blushes and smacks his chest lightly. He laughs and kisses her again.

The whole room feels like love; messy, loud, genuine love.

Somehow, that's the part that hurts the most.

I should be happy for my brothers. I am. But when all you want is your own family, it hurts when the one woman you truly want gives you only pieces of herself.

Continuing to watch them all, their laughter, the way their bodies lean toward each other instinctively, I can't help but imagine what it would be like to have that.

Someone waiting at home. Someone whose voice fills the quiet.

Not just warmth borrowed through a phone screen.

Layla facetimed me last night.

But after the call, when the screen went black, I sat in my office, surrounded by receipts and silence, wondering whether I'd made her feel something real, or if I'm just some sort of convenience for her.

Maverick claps a hand on my shoulder hard enough to jolt me back. "You good, bro?"

"Fine," I say, managing a half-smile. "Just tired."

He squints, unconvinced. "Mmmm, no, you got that thousand-yard stare again. What's goin' on?"

"Nothing worth talking about."

"Bullshit." He grins, looping an arm around my neck and shaking me roughly. "You're thinkin' about that bar of yours again, aren't you? Or a woman. It's always one of those."

"You're going to break my glasses, you fuck."

He laughs and releases me. "Still got that QB1 strength, baby."

Amelia's laughing too now, calling him a menace. Carter joins in, teasing him about burning half the pancakes. Catalina's humming softly, setting the table.

I pick up Leo when he begins fussing, gently settling him against my shoulder. He calms down immediately, his tiny fingers curling into my shirt.

"Yeah," I whisper, mostly to myself. "You've got it figured out, huh?"

Carter glances over, smiling faintly. "Look at you, he likes you."

"Guess I'm good with quiet company," I say, bouncing Leo gently.

The truth burns underneath my words.

I *want* this.

The mornings, the laughter, the peace.

But what if that's not meant for me?

Layla's world is quick and vibrant, filled with cameras and flashing lights.

Mine's slow and quiet, built from ashes and barstools.

Maybe I'm her escape, the safe place she runs to when everything gets too loud. And maybe when she finally finds her footing, she'll realize I was never meant to stay in her story.

Leo babbles softly against my shoulder, and I close my eyes, breathing him in. The smell of baby lotion and pancakes fills the air.

I wish I could hold on to this moment a little longer.

Maverick's voice booms again, dragging me back. "Hey, Reedddd, you gonna eat?"

I force a smirk. "God, you're so loud, I'm comin'."

He grins, flexing his biceps, smirking like the idiot he is.

They all laugh again, loudly and effortlessly.

I smile with them, convincingly and rehearsed. But inside, it feels like standing in the middle of everything I've ever wanted, knowing it might never be mine.

THIRTY-EIGHT
LAYLA

Brian's laughter echoes through the hallway, muffled by his gaming headset.

He's been at it for hours, yelling into the mic at his friends, cursing, laughing, swearing he's "almost done."

He always says that.

I stand in the doorway for a long minute, with my arms crossed, watching him.

He doesn't even look up.

"I'm going to check the mail," I say.

He doesn't glance over. "Yeah, whatever."

My chest tightens, not from surprise, but from the dull familiarity of it.

I grab my keys and leave quietly.

The hallway smells of citrus and vanilla as I walk through it, heading to the elevator.

I finally arrive at the lobby, where early-morning light spills across the white and gray marble, golden rays streaming through the glass doors.

The mailboxes line the far wall; I walk over to mine, unlock it, and start flipping through the envelopes.

Bills, so fun. Ads, gross. And a magazine I didn't remember subscribing to, I need to cancel this shit.

My fingers pull out the last envelope, a simple one with a Ruby Ridge, TN stamp.

My heart stutters.

Reed's handwriting curves across the front, a little messy, but it's *him*.

I slide onto the wooden bench in the lobby corner, carefully tear open the envelope, and unfold the page.

Layla,

I'm not sure why I'm writing this, maybe because I'm better at saying things when you're not looking at me. Maybe because I miss you, and this feels like the only way to quiet my mind for a while.

The bar feels too still without you. I keep expecting to hear your laugh, you filming around the bar, you stealing my drinks and pretending it's an accident. You left pieces of yourself all over my place, and each one makes it harder to breathe.

I've been thinking a lot about what this is between us, how it feels so good, so easy, and how that frightens me. I'm not used to good things lasting. I keep waiting for you to realize you could do better than a man who avoids his reflection.

But then I remember the way you look at me—like I'm something worth keeping—and for a moment, the fear quiets down.

You once told me I made you feel safe.

You do the same for me, sunshine.

If you ever wonder how I feel, just remember

this: you've got a man in Tennessee who hasn't stopped thinking about you, not even for a day. And no matter what happens, I'll always be waiting for you, baby.

– Reed

I'm barely able to reach the end without my vision blurring. A tear slips down as I press my hand against my mouth, my heart splintering wide open.

He thinks I'm going to leave him. He thinks it's temporary. And I've been letting him believe that.

Because I'm still here, trapped in this apartment with a man who stopped loving me long before I stopped pretending, I've been too scared to leave and finally choose myself.

Looking down at the letter again, at the ink smudge where his hand must have hesitated, at the line that says *you do the same for me, sunshine.*

I have to call him.

My hands tremble as I grab my phone.

I scroll to his name, my thumb pausing briefly before I press call.

It rings for less than five seconds before his warm voice and southern drawl flood the line.

"Hey, sunshine."

I swallow the lump in my throat. "You wrote me again."

He's quiet for a second. "Yeah," he says softly. "Didn't think you'd get it this fast."

"I just read it." I glance down at the page still clutched in my hand. "You don't ever have to be scared with me, Reed. I'm not going anywhere."

He lets out a slight sound, relief, maybe, and when he finally speaks, his voice cracks. "You sure about that?"

"I'm sure," I whisper. "I miss you. Every single day. And I'm coming home soon."

He exhales slowly. "Guess I'll start makin' room for you here, then."

"You already have."

I close my eyes, leaning against the cool tile wall, with the letter pressed to my heart.

I stay in the lobby for a few more minutes after Reed hangs up, clutching his letter.

His voice still hums in my chest, soothing the ache that's been sitting there for weeks.

Folding the letter carefully, I tuck it back into the envelope and take the elevator up.

My reflection looks back from the mirrored doors—tired eyes, mascara smudged, the ghost of a smile lingering from hearing his voice.

The large, metal doors slide open, and I stroll to my apartment, reluctant to go inside.

As I step back in, it's quiet—no shouting, no laughter, just the low hum of a TV game menu looping repeatedly.

Brian's off his game now, sitting on the couch with a beer in his hand, scrolling through his phone. The screen's glow illuminates his face, making the bags under his eyes look deeper.

He glances up as I walk in, his gaze sweeping over me from head to toe. "You look like shit," he says flatly.

I blink, clutching the mail tighter.

Yeah, I think, *he's definitely changing his ways.*

"So kind of you," I murmur, setting the small stack of mail on the counter.

He nods toward it without looking up. "Anything for me?"

"No," I say. My voice remains steady, even though I can still feel Reed's words pressed against my ribs.

"You do the same for me, sunshine."

He makes a grumbling sound, like he doesn't believe me or thinks there's no point in asking. He puts his beer down and moves toward the counter.

Fuck, I think he's going to grab the mail, or maybe come back to me, but he doesn't as he just stares at the envelopes, unreadable, turning away.

"Whatever," he mutters as he walks back to his setup. The chair squeaks, the headset clicks, and his friends' voices fill the air once more.

I stand there, still holding Reed's letter in my hand, watching the man I used to know fade away behind a glowing screen.

The pain inside me doesn't hurt the way it used to. It's quieter now. Resolved. For the first time, I'm not wondering whether I'll leave.

Now that I know I can create content without him, I can definitely leave him for good.

I turn away, slipping into our bedroom, the letter pressed close to my heart.

The noise fades behind me, the shouting and the laughter that aren't mine.

In the stillness, I whisper to myself again, this time a promise instead of a hope.

"I'm going to do it."

Brian sits beside me on the couch, scrolling through his phone with one knee bouncing, while the hum of his console continues in the background.

I'm half-curled into myself, thinking about Reed's letter still, and how desperately I want to text him right now.

I draw a breath, smoothing my palms over my thighs before I speak.

"I was thinking," I say, keeping my voice light and careful. "Maybe I should head back to Ruby Ridge for a bit."

He continues scrolling, not paying an ounce of attention to me.

"For what," he says, not looking at me.

I hesitate, angling my body toward him anyway. "I miss the girls. Catalina, Amelia. It's been a while."

That part is true. It's just not the part that hurts.

He exhales through his nose, finally glancing over. "You were just fucking there," he replies.

"I know," I reply quickly, filling the silence before it stretches. "I just—there's a lot going on, and—"

"Fine."

I blink. "Fine?"

He places his phone on the coffee table with a deliberate tap and leans back, spreading his arm across the couch.

"If you're going," he says evenly, "I'm coming with you."

My stomach drops.

"Oh," I say softly, shaking my head. "You don't have to do that. I was just thinking it'd be nice to have some girl time, you know?"

He shifts closer, angling his knee toward mine, crowding my space without touching me.

"No," he says, reaching out to grip my throat, squeezing. "That's not fucking happening."

I gasp for air, raking my nails down his forearm, trying to escape. "Brian—"

He squeezes harder. "No ifs, ands, or buts," he says. "If you go, I go."

"I just thought—" I try to get the words out, but he keeps squeezing harder, cutting off my air.

He releases his grasp. "You don't need to think about it," he says. "I'll handle it."

I nod automatically as I rub my throat, coughing. "Ok—Okay."

He relaxes back into the couch like the conversation never mattered, reaching for the remote.

"Good," he says, his eyes back on the screen. "I'll book something later. And, baby?"

"Y-Yes?"

He smirks, caressing his hand across my thigh, causing me to flinch. "You can take me to that freak's bar."

No.No.NO.

I stare ahead, nodding in agreement as the TV light washes over the room, and tell myself to breathe normally. To stay calm. To not let the ache show on my face.

All I was trying to do was go back to myself and to someone who never once told me what I was allowed to want.

THIRTY-NINE
REED

The bar is alive the way it always is on a Friday; boots scuffing across the worn floorboards, laughter crashing over the jukebox's low thrum, glasses clinking.

My brothers are both home tonight, tucked away in their warm houses with their wives and quiet routines, while I'm here behind the scarred oak bar.

I've been pouring drinks on autopilot for hours, nodding to regulars, flashing the half-smile they expect, pretending the last couple of months haven't carved a hollow space in my heart.

Two months since I last saw Layla.

Two months without hearing her sweet voice around this bar. Two months without feeling her soft hands wrapped around mine or the sweet taste of her.

I've checked my phone so many times that the screen should be worn thin. I've reread her messages until they no longer made sense. I've told myself she's fine, that she's figuring things out, and that she's still wearing his ring.

I knew what I was getting myself into, but it still doesn't stop the ache.

The front door swings open again.

I don't look up immediately as another group of guys yell for another round of Fireball, but the air shifts.

A prickle runs down the back of my neck.

Adjusting my glasses, I quickly glance over at the wooden doors, and my heart stops.

Layla stands just inside the entrance.

She's wearing the pastel yellow dress I've always loved, the one that clings to her hips and ends mid-thigh.

Tonight, it looks off because it's wrinkled across her waist and the hem is slightly crooked.

Her hair is pulled back into a messy ponytail, with strands falling loose around her face, making her look more exhausted than effortless.

My gaze travels along her delicate face and nose, and I notice that concealer sits heavily along the curve of her throat, but it can't quite hide the faint purple bloom beneath.

She wraps her arms tightly around her middle, and her shoulders curve inward as if she's trying to disappear into herself.

He steps in right behind her.

His hand clamps around her upper arm, as his fingers dig in hard enough to turn her skin white under the pressure. He steers her forward through the crowd, tugging her along.

His eyes sweep the room and lock onto mine almost instantly.

A cocky smirk flashes across his lips before he tightens his grip and pulls her closer to his side, briefly kissing her on the lips, making me wince.

She stumbles half a step, but she doesn't try to pull away, and it kills me watching her.

Red-hot boiling anger simmers beneath my skin, my fists clenched under the bartop.

They weave through the tables and finally reach the bar, as she keeps her gaze fixed on the floorboards the whole way.

This cocky bastard doesn't, as he watches me while they inch closer and closer to the bar.

Once he reaches the oak top, he taps his fingers on the scarred wood, leaning in, crowding my space.

Layla stands half a step behind him, her arms still locked around herself.

I set the bottle I was holding down with careful precision.

He snaps his fingers in front of my face. "Don't fucking look at her, you freak. Whiskey neat. Now."

Fuck him. My eyes stay on her, watching her subtle movements.

She finally lifts her head, and I'm able to see her clearly now that she's closer.

Her face isn't her natural ivory tone; it's pale under the warm Edison bulbs. Dark circles color her undereyes, shadows now taking over the once-bright spot.

Our eyes finally meet, and I take in her glassy, red-rimmed eyes, carrying the kind of exhaustion that goes deeper than lack of sleep.

My jaw locks so tight my teeth ache.

Turning, I reach for the Maker's Mark and pour three generous fingers into a rocks glass.

No flourish. No ice. Just like this fucker asked.

I slide it across the bar with more force than necessary.

He snatches the glass, takes a sip, and grimaces. "I've had better."

Fuck you.

He sets it down with a deliberate clack, smirks at me, then pushes off the bar, heading toward the restrooms without another word.

The second his back disappears down the dim hallway, Layla steps forward fast.

Her hands shake as they grip the edge of the bar. "I'm so sorry," she whispers, her voice thin and splintering. "I wanted to come alone, he said he was coming, no—"

She cuts herself off, throat working. "I didn't know what else to do. I'm sorry, Reed. I'm so sorry."

I reach across the bar in one smooth motion and catch her trembling hand between both of mine, my thumbs stroking slowly once, twice, over her knuckles.

"Baby," I say, my voice low and rough. "Don't apologize. Not to me. Not ever. Please."

Her eyes fill instantly as a single tear escapes, tracking down her cheek, and catches the light.

I lean over the bar, stretching far enough to reach her face as my thumb brushes the tear away.

"I'll be right back," I tell her. My voice stays steady even as my pulse roars in my ears. "Stay right here."

She gives me a small nod, holding tightly onto my hands before she reluctantly lets go.

I push through the small side door, my boots hitting the floorboards hard enough to draw a few whoops from the regulars.

The hallway comes into view, lit by a single buzzing bulb that flickers every few seconds.

I pass my office, rounding the corner just as Brian steps out of the men's room, zipping his fly, still wearing that smug half-smirk that makes my blood boil.

I don't slow down.

My forearm slams across his chest, driving him back

into the wall. His head snaps back; the thud is loud in the tight space.

Air punches out of him in a rough grunt.

I pin him there, my forearm pressing across his windpipe as my body crowds him with my weight forward so he can't twist free.

He's stunned for half a second, then his eyes narrow, and the shock turns into fury.

He shoves hard, as both his palms slam into my chest.

I stagger back one step before I plant my boots and shove right back. His shoulders hit the wall again, harder this time.

The impact rattles the framed poster of a long-dead country singer, crooked above his head.

"Get the fuck off me, you freak," he snarls.

Freak. That word. Freak. Freak. *Freak.*

I lean in close, just inches away, but he still has to tilt his head back to look up because I'm taller.

My forearm stays locked across his throat, with just enough pressure to remind him how easily I could snap his neck.

"Put your hands on her again," I say slowly, looking down at him. "I'll break every bone in your fucking hand. Then I'll do the same to the other. After that, I'll move on to your knees, elbows, ribs—until you're crying and can't stand. And I won't stop until you're begging."

His lips peel back in a sneer as he shoves again, harder this time, twisting his hips so his shoulder drives into my chest.

I lean back slightly, but I'm not someone to be underestimated.

Just because I'm quiet doesn't mean I won't fuck you

up, especially noticing how Layla flinches around him—*my* Layla.

He uses the space to wrench his arm free and shove his forearm under my chin, trying to reverse the hold.

I catch his wrist mid-motion, twisting it down and out, slamming my free hand into the center of his chest.

He hits the wall a third time, his breath exploding from him again, but he doesn't fold.

He snarls and swings.

I duck his wild hook.

Coming up inside his guard, I plant my palm on his throat, not a punch, just a hard shove that pins his head back against the paneling.

"Listen to me very carefully," I growl, my voice dropping so low it barely cuts through the muffled music leaking in from the bar. "You don't own her. You don't get to mark her. You don't get to drag her anywhere like she's your fucking property."

His eyes are wild, pupils blown wide with rage and adrenaline.

He spits the words through clenched teeth. "You think I hit her? You're imagining things. Besides, she's my fiancé, asshole." He wriggles in my hold. "Not yours. Never yours. You're just the bar trash she fucks around with when she's bored."

My vision tunnels as I slam my forearm harder across his throat.

His face flushes a dark red; veins stand out at his temples.

"You think those bruises make you a man?" I ask, my voice shaking with the effort to keep it quiet. "You think putting your hands on her when she's scared makes you strong? You're a fucking coward."

He tries to knee me, a pathetic attempt.

I shift my hip, take the blow on the outside of my thigh rather than the groin, and drive my knee into his inner thigh, hard enough to make his leg buckle.

He grunts, sags for a second.

I don't let up.

"You touch her again," I say, leaning in so close our foreheads almost touch. "And I will end you, slowly. I will make sure every time you look in the mirror, you remember exactly who did this to you. Nod if you fucking understand."

"I didn't fucking touch her, you fucking loser." He spits out, struggling. "And every time I look in the mirror? Look at you, you're disgusting."

I push him against the wall harder, cutting off his oxygen.

His hands claw at my arm, trying to pry my forearm from his throat.

I don't move as I keep pushing, until I finally let him go.

He slides down the wall a few inches before catching himself, coughing violently, bracing his hand on his knee, as the other clutches his throat.

Before I walk away, he calls out to me in a hoarse voice. "You'll never have her. Who would want to look at someone like you, let alone love you?"

His words hurt, but I keep pushing, shaking off the adrenaline coursing through my veins.

I step back into the main room, and the hallway light fades behind me as the noise of the bar swallows me whole again—laughter, clinking bottles, the radio kicking into the last chorus of *Siren Sounds by Tate McRae.*

My chest is still heaving, adrenaline burning through me.

I flex my hands once, twice, trying to shake the feeling of Brian's throat under my forearm.

I don't go straight back to the bar, I can't.

If I see her sitting at that bar with those sad blue eyes and that brave little smile she tries to wear when she's hurting, I'm done for.

I'll crumble.

I can't fucking look at the only woman who's ever made me feel alive, not when every part of my soul is still reaching for her.

Moving to the far end instead, near the stack of clean pint glasses and the ice well, where the crowd thins and the pendant lights don't shine quite so brightly.

From here, I can see the whole room.

I watch, and my gaze lands on her.

Always *her*.

She remains in the same spot I left her, her hands resting on the bar top with her shoulders hunched as her eyes are fixed on the hallway.

Brian appears a few seconds later.

He's walking slower than before, no swagger, no smirk, his hand resting at his throat, rubbing absently where my arm pressed.

His face is already smoothing back into something neutral, something practiced.

He walks straight to her, and I wait for him to snap.

The yank, the possessive clamp on her arm again. It doesn't come.

He stops beside her, leaning down close enough that his mouth brushes her ear, whispering.

Whatever he says is inaudible from where I'm at, but I see her flinch, small and almost invisible, the plain eye wouldn't notice, then she nods once.

His hand settles on the small of her back in this sickly gentleness.

The way you touch someone when you're trying to prove you're not the monster everyone believes you are.

My stomach turns over as I watch the light of my life leave with him.

She lets him guide her toward the door. Her steps are small and hesitant, but she doesn't pull away. Doesn't fight.

Once they reach the exit, he pushes the door open with his shoulder, holding it for her like any decent man would.

She steps through first, but hesitates.

Right before the door swings shut behind them, she turns, just a fraction.

Just enough that her eyes find mine across the crowded bar.

Our gazes lock, and I wince at the contact and the pure longing in her eyes.

Her face is pale under the neon signs as her lips tremor, like she wants to say something, anything, but the words can't make it out.

The sheen of tears glosses over her eyes, shining with emotion she hasn't let fall yet.

There's no hope in them. Just a deep, quiet sadness that cuts deeper than any scream could.

She looks at me the way someone looks at a house they once lived in, something warm once, something safe once, knowing they can't go back inside.

My hands are locked around the edge of the bar so tightly that the wood creaks.

I feel the tear slip down my cheek before I realize I'm crying.

My throat constricts, a strangled sob clawing its way up before I can stop it.

Pressing the heel of my hand against my lips, I fight myself to keep it together.

Because the second it escapes, the truth hits me harder than anything ever has.

I'm not losing just anyone.

I'm losing the woman I was supposed to spend the rest of my life loving.

Every muscle in my body is screaming to go over to her, to cross the room, to pull her out of his reach and take her somewhere he'll never find.

But I stay rooted, because it isn't my place.

Because she's walking away with him. Because he's touching her gently now, gentle enough that anyone watching would call it love. Because she's letting him.

And because, deep down, I know what that look in her eyes means.

She's not choosing him tonight because she wants to. She's choosing him because she believes she has to.

Because she thinks the only way to keep the peace is to keep swallowing the hurt.

Because she thinks that if she leaves, everything will explode—her life, his temper, her following, the views, the fragile little world she's built around pretending that everything is fine.

I watch the door close behind them, and all I can do is sit here, breathing through the gaping hole she left in my chest, knowing the only woman who ever felt like home just walked out that door.

And I let her.

FORTY
REED

Steam still lingers in the bathroom after my shower. The mirror is fogged up, except for the streaks left by my hand. My reflection stares back at me; pale, hollow-eyed, water still dripping from my hair, with faint red marks on my shoulders from scrubbing too hard.

I stare at the scars running across my skin.

Faded lines, raised patches, the uneven map of what's left. Every one of them tells a story I can't recount without feeling the heat again; the crash of sound, the breath that wouldn't come, the moment everything changed.

I trace them slowly, my fingertips ghosting over the rough spots. I hate that I still remember the pain, not just from that day but from every time I've looked in this mirror since.

There was a time I could stand here and see a man. Now all I see is what's gone.

Brian's stupid face flashes through my mind, Layla's sunshine aura now hollowed into nothing. How she still left with him, leaving me to bleed in silence.

What killed me the most was how she looked at me

right before they left, like she wanted to explain something but couldn't.

I can still feel the burn of it in my chest.

I try to breathe, but my lungs won't cooperate.

Clenching my jaw against the anger that begins to crawl under my skin, not just at him but at myself, for believing, for wanting, for thinking someone like her could ever truly choose me.

Turning on the faucet, I feel the cold water hit the porcelain. The sound should drown out my thoughts, but it doesn't.

They come one after another—the doubt, the insecurity, the pain.

You're not enough.

You're a freak.

Why would she choose someone like you?

She deserves better. Everyone does.

My hands grip the edge of the sink until my knuckles blanch. The glass trembles in its frame, and my reflection blurs through streaks of condensation.

"Stop," I whisper, the tears beginning to well. "Just fucking stop."

But the thoughts never stop, a consistent reminder every single day of what I am.

A fucking monster.

Everything I've buried for years claws its way to the surface—the loneliness, the scars, the way people look at me and then look away.

The weight of it hits all at once as I let out a guttural scream before I shove my hand through my hair, pulling hard as I pace the small space, breathing hard, trying not to drown in my thoughts.

Trying so desperately not to let myself go back into that dark place again.

My breath comes in quick pulses, and without a second thought, I smash my hand through the mirror, glass shards falling into the sink.

I lower myself to the floor, watching the blood trickle from my knuckles.

Reaching up, I grab my phone off the counter.

I scroll until I find Maverick's number. My finger hesitates for half a second before I press call.

It rings once, twice.

"Yo, what's up, man?" His voice is loud, bright, the sound of life still happening somewhere else.

I can't get the words out right away as I press my phone harder to my ear. "Y-You home?"

"Yeah. Everything okay?"

I glance at my bloody knuckles and the tremor in my hand, reminding me of the dark thoughts that constantly dwell in my mind.

"No," I whisper. "It's not."

There's silence on the other end, then the sound of a door closing, voices fading. "Talk to me, bro. What happened?"

I swallow hard, my throat burning. "I just... I can't do this anymore. I can't keep pretending I'm fine."

"Okay," he says softly now. "Okay. I'm coming over."

The line clicks.

Dropping my phone to the floor, I lean down and rest my head between my knees. My sobs fill the room as the tears fall freely, landing on the aged oak floors.

I allow myself to cry, not because of Layla, the fire, or the scars, but because I finally said it out loud.

I can't do this anymore.

Not even five minutes later, I hear a truck's doors slam outside.

The front door opens and clicks shut. Two pairs of footsteps echo through the hallway.

Maverick is first through the door, with Carter right behind him.

Carter's wearing his ranch jacket, his hair still damp from a shower, and his face looks like stone. The moment he sees my hand and the crack in the mirror behind me, his jaw clenches.

"Goddammit, Reed," Carter mutters. "You could've called both of us."

"I called one of you," I rasp, glancing at Mav, pinching my brows together.

"Yeah," Carter says. "And he called me. That's how this works. You fall apart; we show up."

They move into the bathroom as if they've done this before, because they have.

Maverick grabs a towel, crouches, and applies pressure to my hand, while Carter leans against the doorway with his arms crossed, his blue eyes sharp but tired.

Nobody talks for a while. The only sounds are our breathing and the faint creak of the floor beneath Carter's boots.

Maverick breaks the silence first. "What's going on, Reed?"

Carter's brow furrows, sadness flashing in his eyes. "Reed, please, we can't lose you. We almost lost you once."

I stare down at my shaky hands, watching Maverick apply pressure to the other. "It's about Layla."

Carter stills. "Catalina's Layla?"

"Yeah."

Maverick lets out a breath. "She's engaged, dude."

Carter blinks once, slowly, as if he's trying to process this information.

Maverick keeps his eyes on me, waiting.

I drag a shaky breath. "I've been seeing her."

Carter's expression flickers, shock, disbelief, then concern. "You what?"

"We've been together," I say quietly. "Secretly. For months."

Maverick shifts beside me but doesn't interrupt.

"She reached out about filming that video for the bar," I continue. "We started talking. Then she came down to shoot, and we grew close. It just... happened. I didn't mean for it to. But I—" My throat tightens. "I love her."

Carter exhales hard, dragging his hand down his face. "Jesus Christ, Reed."

"I know."

"She's engaged," he repeats.

"I know," I whisper. "I tried to stop it, but every time I looked at her, it felt like something inside me finally made sense again. Like I could breathe."

Maverick leans forward, his elbows resting on his knees. "You think she feels the same?"

I squeeze my eyes shut. "I-I hope so. She just... she can't do anything about it right now. I can see it in her eyes, in the way she looks at me, as if she's begging me to understand."

Carter's quiet for a long moment before he speaks softly. "That's why you broke the mirror?"

"Yeah."

He nods once, rubbing the back of his neck. "You love her, and you can't have her. I get that. But Jesus, Reed, you can't let it eat you alive like this."

I laugh. "Too late for that."

Maverick runs a hand through his hair. "Cat and

Amelia begged to come. You know that, right? They were worried sick. Cat was screaming on the phone when I called Carter."

Carter snorts softly. "She was ready to drive here herself."

That makes me smile a little, broken. "Tell her I'm fine."

"You're not," Carter says softly. "You don't have to be. You don't have to be the one who fixes everything."

I stare down at my hands, the towel darkened where the blood's seeped through. "I shouldn't have done this to her. To any of us. But I can't regret it. I can't regret her."

Maverick nods slowly. "You always were the one who loved hardest."

"Yeah, well," I mutter, voice cracking, "look where that got me."

Carter steps forward and rests a hand on my shoulder. "It got you here. Alive. Still fighting. Don't you forget that."

The weight of his hand steadies me.

I can almost breathe again, almost.

Maverick's voice cuts through the silence, softer now. "You're not a bad man for loving someone who made you feel alive. Don't twist it into something ugly just because it's complicated."

I blink hard, fighting the burn in my eyes. "I just don't know how to stop."

"You don't," Carter says simply. "You learn to carry it. And when she's ready, you'll be the one waiting, because that's who you are."

I nod, barely holding it together. "I can't watch her suffer anymore."

Carter's hand tightens on my shoulder. "Then we'll help her. We'll figure something out. But you don't do this alone. Not anymore."

Maverick stands, pulling me up with him, his grip firm and brotherly. "You're ours, Reed. No more hiding. If you fall, we catch you. That's how this works."

I let out a broken laugh, tears spilling before I can stop them. "You two are exhausting."

Carter gives a faint grin. "Yeah, well, so are you."

I huff out a laugh. "Please don't tell the girls."

Maverick grins, patting my shoulder. "Don't worry, bro."

For the first time in weeks, I feel the weight of everything I've been carrying beginning to lift, just a little.

The ache's still there, but it's softer now.

Because I'm not alone in it anymore.

I've been outside since sunrise with my sleeves rolled up to my elbows, my boots caked with soil.

The patch behind the wooden beams has half-tilled, uneven rows lined with empty seed packets.

Sunflowers.

Her favorite.

The first time she mentioned them, we were playing twenty questions in my truck, and she had said *how they always face the light, even when it rains.*

So now, I plant them because I don't know what the fuck else to do.

My knuckles sting where last night's cuts reopened. I press them into the dirt anyway, as if I can bury the pain under it.

Buzz. Buzz. Buzz.

My phone buzzes in my back pocket, breaking the quiet.

I reach into my pocket and pull it out, seeing her name flash across my screen.

For a minuscule second, I consider letting it ring out, about protecting what's left of me.

But I can't. I never could when it comes to her.

I swipe to answer, bringing it to my ear. "Hey."

There's a pause on the other end, soft static, and faint sounds of the city traffic and distant laughter.

"Hey."

"You still out here?"

She exhales, and it sounds like she's been holding her breath for days. "No, I'm back in LA."

Shit.

I sink down on the edge of the old wooden step, dirt smeared across my palms. "Baby, please be safe."

"I-I am safe," she says quickly, her voice cracking. "I'm so sorry, Reed."

I close my eyes, jaw clenched.

"You don't have to be sorry, baby," I say softly.

She falls silent for a long moment, then I hear her sniffle. "I-I miss you so much."

My throat tightens at the stutter in her voice. I stare at the half-dug row of dirt as if it might give me the words I can't find. "I miss you more, sunshine, more I can put into words."

"I know you're mad at me—"

"Baby, why would I be mad?" I say softly. "I'm just worried. That's all I ever am when it comes to you."

She becomes quiet again, and I can hear her swallow through the line. "I don't deserve that."

"You deserve everything and more, baby."

She lets out a shaky laugh, the kind that sounds more like a sob. "You're too good to me, you know that?"

"Not sure anyone's ever said that to me before," I murmur, glancing at the sunflower seed packets beside me. "But you deserve it."

I hear the shuffle of her footsteps and a door closing, the faint sound of her sniffling. "I just needed to call. I'm sorry if I shouldn't have. I just, fuck, Reed, I need you."

Those three words hit me straight in the gut.

I can't even answer right away as I stare at the ground, at the seeds scattered across the dirt.

"Fuck," I say finally, my voice breaking a little. "I need you more than my next breath."

There's another pause, and I hear her take a trembling breath. "What are you doing right now?"

I glance around the empty lot, sunlight beginning to break through the clouds. "Plantin' sunflowers."

She lets out a soft laugh, small but real. "For me?"

"Yeah, baby," I say quietly. "For you. Something to look forward to when you come back home."

The line goes silent again, and I hear her sniffling. "I don't deserve someone like you."

I shake my head, even though she can't see it. "You deserve someone who cares, I do."

She sniffles again, voice trembling. "You always say things like that. And every time, it makes it harder to hang up."

"Then don't," I whisper.

She sighs softly. "I don't know how much longer I can do this."

My stomach knots. "You mean—"

She cuts me off. "I just mean pretending everything's okay."

The sound of her scared voice nearly breaks me.

"Then don't pretend," I whisper. "Not with me."

"Okay."

We stay like that for a while, just breathing, not talking, not hanging up, because if we stay still long enough, the world won't pull us apart again.

FORTY-ONE
LAYLA

"What the actual fuck, Layla!" he yells, slamming our bedroom door shut behind us so hard the framed photo on the dresser jumps and clatters face down. "That fucking freak threatened me!"

My suitcase is already open on the bed.

I started packing at dawn, before he woke up, before I even knew I'd have the courage to finish. My hands tremble as I reach for a folded cardigan I haven't worn in months.

"I didn't know he did that," I say. The words come out small, barely audible over the pounding in my ears. "I didn't ask him to."

"Didn't ask him to?" He laughs, walking towards me. "You think I'm blind? You think I didn't see the way you looked at him across the bar, like he's your fucking knight and I'm the monster?

You are a monster.

I keep moving, packing methodically.

My favorite jeans, my pastel yellow dress, the one my sweet Reed loves, anything and everything to get me the fuck out of here.

"I'm leaving you, Brian!" I yell, squeezing my jeans as I pack. "I can't do this anymore!"

The room goes eerily still, as if all the oxygen has vanished, and suddenly I can't fucking breathe.

He grabs the bedside lamp and hurls it; its ceramic base shatters against the wall, a shower of jagged white shards.

Moving across the room, he kicks over the laundry basket as clothes cascade onto the floor in a tangled heap. His arm sweeps the dresser top, causing perfume bottles to crash, a glass jewelry tray to flip, coins and earrings, scattering across the vinyl wood.

"Leaving me?" he screams. "After everything I've put up with? After I dealt with your moods, your crying jags, your 'I need content' bullshit every time you left for Tennessee, when I knew you were fucking him!"

I don't answer as I reach for the small wooden box hidden on the top shelf of the closet, behind the winter coats I never needed because of SoCal weather.

He sees me fumbling with it and lunges toward me. He smacks the box out of my grasp, pushing me hard as I fall onto the floor, screaming.

The box clatters all over the floor as the lid springs open, and letters spill everywhere.

Dozens of them.

Folded notebook pages, every single letter Reed has ever seen. Every "*I miss you,*" scrawled in his messy handwriting. Every "*I'm waiting for you, sunshine.*"

They flutter across the carpet like promises.

He drops to his knees as he snatches the nearest one and unfolds it with shaking fingers.

His eyes scan the page, then he begins to read aloud in a mock tone. "*If you ever wonder how I feel, just remember this: you've got a man in Tennessee who hasn't stopped thinking about you, not even for a day. And no matter what happens, I'll always be waiting for you, sunshine.*"

He laughs, a venomous, nasty, mocking laugh. "Jesus Christ. Forever? This guy's got a death wish."

He grabs another one. "*I keep thinking about you. About the way you laughed that night. About the kiss. I don't think I realized how much it would stay with me. I miss you more than I expected to.*"

He looks up at me, eyes glittering with something dangerous. "What the fuck are these?"

I take a step back as my heel crunches on broken glass. "Brian—"

He stands slowly, clutching the papers so tightly they tear at the edges.

"You fucking whore!"

I turn and bolt, barely making it three steps down the hallway before his hand fists in my hair.

He yanks hard.

My scalp screams as my back slams against his chest.

His arm snakes around my chest, tight enough that each breath burns.

"You think you can just walk out?" he hisses in my ear. "After I put up with your whining, your crying, your pathetic videos? You think you get to leave me like I'm nothing?"

I try to wriggle out of his hold, but it's useless.

"You're nothing without me," he whispers in my ear, wrapping his arms tighter around my chest. "No one is going to believe a word you say about me."

He twirls me around, and I can smell the sharp mix of beer and anger on his breath. He pushes me against the wall, my spine slamming into the drywall as pain blooms.

"After everything I've done for you," he says, gripping my throat, voice rising, "You embarrass me like this?"

I open my mouth to speak, but nothing comes out. He doesn't want my answer anyway as he tightens his grip.

Seeing the flash of fury in his eyes, I know, this time it's different.

He lets go of my throat and hits me, his fist connecting with the peak of my cheekbone.

I stumble back against the wall, the impact sending a shockwave of pain through my skull.

Feeling a sharp pain shoot across my cheek, my hand automatically rises to cradle my throbbing face. The taste of blood floods my mouth, and I feel a warm trickle run down my nose.

He looms over me, his breath ragged. His eyes are wild, and his hands are clenched into fists, ready to strike again.

"You fucking whore," he snarls. "How long has this been going on? How many times have you fucked him behind my back?"

My vision blurs as I struggle to focus.

All I see are the letters scattered across our bedroom floor, the words of love and longing between Reed and me now twisted into weapons of betrayal.

"Brian, please," I whisper, my voice trembling. "It's not what you thi—"

"Bullshit!" he roars, cutting me off. He grabs my shoulders, his fingers digging into my flesh. "You think I'm stupid? You think I can't see how you look at him? You've been fucking him for months, haven't you? Admit it!"

He shakes me violently as my teeth click together.

I feel panic rising in my chest, my fight-or-flight response screaming at me to do something.

"Brian, please!" I yell, pushing weakly at his chest.

He doesn't listen to my pleas, and this time I know he isn't holding back anymore; he has murder in his eyes.

With a swift flick of his wrist, he backhands me across the face, and I cry out in pain.

The room spins, and my knees buckle as I struggle to stand.

Before hitting the ground, he catches me, his grip rough and demanding.

He pulls me against him, his face inches from mine. "You're mine, Layla," he whispers. "You're my fucking fiancé, and you'll never leave me. Do you understand?"

I nod weakly, tears streaming down my face as they mix with the blood from wherever I'm bleeding.

He presses his weight against me, and I feel the hardness of his erection against my hip.

"Brian, please," I think to myself, but the words don't come out.

With a sob, I close my eyes, surrendering to the inevitable. His hands roam over my body, and I know this is my punishment for betraying him.

His hands keep roaming, and a wave of nausea washes over me. His touch is rough and brutal, a stark contrast to the tender caresses I've shared with Reed. His breath is hot and heavy against my ear as he mutters obscenities and threats, his voice a low, menacing growl.

"This pretty cunt is mine, and I'll show you how much I fucking love you, Layla."

He shoves me roughly against the wall, his body pinning mine and trapping me.

My heart races in my chest, and I feel the cold sweat of fear slide down my back.

I turn my head to the side, trying to avoid his lips, but he grabs me by the hair, forcing me to look at him.

"Look at me, you fucking bitch," he snarls, his eyes wild with rage. "You're going to pay for what you've done. You're going to pay for every fucking time you spread your legs for that freak."

With a cruel laugh, he grabs the hem of my dress and slowly pulls it up, his knuckles grazing my thighs.

I whimper and try to squirm away, but he holds me fast, his grip bruising. He pushes my panties aside and shoves his fingers inside me.

Tears stream down my face as he suddenly invades me. I push against his shoulder, but he pushes me harder against the wall, grunting as he forces his fingers inside me.

He finally pulls away, licking his fingers clean of me, his eyes cold and distant as he watches me. "Remember this, Layla," he says, his voice a low, dangerous purr. "Remember what happens when you try to leave me. You're mine, and I'll never let you go. I'll kill us both if I have to."

I slide down the wall, tears flowing freely as my body trembles from sobs.

He laughs, grabs his keys, walks to the front door, then slams it shut.

The apartment doesn't feel like mine anymore.

I raise my head from my knees and take in my surroundings.

The torn letters are scattered across the floor like ghosts, fragments of my handwriting staring back at me in looping ink.

My pulse pounds in my ears. I ache everywhere, my head a little foggy, but my body moves before my brain catches up, the adrenaline pushing me to move.

Standing, I move as fast as I can and go to our bedroom, grabbing my half-packed suitcase.

My hands are shaking so badly that I can barely hold

onto anything. My vision tunnels, my breathing is shallow and rapid, and my head hurts so fucking bad, but I can't stop. If I stay here, I'm as good as dead.

I whisper to myself, *move, Layla, move. I know you're hurting, baby, but we have to leave NOW*.

Yanking open my nightstand, I stuff my wallet into my tote. I find my phone charger and a small velvet pouch holding my grandmother's ring. My hands hover over it for a second before I tuck it into my pocket.

I slip my feet into my sneakers without untying them. The soles crunch over glass as I make my way to the front door and grab my car keys off the counter.

Turning back to look at the apartment I earned on my own, I feel a sense of loss, but I shake my head. This is going to be a new beginning, and if I stay here, I know I won't make it out alive.

My reflection appears in the mirror—puffy eyes, red cheeks, mascara smudged halfway down my face, faint bruises beginning to form around my neck and eye.

I look hollowed out.

Still, I turn the handle. Still, I go.

The hallway outside feels endless as my footsteps echo loudly, dragging whatever I can carry to get the fuck out of here.

The elevator chimes, and I flinch.

By the time I reach the parking garage, the tears I've been holding back start to fall.

My car sits beneath the dim yellow lights, dust settling on the hood because I haven't driven anywhere important in months. My hands shake so badly that I drop my keys once, twice, before I finally manage to unlock the door.

The stench of my old perfume and air freshener hits me

as I slide into the driver's seat and shut the door, sealing myself in with the sound of my heartbeat.

I fucking break.

The sobs burst out of me before I can control them. My whole body trembles as my breath comes in quick, uneven gasps, blurring my vision.

It's everything all at once—fear, guilt, grief, exhaustion. The years of pretending, the months of tiptoeing around his temper, and the ache of losing Reed again and again in silence.

My fingers dig into the steering wheel as another sob escapes, and I fold forward until my forehead presses against it.

The horn blares, and I choke out something between a laugh and a scream.

As my tears finally start to slow, I lift my head, wiping my face with the sleeve of my hoodie.

My reflection in the rearview mirror looks like a stranger, but I made it out.

I take out my phone, my fingers shaking as I open my airline app.

The confirmation for tomorrow's flight stares at me.

LAX to Nashville, 6:00 A.M.

Tomorrow feels too far away.

I whisper to myself. "I can't stay here another night."

Scrolling through the flight options, I finally find a 'change flight' option and click on it to check their availability.

My hands are shaking so badly I can barely type.

The screen loads for what feels like an eternity, showing no available flights until tomorrow.

Fuck.

I press my shaking hands to my face, trying to steady my

breathing as my chest becomes rigid, the walls of my car closing in around me.

Steadying my breathing, I look around my surroundings one last time, the one where I curated my life, where I thought I'd spend it with Brian forever.

It's the place where I used to be happy and make videos.

My hands tighten on the wheel. "No more," I whisper.

I start the car. The hum of the engine fills the silence. Backing out slowly, I check my mirrors even though no one's around.

Every red light feels too long. Every passing car is too loud. But the farther I go, the easier it becomes to breathe.

I don't even realize where I'm headed until I'm on the freeway, the city lights fading in the rearview mirror.

The 405 extends ahead of me, and I roll down the window, feeling the cool air sting my face.

Salty breeze wraps around, and I let myself scream, releasing everything I have been holding in.

I stop at a red light, the glow washing the inside of my car in a dull, pulsing crimson.

My hands are still shaking when I pick up my phone.

I shouldn't be doing this while stopped in traffic, but I do it anyway.

The map loads again, that thin blue line stretching impossibly far across the screen. I zoom out once, then again. The distance feels unreal, like something meant for someone braver than me.

A twenty-nine-hour drive from Santa Monica to Tennessee. Fuck.

I let out a shaky breath, staring at the number.

Twenty-nine hours of driving. Of gas stations, roadside

bathrooms, and cheap coffee—twenty-nine hours of being alone with my own thoughts.

I glance back in the rearview mirror and imagine staying.

No.

My grip tightens on the steering wheel.

Twenty-nine hours suddenly feels manageable.

The light stays red, the seconds ticking by on the crosswalk sign. I watch a couple cross the street, laughing, completely unaware that I'm about to change my life in the middle of the intersection.

I tap the screen again, tracing the route with my thumb. It's a long drive. It's exhausting. It's better than fucking staying.

The light finally turns green, and the sound of horns behind me snaps me back into my body. Dropping my phone into the cup holder, I ease off the brake.

As I press the gas, my chest loosens just a little.

Twenty-nine hours is nothing compared to a lifetime of feeling trapped, manipulated, hated, and unloved.

I pull into the flow of traffic heading east, and for the first time in eight years, I don't look back.

The city passes me in a blur, buildings thinning and lights growing farther apart as I head east.

I keep my eyes on the road, my hands steady on the wheel, even as my heart still races.

And in the quiet of my car, I hear Reed's voice, the way it always is when he is trying to ground me without taking anything from me.

You're safe now, sunshine.

FORTY-TWO
REED

I couldn't sleep at all last night.

It's about eleven in the morning, and sports news is blaring on the screen about a young NHL rookie, Beckett Walker, joining the Opal Springs home team, The Renegades.

The bar is closed today. I told everyone to take the day off; I couldn't stand working with the way I feel.

I'm half-dozing when I hear three soft knocks on the front door.

My brow furrows.

Probably Maverick with his foolishness.

I groan, pushing off the couch. "If that's you, Maverick, I swear to God–"

Gripping the handle, I force the door open, ready to be manhandled by my oaf of a brother, but when I open the door, the words die on my tongue.

Layla's standing there.

She looks like hell.

Her eyes are red, her mascara streaked as she's clutching

her suitcase handle. Her blonde hair's tangled, her lip split, and under the porch light, I notice faint bruising along her neck, jaw, and under her eye, but I can barely see it without my glasses.

"Layla?" My voice breaks on her name.

She tries to smile, but it comes out as a tremor. "Reed."

My body moves before my mind catches up.

Two steps are all it takes before I scoop her up into my arms, and it takes everything in me not to break down right here.

Shit, she's shaking.

It's not from the crisp autumn bite, but from fear, and my heart shatters each time her body trembles against mine.

I wrap her tighter as my hand cradles the back of her head, brushing the strands of her golden hair, trying to comfort her.

"It's okay," I whisper into her hair, pushing the front door open with my foot. "I've got you, baby. I've got you."

She let out this tiny, broken sound, and I feel it straight in my ribcage.

"Let's take you inside, baby," I murmur, carrying her across the threshold. "You're safe now. I promise. You're with me."

And God help me, I meant every word.

I close the door, and the silence between us feels deafening.

Setting her down gently, I grab my glasses from the end table by the front door and slide them on. I flip the light switch, and my stomach drops when I can see her clearly.

Bruises on her face, neck, and wrist.

"Jesus Christ," I whisper, my voice barely steady.

I move closer, my hand hovering near her cheek without

touching until she nods. When I do, she flinches, so softly I almost miss it, and my chest cracks open.

"Layla, baby..." I swallow hard, tears stinging the backs of my eyes. "Who did this to you?"

She's trembling. Her voice is quiet and fractured. " I-I'm sorry, Reed. I've been driving for days. I—"

"Don't apologize," I say quickly. "You never have to apologize to me. Just tell me who did this."

Her lips part, trembling. "B-Brian."

I close my eyes, my jaw tightening.

A thousand violent thoughts race through my mind, but none of them matter right now. She's standing here, trembling, and she needs me to stay calm.

"Okay," I murmur. "You're safe now, sunshine. You hear me? You're safe."

She nods, tears silently streaming down her face.

I reach for her hand. It's cold, small in mine. "Come on. Let's get you cleaned up."

Her body moves on instinct, trusting me as she always has. I guide her down the short hall to the bedroom and my en-suite bathroom, the old floorboards creaking beneath our feet.

I flip the light switch on, its bulbs humming softly. Steam fogs the mirror as I turn on the shower, testing it until it's just warm enough.

She's still shaking, sitting on the edge of the counter, with dazed, distant eyes.

"Layla," I whisper, kneeling before her. "Look at me."

Her eyes find mine, and my chest aches all over again.

"I'm gonna help you, alright? You're not alone anymore."

She nods, and when I offer my hand, she takes it. I help her stand, guiding her gently toward the shower.

"Can I stay?" I ask.

She nods again, barely audible. "Please."

I slowly undress her, helping her out of her clothes. The fabric falls to the floor, leaving her bare.

My eyes sweep over the semi-healed bruises and the new ones forming. I press my hand to my mouth, fighting back tears.

Keeping my clothes on, I gently guide her into the shower.

The water begins to fall on us as I grab a washcloth, wetting it, and gently scrubbing her arms. "You just breathe. Let me do the rest."

I gently run the cloth over her face, wiping away streaks of makeup, grime, and faint traces of blood.

She winces once but doesn't pull away.

My fingers tremble as I brush a strand of hair from her forehead, and I can't help it; the tears blur my vision until I can barely see what I'm doing.

Her voice cuts through the sound of running water. "He said no one would believe me."

"I do," I whisper. "I always will, baby."

She finally breaks down. A sob racks through her body as she collapses into me, her hands clutching my wet shirt.

I hold her closer, pressing my lips to the top of her head. "It's over, sunshine. He's never gonna touch you again. Not as long as I'm breathing."

Her tears keep falling, and I don't mind. I let her cry until her breaths slow and become shallow again, until the shaking calms down.

I turn off the water, hearing the pipes' faint squeak.

Grabbing a towel, I wrap it around her shoulders, tucking it close.

"You're gonna be okay," I murmur, brushing my thumb along her cheek. "You did the hardest part already. You left."

She nods weakly, her eyes glimmering with tears.

"I don't deserve you," she whispers.

"Yeah," I say softly, "you do, baby. You always did."

I help her with one of my old flannels. Grabbing a brush, I brush her hair, detangling a few knots. Once done, she stands there waiting while I quickly throw on some dry clothes.

Throwing on some sweats, I walk over to her and scoop her up without asking, carrying her down the hall.

She doesn't protest as she buries her face in my chest, sobbing.

I gently lay her on the couch, pulling a blanket over her; her eyes are already half-lidded, exhaustion finally winning.

Sitting beside her, I gently brush my thumb along the edge of her jaw. "You sleep, baby. I'll be right here."

Her voice is barely a breath. "Don't leave me."

"Never," I promise.

She drifts off, her hand still tangled in my shirt, and I remain there long after her breathing evens out, watching her chest rise and fall as the fear finally leaves her face.

The highlight reels of their new player are flashing on the screen, but I can't hear the commentators.

All I see is her.

And all I can think is that I'd burn the whole damn world to keep anyone from hurting her again.

She finally fell asleep; her face soft, her lashes casting tiny shadows, one fist curled against the blanket. Every rise and fall of her chest is a small, perfect thing I want to protect with my whole body.

My house is absurdly quiet as I watch her sleep.

Heat simmers in my chest, rising mercilessly. It begins behind my ribs and blooms until my hands form fists without my willing them to.

My jaw tightens as I chew the inside of my cheek, and the taste of copper blooms on my tongue.

For a ridiculous, glorious second, that's all I want, him on my floor, the two of us with no witnesses, and the rest settled with my fist in his face. I can already hear the hollow punch of it in my head.

I imagine how it would feel to let that anger land on someone else, to trade the ache in my chest for the sound of him caving under it.

It's terrifyingly tempting.

I can feel my blood pulsing at my temples as my hands twitch at my sides.

Taking a deep breath, I look at Layla, at the tear tracks on her cheeks, at the small tremor in her sleeping fingers, and the fantasy grows uglier.

Violence only breeds more violence. It wouldn't fix her; it would diminish her again, shrinking her room to the size of his fists. I refuse to let her become collateral damage in my rage.

So the fantasy ends there, as sharply as it began. I let out a long, deliberate exhale and unclench my fists.

My knuckles still ache from punching the mirror; they remind me that hurting myself or someone else doesn't fix anything.

I stay there until my legs ache, my back pressed against the edge of the couch.

The sun's higher now, spilling soft light across the floorboards, catching the strands of her hair that glint like gold against the pillow.

She shifts in her sleep just enough to make a quiet sound, and her hand slides out from under the blanket. I catch it instinctively, threading my fingers through hers.

I ease down beside her, careful not to jostle the couch. My feet thud softly to the floor, and my body feels heavy like I haven't felt in years.

The exhaustion that's been riding me for months finally catches up; all the sleepless nights, the fear, the rage that wouldn't quiet down.

She mumbles something I can't make out, her brow furrowing. I reach up and smooth it away with my thumb, whispering, "It's okay, sunshine. I'm right here."

Her breathing evens out again.

I continue staring at her, each bruise, each faint mark, a reminder of what she survived.

Pressing a gentle kiss to her forehead, I whisper. "You don't have to be afraid anymore."

My eyes burn, but I let them close.

The warmth of her body, the faint scent of her shampoo, and the way her fingers unconsciously curl around mine it's enough to pull me under.

I let myself rest.

She's at the table, one of my old flannels hanging off her frame. Her hair's still damp from the shower, pulled into a low braid. She hasn't said much since she woke up.

"Hey, sunshine," I say gently, glancing over my shoulder. "You want some French toast?"

She hesitates, twisting the edge of the flannel's sleeve between her fingers. "Um...yeah, sure."

I nod once, flipping the spatula in my hand. "Comin' right up."

The smell of coffee fills the air, rich and bitter—just as she used to rave about when she first came here.

Pouring a cup, I catch myself smiling at the way she likes it, iced with hazelnut creamer.

I set the glass in front of her, and she gives a tiny nod, her fingers curling around the cup. Her hands are still shaky, but she doesn't let go.

"Thanks," she mumbles, her eyes fixed on the ice clinking against the cup.

"You're welcome," I say, pushing my glasses up the bridge of my nose.

I slide the plate of French toast toward her, sitting across the table, my elbows resting on my knees. "You feelin' okay? Need me to take you to the doctor?"

She shakes her head almost immediately, her voice barely audible. "No."

"Alright," I murmur, nodding.

I watch her quietly, noting how her shoulders slump and how she keeps her eyes on the plate rather than on me. "You sure, sunshine? Police, doctor, anybody. You say the word, and I'll drive."

She grips the fork tighter, her throat bobbing. "No cops," she whispers, her eyes flicking up in a plea. "No doctors. I just..." She swallows, her words breaking apart. "I just want to be here."

I exhale slowly, nodding again. "Okay," I whisper, leaning in slightly. "Here's where you'll be, then."

She tries to smile but can't quite manage it. Her hand

shakes as she lifts the fork, her eyes flick to me as if she's afraid I'll say something else.

"You didn't have to do all this," she says finally, her voice soft yet frayed at the edges.

"I wanted to," I answer, reaching up to scratch the back of my neck. "I couldn't just sit around while you slept. I needed to make sure you'd have somethin' warm when you woke up."

She looks down again, a quiet sniffle catching in her throat. "You're always so patient with me."

I lean forward, resting my forearms on the table. "You don't owe me nothin', Layla. Take all the time you need."

Her hand slips across the table as her fingers brush mine. I inch my hand forward, letting her rest her hand there. Her thumb traces the rough skin of my knuckles, then stops at an old scar.

"You're too good to me," she whispers.

I shake my head, smiling faintly. "Baby, you just haven't had anyone treat you right before."

Her lip trembles, eyes glistening. "I don't know what I'd do if I hadn't come here."

"Hey," I murmur, squeezing her hand gently. "Don't think like that. You're here now. That's what matters."

The silence between us feels delicate.

Her eyes drop to our clasped hands, and I notice the slightest tremor in her breath. My own eyes begin to sting before I even realize.

I reach up, lifting my glasses as I wipe a stray tear with my thumb.

She notices, her voice breaking. "Reed... don't cry."

I chuckle, blinking quickly as I look down. "Sunshine. I —" I exhale, shaking my head. "I'm just glad you're safe."

Her fingers grip mine. "I feel safe," she whispers. "With you."

I look up at her, my vision blurred, my chest full. "That's all I'll ever want," I say softly.

And right there, with the skillet still crackling behind us and her hand in mine, I know I'd spend the rest of my life making sure she never has to whisper that word like a prayer again.

FORTY-THREE
LAYLA

A raw, guttural scream escapes me before I even realize it's happening.

The nightmare has been the same every night—his hand around my throat, his fist connecting with my face, and the hiss of his voice in my ear, whispering obscenities in my ear, all while he was threatening me.

"Layla!"

Reed's voice cuts through the darkness as his footsteps thunder down the hall. He appears instantly, barefoot and half-dressed, eyes wide and wild, pausing in the doorway, hesitating, unsure whether he can come near me.

My chest heaves as I sit upright in bed, the blanket tangled around my legs as my hands clutch my throat.

It feels like I can't breathe; I claw at my throat, struggling for air as the ghost of Brian's hands squeeze around my neck.

"Hey, hey, sunshine," he says quietly, his tone shifting from alarm to gentleness in a breath. He lifts his hands slightly, palms out. "You're okay. You're safe. It's me."

I shake my head, struggling to hold back a sob. "He was here, Reed—he—"

He takes a slow step forward. "No one's here, baby. I checked the locks before I went to bed. You're safe, Layla."

I can't stop trembling. My entire body shakes as if it's about to fall apart.

He lingers by the door for a moment longer before crouching down low, his voice soft and gentle. "You want me to come closer?"

I nod quickly, tears spilling over.

He crosses the room in two quick steps. The mattress dips when he sits on the edge, close but not touching. "You're okay, sweetheart. You're just dreamin'. Look at me, baby."

I force my gaze upward. His hair's a mess, sticking up in every direction as his chest rises quickly. His hands are trembling too, but his steady, green eyes hold me there.

My voice cracks. "It felt real."

He nods, his throat working. "I know. It's gonna feel that way for a while." His voice catches, softer now. "You've been through too damn much."

I press my hand to my chest, trying to slow the pounding rhythm against my ribs. "I can't—I keep seeing him. I can't make him stop."

He exhales shakily, running a hand through his hair. "I know, baby, but you're safe here, I promise."

I wipe my face, the words barely coming out. "What if he comes here? The letters, the ones I left, they had your address."

He shifts a little closer, still giving me space. "He'd never make it past my property line, Layla. I'll make sure of it."

My lip trembles. "I don't feel safe."

His expression softens, and his voice becomes gentler. "Then I'll stay right here until you do."

I blink up at him, exhausted. "You don't have to—"

"Not leavin' you like this," he says firmly, shaking his head. He leans forward slightly, his elbows on his knees. "Not tonight."

I take a shaky breath. "Can you just talk? Please?"

He nods, clearing his throat, his eyes glancing to the window before returning to me. "Well," he murmurs, "you've successfully scared the shit outta me. Thought someone broke in."

A faint laugh escapes me, more air than sound. "Sorry."

"Don't be sorry," he says softly, his mouth twitching into the faintest smile. "I'm just glad you scream loud enough to wake the dead. Means I'll always hear you."

My lip curves, just barely.

He grunts, looking away for a second, his jaw flexing before his voice drops low again. "Layla... you're safe now, you hear me? He ain't ever touchin' you again."

I nod, but my shoulders tremble. "It doesn't feel over."

He swallows, his eyes shining in the dark. "I know." He pauses, then softly asks, "Can I—?" He makes a faint gesture toward me.

My voice cracks. "Yeah."

He moves slowly, carefully, sitting beside me, wrapping his arm around my shoulders, it's light, tentative, giving me space to pull away if I want to.

I don't as I lean in, pressing my forehead to his chest, the soft cotton of his shirt damp beneath my cheek from tears.

His hand gently circles against my arm. "Breathe with me, sunshine," he says, taking in a breath of his own, coaching me. "In and out. That's it. You're here. Not there."

My breath finally evens out against him, and my body feels heavy with exhaustion.

"You did good gettin' out," he murmurs, voice low and rough. "You're stronger than you think."

"Doesn't feel like it," I whisper.

He doesn't respond as he presses me tighter against his chest.

Silence falls around us; just our breathing, filling up the space.

The fear still lingers, but it's quieter now, softened by his voice and the steady rhythm of his heartbeat beneath my ear.

For the first time in years, I let myself believe that maybe he's right.

Maybe I really am safe.

"Mornin', sunshine."

My gaze moves toward the doorway, and I spot Reed, barefoot, with a tray in his hands.

There's French toast, powdered sugar dusted over it, a side of strawberries, and an iced coffee packed with ice. He gives me a small smile that doesn't quite reach his eyes.

"You brought me breakfast?" I whisper, my voice scratchy.

He nods. "Yeah, and I made it myself," he says jokingly.

I almost smile, but it fades too quickly, my throat tightening. "I'm not really hungry."

He places the tray on the nightstand, moving towards me cautiously before sitting gently on the edge of the bed.

The mattress sinks under his weight, and the clink of the plate against the wood fills the quiet.

"I know," he says softly. "But you need to eat, baby."

The way he says 'baby' with his Southern drawl makes something in me ache.

"I just..." My voice trails off. "I can't make myself move."

He exhales slowly, nodding as if he understands, because he does. He's never pushed me, not once.

"Alright," he says after a moment. "Then we'll do it together."

He reaches out slowly, waiting until I nod, before his hand touches my arm. He helps me sit up, fixing the pillow behind my back.

"There we go," he murmurs. "See? Not so bad."

He adjusts his glasses, then cuts a piece of French toast into smaller bites, holding it out to me. "Just start with this."

It's ridiculous being fed like this, but I don't stop him. I open my mouth and take a small bite.

"There you go," he says, voice gentle but relieved. "You're doin' good, sunshine."

My throat burns as I swallow. "You don't have to take care of me like this."

He gives a quiet chuckle, shaking his head. "Yeah, baby, I do."

That's what breaks me down. The tears come quickly, initially silent, then grow stronger until my breath catches.

"Hey, hey," he whispers, setting the plate down and moving closer, but not too close. "Talk to me, baby."

"I just—" I press a trembling hand over my face. "I need my girls. I need to tell them everything. I can't hold it in anymore."

He nods slowly, his eyes gentle. "Then we'll call 'em, alright?"

I nod, wiping at my eyes. "I don't even know where to start."

"Start wherever you need to. They love you. They'll listen."

He reaches out again, softly brushing his thumb across my cheek, catching a tear before it falls. "You don't gotta do it alone anymore, sunshine."

I nod again, a broken sound escaping my throat as I lean forward, just enough for my forehead to rest against his shoulder.

He remains still, his hand lightly resting on my back as the other is steady on the blanket beside me.

I feel something that nearly resembles *hope.*

He doesn't move immediately as he stays still, his hand steady against my back while I try to calm my breathing. My tears slow down, but the heaviness doesn't go away.

He pulls back slightly, enough to look at me. "You want me to call them for you?"

I sniff, nodding. "Yeah. I can't—I don't think I can talk yet."

"Alright, baby," he murmurs, brushing a strand of hair from my face.

He stands and reaches for his phone on the nightstand, the mattress creaking as he moves.

His thumb swipes across the screen, and for a moment, the faint ring fills the room. I watch him pace near the window, sunlight spilling over his shoulder and bathing him in soft gold.

It takes three rings before someone answers.

"Hey, Cat," he says softly, his tone shifts, but with an undercurrent that makes my stomach churn.

A pause. Catalina must have said something, because his jaw tightens, but he keeps his voice gentle. "Layla's here." He glances back at me, eyes soft.

I can't hear what Catalina is saying, but I can picture the sharp inhale, the way she probably presses her hand to her chest. She's always felt things too deeply.

Reed nods slowly. "Yeah. You, Amelia, Mav, and Carter. Just get here, alright? She needs you."

There's a pause again. His thumb moves over his bottom lip as he listens. "Yeah, Cat. She's okay. But... she needs her girls right now."

I close my eyes, swallowing hard.

My girls.

Catalina's fiery warmth. Amelia's quiet steadiness. The kind of love that doesn't ask or judge. Just shows up.

"Alright," Reed finally says, his voice dropping to nearly a whisper. "We'll see y'all soon."

Ending the call, he gently places his phone on the dresser. For a moment, he doesn't turn around, just stands there with tense shoulders, breathing slowly.

He turns slowly, his eyes meeting mine. "They're on their way."

My throat tightens again, but nothing escapes my lips as quiet sobs wrack through my body.

He crosses the room, crouching down to be at my eye level, his hand hovers before gently resting on my knee. "You did the right thing, sunshine. You don't have to face this alone anymore."

Tears blur my vision. "What will they think when they see me like this?"

He tilts his head slightly, voice quiet but certain. "They'll see a woman who got out. A woman who's still standin'. That's what they'll see."

Something in me opens up again, but this time, it's not from fear. It's relief.

He gently squeezes my knee, then stands, brushing his palms on his jeans. "I'll get some more coffee going. They'll be here soon."

I watch him walk out of the bedroom, into the narrow hallway, and into the kitchen, hearing the sound of him opening the cabinets and glass clinking as he starts the coffee pot.

My girls will be here soon, and finally, I'll tell them everything.

About five minutes later, the muffled sound of engines breaks the morning silence, followed by the closing of doors and quiet voices outside.

I haven't moved from the bed since Reed left the room to make coffee.

The front door opens with a familiar creak that echoes down the hallway. I hear quick footsteps scatter into his home, and frantic voices are muffled by the walls.

"Where is she?" Catalina's voice I recognize first, laced with panic.

Reed's quiet response comes, steady but weary. "Bedroom. She's resting."

The floorboards creak closer and closer until the doorway is filled with soft light and familiar faces.

Catalina stops first, her chestnut eyes widening the moment she sees me sitting against the headboard.

She's wrapped in Carter's enormous hoodie, her hair's tangled, and her eyes are swollen from crying as she gently touches her small baby bump.

Her eyes flick from the bruises starting to heal, and she lets out a sharp gasp.

"Oh, baby," she whispers. Her voice cracks as she

crosses the room and drops onto the mattress beside me before I can even process it.

The bed dips under her weight, then she's holding me, wrapping her arms around my shoulders.

"Cat—" I start, but my voice breaks on the first word.

"You don't have to say anything," she says quickly, her breath shaky against my hair. "You don't owe us an explanation. You're safe now, that's all that matters."

The scent of her lavender-and-vanilla perfume hits me, and it's enough to finally break me open. The tears come suddenly and silently, and my body trembles as I clutch the front of her hoodie.

Amelia steps forward next, quiet as usual.

She kneels by the bed, her hand brushing my leg, then gently wrapping around my wrist. Her eyes shine, but her voice remains soft and steady. "We're here, babe. We're right here."

I can't stop trembling. "I—I didn't know what to do," I whisper, my words spilling out between gasps. "I thought maybe he'd change, that, ma-maybe he'd be different, but he just got worse."

Amelia's grip tightens on my wrist. "They always say they're going to change," she says softly. "They promise things will get better, but as soon as they get mad, they blame anyone but themselves. It's not your fault, Layla. None of this is."

Behind them, Maverick lingers in the doorway, shoulders tense, jaw clenched. He's not his usual loud, chaotic self. His voice is calm as he asks, "You okay, sugar?"

I give him a small nod, tears forming in my eyes.

Carter steps in beside him, his expression grim yet gentle. "You're safe here. We'll make damn sure that fucker doesn't get anywhere near you."

Reed finally walks over and stands next to Carter, watching everything with red-rimmed eyes. He's trying to stay steady, but I can see the tension in his shoulders and the way his hands keep flexing open and closed.

Catalina finally pulls back just enough to look at me, brushing the hair from my face. "You want to sit up, baby? You look pale."

I nod feebly, and Reed steps forward quietly.

He adjusts the pillows behind me, being careful not to touch too much. The mattress dips slightly as he helps lift me upright, his arm steady at my back but never pressing.

"Easy," he murmurs, voice barely above a whisper. "You're okay."

I look up at him through tears, my chest twisting. "I'm sorry," I whisper. "For bringing all this here."

Reed shakes his head instantly. "Don't you dare apologize, sunshine. You didn't bring this. He did."

Catalina wipes her eyes and looks toward the boys. "Coffee," she says, her voice shaking but determined.

Amelia nods and stands up slowly. "And something to eat. I'll help."

As they leave, Reed sinks back onto the edge of the bed, his elbows resting on his knees. "You did the right thing, baby," he says softly. "You did the right thing comin' here."

Catalina gives Reed a curious look after he just called me "baby," then smirks, staying seated beside me, rubbing small circles into my back while whispering soft reassurances as the others move around the house.

Being surrounded by them, by their warmth and quiet presence, I feel something close to steady.

And when I glance over at Reed, his eyes already on me, I realize he's the reason I made it out at all.

FORTY-FOUR
REED

The entire family has been stuck here for the past few days since Layla shared what she's been through; they're just acting like a family should.

Maverick is lying on the rug next to Leo on his baby mat, babbling at him while Amelia sits crisscross, gently rubbing slow circles along his back.

Carter and Catalina sit together on the couch, with her reading her gossip blogs while he rubs her growing belly.

Layla looks better today; she finally got out of bed and is sitting on the floor with Mav, playing with Leo.

She looks brighter, her smile slowly returning.

The bruises might be fading, but I know this will never truly go away. And I'll make damn sure I spend the rest of my life ensuring she always feels safe in my home, in my arms, with me.

I yearn to touch her, to hold her, but the girls don't know about us, and there's never a right time to say it. I'll let her take the lead; she's been through enough.

Catalina's laugh rings out. "Reed Hayes, are you just

gonna stand there starin' at her, or are you gonna come sit down like a normal person?"

Maverick snorts, glancing over his shoulder. "Yeah, man, you're creeping."

"Watch it," I mutter, but there's no heat behind it.

Amelia smirks. "You are kinda brooding."

"Brooding?" I arch a brow. "You all share the same vocabulary."

"Maybe," Amelia says, grinning.

I shake my head, attempting to dismiss it, but the reality is—I am brooding. I can't escape it.

Layla seems more vibrant today, lighter, like she's beginning to find herself again. However, I notice the ghosts lingering in her eyes when she believes no one is looking.

And every time I see them, I want to pull her into my arms and promise her that no one will ever hurt her again.

So I remain where I am, allowing her to laugh with them and gradually rebuild parts of herself in her own time.

Until then, I'll keep standing here, memorizing the sound of her laugh, how she runs her fingers through Leo's soft hair, and the subtle curve of her smile when she notices me looking.

It's enough, for now.

By noon, the house smells like a Sunday cookout. Carter's infamous ribs are slow-roasting in the oven, Catalina's got three pots on the stove, and Maverick's been caught "taste-testing" at least six times.

"Swear to God, Mav," Catalina warns, pointing a wooden spoon at him. "If you touch that mac and cheese one more time, I'll break your hand. The baby is craving this. I'll hurt you."

He grins, already backing away with a bite in his mouth. "Worth it."

Amelia rolls her eyes from the counter where she's slicing cornbread. "You have no self-control."

"Funny, you don't seem to mind when I'm deep in—"

She bumps his hip with hers, cutting him off. "MAVERICK!"

Carter snorts from his spot at the sink, drying a dish. "Y'all are exhausting."

"Don't act like you're any better," Catalina says, tossing him a dish towel. "You were on your knees earlier begg—"

"Darlin'," Carter warns, rubbing her belly when she passes.

The entire room hums with that familiar Hayes energy.

And right in the middle of it all is Layla.

She's at the table with her sleeves rolled up, carefully arranging plates and laughing at something Amelia said.

Her hair's down now, brushing against the collar of my flannel. There's color back in her cheeks and a subtle spark in her eyes.

She laughs at something Maverick says now, and the sound nearly knocks the air out of me.

"Reed," Catalina calls, breaking through my daze. "You just gonna stand there starin' or help pass out drinks?"

I clear my throat. "Right. Drinks."

Maverick smirks. "Bro's in another galaxy."

"Shut up," I mutter, grabbing the pitcher.

Layla glances at me as I set a glass in front of her, that same little smile tugging at her lips. "Thanks," she says quietly.

"Anytime, sunshine."

When the food's finally ready, everyone gathers around the table.

Catalina sets down a bowl with a triumphant grin. "All

right, nobody move till I say grace, or Maverick's gettin' another lecture on manners."

"C'mon, I was starving," he grumbles, but bows his head anyway.

Lunch becomes a blur of laughter and clinking silverware.

Maverick tries to convince everyone that he makes the best potato salad, until Amelia points out that it came from the store.

Carter shares a story about Leo learning to crawl and nearly getting into Cupcake's water bowl, and about Catalina's cry-laughing so hard she almost spills her tea.

And Layla is laughing with them, her shoulders relaxed and eyes bright.

She looks at me across the table, smiling in that gentle, private way. I don't smile easily, but damn if she doesn't make it look effortless.

Catalina notices, of course. "Layla, you look happier today," she says, her tone genuine and warm.

Layla tucks a strand of hair behind her ear. "I feel lighter, like I can breathe again."

Carter nods, showing seriousness for a moment. "That's all we want for you."

The table falls quiet for a beat.

Maverick, unable to stand the silence, points his fork at me. "Reed's finally smilin' again, too. I was startin' to think his face was stuck like that."

"Keep talkin', and I'll feed you your fork," I shoot back.

Everyone laughs.

I glance around the table—my brothers, their wives, and the people who make this old house feel like home—then back to her.

She fits in here as if she's always belonged.
Her spark, her fire, is finding its way back.

FORTY-FIVE
LAYLA

I thought I was making progress, but this morning I find myself back at the same dread and despair.

He's still out there.

Reed's arm tightens around me as I lie there, trying to steady my breathing. The gentle brush of his lips against my shoulder pulls me back to the present.

"You still awake?" he murmurs, his voice rough with sleep.

"Yeah," I whisper.

He hums and shifts closer until his forehead rests against the curve of my back. One of his hands slides down, and his palm settles over my stomach as his thumb moves in slow circles, so gentle it almost overwhelms me.

"You hurtin'?" he asks quietly.

"Just tired," I say, my voice barely there.

He nods, pressing a gentle kiss to my temple. "This takes time, baby, and I'll be here every step of the way if you'll let me," he whispers, nuzzling his face into the crook of my neck.

His words bring tears to my eyes. I place my hand over

his, feeling the roughness of his knuckles against my fingertips.

I want to believe him, but how can I when this maniac is still out there with Reed's address? His silence is starting to scare me.

My phone buzzes for the fourth time.

Reed lifts his head slightly, brow furrowing. "You need to check that?"

I hesitate, then nod. "Yeah... just in case."

Reaching for my phone, I click the side button, seeing the flood of messages coming in from none other than the psycho himself.

BRIAN

You really think I'd let you run away from me?

You dumb bitch.

His address was on those letters.

I'm coming, Layla.

My hand shakes so hard I nearly drop the phone.

He notices immediately. "What is it?" he asks, his voice low but edged with alarm.

I can't speak, so I turn the screen toward him. He grabs his glasses from the nightstand and quickly puts them on.

His eyes darken as he focuses on reading, his jaw tightening and every muscle in his body going still.

"Layla," he says softly, like he's forcing himself to stay calm. "When did this come in?"

"Just now." My voice cracks.

He exhales slowly, taking the phone from me, setting it on the nightstand, before he pulls me close.

His hand returns to my waist, protective, while the

other cups the back of my head. "He's not coming anywhere near you," he says, "I promise you that."

The tears come as I clutch his shirt, bury my face against his chest, and listen to his heartbeat pounding beneath my ear.

He presses another kiss to my hand, then to my forehead. "You're safe here," he whispers. "I swear it."

And even with fear crawling under my skin, I believe him.

He quietly gets up, still half-dressed from sleep, and pulls on the first flannel he finds. "Come on," he murmurs, reaching for my hand. "You need to eat somethin'. I'll make breakfast."

The aroma of espresso and syrup interweaves in the air.

He tiptoes through the kitchen, barefoot, hair still messy from sleep. He hasn't said much since the messages came in, but he doesn't have to. The way he hovers close, the way his hand occasionally grazes the small of my back as he passes, says it all.

"Sit," he murmurs when I try to help. "You need to eat."

I sit on one of the barstools, wrapped in his hoodie, watching him flip French toast, my favorite. His shoulders are tense, his jaw clenched, but his movements are gentle.

He slides a plate in front of me, and a few minutes later, it's perfectly cooked. "You've barely eaten since yesterday."

"I know," I whisper. My voice sounds small in the quiet kitchen. "Thank you."

He nods and starts pouring coffee into a glass. "You're welcome, baby."

Before I can answer, a loud knock rattles the front door —quick and impatient, then another.

Reed frowns, wiping his hands on a towel as he heads over. "Oh my—"

The door swings open before he finishes, and Maverick's voice booms through the house. "Heyyy, favorite Hayes brother is here. Everyone, clap."

I freeze, fork halfway to my mouth.

Behind him, Carter walks in, calm as always, with Leo perched on his arm and babbling happily. Catalina follows, her belly now slightly more visible beneath a soft lavender dress. Amelia is close behind, wearing her signature oversized band tee, tattoos on display, holding a coffee, her scowl intact.

Reed blinks. "Jesus, y'all ever heard of knockin'?"

Catalina spots me and gasps. "Heyyyy," she says, a mischievous look on her face.

"Hey," I manage, my voice trembling slightly. "I need to talk to you guys again."

Amelia's expression shifts quickly from confusion to concern. "Wait. What's going on?"

Reed exhales, rubbing the back of his neck. "It's... a lot. Sit down."

I shake my head. "No. I should be the one to tell all of you."

Everyone finds a spot; Carter leans against the counter as Leo wiggles in his arms, cooing softly. Maverick paces as he always does when restless, Catalina sitting beside me, and Amelia beside her.

I take a deep breath, glancing at Reed before I begin.

They already know most of it—that Brian hurt me and that I've been staying here ever since, but there's still one truth weighing heavily on my chest, and I refuse to keep it buried.

I glance up, catching Reed across the room. He's standing by the counter with his arms crossed, pretending to listen to Carter and Maverick talk about random shit. But I can tell he's not really paying attention. His eyes keep flicking toward me.

Catalina must feel it too, because her hand stops. "Layla?" she says softly.

I swallow hard. "There's something else I need to say."

Reed immediately straightens, shoving Maverick's beefy arm off of him.

Amelia tilts her head. "You can tell us anything, babe."

My fingers knot in the sleeve of Reed's yellow flannel, the same one I've been living in since I arrived. My pulse pounds so loudly I can barely hear myself.

"I wasn't just staying here because I was scared," I whisper. "I was here because... because I wanted to."

Catalina blinks, her eyes flicking between us. "What do you mean?"

I force myself to look at her, at Amelia, at the sisters I've come to love like family. "We've been seeing each other," I reply, my voice trembling. "For months, before everything happened."

Catalina's eyes widen, and her hand flies to her mouth in feigned surprise. Amelia's eyebrows shoot up, but she doesn't look surprised either.

Reed remains by the counter, jaw clenched, but his eyes soften as he looks at mine.

Catalina finally exhales, a quiet sound. "Finally, fuck, you act like we didn't notice."

I huff out a laugh. "Wait, what?"

Amelia's lips twitch into the faintest smirk. "Babe, we literally figured it out, and our husbands told us."

Catalina swats her arm lightly, still blinking through tears. "Amelia."

"What?" Amelia says, smiling gently at me. "They did."

Glancing at Reed, he furrows his brows at his brothers

as Maverick snickers in response, and Carter pinches his brows between his fingers.

I laugh, a watery, nervous sound, and shake my head. "Oh, well, what a relief."

Catalina's expression softens immediately as she squeezes my hand. "You don't ever have to explain to us for finding someone who makes you feel safe; we won't judge you for how it happened."

My throat burns. "It wasn't just about safety," I whisper. "It's him."

Reed then moves, crossing the room slowly until he's standing directly in front of me as he slides his hands into his pockets.

"You don't have to—" he starts, but I cut him off.

"I do."

He stops, his eyes searching mine.

The tears come before I can stop them. "You've done everything for me, Reed. You've held me together when I couldn't even breathe. You've protected me, loved me, and seen me when I didn't want anyone to look." My voice cracks, and I press a hand to my chest, trying to hold it in. "I can't hide it anymore. I love you."

Reed's jaw tightens, his eyes growing glassy before he finally moves. He doesn't say anything at first, cupping my face in both hands, his touch trembling.

His forehead rests against mine, his voice low and breaking. "Say it again," he whispers.

"I love you," I breathe.

A tear rolls from his cheek onto mine. "God, Layla," he says, his voice trembling. "I love you too, baby. I've loved you since the day you walked into my bar with your wild smile and a proposition to film it."

Catalina is already openly crying, and Amelia is wiping at her eyes with a grin.

Maverick mutters something about the "Hayes house being a goddamn soap opera," earning a soft elbow from Carter, who's smiling despite himself.

But I barely hear any of it.

All I can feel is Reed's hands cradling my face, the steady rhythm of his breathing against mine, and the quiet, unshakeable truth between us.

For the first time, I'm not afraid to say it.

For the first time, he doesn't have to guess.

I love him.

And I'm finally free to let the world know.

Reed's thumb circles slowly against my cheek, his forehead pressed to mine, as we share the same fragile breath.

By the time we sit down to eat, the house smells of bacon, coffee, and something more stable than fear.

The kitchen's alive again; chairs scraping, plates clinking, and Maverick raiding the fridge as if he hasn't eaten in days.

Catalina sits on a stool next to me, her hand casually resting on her belly as she teases Carter for oversalting his eggs. "You're gonna give the baby high blood pressure," she mutters.

Carter chuckles, flipping a pancake. "Darlin', they're my eggs, I made a special batch for you."

Amelia snorts softly from across the counter, sipping her coffee. "Catalina, stop complaining."

Catalina squints. "Can you not?"

"Shut up," Amelia smirks, and Maverick nearly chokes on his toast laughing.

It's ridiculous, warm, and perfect.

Reed slides a plate toward me and sits beside me, his

knee brushing mine under the table. His small touch sends a quiet thrill through me, a reminder that it's okay to be here now, in the open, in the light.

Catalina notices the look we exchange and smiles softly, her voice gentle amid all the noise. "I'm really happy for you, Layla."

I blink, caught off guard. "You are?"

"Of course I am," she says, resting her chin on her palm. "You both deserve to be loved this way."

My throat tightens. "I didn't think I'd ever have this again. Not after everything that happened."

Reed's hand finds mine beneath the table, our fingers intertwining, his thumb gently brushing my ring finger like a silent vow. "You've got it now," he says softly.

The chaos persists around us—Amelia rolling her eyes at Maverick's boasting, Leo happily babbling in Carter's lap, and Catalina laughing so hard she almost spills her juice.

And somehow, in the middle of it, my heart finally slows.

I catch myself laughing too, really laughing, the sound light and unfamiliar to my own ears.

Reed watches me with that quiet smile, the one that shows he notices the little things and says he's never going to let me go again.

I squeeze his hand and look around the table—my girls, their husbands, the man I love, and the life I never thought I'd get to live.

FORTY-SIX
REED

Layla's still asleep when I slip out back, coffee in hand, the air cool enough to see my breath.

She's been doing better, laughing again, eating, sleeping in longer stretches without waking in a cold sweat.

But I still notice the shadows behind her smile, the way her hands sometimes tremor when she thinks no one's watching.

So today, I wanted to give her something special, something that feels like her.

I spent the morning dragging an old table from the shed and setting it up under the oak tree. I covered it with a white sheet Catalina brought over last week and laid out brushes, jars of paint, and a large canvas still wrapped in plastic.

By the time I finish lining up the paints by color, I hear the screen door creak open. Her bare feet pad across the porch, and her soft voice drifts through the quiet.

"Reed? What are you doing out here?"

I turn, and there she is, sleepy-eyed, wearing one of my flannels and shorts.

The morning light highlights the faint bruises along her legs, but they're healing, fading into the past where they belong.

"Hey, sunshine." I nod toward the table. "I figured we could get some sun and paint today."

Her brow furrows as she steps down onto the grass, barefoot, the hem of my shirt brushing her knees. "You set all this up?"

"Sure did." I take a sip of my coffee. "C'mon, baby, paint with me."

Her lips part slightly as she looks at the table—the neat rows of colors, the glass of water I set out for the brushes, and even the small bouquet of wildflowers I picked from the edge of the fence line.

"Reed..." she says softly, her eyes glassy. "You didn't have to do this."

"I know," I say quietly. "But I wanted to."

She steps closer, her fingertips brushing the handles of the brushes. "You even got canary yellow," she murmurs, a small smile tugging at her lips. "That's my favorite."

"Lucky guess," I lie, even though I'd spent half an hour scrolling through her old videos online, trying to figure out which shade she used most.

Layla laughs under her breath, a sound that warms me to the core. "You're ridiculous."

"Maybe." I grin faintly. "But I like seein' you smile, so I'm not stoppin' anytime soon."

Her eyes lift to mine, and for a moment, the world stops.

The way she's looking at me is the same as the first time she walked into my bar years ago.

"Come on," I say, clearing my throat. "Before the wind dries the paint."

We spend the next hour outside, sunlight filtering

through the branches and casting streaks of gold across her hair.

She hums softly as she works, her tongue peeking out between her lips, her brush gliding over the canvas in long, deliberate strokes.

I don't really paint, but I sit beside her anyway, sketching random shapes in the corner just to make her laugh. Whenever I mess up, she giggles softly and shakes her head.

At one point, she glances at me, her eyes shining. "You're actually kind of terrible at this."

"'Kind of'?" I snort. "That's generous."

Her laughter spills out, and I swear I'd do anything to keep hearing it.

She leans back, wiping a streak of yellow across her cheek with the back of her hand.

I glance at her painting. It's abstract; swirls of lavender, blue, and peach.

"It's beautiful," I say honestly.

She looks down, cheeks warming. "It's just colors."

"Yeah," I murmur, watching the sunlight dance across her face. "But they look like you."

She blinks, caught off guard, then smiles. "You always know exactly what to say, don't you?"

"Not always," I admit. "Just when it comes to you."

She looks away, biting her lip, but I notice it, that spark. That part of her that's finally beginning to believe she deserves happiness.

We sit there until the light begins to fade, our hands covered in paint, our brushes drying in the breeze.

She's sitting cross-legged in front of me, her hair caught in the breeze, a pale yellow streak smudged across her cheek. She's been quiet for a few minutes now, the brush resting in her lap, watching the light shift through the trees.

I lean back on my palms, trying not to stare too long. Her tank top's speckled with color, her knees dusted with dirt.

She looks—God, she looks like peace.

"You did good, sunshine," I murmur.

She glances up, her lips curling. "You mean we did. You made that weird-looking cloud, right?"

I chuckle. "That's supposed to be a mountain."

"It looks like mashed potatoes."

I grin. "Guess I'm more of a mashed-potato kinda artist."

Her laugh fades into a quiet smile. "You always know how to make me feel normal again."

"You are normal," I say softly.

She studies me for a long moment, her eyes tracing my face as if memorizing it. She sets her brush down and crawls closer across the grass, her knees brushing mine.

"Layla," I whisper, voice rough. "You sure?"

She nods, just once. "Yeah. I'm sure."

Her hand rises slowly as her fingertips skim the paint from my scarred jaw. Her touch is gentle, slightly trembling, and it sends a shiver straight through me.

"You've been so gentle with me," she says, barely above a whisper. "You never ask for anything."

I swallow hard, my heart pounding. "You don't owe me a thing, baby."

"I know." Her thumb gently traces my lower lip, smudging a yellow streak. "But I want this."

I can smell the faint cherry note of her shampoo and the sun's warmth on her skin. Her gaze flicks to my mouth, and then she leans in.

I don't move until she closes the distance.

Her lips are soft and hesitant at first, tasting faintly of hazelnut and something sweet that's uniquely hers. My hands twitch against the grass, every instinct screaming to touch her, to pull her closer, but I don't.

Not yet. I let her lead and decide.

She kisses me again, this time deeper, her fingers sliding into my hair and tugging just enough to make me exhale into her mouth. When she finally pulls back, her breath catches, and her eyes are glassy yet steady.

"Sorry," she whispers, though her voice holds a hint of a smile. "I couldn't stop thinking about it."

I shake my head, a soft laugh escaping me as I cup her cheek, my thumb tracing the faint paint streak there. "Don't you dare apologize for that."

She leans into my touch, her eyes closing for a moment.

When she opens them again, she's smiling. "You've got paint all over your face."

I grin. "Worth it."

The sun slips lower, bathing us in gold. She presses her forehead to mine, and our breaths mingle as we stay silent for a long moment.

I breathe her in and whisper, "You don't ever have to run again, sunshine. You're home now."

She sinks back onto her heels, blinking up at me with that quiet spark I haven't seen since everything went wrong. There's color in her again, warmth.

"You okay?" I ask softly.

She nods, biting her bottom lip. "Better than okay."

A brief silence passes before she looks toward the side of the house—where my motorcycle sits, gleaming in the fading light.

She tilts her head, her eyes narrowing as if she's considering something she knows she shouldn't.

I catch it instantly. "Don't even think about it."

She gasps dramatically, feigning offense. "Think about what?"

"You know damn well what," I say, smirking. "That look's dangerous."

Her grin widens, mischief flashing across her face. "Come on, Reed. Just a quick ride. Please?"

I groan, already shaking my head. "You're barely healed, sunshine. I'm not riskin' you fallin' off the back of my bike."

"I wouldn't fall," she argues, standing and brushing grass off her legs. "You'd never let me."

She's right. I wouldn't.

She tries to hold back a grin but fails spectacularly. "Reed, come on. Please. Just a short ride. You promised when I was feeling better."

"I said maybe," I correct, pointing a paint-stained finger at her. "And you're still—"

She steps closer, the hem of my flannel grazing her bare legs. Her voice drops to that soft, teasing drawl that always gets me. "Please?"

Hell. There goes my resolve.

I drag a hand down my face, sighing. "You're impossible."

Her grin spreads wide, bright as the damn sun. "You love it."

"Yeah," I mutter, pretending to be annoyed. "That's the problem."

Out by the bike, she doesn't even wait for me to grab the helmets—she already knows which one's hers.

She picks it up gently, her fingers tracing the design as she always does before slipping it on.

"You ready?" I ask, voice rougher than I intend.

She tilts her head, the painted flowers shining gold in the late afternoon light. "I've been ready since you made me my helmet."

I chuckle. "Guess I set myself up for this, huh?"

"Yep," she says, popping the *p*.

Throwing my helmet on, I settle onto the motorcycle, reaching out my hand, waiting for her to grab it. She intertwines her fingers with mine, guiding herself onto the bike.

She wraps her arms around my waist, settling into place.

"Hold tight, sunshine," I say, glancing over my shoulder.

"Always do," she murmurs through the wired Bluetooth.

That small smile of hers flickers through my mind as I ease us down the driveway, the bike rumbling beneath us.

It's just us and the open road.

Her arms tighten as I take the first turn, the wind tugging at her hair where it slips past the helmet's edge.

She lets out a small, breathless laugh—God, I haven't heard that sound in so long.

"You good back there?" I say through the Bluetooth connected to our helmets.

"I'm perfect," she squeals, laughing again, and it hits me right in the chest.

A smile tugs at my lips as I reach back with one hand, just for a moment, and my fingers find the smooth skin of her thigh where the hem of my flannel rides up.

She stiffens for half a heartbeat, then relaxes, her hand covering mine.

I give her thigh a slow squeeze, my thumb lazily circling, a quiet reminder that she's safe, right here with me.

She presses closer. "Don't let go."

"Never," I promise.

We ride like that; her laughter carried on the breeze, her hand still over mine. The world around us blurs into streaks of green and orange, a view that doesn't look real.

Every few miles, I glance down at our hands linked together, watching how her fingers twitch against mine as if she's trying to memorize the feel of it.

We finally pull up to the ridge. The engine goes silent, and the world breathes a sigh of relief.

She slides off first, removing her helmet, her hair tousled by the wind. She's flushed, with bright, shining eyes as she looks up at me, smiling so wide it takes my breath away. "That was—"

"Worth it?" I finish for her.

She nods, still breathless. "Every second."

I set my helmet down and step close enough to tuck a loose strand of hair behind her ear. "Told you I wouldn't let you fall, sunshine."

"I know," she whispers, "You never do."

FORTY-SEVEN
REED

The girls insisted on a movie night. Now that Layla is here, they can't get enough of her.

Fuck, I can't either. The hole in my heart that I've carried for years is finally beginning to heal because of her.

Catalina has her fuzzy blanket wrapped around her, leaning into Carter on the couch as he kisses her every few minutes; he's clearly forgotten that other people exist.

Maverick gags looking at them as he's sprawled on the floor, a bowl of chips balanced precariously on his stomach. Amelia's beside him, stealing them one at a time just to watch him complain.

They're child-free tonight, so they're acting like complete fools.

I'm in the recliner with Layla nestled against my side, her head resting on my heart as I gently run my fingers across her shoulder.

On TV, Texas Chainsaw Massacre is playing; Maverick's idea of hell.

"Turn this sick shit off!" he yells, shielding his face with a throw pillow, a muffled gag escaping him. "I swear to God!"

Amelia's doubled over laughing. "You're such a baby!"

"The fuck I am!"

Catalina giggles. "You're literally quivering over there."

Carter smirks. "Maverick, shut up."

I can't help but laugh. Layla's laughing too, her hand resting on mine.

Three sharp knocks on my front door draw everyone's attention away from the movie. Layla tenses next to me, gripping my hand.

"Layla!"

She grips my hand tighter, the color draining from her face.

"I know you're in there! Open the fucking door!"

Maverick leaves the floor before the echo dies, the chip bowl spilling. Carter's already up, telling Catalina to stay put.

I move toward the door with them. "Stay with Cat," I tell Layla, my voice lower than I recognize. "Don't move, baby."

Swinging the door open, I feel cold night air hit my face, and there he is.

Brian stands on the porch, eyes wild, lips twisted in a sneer. His clothes are wrinkled, and his pupils are dilated.

"Well," he spits, "there she is, hiding behind the burn-marked freak."

His words hurt, but I don't flinch.

Maverick steps forward, voice a growl. "You better start prayin', man."

Brian laughs. "Get the fuck out of my way!"

Carter's hand shoots out, grabbing Maverick's arm. "Don't," he warns, but it's too late.

Maverick shoves him hard as he staggers back down the porch steps, gravel crunching under his boots. He catches himself, jaw clenched. "She's mine!" he shouts. "She doesn't get to leave me!"

He lunges toward the doorway with his hands outstretched. I catch him mid-step, my palm against his chest, the impact vibrating up my arm.

"Get your ass off my property," I snarl.

He swings wildly as the hit ricochets off my shoulder.

I push him back again, this time with greater force. Maverick blocks his second charge and shoves him sideways into the porch railing.

"Enough!" Carter steps in, grabbing Brian by the collar and throwing him on the floor. "You're done!"

Brian's chest heaves, his breath ragged as he pushes himself to stand, wiping the dirt off his pants. "You think she wants you? Look at you!" he spits at me, his face twisted. "You hide those scars, right? You keep the lights off so she doesn't flinch while you're fucking her?"

Something inside me flashes hot, but I don't move. My jaw locks, and every muscle screams to end it.

"Reed," Carter says quietly, warning in his tone.

Brian's voice drops to a snarl. "You think she loves you? She pities you."

Maverick moves again, his fists clenching in Brian's shirt as he slams him back against the siding, making the porch shake. "You don't talk about my brother like that," he growls.

Brian pushes at him, but Carter is already there, stepping between them, gripping Brian's chin. "You've got two choices, fucker. You leave right now, or we call the sheriff and let him drag your bitch-ass out."

For a long moment, Brian's breath comes in short, trembling as he looks past us toward the living room, his eyes settling on Layla.

"You'll regret this," he says.

I told myself that violence wasn't the answer, well fuck him because he's about to eat my fist.

I step into his line of sight, blocking it completely. "You're not welcome here, Brian," I say, my voice low and dangerous. "You need to leave and stay away from Layla. She's done with you, and so am I."

Brian lets out a harsh chuckle, a mocking sound. "Done with me? She'll never be done with me. She's mine, and she always will be. And if you think you can keep her from me, you're sorely mistaken."

He lunges free from Maverick and Carter's grip, his fist flying toward my face.

I dodge just in time, and the blow grazes my cheek as I counter with a quick uppercut to his jaw.

Brian stumbles back, his eyes wide with surprise, but he quickly regains his footing and charges in again.

We both start fighting, and our fists collide in a flurry.

I feel the adrenaline coursing through my veins, my muscles coiled and ready for his next strike. I manage to land a solid punch to Brian's ribs, and he grunts in pain, his breath rushing out.

That still doesn't stop him; he looks at me with wild, unhinged eyes, with rage dancing in his irises.

He lunges at me again but misses.

As he stumbles, I grab him by the collar of his flannel, my fist flying and connecting with his eye socket, then his nose and mouth. Blood splatters across the porch floor.

I don't fucking care that I'm acting like a wild animal, and I'm not going to stop until he's a bloody, broken mess.

Continuing to pummel him into the ground, my fists

move on instinct, a blur of motion, until his body is limp and unmoving.

Standing over his prone form, I let out ragged exhales, shaking my fists as they ache from each punch. Blood stains my knuckles, but that's the least of my worries.

Carter grips my shoulder. "Reed, stop. You've won. He's not getting up."

I shake my head in agreement, turning slightly to see Maverick standing in the doorway. His eyes are hooded, but a flash of pride shows in them. "That's what that fucker gets."

A smile touches my lips; it's exactly what he deserves.

Brian's still lying on the grass, out cold, his cheek pressed into the dirt.

Maverick's already got his phone out, pacing near the steps. "Yeah, we need a unit out at Creek Way. Now. We have an idiot trespassing."

He hangs up, jaw clenched. "They're on their way."

The porch door creaks open behind us, and Layla steps out slowly, with Catalina's hand steadying her. Her eyes are wide, her face pale, yet she stands on her own.

"Baby, go inside," I tell her gently.

"I just..." Her voice shakes. "Is he—?"

"He's fine," I say, forcing calm into my tone. "Just not gonna be yellin' for a while."

Her gaze falls on Brian's limp figure, the bruises on her throat still faint but visible. She swallows hard, tears welling in her eyes.

Maverick places a hand on my shoulder. "The sheriff will be here in five."

We wait in silence, crickets filling the space between us.

Carter leans against the railing, arms crossed, every muscle in his body tense. Maverick paces again, muttering under his breath about "no one messes with the Hayes brothers."

Flashing red and blue lights finally pierce the darkness, and the tension in my chest eases, just barely.

Two deputies step out of the cruiser—Harris and Boyd, both locals and men I've known since high school. Good men. They glance at Brian and exchange a silent question.

Harris steps onto the porch, his voice calm yet firm. "Evenin', Reed."

"Evenin'," I say, crossing my arms. "He showed up screamin' and tried to force his way in."

Boyd crouches next to Brian, checking him over. "Looks like he didn't get far."

"No," I say flatly. "He didn't."

Harris glances at me, then at Layla, who's partially hidden behind Catalina near the door. He sees her crouched behind Catalina and notices the faint bruise on her neck. "You the one he hurt?" he asks softly.

Layla nods once. "Yeah." Her voice cracks. "He followed me here."

Harris's jaw tightens. "We'll make sure he doesn't again."

They lift Brian upright. He groans, blinking sluggishly, then his eyes focus on me, on Maverick, and on the woman he can no longer reach.

He spits, his voice hoarse. "You think this fixes anything? You think she'll stay with you?"

Maverick takes a step forward, but Carter grabs his arm. "Shut the fuck up. Have fun being someone's bitch," he mutters.

I step close enough that Brian has to tilt his head to meet my gaze. "You're done," I tell him. "If you come near her again or say her name again, I'll make sure you don't walk away next time."

His lip curls, but Harris pulls him back toward the cruiser. "That's enough, Brian," he says. "You're under arrest for trespassing, harassment, and domestic violence."

Brian stumbles, cursing under his breath as they cuff him.

Before they shut the door, I call out to Harris. "Make sure the report includes everything—what he did to her, the messages, and tonight. I want it in writing that he's not allowed in this state."

Harris nods in agreement. "You got my word, Reed. We'll take care of it."

Boyd gives a quick nod, too, his eyes flicking toward Layla. "She's safe here. We'll make sure of it."

The cruiser's doors slam shut. The gravel crunches beneath the car as it pulls away, its taillights fading down the long driveway.

The moment they're gone, the silence returns.

Maverick exhales sharply, rubbing his hands over his face. "Phew! What a fucking adrenaline rush!" he yells, running toward the door as he calls out to Amelia. "Baby! Did you see Daddy fucking that guy up?!"

Amelia rolls her eyes as she jumps, looping her arms around his neck as Maverick holds her with one arm, giving her steady kisses.

Carter grunts, walking back towards his wife as he pulls her close to his chest.

I linger on the porch a little longer, watching the dust settle on the empty road. My fists still ache, and my heartbeat is finally slowing.

Stepping back inside, Layla is waiting for me in the doorway. Her eyes are red, but her hands are steady.

"He's really gone?" she asks softly.

"For good this time, baby," I promise.

She nods, moving closer, as she wraps her arms around my waist.

I pull her in, burying my face in the crook of her neck, peppering kisses.

Inside, the family's laughter begins again. Catalina hums a tune while caressing Carter's face. Maverick and Amelia run down the hall, giggling, talking about how he brought her favorite mask.

Normal. Safe. *Home.*

FORTY-EIGHT

REED

FIVE MONTHS LATER

Five months.

That's how long it's been since she showed up at my door, broken, bruised, and shaking so hard I thought she'd splinter on my porch. Five months since she whispered my name like it was the last safe thing she knew.

Now she's here, with *me.*

Layla has made this place feel alive again, has made me feel alive again. She's barefoot most of the time, wrapped in one of my shirts, editing videos at the table with a cup of coffee with more ice than the actual drink, but I love her for it.

She still makes content, but it's no longer the glossy, filtered kind.

It's *real.*

She speaks about healing, leaving, and starting over when the world says it's too late. She uses her voice for something meaningful; to reach women and men who have been in her place, telling them it's okay to begin again.

Her following doubled. Shit, maybe tripled.

She doesn't even seem to notice anymore. She used to

be so worried about her followers, her content, how she looked, whether they'd like her without Brian.

Every time I watch her record, I see the strength it takes for her to say the words out loud.

The slight tremor in her hands before she presses record. The calm that washes over her when she finishes.

I'm so fucking proud of her.

Brian's in jail now, good, that's what he deserves.

He has been since that night at my house, when he pounded on my door.

The cops made sure the charges stuck—assault, trespassing, domestic violence. He's got time to think about what he did.

But if he ever shows his face in Ruby Ridge again, it won't be the law he'll answer to; he'll answer to me again, and I'll fucking break him to keep her safe.

She's safe now, and I'll make damn sure it stays that way.

Still, the nightmares come.

She'll wake in the middle of the night, trembling, her breath caught in her throat.

Sometimes she doesn't even realize she's crying until I wipe away her tears. I'll pull her close, press my lips to her hair, whispering gentle words until her heartbeat slows.

She always apologizes for it, and I always tell her the same thing. *"You don't have to be okay all the time to be safe."*

And the truth is, I get it, I understand it more than she knows. This ache I've dealt with for years comes back to haunt me, too.

Because I still wake up some nights, too. Not because of her screams, but because of my own.

Beau's voice still rings in my mind, the moment he stopped talking, the hiss of gas, the flash that took him.

My brother in the firehouse, my best friend.

I survived. He didn't. And some nights I still hate myself for it.

I'll catch my reflection in the mirror, the scars that crawl up my neck, the twisted ones on my shoulder, and all I can think is *monster*.

I see the damage before anything else.

The melted skin, the uneven lines, the reminders that I wasn't fast enough.

Layla never looks away.

The first time she saw me without my shirt, I flinched instinctively, trying to hide what I could.

But she stepped closer, her hands trembling, eyes soft. She traced the scars with her fingertips, slowly as if she was learning them by heart.

"You survived this," she whispered. "That means you're stronger than what tried to break you."

I wanted to believe her, and I still try to with the daily reassurance she gives me.

But some nights, when I'm alone in the shower, I trace those same lines and wonder why I get to keep breathing when Beau didn't.

Grief is a strange thing. It doesn't truly end; it just settles somewhere deep and surfaces when a particular smell hits you or when you see something that reminds you of them.

But Layla makes the weight easier to carry.

She doesn't try to fix me; she just sits beside me in silence as she rests her head on my shoulder, her thumb absentmindedly tracing circles over the old burns, silently reminding me that she sees me, not the scars.

We're both rebuilding our lives here together in Ruby Ridge, and she finally has the power to do it her way.

She paints again, barefoot in the backyard on Saturdays. She laughs more, eats better, and teases me at the bar when I'm too serious.

Some nights, she'll work beside me, helping close up. And closing time... well, let's just say we've turned that into something worth staying late for.

But even outside the heat and laughter, it's her quiet moments that get to me. The way she holds herself now.

She left, and she chose herself. And while choosing herself, she built a new life from the ashes.

I know something about that because when she showed up, I was still stuck in mine.

I'll still see ghosts in every corner—my mama, Beau, the man I used to be before everything burned.

I'd convinced myself I was too scarred to be loved again. Too broken. But then she looked at me and saw something worth saving.

Some nights, when we're closing up, and she's perched on the bar counter with paint still on her fingers, she'll reach for me, her eyes soft and full of mischief.

I'll press a kiss to her scarless shoulder, my hands memorizing the feel of her, and I'll think, maybe this is what healing looks like.

It's not about forgetting, but about finding someone who makes the pain easier to bear.

She's still carrying her scars on the inside. I've got mine on the outside.

Somehow, they fit together.

And every morning I wake up beside her with her hand curled over mine, and I whisper a thank-you to the ghosts that stayed behind.

Because they led her here.

And for the first time since that fire, since my mama's last breath, since Beau's name became a whisper in my chest...I'm not surviving anymore.

I'm living.

"Reed."

I blink, looking up; she's watching me from across the bar, eyebrow raised.

"You okay?" she asks, snapping her fingers once, teasing but gentle. "You've been staring at that receipt for five minutes, baby. It's not gonna give you life advice."

I let out a laugh, rubbing the back of my neck. "Sorry, sunshine. Got lost in my head."

She smirks, setting the rag aside, and leans on the counter, her chin resting on her hand. "Must've been something deep. You had that faraway look going on again."

I can't help but grin. "You mean rugged and mysterious?"

"I mean brooding and distracted," she fires back, her eyes glinting with mischief.

"Same thing," I mutter.

She rolls her eyes and walks around the counter. "You've been thinking again," she says softly, sliding between my knees where I'm sitting on the stool. "About Beau?"

I nod slowly, wrapping my hands around her waist. "Yeah. Him. Mama. All of it."

Her hands come up, looping around my neck. "You miss them."

"Every damn day." My voice roughens, barely a whisper. "Some days it's easier. Some days, I see his face in the flames again. Or I hear Mama's laugh when I'm closing up. I just... wish they could see this. You. Us."

Her eyes soften as she presses a kiss to my forehead. "I think they do, Reed."

I shake my head, my throat tight. "I don't know. I still ain't sure I deserve any of this."

She frowns and moves closer. "Don't say that." She gestures with her hands, tracing the scar that runs over my jaw. "You do. You more than do. You kept going. That's what they'd be proud of."

Her touch burns in the best way, anchoring me.

I hold her hand with mine, keeping it there. "I love you."

She smirks, kissing me ever so softly. "I love you more."

I tug her closer until there's no space between us. "Not possible," I murmur.

We stand there for a brief moment in the glow of the bar lights; her breathing steady, mine trying to keep up.

She tilts her head, smiling softly. "You always go quiet when you start thinking too hard."

"Maybe I also like watching you work," I tease, my thumb brushing her hip.

"Oh yeah?" she says, grinning. "Pretty sure you've been staring at the same stack of receipts since we opened."

I chuckle, leaning forward so my forehead rests against hers. "Can you blame me?"

She laughs quietly, her breath ghosting over my lips. "You're impossible."

"Yeah," I say softly. "But you're the one who keeps showin' up for it."

Her eyes sparkle, and I swear the whole world slows down. "Guess I'm just a sucker for a man who makes good cocktails."

"And locks up late," I murmur softly, "so no one interrupts when I kiss you."

Before she can respond, I tilt my head and kiss her, full of all the unspoken things I don't know how to say out loud.

She melts into me, her hands sliding up my neck, gentle over the scars.

When she finally pulls back, she's smiling, cheeks flushed. "Bar's supposed to close at midnight, we're on the clock."

I grin, brushing my thumb along her jaw. "Then I guess we're gettin' some overtime."

She swats at me, laughing, but doesn't move away.

And for the first time in a long damn while, I'm not haunted by what I've lost.

I'm anchored by what I found, *her*.

Her laughter lingers, bringing me back to the present, echoing off the old wood and neon hum.

Fuck, I'm about to propose to her, and I'm nervous.

"Reed," she says softly, a small crease forming between her brows as she taps my forehead. "What's going on in that head of yours? You look like you're about to give me bad news."

I huff out a laugh, shaking my head. "No bad news, sunshine. Just trying to get this right."

She narrows her eyes playfully. "Trying to get what right? Oh my God, are we going to have some fun on the mechanical bull, again?"

Her teasing is gentle, but it's the exact push I need. My heart pounds so loud I swear she can hear it.

"No, baby," I admit, gently pushing her forward as I step back, my boots heavy on the wood floor. "It's something else."

She blinks, her lips parting slightly as I stand to my full height and stop in front of her.

My hand rises to cup her jaw, my thumb brushing the

corner of her mouth. "You have no idea how much light you brought into this place," I mumble. "Into me."

Her voice drops, barely audible. "Reed..."

I take a slow breath and drop to one knee.

Her hand quickly moves to her mouth, eyes wide and shimmering immediately.

The bar falls silent except for the rain and the faint thrum of my heartbeat in my ears.

I reach into my pocket, pulling out the small velvet box I've been carrying for weeks, through bar shifts, nights in bed with her head on my chest, and every moment I wanted to tell her how much I love her.

With careful fingers, I flip it open, and she gasps. The ring isn't flashy; it's gold, carved with tiny sunflowers all around the band, with an oval diamond sitting on top.

The carved sunflowers are just like the ones she plants by our porch; the same ones I grew for her when I didn't know how else to show love.

"Layla," I begin, voice low and trembling, "I used to believe the fire took everything I had. My home, my purpose, my family. I looked in the mirror every day and saw a man too broken to deserve anything good again. But then you walked in here years ago, smiling, glowing, proposing this idea to flim here, and I swear, sunshine, you turned my whole world upside down."

Tears fall down her cheeks, catching on her trembling lips.

"You didn't just walk in here," I continue, "you walked right into my heart. Into the quiet I'd been drowning in. You made me laugh again. You made me *want* again. You took all the pieces of me that were burned, scarred, and treated them like they were still worth somethin'. And now..." I swallow hard, caressing the backs of her legs. "Now I can't imagine breathin' without you beside me."

I look up at her, my eyes watering. "Marry me, Layla. Let me spend the rest of my life making sure you never doubt what love feels like. Let me be your home."

She's crying before I even finish, her knees hitting the ground as she drops in front of me.

Her fingers cradle my face, her thumbs brushing away my tears, though hers are falling faster.

"Reed Hayes," she whispers, voice trembling yet steady, "you have been my home since the moment you opened that damn bar door for me. You were the first man who didn't want to change me. You saw all of me—the broken parts, the scared parts, the pieces that still shake at night—and you never looked away."

Her breath catches. "You make me feel safe. You make me feel seen. You remind me every day that even wrecked things can still be beautiful. You're my light, my safe place, my best friend. And yes, I'll marry you. I'd marry you a thousand times over."

The box trembles in my hand as I slide the ring onto her finger. It fits perfectly, because it was made for her.

She gazes at it, then looks up at me through wet lashes, laughing breathlessly. "Reed," she murmurs, "you didn't have to get me sunflowers."

I smile, brushing my thumb over her cheek. "Sunshine, you're the reason they grow."

She laughs as she leans in and kisses me.

It's slow at first, filled with salt, warmth, and years of pain melting into something new.

Her hands tangle in my hair as mine press into her back, holding her close as the kiss deepens.

We finally part, her forehead rests against mine, breaths mingling in the dim light.

"This place started it all," she whispers.

"Yeah," I murmur, glancing around the quiet bar. "Guess it's only right we promise forever where we found it."

Her smile breaks through her tears. "Forever sounds good."

"Forever's already yours."

She's beaming, that radiant smile lighting up my truck, and I can't stop stealing glances at her, my *fiancé*, the woman who has my soul wrapped around her little finger.

We barely make it through the door of our home before I'm on her, kicking it shut with my heel, our bodies colliding in the entryway.

She's pressed against the wall, my hands framing her face as I kiss her deeply, savoring it, our tongues sliding together in a rhythm full of promise and heat.

"Layla," I whisper against her lips, my voice thick with emotion. "You're everything. Say yes again."

She laughs softly, her arms wrapping around my neck. "Yes, Reed. A thousand times, yes."

I scoop her up, her legs instinctively wrapping around my waist, and carry her to our bedroom, our mouths never breaking contact.

Our room is dimly lit by the bedside lamp, casting warm shadows over the rumpled sheets where we've made so many memories.

I gently lower her onto the bed, following her down, our bodies perfectly aligned as I hover above her, gazing into her eyes.

She's flushed, her lips parted as I trace the line of her jaw with my thumb, gliding it down her neck, feeling her pulse flutter beneath my touch.

"Let me show you how much I love you," I whisper, planting kisses along her collarbone as my fingers lift the hem of her tank top, pulling it over her head.

Her bra comes off next, unclasped with a flick. I peel it away to reveal her breasts as her nipples pebble in the cool air.

I cup it gently, my thumb brushing the tip, then lean in to take it into my mouth, sucking softly as my tongue swirls around the hardened bud.

She arches beneath me, a soft moan escaping as her hands slide into my hair, holding me there.

I move to the other side with the same care, nipping lightly, drawing out her sighs, and her body responds with subtle shifts and tremors.

My mouth moves lower, kissing her ribs and stomach, while her hands skillfully unbutton her jeans, sliding them down her hips, along with her panties.

She's bare now, her legs parting as I settle between them, my breath ghosting over her clit. Her pussy is already slick and glistening, and I part them with my fingers.

"Such a pretty pussy, baby," I breathe, dipping my head as my tongue flicks out to taste her.

She gasps, her hips lifting, and I steady her with my hand on her thigh while the other spreads her wider.

I lick her slowly, long strokes from her entrance to her clit, savoring her tangy sweetness as I focus on her sensitive clit, circling it with the flat of my tongue.

Her thighs quiver around my ears, her moans growing breathier as I suck gently, alternating with flicks that make her buck.

"Reed, shit!"

I hum against her, the vibration drawing a whimper as I slide two fingers inside her, curling them to stroke that inner spot while my mouth works her clit relentlessly.

She's clenching around me, pulling me deeper as her arousal coats my hand.

I build her up slowly, moving my fingers in a gentle rhythm, tongue lapping faster now until she's trembling on the edge. "Come for me, baby, give me one."

She does, crying out my name, her pussy pulsing around my fingers, her juices flooding my palm as waves of pleasure crash through her. I soothe her through it, licking softly as her thighs twitch in my grasp.

As I rise, I strip off my shirt and pants, my hard cock springing free, its tip leaking pre-cum at the sight of her.

She reaches for me, her eyes dark with need, and I climb back over her, settling between her legs.

Our gazes lock as I run the head of my cock along her slit, coating myself with her wetness, notching at her entrance. "I love you," I say, pushing in slowly, inch by inch, feeling her stretch around me.

She bites her lip, nodding as her hands rest on my shoulders. "God, Reed, I love you so much."

I begin moving with deep, unhurried thrusts that rub against her clit with each pass. "You think I don't know every sound you make, every shiver? I've memorized 'em all."

She moans in response, wrapping her legs around my waist and pulling me closer.

I kiss her deeply, swallowing her gasps, while my hand

tangles in her hair and the other caresses her breast, pinching her nipple just enough to ignite more heat.

The pace I set remains tender yet intense, each plunge drawing out her wetness, the wet sounds of us joining filling the room.

Her walls flutter, building again, and I angle my hips to go deeper, brushing that sweet spot.

"That's my good girl, takin' me so well."

She clings tighter as her nails graze my back, our breaths mingling as we chase the peak together.

Her orgasm hits first, her pussy clamping down and milking my cock in rhythmic squeezes.

I follow seconds later, thrusting deep and spilling inside her, filling her as I groan her name.

We stay close together, my weight a comforting blanket over her, as we press our foreheads together, hearts beating in sync. I kiss her softly, before rolling us onto our sides, remaining buried inside as my hand finds hers, my fingers lacing over her new ring.

Mine.

EPILOGUE

Reed

One Month Later

I glance back at the clock on the nightstand, my heart racing, not just from the heat building between her thighs because of me, but from the minutes slipping away.

Our wedding is in two hours, and here I am, tangled in the sheets of our hotel suite, my hands roaming her body as if I can't get enough, because I can't.

My soon-to-be wife couldn't wait until after the ceremony, and truthfully, neither could I; I needed to see her now.

She's already in white lace lingerie, the delicate fabric hugging her thighs, and the sight of her steals my breath away.

"Reed," she breathes, half-laughing, half-protesting, as I trail hot kisses down her neck. "We're going to be late to our own wedding."

I lift my head, my dark-framed glasses slightly askew yet still perched on my nose, a soft smile tugging at my mouth.

"Shh, my love," I murmur, my voice low and soothing as I bare her breasts, the cool air pebbling her nipples. "We've got time. Let me worship you one last time before you're mine forever."

I slide my hands up the insides of her thighs, my thumbs brushing the tender skin just beside where she's aching most.

Spreading her wider, I open her completely to my gaze.

"Look at you, baby," I murmur, kissing her inner thigh. "So fucking pretty, and so wet for me already."

She bites her lip, her cheeks blooming pink as her fingers twist in the sheets.

"Reed..."

"Shh." I lean in, letting my breath ghost over her clit. She jolts anyway, her hips lifting toward my mouth. "I've got you. Just let me taste what's mine."

I press the flat of my tongue against her entrance first, lapping up her arousal already dripping toward the sheets.

She tastes of salt, honey, and pure need. I groan against her, the vibration making her whimper.

"God, baby," I rasp, pulling back just enough to look at her. "You taste so fucking good. I've been thinking about this all morning, getting my mouth on you one last time before we make our vows."

I drag my tongue through her tight heat, stopping just short of her clit. Circling it, teasing, never quite touching.

Her hips chase me. "Please, Reed—"

"Patience, baby. I want to savor every second of this." I say, smiling against her skin.

I flatten my tongue again, licking a long, firm stripe from

bottom to top, sealing my lips around her clit, sucking gently.

Her back arches off the bed; a broken moan spilling out.

"That's it," I murmur, my voice muffled against her. "Let me hear you. Let me feel how much you love my mouth on this pretty pussy."

I flick the tip of my tongue over her clit, quick little licks, sucking again, harder this time.

Easing two fingers inside her, I curl them upward, stroking that soft, ridged spot that makes her thighs shake.

"Reed, fuck, right there—"

I hum in approval, the vibration sending another jolt through her. My fingers pump slowly as my tongue works her clit in steady circles. I can feel her walls fluttering around my fingers, feel her beginning to tighten.

"You're gonna come for me like this?" I ask between licks. "Gonna give me one right before I slide inside you and make you mine forever. Can you do that for me, baby? Can you give me one more before the dress, the vows, and everyone else sees how beautiful you are?"

She's nodding frantically now, her hips rocking against my face as her fingers tangle in my hair so tightly it stings in the best way.

"Yes, yes, Reed, please—"

I add a third finger, gently stretching her while I suck her clit harder, rhythmic pulses, as my tongue flicks fast against her swollen bud.

Her whole body locks up.

She comes with a cry that's half sob, half my name as her pussy clenches hard around my fingers, flooding my tongue with her arousal.

I don't stop as I keep licking her through it, slow and gentle now, drawing out every aftershock until she's whimpering, oversensitive, her thighs trying to close around my head.

With one last soft kiss to her clit, I crawl back up her body, trailing kisses until I meet her mouth and give her a gentle peck.

She's flushed from chest to cheeks, eyes glassy, lips parted. I settle between her legs, my cock heavy and leaking against her inner thigh.

I brush a damp strand of hair off her forehead, kissing her again.

"Mine," I whisper against her lips. "Every inch of you. Every sound you just made. Every drop I just swallowed."

She smiles against my lips. "Yours," she breathes. "Forever yours."

I notch myself at her entrance, pause, as my forehead presses to hers.

"Ready to let me in, Mrs. Soon-to-Be-Hayes?"

Her laugh is soft, breathless, perfect. "Been ready since the first night I walked into your bar."

I push in slowly, letting her feel every inch. When I'm buried to the hilt, when she's wrapped around me like she was made for this exact moment, I kiss her like it's the only promise that matters right now.

"I do," I whisper against her lips.

She smiles through fresh tears. "I do."

Her nails rake lightly down my back as her lips part on a shaky exhale. "Reed..."

I brush my lips against hers, pulling back just enough to look into her eyes.

"Feel that?" I whisper. "Every inch in this sweet cunt."

She nods, her eyes glassy as her hips rock in tiny, helpless circles.

"I need—" Her voice cracks. She swallows, trying again.

"I need it harder, Reed. Please. I want to feel you as I walk down the aisle."

Fuckkk. My cock twitches hard inside her.

I rest my forehead against hers. "You beg so pretty, baby. Don't stop, let me hear you."

She whimpers as her hands slide down to my lower back, urging me closer, deeper.

"Harder," she breathes. "Please, fuck me harder. I want it rough. Can you do that for me?"

I groan, pulling my cock almost out, until just the tip is stretching her entrance, before I snap my hips forward.

The bedframe knocks against the wall as her cries echo throughout the room.

"Yes, yes, like that—"

I do it again, setting an intentional but brutal rhythm. Every thrust bottoms out, my balls slapping against her, as my cock grinds against her sweet spot that makes her sob my name.

"Harder," she begs again, her fingers pulling my hair gently. "Reed, please, don't hold back—"

I shift my angle, hooking one of her legs over my shoulder so I can go deeper, open her wider.

"Like that, baby?" I rasp against her ear, picking up the pace as my hips snap with real force now. "You want me to fuck you like I own you? Like this cunt is mine to ruin before I put my ring on your finger?"

"Yes, God, yes—" Her nails dig into my shoulders hard enough to leave half-moons. "Ruin me."

I give her what she's begging for.

My thrusts turn punishing, each one driving the air from her lungs in sharp little gasps. The headboard bangs rhythmically against the wall as the bed creaks under us.

Her breasts bounce with each thrust as her pussy grips

me so tightly I can barely control myself from coming right now.

"You feel that?" I growl, my voice shredded. "Gonna leave you sore, baby."

She's crying now; happy, overwhelmed tears slipping down her temples.

"R-Reed, I'm, I'm gonna—"

"Come," I command, slamming in hard, reaching down to touch her clit, giving her that extra pressure she needs. "Come on this cock, baby."

Her whole body seizes as her back arches, her pussy clamping down so hard I see stars.

She screams my name as her walls pulse violently around me, milking every inch as she comes apart.

Wetness floods between us, soaking my cock, my thighs, the sheets.

I can't hold on anymore.

Burying myself as deep as I can, I groan gutturally, my cock pulsing, spilling inside her. Pulse after pulse until I'm shaking, until I've filled her so full I can feel the excess leaking out around me.

We stay locked together, panting, trembling, as our foreheads press together.

I kiss her tears away, soft now, tender.

"You're so fucking beautiful," I whisper. "And you're all mine. Forever."

She smiles through the tears and pulls me down until my full weight is on her.

"Forever," she says, caressing the scarred skin along my cheek, "I can't wait to marry you."

I kiss her slowly as I'm still buried inside her.

"Two hours," I murmur against her lips. "Then you're officially Mrs. Hayes."

LAYLA

As the doors creak open and all sounds seem to fade, the soft shuffle of dresses, the quiet hum of a piano somewhere behind me, until all I hear is the pounding of my own heartbeat.

Reed's at the altar.

Fuck.

He's standing there in a black suit, his hair slicked back, his scruffy mustache tamed yet still him.

His brothers flank him, Maverick grinning like a fool, Carter's hand steady on his shoulder.

Amelia and Catalina stand on opposite sides, their tears shining through.

And there's Reed. My Reed.

The man who held me when I was nothing but broken pieces and made me believe I could be whole again—the man who never once looked away from the scars, his or mine.

I take a breath and begin walking, each step sinking into the old wooden floorboards as the train of my lace gown whispers behind me. The veil catches the sunlight, turning its edges into soft white fire.

In my hands, the sunflower bouquet feels vibrant and warm, with its bright yellow standing out against the pale ivory of my dress.

Reed's eyes lock onto mine, and for a moment, he seems like he might stop breathing. His lips part, revealing the tears he's desperately trying to hold back.

Maverick nudges him gently, whispering something that makes Reed let out a shaky laugh, but his eyes remain fixed on me.

Every step closer feels like a lifetime of memories—the morning I showed up at his door, the paint-stained afternoons, the motorcycle rides through open fields, and the nights at the bar when the world finally felt safe again.

It all led to this.

I finally reach him, and he exhales as if he's been holding his breath since we first met.

His hand reaches out, palm open. I slip mine into his, and it feels exactly as it did that first time, steady, sure, *home.*

The officiant's voice fades into the background as the sunlight shifts. It's warm on my face and bright on the scar along his jaw. I swear Mama Hayes is somewhere in that light, smiling.

"Marriage," the officiant says, smiling gently, "is a promise to keep choosing each other every day, in every way."

Reed's thumb brushes the back of my hand. He leans in slightly, his voice low and rough.

"You look so beautiful, baby."

My heart pounds against my chest as the world shrinks down to just him and me.

The officiant nods. "Reed, your vows."

Reed clears his throat, his voice already thick with emotion.

"Layla," he starts, his voice gruff and soft at the edges. His hand shakes a little as he intertwines our fingers, his palm's warmth calming my hand.

His thumb gently moves over my knuckles, slowly and

with reverence. "I used to believe I was done," he says, inhaling sharply. His eyes briefly glance down, catching the light, then return to mine, brimming with unspoken feelings. "I thought the fire had taken everything worth loving."

His throat works as he swallows hard, a faint sheen of tears gathering along his lashes. "Thought I was gonna spend the rest of my life patchin' holes that couldn't be filled." His voice cracks on the last word, and he huffs out a breath, his mouth twitching at the corners.

He meets my gaze and looks at me—truly looks—and a soft, trembling smile appears on his lips. "Then you showed up," he murmurs, gently squeezing my hand. "You looked at me, and suddenly I didn't feel broken anymore."

He exhales slowly, his forehead nearly touching mine. "You stitched me back together just by stayin'."

His voice cracks, and he swallows hard as tears start to surface. "You're my home, sunshine. My reason. The proof that even the burned-out parts can bloom again."

My vision becomes completely blurred.

I hear Catalina sniffling somewhere behind me, and even Carter is pretending to rub his eye.

When it's my turn, I can barely get the words out.

"Reed," I whisper, my voice trembling as I look up at him. My hands shake, so I tighten my grip on my bouquet, trying to steady myself. My chest rises and falls with shallow breaths, every word caught in my throat.

"When I first met you, I was quietly hurting," I whisper, with trembling lips and tears blurring my sight.

Reed's thumb softly brushes the back of my hand, providing comfort and silent encouragement to continue. "I was afraid, truly convinced that love existed only in other people's stories."

His gaze softens, his green eyes shimmering with unspoken emotion.

I swallow hard, my voice breaking as I go on. "But you saw me, really saw me, and you called me beautiful."

Reed's jaw tightens, a flicker of emotion passing over his face. He softly squeezes my hand.

I softly say, "You showed me that strength isn't loud," as I wipe away a tear trailing down my cheek. "It's gentle. It's steady. It's you."

A shaky breath escapes me as I lift his hand between us, my thumb gently tracing the small tattoo on his ring finger—444. The same number is also on my finger, concealed beneath lace and gold, symbolizing soulmates, protection, and divine alignment.

My voice softens to a whisper, trembling with emotion. "We were always meant to find each other," I whisper, gently touching his scarred knuckles. "The universe connected us long before we met—an invisible thread that guided me directly to you."

Reed's breath catches, his eyes shining as he presses our intertwined hands against his heart. The space between us vibrates, alive with all we've endured, created, and still have to face.

He smiles through tears, his eyes gleaming. "I love you, baby."

"I love you more."

The officiant's voice resonates through the chapel, gradually turning into a gentle hum in my mind. He discusses promises, forever, and love as a daily choice—yet all I focus on is him.

Reed's thumb slowly circles my hand, his rough skin against mine, grounding me when I feel like I might drift away. His chest rises and falls unevenly as he breathes, and his lips tremor into a smile he can't suppress—a tear balances on his lashes, catching the sunlight through his glasses.

The officiant finally says, "Do you, Reed Hayes, take Layla LeBlanc to be your wife?"

Reed's smile widens, trembling yet confident. "I do," he says, his voice breaking in the most beautiful way.

The officiant nods, turning to me. "And do you, Layla, take this man to be your husband?"

My throat tightens, my heart pounding against my ribs, and all I can do is stare at him—his scarred jaw, his tearful eyes, the way his thumb never stops tracing along me as if he's afraid to let go.

"I do," I whisper, voice barely holding together.

We say I do, and it doesn't feel like a ritual or a formality. It feels like a heartbeat—two finally syncing after years of searching. His fingers tighten around mine, anchoring me to everything good and real.

Maverick's voice booms on Reed's side. "Hell yeah, they do!"

The entire chapel bursts into laughter. Even the officiant smiles and shakes his head.

Reed laughs through his tears, pressing his forehead to mine as the room fills with joy and applause. "There's my damn brother," he murmurs, chuckling softly.

The officiant adjusts his glasses and mutters, "You may now kiss the bride."

He kisses me, gentle at first, then deep enough to steal the air from my lungs.

The crowd cheers, but everything blurs—the music, the light, the sound—until it's just us, standing in front of the tall glass windows, sunlight pouring over the pine trees.

Wrecked hearts. Stitched together.

Two souls who made a home out of the ruins.

He presses his forehead to mine, whispering, "You and me, always."

I know that invisible string never stood a chance of detaching us.

The reception feels like a dream as the chapel is cleared for the dance, and warm strands of lights hang from the beams, enveloping the room in gold.

Our song floods the chapel, and Reed turns to me, his hand outstretched, that boyish grin tugging at the corner of his mouth. "Dance with me, Mrs. Hayes."

Mrs. Hayes.

My heart actually skips a beat.

I laugh, slipping my hand into his. "God, that sounds so good when you say it."

He pulls me close as his hand settles at my waist, the other lacing with mine. "Better get used to it, sunshine. You're stuck with me."

The first notes of *Fade Into You by Mazzy Star* drift through the air, the same song that played the night we danced under the stars before I left for LA.

I sink into him, my head resting against his chest, and feel his heartbeat beneath my palm.

Reed's eyes are glossy, revealing the quiet storm of emotion he no longer hides from me.

"My wife," he murmurs against my temple, his voice thick with awe. "You're my damn wife."

The way he says it makes me press closer. "Your wife," I whisper back, smiling into his shoulder. "Guess you're stuck with me, too."

He chuckles softly, guiding me gently across the wooden floor.

Life hums softly around us.

Catalina and Carter are slow dancing near the windows, her hand resting on her belly, his other hand covering hers as if he's holding the world there. She laughs at something he whispers, glowing in a way only she can.

Maverick spins Amelia near the center, his blonde hair catching the light. Leo's in his arms, giggling as his parents sway. Amelia's dress skims her small bump—pregnant again, radiant as ever—and she leans her head against her husband's chest, love spilling from every look.

I stand there, my chin tilted toward Reed's chest, taking it all in.

Family. Safety. Peace.

All the things I once thought I'd never have.

The song slows as Reed's thumb moves in slow circles on the back of my hand.

I've been keeping this secret for a couple of weeks, and I think I can finally tell him.

"Baby," I whisper, my breath trembling as I find the courage.

He leans down, his brows furrowing. "What is it, sunshine?"

I press my lips together for a moment, looking up at him, my voice barely a whisper. "I need to tell you something."

His grip tightens slightly, worry flickering. "You're scarin' me."

A tear slides down my face, but it's a happy one."I'm pregnant."

He stares, like he's trying to make sure he heard right.

His eyes widen, glassy with disbelief. He laughs, cupping my face, and kisses me once, twice, and again, whispering against my lips, "You're serious?"

I nod, smiling through tears. "Yeah. We're having a baby, Reed."

He closes his eyes as he presses his forehead to mine, tears sliding down his scarred cheek. His voice cracks when he says, "You just gave me everything I never thought I'd get."

Around us, the song fades, but he keeps swaying, his thumb brushing my jaw. "You saved me," he whispers. "You took a wrecked man and made him whole. Now you're giving me a family."

I shake my head, tears catching in my throat. "No, Reed. We saved each other. Two wrecked hearts, we stitched them back together."

He smiles, resting his hand on my stomach, his fingers trembling. "Guess that's what we do, huh? We build somethin' beautiful from the wreckage."

Two souls rediscovering their path through the ruins.

Two hearts that refused to stop beating.

And when Reed kisses me again, tender, trembling, and reverent, I know deep down that *Wrecked Hearts* isn't just our story.

It's our beginning.

Two wrecked hearts. One steady rhythm. Forever beating as one.

THE END.

BONUS CHAPTER

Mama Hayes
9 years prior to Wild Hearts

Bacon sizzles in the pan as morning light pours through the window, catching the deep red roses Carter set on the counter a few minutes earlier. I'm still trimming the stems when the door shuts behind him.

"My oldest troublemaker," I say without turning.

Carter exhales a soft laugh.

Twenty-five years old, shoulders broad, beard darkening every time I see him, and eyes that look older than they should, until he's standing in my kitchen.

Here, he smiles more easily. Here, he still looks like my boy.

"They reminded me of yours," he says quietly, nodding toward the roses.

"They're beautiful," I tell him, brushing my fingers over the petals.

He shrugs, but the corner of his mouth lifts.

Before the moment can settle, the back door explodes open.

"MAMA, I HAVE ARRIVED. HOLD YOUR APPLAUSE."

I laugh, whispering to myself. "My wild boy."

Maverick storms in like he's entering a stadium rather than a kitchen.

Twenty-three years old, newly in the NFL, and louder than the coffee pot, he nearly collides with Carter, who catches him by the back of his shirt without even looking.

"Use your feet," Carter mutters.

"I am using my feet," Maverick argues.

"You're fucking reckless," Carter replies.

"Carter Hayes, watch your mouth."

Maverick giggles as Carter pushes him, and Reed quietly slips in behind them.

Twenty-one years old, his smile already threatening at the corners of his mouth as he watches his brothers act like fools.

"My quiet storm," I tease.

He nods once, taking over flipping pancakes like he always does when he visits.

Maverick reaches straight into the pan and steals a strip of bacon.

"Plate," Carter says.

"I don't need a plate, I have hands, duh," Maverick repeats proudly.

"You're disgusting," Carter shoots back.

"Jealousy doesn't look good on you," Maverick replies, pointing a greasy finger at him.

I smack his hand lightly with a wooden spoon. "Don't you dare touch anything else with bacon grease."

He gasps dramatically. "Violence in this household? Mama, I thought you raised us better."

"I did," I say sweetly.

Reed snorts, his shoulders shaking as he tries not to laugh.

Maverick points at him. "You laugh now, but when I'm rich and famous, I'm buying a house and banning both of you."

"You'd forget to pay the electric bill," Carter says dryly.

"Nuh uh!"

"It's true," Reed adds softly.

Carter steals a pancake off Reed's plate.

"That was mineeeee," Maverick whines.

"You were giving a speech," Carter replies.

"I was motivating the household."

"You were yelling."

"There's a difference," Maverick insists, climbing onto a chair backward. "All right, Mama, settle this: who's your favorite? Clearly, me, because we're both blonde."

I glance between them, pretending to think.

"The one who brought me roses," I say.

Carter hides a smile.

Maverick clutches his chest. "Oh my God. Is this what rejection feels like?"

"You bring me noise," I reply. "Which I also love."

Walking over to Reed, I squeeze his shoulders, whispering. "And you, my gentle boy, bring me solitude."

Reed smiles, sliding a plate toward Carter without asking. Carter nods once in thanks, and Maverick groans loudly.

"See? He gets silent appreciation. I, for one, get shit on."

"Maverick James," I tell him, tapping his shoulder when he leans too far back. "Watch your goddamn mouth."

The kitchen fills with laughter; Carter's deep and easy, Reed's soft and bright, Maverick's loud enough to shake the cabinets.

I lean against the counter, watching them bump shoulders and argue over nothing, and my chest aches in that familiar, full way.

"You know," I say suddenly, quieter this time.

They don't notice at first as Maverick reenacts a touchdown celebration that almost knocks over a chair.

"Boys," I repeat.

Three heads turn toward me.

"When you were little," I begin, "you used to ask me how you'd know I was still with you when you couldn't see me."

Maverick rolls his eyes dramatically. "Mama, you're not going anywhere."

If only I could stay forever, moving through life with my boys.

Carter's smile fades just a little as his gaze sharpens.

Reed leans forward, listening.

I set the wooden spoon down and press my palm gently to my chest.

"Our hearts," I tell them softly, "are reminders that we're never alone. If you ever miss me, or each other, you put your hand right here." I tap my sternum. "And you listen."

Maverick tilts his head, suddenly quieter.

"That beat?" I continue, smiling at them. "That's me saying you're *always loved.*"

The kitchen stills for a moment.

Carter looks down at his chest as if memorizing the words. Reed's smile softens into something deeper, his eyes bright. Even Maverick doesn't joke right away, which might be the loudest reaction of all.

Maverick clears his throat. "Well," he says, louder than necessary, "that was emotionally aggressive before breakfast."

I laugh, shaking my head. "Sit down before you fall off that chair."

He falls anyway, screaming while Carter smirks and Reed laughs quietly under his breath.

I grab a pen from the drawer and scribble a note on a small piece of paper, sticking it to the fridge.

Always loved.

Carter notices first. His gaze lingers on the words, a steady look passing through his expression before he taps the note once.

Maverick reads it next and groans. "You're trying to make me cry."

"You cried at a dog commercial," Reed reminds him.

"What! I want a puppy!" Maverick argues.

I laugh, shaking my head, and that's when Carter steps forward.

He wraps his arms around me first.

It's neither quick nor casual. It's tight and protective, as if he's trying to anchor himself. I feel the strength in his hold, the quiet way he presses his forehead to the side of my head.

"Love you, Mama," he murmurs, voice low enough that it almost sounds like a secret.

My chest aches.

Maverick doesn't wait long. He barrels into us next, his arms wrapping around both of us, and nearly knocks us sideways.

"I also love you," he says loudly, squeezing too tightly. "And I'm definitely the favorite, just so we're clear."

"You're crushing me," Carter mutters.

"That's what affection feels like," Maverick replies.

Reed hesitates for half a second before stepping in, too, his arms wrapping gently around all of us. His hug is quieter, more careful, but it holds just as much love.

"I love you, Mama," he says softly.

My boys, grown, loud, and stubborn, are holding onto me like they're still small enough to fit on my lap.

I close my eyes and memorize it.

Carter's steady strength.

Maverick's chaotic warmth.

Reed's gentle heart.

"Alright," I laugh after a moment, pretending to struggle. "Someone's going to burn the pancakes if you don't let me go."

Maverick releases me last, wiping his eye. "Don't ever leave us, Mama."

I glance at him, grabbing his face in my hands, kissing his cheek.

Carter smiles as Reed settles back into the chair.

Maverick pulls away with a light sheen in his lower lash line as he joins his brothers, torturing them with his chaotic self.

I stand in my kitchen, watching them argue over who gets the last piece of bacon, knowing one truth deeper than anything else.

They're loud. They're chaotic. They're mine.

And they are *always loved.*

DELETED SCENE

Did you ever wonder what it was like when Reed took Layla shopping? Here's the deleted scene!

LAYLA

I'm already flying through the clothing racks, my fingers pushing through the soft cotton as I find what I need.

My arms are loaded in under three minutes—dark-wash Levis that look like they'll hug my hips just right, a couple of soft cotton tees in cream and faded yellow, and a chunky sweater that feels like a hug when I press it to my cheek.

I'm moving quickly, almost frantically, as if slowing down might let the embarrassment from earlier catch up to me again.

Reed's leaning against the wall near the fitting rooms with his arms crossed, holding my iced coffee.

He observes me with a subtle, private smile, seeming willing to stand there endlessly if that's what I want.

I spin toward him, holding up the jeans and a tee. "These okay?"

His smile widens as his eyes crinkle at the corners. "You'd look good in a paper bag, sunshine. But yeah, they're good."

Heat flushes my neck, spreading to my cheeks. I swiftly duck behind the thick cream curtain of the first fitting room to hide how red my face is from him.

I quickly try on all the clothes, starting with jeans that fit perfectly, then the soft, flattering T-shirts, and finally the cozy sweater I want to wear nonstop.

Each time I step out barefoot onto the cool hardwood floor, I do a small spin or stand there awkwardly, waiting for his opinion.

Every time he looks at me, it's like I hung the moon.

The first outfit I showcase is a pair of worn denim jeans paired with a cream tee.

He leans forward, his elbows resting on his knees, eyes slowly scanning me from my bare toes up to my face. "Jesus, Layla. Those jeans, fuck."

I feel the blush creeping back again, as I snicker in response, running back into the changing room to show him the next outfit.

Keeping the jeans on, I throw on the pale yellow tee, pairing it with the oversized sweater.

I walk out again, turning around in a small circle for him."Well?"

He exhales through his nose as he tilts his head back for a moment before meeting my gaze. "You're killing me, baby. I love it when you wear yellow; it makes the honey in your eyes shine."

He's the only person who truly noticed my eye color, a trivial detail, but somehow it means everything.

Giving him a small smile, I finally respond. "You're so sweet, Reed, stop." I joke, holding my hand to my chest.

"You deserve it."

Damn him.

Before I can cry in front of him again, I make my way back to the dressing room for the third time.

The last item of the evening, hanging alone on the far hook, a long, butter-yellow sundress.

It has a flowy chiffon skirt, a delicate lace overlay on the bodice, and thin straps that crisscross in the back.

I undress quickly, taking the dress off the hanger with shaking fingers.

Finally stepping out, the curtain swishes behind me. I clear my throat, grabbing Reed's attention.

He lifts his head, adjusting his glasses, and he just stares.

For a full five seconds, he doesn't move as he continues staring with his lips parted, and his eyes wide in utter disbelief.

He lets out a long, shaky exhale. "Sunshine..."

Slowly standing, he walks toward me until he's close enough that I can smell the coffee on his breath and the faint leather of his jacket.

He leans his frame down, reaching out his fingers as they brush the hem of the dress where it skims my thighs, then trailing up to trace the lace over my ribs.

"You look..." He swallows. "You look amazing."

I feel tears creeping in again, but I laugh instead to shake them off before I throw myself at him.

He catches me mid-step, his arms banding around my waist, lifting me just enough that my toes leave the floor.

I don't care that we're in a small boutique in Ruby Ridge, I don't even care if my friends or their husbands see.

I kiss him desperately, pouring everything I don't know how to say into gentle kisses.

He kisses me back as his hand cradles the back of my head, and the other splayed wide across my lower back.

We finally pull away from each other, both breathing hard, and he rests his forehead against mine.

"Grab everything," he says, setting me down gently. "The jeans, the tees, the sweater, that dress; whatever else catches your eye. Whatever you want, baby. It's yours."

I look up at him, my heartbeat so loud I'm sure he can hear it.

"You don't have to—"

"I want to." He says, brushing his nose against mine. "Let me spoil you a little. Let me do something nice for the woman I can't stop thinking about. Please."

I nod because I can't speak as tears slip free again.

He kisses them away, one by one, with a patience he surprises me with the more and more we spend time together.

I run back into the dressing room, throwing on my original outfit, and grabbing all the clothes I tried on.

He smiles at me when I walk back out, grabbing all the clothes I'm holding and nodding towards the register.

The girl behind the counter smiles and rings everything up without comment.

Reed hands over his card without even glancing at the total.

We step back outside, bags swinging from his hands, and the late-afternoon sun bathes everything in gold.

He stops me on the sidewalk, setting the bags down as he pulls me into his arms.

I wrap my arms around his waist, pressing my cheek to his chest, feeling his heartbeat thump in perfect rhythm.

Inside my mind, something long gone cracks open and begins to breathe once more.

This man, this gentle, steady, ridiculous man, sees *me*.

Not this version I've curated online, not the version I think I should be. Just... me. Babbling when I'm nervous, crying too much, insecure, hopeful, scared—all of it.

And he doesn't flinch. He doesn't try to fix me. He just wants me as I am.

I've never experienced that before.

I didn't realize it could feel like this, like safety and wildfire all at once.

I tip my head back, looking up at him. "Thank you," I whisper.

He smiles, slightly leaning in as he presses a kiss to the tip of my nose.

"Anytime, sunshine."

ACKNOWLEDGMENTS

To everyone who picked up Wrecked Hearts, thank you.

This book was heavier than the others. It came from a quiet place inside me that once didn't believe peace was possible. Writing it hurt at times, but it also healed. It reminded me, and maybe you, that even when life falls apart, there's beauty in the rebuilding.

If you've ever loved through chaos, started over when it seemed impossible, or simply chosen to keep going when you were tired of trying—I hope you found a piece of yourself in these pages. Thank you for holding space for these stories that aren't perfect, but real.

To Layla and Reed, you two hold parts of me I didn't know how to express until now.

Layla, your heart proves that softness is strength. That even after pain, love can bloom again, gently, over time.

Reed, you embody the quiet lesson of what it means to love yourself, even when it feels like you don't deserve it. You reminded me that peace isn't something you stumble into; it's something you choose, again and again, even on the days you don't feel worthy.

You both taught me that healing isn't about becoming someone new, it's about remembering who you've been all along and loving that person completely.

To the readers who've been with me from the beginning, thank you for trusting me with your hearts. Thank you for picking up Wild Hearts, falling in love with the Hayes brothers and their wild wives, and for continuing to read their stories. Thank you for embracing love that's messy, human, and honest.

You are the reason these stories exist.

And to anyone still learning how to love themselves—you are not behind. You are not broken. You are enough, just as you are.

Thank you for loving these couples with all your hearts. I will miss Ruby Ridge and the Hayes family dearly as they mean so much to me.

With all my heart,

xoxo, A.M. Fernandez

Get ready for what's coming. ;)

SOCIALS

Follow me on my socials to stay in the loop!
Instagram/Tiktok: @authoramfernandez

www.ingramcontent.com/pod-product-compliance
Lightning Source LLC
LaVergne TN
LVHW100501110826
845146LV00002B/475

* 9 7 9 8 9 9 4 0 0 4 0 2 9 *